PLAYING
GOD

PLAYING GOD

A JOE BURGESS MYSTERY

KATE FLORA

Five Star • Waterville, Maine

First Edition
First Printing: September 2006

Published in 2006 in conjunction with
Tekno Books and Ed Gorman

Set in 11 pt. Plantin.

Printed in the United States on permanent paper.

Library of Congress Cataloging-in-Publication Data

Flora, Kate Clark.
    Playing god / by Kate Flora.—1st ed.
        p. cm.
    ISBN 1-59414-461-3 (hc : alk. paper)
    1. Police—Maine—Fiction. 2. Maine—Fiction. I. Title.
PS3556.L5838P57 2006
    813′.54—dc22   2005030207

For my sister, SARA

If they laugh in heaven,
you will get this joke.

Acknowledgments

Playing God was born over breakfast with Newark, Delaware, police Lt. Tom LeMin at a Mid-Atlantic Mystery Conference in Philadelphia. Over time, many people have helped me shape it into the book it finally became. For police procedure, I am indebted to Captain Joseph K. Loughlin, Sgt. Jon Goodman, Sgt. Dean Mazziotti, Det. Joseph Fagone, and Officers Chris Sibley and Michael Porter, of the Portland, Maine, police department; Lt. Joe Brooks, of the Waltham, Massachusetts, police department, and the City of Waltham for their Citizens' Police Academy; Lt. Albert Joseph of the Rochester, New York, police department; Sgt. John Franicevich, of the San Francisco police department; and Concord, Massachusetts, police chief Len Wetherbee. For making me ruthlessly cut and rewrite, my writer's group, Hallie Ephron, Sarah Smith and Linda Barnes, and my agent, Joshua Bilmes. For a critical eye and moral support, thanks to my readers: Peter Rogers, Skye Alexander, Jack Nevison, Nancy McJennett, Brad Lovette, Diane Englund, Robert Moll, and my brother, John Clark. During the dark years, your faith in this book kept me going. A special thanks to my mother, A. Carman Clark, for showing me what it means to be a writer. Finally, thanks to all those on MELIB, the Maine Librarians List, for responding to my call for help about their special places in Portland. No writer can function without librarians on her team.

CHAPTER ONE

The small black dog skittered into the street, shining eyes registering canine astonishment that a vehicle dared to be out at this hour. Burgess stomped on the brakes, the Explorer responding with orgasmic ABS shudders, stopping just short of the beast. Four-wheel drive beating out four-foot traction. With a look Burgess decided to take as gratitude, the dog turned and trotted away. A good result. The cops waiting with the body wouldn't have taken kindly to freezing their nuts off while their detective worked a dead dog scene.

Dog was right. Three a.m. on this icy bitch of a February night, even a murderer should have known enough to stay home. February in Portland, Maine, wasn't a benign month. Tonight, with the temp at minus ten, a roaring wind and black ice under foot, it was winter at its worst. But that was the cop's life. Get a call there's a dead body in a car on a lousy night, you don't roll over and go back to sleep, planning on working it in the morning. You get up and go.

Not that Burgess had been asleep when Remy Aucoin called it in. He'd been finishing the report on an unattended handgun death, detailing the reasons they'd concluded it was suicide. He preferred working nights. He liked his landscape gray and quiet, regarded the day's flurries of activity—all those sounds and smells and people—as intrusions into the peace that was possible at night. Some cops didn't like nights. They got used to it—when you were low man on the totem pole, you got stuck on late out—but always found it a little spooky. He'd seen it. Touch a guy on the arm in the afternoon and he'd act one way, touch him the same way at night and he'd wheel around, hand on his gun, a little wild around the eyes.

The brass preferred him working days. Their grudging compromise was some of each. So Burgess, already well into a double shift, had gotten the call. He'd put on his expedition-weight underwear, lined, waterproof boots, and a snowmobile suit. A hard-faced, middle-aged Michelin Man. But not everyone would dress for the weather and they were going to suffer. Crime scenes didn't take less time because it was cold. Ninety above or ten below, the job required the same slow, meticulous work. You had to give the dead their due.

In fiction, crime scenes were the pristine springboards of the mystery. People didn't move bodies and carry away souvenirs, cops didn't stomp on footprints, track blood everywhere, litter the scene with their own hair and fibers. In real life, anything could happen. He'd been to scenes so compromised by cops that the perp couldn't have asked for better. Once he'd found two EMTs and a fireman handling the murder weapon. Another time a patrolman washed the glasses the victim and her killer had used "so her parents wouldn't know she'd been drinking." Hell of a piece of numbskull chivalry, with the girl already dead. He'd said that loud enough to make the papers. Gotten called on the carpet for making the department look bad. He didn't care. Truth was truth. At least the hour and the weather would keep spectators away.

He passed the neon lights of the hospital, moving fast as the slippery streets allowed. Saw the flashing light bar, only sign of life at this dismal hour. He stopped well short of the cruiser and the parked Mercedes. Stepping carefully in the existing tracks, he went to meet Remy Aucoin, the young patrol officer who'd found the body. Aucoin got out, head down and shoulders hunched defensively, like a kid expecting to be yelled at. Burgess wanted to slap a hand on his shoulder and tell him it was okay, but held back. He didn't know if it was okay, or if the kid had fucked up somehow. Looked like the kid thought he had. It usually wasn't the end of the world, but he'd never let on he thought that. He'd never have another crime scene go right if word went around he was getting soft.

The wind whistled up the hill and tore into them, rattling the ties on his hood and stinging his eyes. "What have we got?" he asked, raising his voice.

Aucoin was hanging on to his uniform cap, trying to keep it from blowing away. "Dead guy in the Mercedes. Looks like someone jammed a rod down his throat." There was a faint whiff of sickness on his breath.

An ugly corpse, maybe the kid's first, or the prospect of getting reamed by Portland's meanest cop? He'd find out soon enough. "Rod. That a euphemism or are we talking about a piece of metal?"

"Metal, sir."

"There's crime scene tape in a bag on the front seat. Mark it off and then I want you to be the recording officer. You got your notebook?" Aucoin nodded. Burgess raised his flashlight and examined the kid's face. His color was bad. Despite the sour breath, Burgess decided it wasn't distress, that would be green. This was the blue of hypothermia. Kid probably wasn't wearing thermals. Didn't want to look fat in his uniform. Young guys were like that, and this was Aucoin's first winter. He'd learn. "There's a watch cap, a heavy sweater and wind pants on the back seat. Put 'em on."

Aucoin hesitated, pride warring with common sense, then nodded. Burgess watched Aucoin grab the gear, then look around for a dressing room, like he wasn't standing in a snowy street. "Out here or in your car, I don't care, but hurry it up. Like to get things under control before I turn into a Popsicle."

While Aucoin opened his cruiser door and sat on the seat to pull on the pants, Burgess got the crime scene tape, a mallet and a handful of wooden stakes and dumped them in Aucoin's lap. "Ground's probably too hard for stakes. Trees. Poles. Use whatever you can," he said. "How'd you happen to find him?"

The young patrolman looked like he wanted to be anywhere else on earth. "I'd noticed the car earlier, sir. It had been there a while. I thought I'd better check."

"How much earlier?"

"Three hours, sir." The words came out a little bit strangled.

"You waited three hours to check on him?"

"Man's a regular, sir."

Burgess shined his light on the MD plates. "So our victim's a doctor. What's this regular do here?"

"Sex, sir."

He didn't like it that the kid had let so much time pass. That this doctor was allowed to park on a residential street and have sex in his car. "You know of any sex act that takes three hours?"

"No, sir." Aucoin's teeth were chattering.

No sense wasting time out here on things they could do inside later. Like talk. "You run the plates?"

"Pleasant. Dr. Stephen Pleasant. Radiologist over at the hospital. Pine State Radiology. Car's leased by the business."

The shiver he felt wasn't from the cold. He'd run into

Pleasant before. "Live around here? This neighborhood?" In this part of town, the West End, there were some lovely houses.

"Cape Elizabeth."

"Surprise, surprise." His cousin Sam, chief down in Cape Elizabeth, wouldn't take kindly to *his* citizens parking on the streets and getting blow jobs. Burgess didn't either. "Speaking of hospitals, our friends from down the street are taking a damned long time, aren't they? You get that tape up while I look at our victim."

"Car's locked, sir," Aucoin said.

"Locked? How'd you get into the car? Break a window?" Aucoin's uncomfortable squirm was all the answer he needed.

"How do you know he's dead?"

"Oh, he's dead all right. Doesn't look like he died happy, either."

"Jesus Christ, Aucoin. You must be damned gifted if you can declare death through a closed car window. How long you been on the force?"

"Seven months, sir."

"A word of advice," Burgess said. "Don't start cutting corners. It's the quickest way to screw up any investigation . . ." He held up a hand to ward off the young officer's protest. "I know it's a miserable night. No one wants to get out of the car on a night like this. But the scumbags count on that. We don't wanna be playing the game their way."

Wind-whipped tears had turned to ice in the young cop's mustache. "Keep moving," Burgess said. "It helps. For starters, get me a scraper, okay? And don't make any new tracks." He strode over to the car, sliding on black ice under the powdery snow. The night was empty but not quiet. Wind rustled frantically through a nearby oak and shrieked around the buildings. Ice had re-formed on the window where Aucoin had cleared it. He grabbed the scraper. "Give me a big perimeter, okay? And watch for footprints." Aucoin, hunched and miserable, crunched away.

He scraped the window, then took his flashlight and peered in, running the beam slowly over the still figure. The sharp light distorted the taut face into planes of yellow-white and dark crevasses. Maine wasn't exactly a hotbed of homicide, but Burgess had been a cop a long time, in Vietnam before that. He'd seen his share of ugly bodies but this was a contender. Dr. Pleasant hadn't gone quietly into that good night. Death had left its mark in the wide, horrified eyes, cocked head with straining neck cords, that metal rod protruding between the teeth like a fire-eater whose act has failed.

Early forensic scientists had believed the dying eye recorded the assailant's picture like a photograph and tried to find a method to recover it. Faces like Pleasant's, with the awful anticipation frozen there, had fueled those theories. The seat was pushed away from the steering wheel and half-reclined, like a dentist's chair. He could hear his dentist's voice. Open wide.

He wondered if the rod had gone through the victim's neck. What the ME would say about the cause of death, assuming the man was dead. Burgess didn't doubt it, but he had to make sure. As a police officer, he had the authority to declare the man dead. He could confirm, for the record, that the victim had no pulse or respiration, so no extraordinary measures would be taken to save his already lost life and screw up the crime scene.

He raised his flashlight, wincing at the desecration of such an expensive car, broke out enough of the window to slip a hand through, and opened the door. He exchanged leather for latex and touched the victim's bare chest. Despite the heater's best efforts, the car wasn't warm. Pleasant was already cooling, his skin gone a waxy yellow. He had no detectable pulse, wasn't breathing. His pupils were fixed and dilated. The blood which had dripped from the corners of his mouth onto his scarf was still wet and red, but coagulating.

This was when training and experience came together, when keeping an open mind and open eyes were essential. Burgess surveyed the rest of the body and the car's spotless, characterless interior—black leather, gray carpet. No change, phone, CDs, glasses, cups, papers or briefcase. Only a dark overcoat, folded carefully on the rear seat, which the drape suggested was cashmere. The car smelled faintly of pizza.

He noted things for the report, things to be collected, the strange choice of weapon, already framing the pictures, though he no longer took them. Who was this man? Why had he been here? Who had been with him? What had happened in this car? And why?

What would he say to the widow? It was a difficult conversation at the best of times. Getting caught—or killed—with your pants down was hardly that. Mrs. Pleasant—and a wedding ring suggested there was one— wouldn't want to know how her husband's body was found. His shirt unbuttoned and his pants unzipped. He wore no undershirt and there were garish lipstick stains around his nipples. His penis, upright and hard with post-mortem tumescence, still awaited its anticipated release. A party atmosphere despite the lack of decorations. On the passenger's seat were two crumpled twenties and a ten. Party favors? One clenched hand held many strands of long blonde hair. Otherwise there were no marks on the hands. No signs of a struggle.

He was supposed to wait for the ME, the photographer, and the rest of the crime scene team before he touched anything, but any second now, the wind might whip in and snatch those hairs away, hairs that, for all he knew, might be a vital clue. Making a mental note to bag the hands, he pulled out an evidence envelope, untangled some hairs from the clutching fingers, and dropped them in, carefully recording the necessary information.

He backed out of the car, slamming the door, just as the crime scene van, an unobtrusive Taurus full of detectives, and an ambulance pulled up. He hoped they wouldn't have to wait long for someone from the ME's office to arrive and release the scene so they could work it. He wondered whether, having met Pleasant briefly in the past, he ought to let someone else work the case. That was something he and the lieutenant could work out later. He was here, the body was waiting, and it would be a pity to drag anyone else out into this icebox of a night.

He shoved the envelope into his pocket and went to meet them.

CHAPTER TWO

They finished the scene at six. A miserable, frost-bitten, chilled to the bone bunch of street cops, detectives and crime scene techs headed back to Middle Street and the promise of warm showers, hot coffee and breakfast. Even though his bones ached, Burgess skipped the shower. No time to waste. He went straight to Lt. Vince Melia's office to brief him on the case. Clutching a cup of coffee between his hands like a hot water bottle, he hunched in his chair and delivered the essentials.

Before he left, he brought up the thing that was bothering him. "Let me run something by you, Vince, see if you think I ought to hand this off to someone else. The victim, Dr. Stephen Pleasant, was my mother's doctor . . . the asshole who misdiagnosed her."

Melia looked pained. The city'd just had a high-profile murder and his most experienced detective looked like he was trying to weasel out of the case. "You sue the man?"

Burgess shook his head. "Threaten to sue him?"

"No."

"Think you'll have any problem working the case?"

"No."

"Then I've got no problem with it, either. Go find me a killer."

By seven, Burgess had changed into jacket and tie and done his initial reports. He was pulling on his coat, heading off to give Mrs. Pleasant the bad news, when Remy Aucoin's Uncle Guy walked in.

"Look, Joe," he began.

"Not now, Guy. Gotta go see the widow." Burgess picked up his notebook, checked his pocket for gloves, and moved toward the door.

Guy Aucoin's nod was spare. "Look, about the kid . . ."

"Not now," Burgess repeated. Guy was getting old. The skin on his face sagged like a bloodhound's jowls above the tight uniform collar, and his neck looked like a plucked chicken. Did he look like that to others? Did looking at him make other people feel tired, their fingers unconsciously poking at their sagging chins?

Guy didn't move. The Aucoin way—stand your ground and stick together. He had a beaky face, forehead and chin receding from the prominent nose, as though it had taken more than its share of bone and cartilage to build that edifice. Chronic circles made his eyes look sad. "I only need a minute, Joe. About the kid . . ."

"About the kid, Guy? What have you been teaching him, that he's letting hookers use his patrol area like that? Not the first time, he says. Pleasant's a regular. And that's not all . . ." Shit. He didn't have time for this.

"He's worried about his record."

"Oughta worry about survival. Kid wants to live through the winter, he better wear thermals. Tell him, next time, break the window, it's the person that matters. Tell him to be more curious. More careful. He's smart. He'll learn. Excuse me." Sighing, the man stepped aside to let him pass. The uncles were taking too much interest in their nephew's career. Ultimately, it fell on Remy. He needed to stand on his own feet, develop judgment, something he'd learn more slowly if his uncles interfered.

Dawn hadn't diminished the cold at all. Crossing the parking lot, the air was needle-sharp, bending Burgess over with a cough like a life-long smoker. He waited for the engine to warm up, watching his breath hang in the air. Too tired to get out and scrape. He used to get a second wind around now, the excitement of the chase buoying him up. Not any more. He carried his weariness like a chronic disease. His doctor offered antidepressants, but a lifetime among criminals, crazies and society's human junk heaps had made him wary of drugs, legal or illegal. He didn't believe in chemicals, he believed in endurance.

He leaned back, staring at the windshield. At the top, the sun peeping over the Old Port's brick buildings illuminated icy etchings, elaborately and intricately beautiful. At the bottom, heat turned the beautiful detailing to opaque mush. Soon the slap of wiper blades would flick it all away, giving him back a clear view of the lot full of salt-rimed cars and dirty snow. *Sic transit gloria mundi.*

This wasn't a day for reflecting on beauty anyway. This was a day for death. Going to see Pleasant's wife. Widow. He hadn't called ahead. He wanted a fresh, unrehearsed reaction. She hadn't reported him missing, so maybe he often stayed out all night, or maybe she already knew why. The widow of a man who frequented prostitutes—Aucoin said the guy was a regular—might, if she were aware of her husband's extracurricular activities, have an interest in stopping them. If so, it was a pretty damned dramatic stop.

Times like this, steeped in death and the reasons for it, when weariness eroded his rigid control, his own issues crept out. It was ironic that his job was to deal competently with death in others' lives yet he dealt with it so badly in his own. Two years since his mother's death and he couldn't put it behind him. Sometimes he'd go weeks, even a month, without that choking sensation, that surprising wave of sadness, but it always came back.

Wallowing. Goddammit! He hated wallowing. Self-pity

was such a useless emotion. Angrily, he jammed the vehicle into gear and skittered backward over the ice, nearly running down an overweight patrol officer mincing carefully across the lot. The man shot him an angry look, then lowered his eyes. His reputation again, Burgess supposed. Bad-tempered hardass who chewed new recruits to shreds the way some guys chewed gum. Despite his own excess pounds, he couldn't stand fat uniformed cops.

Down Franklin and onto Commercial Street along the wharves and the waterfront, sun gilding the windows and glancing off the ice-glazed streets of the restored old shopping district, quiet this early in the day. He took 77 south over the Fore River. On a morning like this, with the air so cold, great columns of sea smoke rose off the salt water, sunlight turning it a soft golden color, so that he might have been driving toward the gates of heaven instead of South Portland. The grim-faced drivers around him had their gaze fixed on the cars in front of them. God had laid on a spectacular performance this morning and no one was watching.

His mother would have noticed. She was the one who'd taught him to see, summoning him to the window and whispering, "Look, Joseph," in her soft voice. He rarely mentioned his mother—once they grew up, men didn't admit they had mothers, except to begrudge the services mothers required of them—but spending so much of his life dealing with death had reinforced the importance of honoring the dead. It was almost certainly his mother's noticing and wondering that had made him a detective.

Pleasant's house was an oversized white monument to success. The doorbell drew a slender young woman who flung the door open with an eager "Steve!" Finding Burgess there instead, she flinched, her face falling like a disappointed child's.

"Sergeant Burgess, Portland police," he said. "May I come in?" She stepped back wordlessly to let him enter, clutching her pink robe together with one small hand, her nervous blue eyes flickering across his face. Her appearance confirmed one thing. Pleasant had liked blondes. As he followed her into the kitchen, Burgess saw that her long, straight hair was held at the nape of her neck with the red wire twist-tie from a bread bag.

The house was new or had recently been redone. Everything was fresh and shiny and had an unused look. No chipped paint or scratches on the woodwork. She led him into a huge kitchen–family room with stunning ocean views, a room that was painfully neat. No papers. Clutter. Life. She waved a vague hand toward an oak table big enough to hold a roasted ox. "You can sit there. I'll make . . ." Her voice failed. She turned away, gripping the granite edge of the counter with both hands.

He gave her the space to do it, pulling out a chair, putting his coat over the back, getting out his notebook. She turned back to him, lips trembling, pale fingers twisting an enormous diamond. "It's about Stephen, isn't it?" she said. "I thought you were going to be . . ." She swallowed. "He didn't come home last night."

"You didn't report him missing," Burgess said. "Is he in the habit of staying out all night?"

Her eyes fell, a delicate pink rising in her cheeks. Instead of answering, she asked, "Has something happened to him?" He said yes and waited. What she did next—how she reacted—was important. "I . . . he . . . Stephen . . ." The pain in her voice was palpable. However she took the news he'd brought, Stephen Pleasant had already hurt this woman badly. "Is Stephen all right?"

Doing this part of the job, you learned to be grateful for

small things. He was grateful he didn't have to ask her to identify her husband's body. By the time she saw him, the protruding rod and the rictus of fear would be gone, the face rearranged into something more composed and human, the body cleaned of lipstick kisses. His job required a certain level of matter-of-fact cruelty—cops couldn't treat people the way people treated people and still do their job— but luckily the ME had known Pleasant. The form of the ID was a career first, though. The doctor had stared at the body and said, "Jesus Christ. He must have really pissed someone off this time."

Burgess had made a mental note to follow that up when they weren't standing around in the cold. He'd met Pleasant under professional circumstances, knew nothing about the man's personal life.

He was ready with the speech that never got any easier, but she didn't wait for an answer. Something else was crowding her mind. "He's never not come home before. What happened?" Trying to be calm and in charge but her voice tripped and stumbled. The pink flush deepened, coloring her neck and face. Her skin was fine, translucent. So vulnerable. She swallowed and looked Burgess full in the face. "Stephen has . . . sees other women. He thinks I don't know but I'm not so stupid as he supposes. But he's never . . . Sergeant . . . Detective Burgess . . . what's happened to my husband?"

"Mrs. Pleasant, maybe you'd better sit down."

"Oh! An accident," she said, nodding to herself, though Burgess hadn't said a thing. Her hand skipped up her body, touching chest, chin, forehead. It stayed there and she tapped her forehead again with two fingers. "I'm forgetting all my manners, aren't I? I'm Jennifer. Jennifer Kelly. Jen. And please don't call me Jennie." The use of a different last name surprised him. Most of the women he met who'd married doctors were proud to be Mrs. Doctor So-and-so. He bet her husband had called her Jennie. "Did you want coffee?"

People confronted with the news of violent death often apologized for their lack of manners, for forgetting civilities. He pitied them, yet admired the old-fashioned quality of hard-wired manners. Mannerly reactions to sad news might be too civilized but they were immeasurably easier to deal with than screaming, cursing and kicking furniture, hysterical tears or a retreat into catatonic silence.

"I'm fine," he said, "unless you were making some anyway."

"I usually . . ." She stopped, quiet tears sliding down her face, making no move to brush them away. Burgess thought she'd often cried like this, silent grief that simply spilled over. He pulled out a clean handkerchief and gave it to her. "Coffee. I usually make it for Stephen. I don't drink much coffee." She opened the cupboard, took out a filter, then pulled a can of coffee toward her. She scooped coffee into the filter, poured in the water, hit the switch. She stood with her back to him, watching the coffee pour into the pot, her face in the handkerchief, shoulders shaking.

He waited. He learned a lot, waiting, that more impatient people missed.

She got out two mugs, poured coffee, and put them on the table. She set a sugar bowl in front of him, and got out a container of half and half. She tried to open the top with shaking hands, then abruptly thrust it at him. "You do it," she said.

He opened the box, poured some in his cup, then set it on the table. It was time to reel her in. "Sit down, please, Ms. Kelly. We need to talk." He pulled out a chair and waited until she had settled into it. Then he took his own chair facing her. "I'm afraid that your husband is dead. We found him early this morning . . ."

"Dead?" she interrupted, grabbing his arm. "You're telling me Stephen is dead? I thought . . . maybe . . . he'd been arrested or something, because of . . ." Her eyes jumped so wildly he thought she might faint, but the grip on his arm was strong. Her voice rose. "Stephen can't be dead. We've got an appointment with our lawyer this afternoon. To make our wills. Because of the baby. We can't miss it."

It wasn't unusual, this failure to hear the bad news. He'd had a mother once who, being told that her son's bike accident was fatal, had responded, "Yes, but what about his leg? He's supposed to race tomorrow."

"I'm sorry," he said. "We found him around three this morning. In his car."

She released his arm and folded her hands in her lap, staring down at them. Once or twice she lifted one, trailed it slowly through the air, and folded it back into her lap again. Finally she looked at him. He saw that she was tired, missing the healthy vigor normal in a young woman. Her skin was dry and blotchy and there were purplish half-moons like bruises under her eyes. "In his car?" she said. She shook her head rapidly, as if anticipating something he was going to say. "Stephen didn't kill himself, if that's what you're thinking. He had no reason to. He was happy." She cradled her coffee with both hands and brought the shaking cup to her lips.

Burgess noted that she didn't say "we were happy."

"Your husband didn't kill himself, Ms. Kelly. He was murdered."

"Murdered!" The cup slipped from her fingers and

smashed on the shiny granite floor. She stared down at the mess and the spreading pool of coffee around her bare feet. "Murdered?" She shook her head in disbelief. "But no one would want to murder Stephen. He's successful. He's important. There are people who are jealous, I suppose, but you don't kill someone for that. And Janet . . . well, she hates his guts, but she loves the almighty buck way too much to kill the golden goose."

"Who is Janet?" he asked, just as the wail of a baby came from upstairs.

"In a minute," she said. "Stevie is awake." She stared helplessly at the broken crockery and pool of coffee, as if it was a lake too deep and dangerous to cross. Burgess grabbed the kitchen towel, threw it over the mess, and held out his hand, the Sir Walter Raleigh of Portland. She took it and jumped nimbly over the mess, more like the twelve-year old she looked than the twenty-three-year-old she probably was. "I'll just pick him up. Be right back."

He cleaned up the spill, threw away the broken cup, and poured new coffee. Her "right back" took about fifteen minutes. She returned in a flannel shirt and yoga pants. She had a nice figure, though a bit thin. If she was fine porcelain, he liked crockery. Something to settle his own bulk against. She carried a baby wrapped in a blue blanket. The baby was only a few months old, which explained the weariness. Childbirth and sleepless nights, compounded by an unfaithful husband, and the future that laid out for her.

"Thanks for cleaning up. You didn't have to," she said, unbuttoning her shirt. "I hope you don't mind." She wasn't wearing a bra, so there were no fumbling preliminaries, she simply let the shirt hang open as she unwrapped the baby. She glanced at him with a look that could have meant many things—see what my husband was giving up, or see how

25

easy-going I am at this nursing business—before she attached the whimpering baby to one small, swollen breast. She closed her eyes, holding her breath as the baby settled into its rhythm, then let it out softly. A damp patch appeared as her other breast leaked on to her shirt. She shook herself, as though suddenly realizing she wasn't alone. "I still find this amazing."

"Who's Janet?" he repeated.

"Stephen's ex-wife. The mother of his child. His only . . . in her opinion . . . real child. Mackenzie. Mackenzie, though you can't tell from the name, is a girl. Seven years old. Rather a nice girl, which, given she's got Janet for a mother, is something of a miracle."

He got Janet's full name and address, unsurprised to learn that Janet was still Mrs. Pleasant. "Your husband's relationship with his former wife was acrimonious?"

"Janet and Stephen could barely be in the same county, let alone the same room. They hated each other."

"What is your relationship with her?"

Jen Kelly shrugged. "We don't have a relationship, other than that necessary to facilitate the transfer of the child." She fell silent, then said, "Excuse me. That was bitchy. Janet does that to me. I tried. Honestly, when Stephen and I were dating, and when we decided to get married and I knew I'd have to deal with her, I tried to establish some kind of working relationship, but Janet hasn't got a compromising cell in her body. If you're looking for someone who might have wanted to kill Stephen, look at Janet. More than once, I've heard her scream she was so sick of fighting about support for Mackenzie, she was going to give up and kill him for the insurance."

The silence was filled with the slurps and sighs of nursing. She stared down at her baby. "Poor little thing," she whispered. To Burgess, she said, "How did he die?"

"He was stabbed."

She detached the baby, closed her shirt, and set him on her shoulder to burp, her movements jerky and uncertain. "Was it . . . did he . . . suffer, do you know, or was it quick?"

He didn't want to tell her much. Not while everyone was a suspect. If she was innocent, then knowing about the expression on her husband's face, the horror there, would only deepen her pain. Burgess had no idea whether this woman might have been involved, but he had an instinctive desire to protect her, one he suspected she brought out in many men. Not, apparently, including her husband. "I think it was quick. I won't know until the autopsy."

She looked stricken. "Autopsy? They'll . . ." She swallowed. "They'll be cutting him up? Stephen would hate that. He is . . . was . . . always so vain about his body. Do they have to?" Her voice was almost a whisper.

"I'm afraid it's necessary. Your husband was a radiologist?" She nodded. "On his own or with a group?"

"Pine State Radiological Associates. At Maine Med. His specialty was oncology." She hesitated. "Cancer. The person to talk to there is Ken Bailey. He's the . . . I don't know what you call it in a group practice . . . the closest thing Stephen had to a boss, I guess. Ken—Dr. Bailey—he's a good man. A kind man."

Did that mean her husband had not been kind? He felt like a rat, taking advantage of her vulnerability. But a well-trained rat. Right now she was talking freely. It was the shock, and her age, and the weariness. Whatever he didn't learn now he might have trouble getting later, when protecting privacy and putting a good face on things had become important. When the family had closed ranks.

27

"When was the last time you saw him?"

"Yesterday morning. Around seven-thirty. He ate break-fast and left. Said not to wait up. That he'd be late."

"Was that his usual schedule?"

"Stephen was a workaholic. He left even earlier when he was going to be in Auburn or Damariscotta. Sometimes we'd meet in the city for dinner. He did a lot of business over dinner, liked having me there. He was frustrated that I didn't like leaving the baby."

"So he left around seven-thirty. On a normal day, when did he return?"

"It varied. Anywhere from six-thirty to nine."

"Did you speak with him during the day?"

She nodded. "He called around noon. Said he'd set up the appointment with the lawyer. Wanted to be sure I had a sitter."

"That was the last time you spoke with him?"

"I . . . he . . . he left a message on the machine while I was changing Stevie, reminding me to get the garage door fixed. We didn't speak."

"When was that?"

"Around four, I think."

"And that's the last time you had any contract with him?" She nodded, her eyes filling with tears. "Did he seem agitated or worried, either time?" She shook her head. "You said your husband saw other women, Ms. Kelly. Any partic-ular woman?"

"He wasn't very particular," she said, then bit her lip. "I'm sorry. That was shabby. Stephen was . . . I don't know . . . hypersexual. His appetites. I couldn't satisfy . . . he picked up women. All sorts of women. Look. Okay. I'll say it." She swallowed. "He paid women to sit in his car and suck his dick. Oh, God!" She blurted it out fast, the way you move something hot so it won't burn you. "Do we have to talk about this?"

"I'm afraid we do," he said. "How did you learn about his infidelity?"

She didn't answer. She looked diminished, sitting there clutching her baby, a small woman made smaller by the things he was forcing her to reveal. He wondered who Jen Kelly, alone in this splendid house, confided in. "I can come back another time, if that would be easier. I wish I didn't have to ask these questions, especially at a time like this, but your husband's been murdered. The first few days are crucial in finding his killer. To do that, we need to learn as much as we can about him."

She lowered the baby to her other breast, closing the shirt modestly this time, and raised sad eyes to his face. "I'm sorry. Even after what you've told me, it's hard to think of Stephen as a victim. He was so cocky. So confident. He ran . . . I'm sorry. You'll think I'm awful to say this, but he could be arrogant in the way he ran over people's feelings. He was so impatient, so certain he was right. He was not . . ." She gazed toward the windows, but not at the restless blue ocean, searching for words. "Despite what he did . . . the people he treated . . . he wasn't a very compassionate man."

Burgess pounced. "His patients didn't like him? Were there complaints?"

"I don't know."

"Was he ever sued? Threatened?"

She shrugged, drooping on her chair. "Not that he ever mentioned."

"Do you know of anyone who might have wanted to hurt him?"

"Besides Janet?" He nodded. "I can't imagine . . . The

29

women in his car got paid, right? Patients are supposed to be grateful for having their lives saved. You don't have to like your doctor." She looked up, shaking her head. "No. Don't get me wrong. He was a good doctor. His nurses? His broker? His mechanic? My father?" She shook her head. "No. No! I don't mean that. My father's a gentle soul. He just doesn't think Stephen treats me well. But look at this . . ." She swept a hand at the room. "I'm kept in lonely splendor."

"Who were your husband's friends?"

She considered, her eyelashes resting on her cheeks in a gesture of utter weariness. "There were a couple doctors at the hospital he played golf with." Burgess wrote down the names. "He and Jon Shorter, he's in internal medicine, lives down the street, are running buddies. The guys in the practice did some stuff together. He didn't really . . . I think most men don't . . . have friends. Not like women do. Do you?"

A feeble attempt to deflect conversation from herself. It was chilly in the kitchen. Her bare feet, neatly aligned on the granite tile, were purple and her pale face had gone white. It was time to stop.

"You ought to have someone with you," he said. "Who should I call?"

"My father." Her voice small and tired. "His number's on the wall by the phone. Jack Kelly." Suddenly, she detached the baby and held it out. "Here. You take him. Burp him." She shoved a cloth into his hand. "Sorry. I'm going to be sick."

I've been at it longer, so I have more of each. But I wasn't Stephen's boss." He shook his big head sadly, clasping his hands as he leaned forward. "How's Jen doing? This can't be easy . . ."

He wasn't here to answer questions. They only had fifteen minutes and Bailey had a phone. He could find out for himself. "What was Dr. Pleasant like?"

"He was a terrifically bright and extremely competent physician." Burgess waited. Bailey shifted uncomfortably. "He was a very ambitious man. Financially and personally. He was the one who persuaded us to open satellite clinics in other parts of the state for the convenience of our patients. It's difficult for people to travel when they're so sick."

Couldn't argue with that. "There are how many in your group?"

"Six of us. There were six."

"And you have how many clinics?"

"Two. One in Damariscotta and one in Auburn. And here, of course."

"And the six of you staffed them?" Bailey nodded. "What was Dr. Pleasant's relationship with his colleagues?"

"Cordial. Everyone is independent, of course. Sees their own patients, but we do a lot of consulting with each other."

"He was well-liked?"

Bailey had been fiddling with the magnets of an executive desk toy, though he didn't seem like either the fiddling or the toy type. Now his head came up. He gave Burgess a searching look. "Well enough, I suppose. It was a business relationship. His colleagues and I appreciated his expertise. Even though he maintained a very busy practice, Stephen was always available to give a colleague advice."

Whether they wanted it or not, it sounded like. "What

CHAPTER THREE

He'd barely scratched the surface of what Jen Kelly knew, or suspected, about her husband, but he had to move on. As he left, stylish studio portrait of Pleasant in hand, a rusty old pickup turned in. The driver, presumably Jack Kelly, wore a blaze orange hunting cap low on his forehead, and a jacket with the collar turned up, so he formed no impression other than short and wide. Burgess noted the license number, hoping, as he watched the truck roll to a stop, that Kelly would be kind.

He called to see when the autopsy had been scheduled—eleven—then transferred to Terry Kyle, and got Kyle's clipped, "Kyle, investigations."

"Lab gone over the car yet?"

Kyle made an affirmative noise. "The lab and Terry Kyle. Thought I'd get in the back seat with Dani Letorneau. Got Wink Devlin instead."

"Find anything?"

"Maybe too much." Except for rare bursts of eloquence, Kyle hoarded his words. "Why don't I have Dani go over it when you get in."

"All right. Can you call Dr. Ken Bailey at Pine State Radiology, ask can he see me? Might as well head over to the hospital, catch some people before I go up to Augusta."

"You want me there?"

Vince Melia, who headed the CID, liked two people at autopsies, just in case one quit the force or got run over by a bus before the matter came to trial. But Kyle was up to his ass processing illegal guns they'd taken from the home of a suddenly deceased local dealer. "Be nice to talk some things over on the way, but forensics'll be there."

"Right. I'll make that call, get back to you." No small talk. No time wasted. The City of Portland could do a lot worse than spend its money on detectives like Terry Kyle.

The sky was clouding up as he drove back into the city. That was New England weather. You had to get up early—get up or be up—to see the sun. Kyle called back as Burgess wound his way uphill to the hospital. Portland was a little like San Francisco, the downtown clustered on a hilly peninsula that sloped down to the sea. The Maine Med buildings dominated the back side of the West End hill, looking out over Back Cove and the Deering flats. "Bailey's in now, Joe. He's holding a fifteen-minute window for you."

"How generous," Burgess said. "Thanks." He parked near the door, nodding to the security guy on duty. "Gotta see a man about a body, Charlie. Don't let anybody steal my ride."

"No problem, sir." God. Even Charlie was getting old. Maybe it was winter. The cold, dry air withered them all up, pinched their faces, reddened their noses, stooped their shoulders defensively and turned their hands into cramped little claws. "It's too bad about Dr. Pleasant," the man added.

"You knew him?"

Charlie nodded.

He'd have to come back and talk to him, Burgess thought. Security people noticed a lot.

He stopped at the information desk and asked them to tell Bailey he was on his way, then stepped into the elevator, surrounded by people whose business he didn't want to know, watching the doors slowly close. He'd watched those

doors so many times, visiting his mother. Wondered if he'd ever ride an elevator in this hospital and not be dragged back to those days. Go to work, spend the day on other people's death and disaster, come here and sit with his own. He shrugged, noticed the woman beside him staring, gave her a "back off" look.

Dr. Kenneth Bailey projected an avuncular competence suggesting you'd be safe in his hands. Big, strong, warm hands, the dominating handshake of a politician. "Detective," he said. He had a growly voice. "We're all shocked by what's happened. Anything we can do to help. Anything. I've told the staff to give you full cooperation." He swept a hand toward an open door. "This way . . ."

Burgess followed him into a spacious office, nicely furnished, but so cluttered with files and journals there was barely room to move. "I'm no housekeeper," Bailey said. "Trying to keep abreast of new developments. Trying to keep my patients alive. The rest . . ." He waved dismissively. "I'll get to it someday. Sit down, detective. You look tired."

He hated being told he looked tired. He moved a thick red notebook and sat, feeling a twinge in his left knee, a legacy from high school football. Damn the aging body anyway! The younger officers were always in the gym, getting buffed and polished. He was too busy taking care of other people's dirty business. If someone developed a form of exercise he could do while sleeping, he'd look into it. Dr. Bailey cleared his throat. Burgess realized he was keeping the doctor waiting. He opened his notebook. "Jennifer Kelly says you're the closest thing to a boss her husband had. I assume you knew him pretty well?"

Bailey looked pained. "We're a partnership," he said. "Naturally there's a sharing of information and experience.

about his staff? Did he get along with them?"

"Stephen was"—Bailey pursed his lips—"exacting. They sometimes struggled to meet his standards."

Not a very helpful answer. "Did *you* like Stephen Pleasant?"

Bailey gave a snort of irritation and glanced at his watch. "What difference does that make? We're professionals . . ."

Professional evaders of the truth? "Look, doctor, I have no interest in tarnishing your colleague's reputation, but someone killed the man. I'm trying to learn enough about him to find the person who did it. To do that, I need your help. If you're not forthcoming, you make my job harder."

The doctor's geniality vanished. Bailey was used to being the one who controlled conversations, gave the orders. Cordial as all get out so long as no one trod on his toes. Burgess had just stomped. "I don't know what you're getting at, but you won't find his killer here," Bailey said. "No one had any reason to harm Stephen. Besides, why stab the man when we could find more subtle methods?"

Stabbed? He hadn't mentioned how Pleasant had died, though it might have traveled through hospital gossip.

"I suggest you look among the hookers he was so fond of," Bailey said.

"Why don't you tell me more about that?"

"About what?"

"Dr. Pleasant and the hookers." It sounded like the title of a play.

"There's nothing for me to tell," Bailey said. "Steve didn't talk about his personal life. We had a professional relationship." His foot tapped restlessly against the plastic rug protector.

"You brought it up, doctor. And you knew him well enough to know his wife."

35

"Of course I know my partners' wives," Bailey said. "And Jen's mother was one of my patients. I've known the family a long time."

"One of your patients? Not one of Dr. Pleasant's?"

"Steve couldn't have dated her if her mother was his patient. That would have been unethical."

"But you can date each other's patients or their family members?"

"Theoretically," Bailey said sourly. "But everyone in the practice is married."

Burgess nodded. Most of his time gone and he hadn't learned much, except the unsaid. Bailey hadn't thought much of his difficult colleague in or out of the office. Hadn't approved of his dating Jen Kelly. And wanted to keep Pleasant's sleazy personal life from coming back at the rest of them.

"You went to their wedding?" Bailey nodded. "Was Dr. Pleasant still married when he met Ms. Kelly?"

"No."

So much for complete cooperation. No big deal. He'd never looked at his job as a popularity contest. He worked for the victims. The dead. "Getting back to Pleasant's hookers. How do you know about that?"

Bailey shrugged. "You hear things. Portland's nothing more than a big small town."

"Hear things from whom?"

"Jesus!" The word hissed out. "You know. Around."

"I don't know. I know how information travels through Portland's drug community. How it moves through the bars. I know where to find a hooker. But I don't know how information travels through your community. We don't have a lot of physicians murdered."

"I should hope not." Burgess waited. "Hell, I don't

know. Staff room or cafeteria gossip. Cocktail parties?" He shrugged again, an angry shifting of his big shoulders. "You hear things, that's all."

"It could be important." Bailey didn't respond. "When you heard he was dead, you immediately assumed he'd been killed by a hooker?"

Dr. Bailey carefully added another magnet to the structure he was building. "Or her pimp. Some low-life type who'd prey on a prosperous-looking man in the wrong place at the wrong time. A matter of opportunity, detective. Stephen was pursuing a stupid and dangerous lifestyle . . ."

"And the thought that followed?"

"That it would be pretty sordid. I hoped it wouldn't reflect too negatively on the practice."

"About the practice. You say you all worked independently?" Bailey nodded. "So was it an eat what you kill kind of thing, or was there profit sharing?"

"A little of each."

"Each of you carried your own malpractice insurance?"

"Yes."

Burgess made a note to look into the insurance. "You said Dr. Pleasant was a competent physician. Was he liked by his patients?"

Bailey pinched a magnet between blunt fingers. "I didn't hear many complaints."

"Had there ever been malpractice suits against him?" A shrug. "Any threats of suits, or matters which were settled to avoid lawsuits?"

Bailey hesitated. "Maybe you'd better talk to our lawyer."

"Why did you hesitate, doctor?"

"You always this big a pain in the ass?"

"Usually." It had been his experience that most doctors were neutral to nice until you pressed them. They felt put upon and oppressed, especially the older ones. It must be hard to start out believing you were God and receiving God-like deference, only to have the whole climate change. "Why did you hesitate?" Bailey didn't respond. "The lawyer. Will he be willing to talk or am I going to run into a stonewall of confidentiality?"

"She. Martha McFarland. Marty. I don't know about the confidentiality thing. You'll have to ask her." He scribbled something and shoved it across the desk.

Burgess examined it carefully. Doctors earned their reputation for bad handwriting. He printed the lawyer's name above the scrawl and repeated the number. Bailey nodded.

"Who are the other doctors in your practice?" Bailey answered by handing him a card. "What about staff? Who worked most closely with Dr. Pleasant, who would be likely to know his schedule?"

"Betty Ling was his appointments secretary. You could start with her. Chris Perlin was his nurse."

"That's here? And Betty Ling can give me information about the other offices?" Bailey nodded. "Getting back to the hookers. It was common knowledge?" Bailey nodded again, looking pained. "You ever see him with a hooker?"

"He didn't bring them into the hospital, detective."

"Any idea how frequently he solicited hookers?" A shrug. "Did you regard it as a serious problem? Was it impacting his work?" Bailey didn't answer. "Did you ever talk to him about his fondness for hookers?"

"Of course not."

"Who were Pleasant's friends on the staff?"

The doctor jerked up his sleeve and studied his watch. "He didn't . . ." Reconsidered. "Tony Stavros and Jon Shorter were golf buddies. Paul Conklin was his rabbi."

"His rabbi?"

"Advisor. Confidant. His guru."

"Where do I find these people?"

"Stavros is in oncology, they worked closely together. Shorter is an internist. Conklin is a surgeon." Bailey stood up. "I'm sorry. We're out of time. I have patients."

Complete cooperation. Burgess stayed in his seat. "When was the last time you saw him?"

Bailey headed for the door. "Yesterday afternoon, five, five-thirty, maybe."

"What was he doing?"

"Standing by the reception desk. On the phone. I was on my way out. I waved. He waved."

"That's your normal time to leave?"

An impatient twitch. "It varies."

"And for Dr. Pleasant?"

"He worked long hours. He was ambitious. Financially ambitious."

"Were any of the other doctors still here?"

"You'd have to ask them. They don't necessarily leave at five. If you have further questions . . ."

"Did anyone in the practice, or here in the hospital, speak with Dr. Pleasant about picking up prostitutes?" Dr. Bailey shook his head. "Was there anything else about Dr. Pleasant's lifestyle that might have put him at risk?" A vehement and totally unconvincing "no." Reluctantly, Burgess put his notebook away. He wouldn't get in the door as easily next time. "Do you know of anyone who might have wanted to harm Dr. Pleasant?"

"Of course not. When you see Jen, please tell her . . ."

Coward. You're her friend. She sees me, it's not going to be for comfort. "You should call her. She'd appreciate your support. Thanks for the help." He left Bailey staring after him, probably wondering if he was being sarcastic. Stopped

39

at the desk to get addresses for the other offices.

Ten minutes for coffee before driving to Augusta. Portland was the biggest city in Maine, two hours north of Boston except in the summer, when the road clogged with tourists, but the medical examiner was in the state capital. Forty-five minutes north on a good day. Today looked like a good day. Following the cop's rule—eat when you can—he grabbed coffee and a sandwich in the cafeteria. That was the difference between a veteran and a rookie. Remy Aucoin wouldn't have been able to eat before an autopsy. Burgess wasn't so cold he could eat while watching, but it had been a while since he'd lost his lunch.

He detoured by the scene and snapped a picture of the empty space, trampled snow, yellow tape flapping in the wind. It was something that he always did. That empty space represented what he needed to fill in. Then he headed north.

CHAPTER FOUR

The Portland forensics officers were just finishing up when he arrived. Dani Letorneau, engulfed by her lab coat and barely recognizable in a shower cap and face mask, nodded and said, "Good thing a Mercedes has a big front seat. Looks like this guy was having a party." Her eyes were tired. Her piece of this job was up close and eye-intensive.

"Party?"

"Curly black hairs. Long blonde hairs. And two shades of lipstick around his nipples and on his penis. Looks like a party to me. Unless it was one woman with weird hair who went from vampire blood black to demure pink lipstick in midstream. So to speak. No wonder he was still standing hours later."

"Saliva?"

"Most likely. We've taken swabs. Maybe some vaginal secretions. Swabbed a pubic hair out of his mouth. And we got a ton of stuff off the car. Prints. Hair. Fibers. Been better if he hadn't had leather seats, but at least he didn't have leather carpet. Funny thing is, he doesn't seem to have fought back. I'm not finding anything under his nails. Not on this hand, anyway. No scratches or defensive wounds of any kind. I'll be curious about what toxicology shows." She raised an eyebrow. "Roofies, maybe?"

Rohypnol, the date rape drug, wasn't often used on men. What did that suggest? A hooker with drug connections? Someone with a medical background? Premeditation? Wink Devlin, the other ET, paused in his meticulous scraping of the fingernails on the other hand. "Does toxicology pick up Viagra?"

"Jerk," Dani said. "Kyle tell you his wallet was missing?"

Burgess shook his head, idly watching her finish with Pleasant's hand. Suddenly he bent forward. "What about these marks on his wrist? You got marks over there, Wink?"

Devlin scrutinized the arm, turning it carefully as he inspected it. "Maybe something here. Hold on." He laid the arm on the table and walked to the other end, bending to inspect the ankles. "I don't know, Dani. What do you think?"

"Morning, everyone. Interesting case you've brought me." Dr. Andrew Lee, the assistant medical examiner, burst through the door, grabbed some gloves, and came up to the body, followed by his silent assistant. He always moved at least twice as fast as everyone else. Sometimes too fast for a Downeast sensibility. People in Maine took their time. Send him to LA or Baltimore, where the bodies piled up in heaps and he'd have 'em sorted out in a week. Still, he didn't miss much and was a brilliant witness. More than one defense attorney had made the mistake of treating this suave New York City native like someone just off the boat.

"My turn?" Lee asked, eyeing the metal rod. "I can't wait to see this thing . . ."

"Two minutes," Devlin said.

"Take a look at his wrists and ankles," Burgess said. "Looks like he might have been tied up."

"In his Mercedes?"

"Maybe it was a busy evening."

Dr. Lee inspected the wrists and ankles. "Very subtle," he said. "Good catch, Joe. You guys check the wrists and ankles for fibers? I doubt if it was rope. More likely it was something silky—scarves or curtain ties, something like

42

that. By the way, you catch that fistful of blonde hair? I were you, I'd be looking for a woman with a bald spot."

"We got the hairs," Devlin said. "Just about had to break his hand to get 'em. He didn't want to let go."

Burgess looked at the man laid out on the table. Was body type a kind of destiny? He'd been big and bulky by age thirteen, automatically steered into football. Pleasant had a compact, efficient runner's body. He hadn't asked Jen Kelly about her husband's habits, but would bet the man was compulsive about exercise and finicky about his diet. A man who would be particular about everything he put in his mouth, and considerably less so about the part of himself he put into others' mouths.

An ugly thought. He scratched absently at his shoulder as he watched Devlin shooting close-ups of the faint abrasions. He needed a shower and a shave and a few hours off his feet. Didn't know when he'd get them.

Lee and his assistant finished measuring and weighing the body, took some photographs, and then Lee dictated some things for the record. "You the primary on this, Joe?" He nodded and introduced Dani Letorneau, who was new to Portland's crime lab. The doc knew Devlin.

"Okay, gentlemen," Lee said, "Excuse me. Lady and gentlemen, you want to get a closer look at your murder weapon?"

Dani cleared her throat, not for the first time, and Burgess turned to look at her, wondering if she might be sick. It was her first autopsy, at least as a member of his department. She shook her head emphatically, waving him off. "I'm fine."

Lee would have already X-rayed Pleasant's head with the rod in place. Burgess approached the table and watched from the other side as Lee seized the metal rod with two gloved hands and tugged until it finally came loose and slid out of Pleasant's mouth. The doctor held it out flat on his palms.

"What the hell is that?" Burgess said, feeling a tingling in his throat. "Looks like a piece of old metal curtain rod sharpened to a point."

"That would be my guess," Lee agreed. "Pretty weird murder weapon, huh? If that's what it is. It doesn't look like some kind of sex toy." He nodded at Letorneau and Devlin. "Okay, kids. It's all yours."

Lee set it carefully on a metal tray and Burgess bent to take another look. The rod was over a foot long, a rough grayish-brown metal, except for the tip, which was sharply pointed and shiny except for clinging bits of bloody tissue. Kind of like a big pencil. Had it been made to use as a weapon? Something a nervous prostitute carried for protection? "Makes you wonder, doesn't it?"

"Wondering," Lee said. "What we do best, detective. Right about now I'm wondering where our killer got his . . . or her . . . hands on this. Someone goofing around in a machine shop?" He dictated a description of the object he'd just removed and proceeded with the autopsy. Letorneau got a little greener when Lee flapped the face down and took a saw to the skull, but she stayed on her feet and didn't make a peep as Lee plied his trade, slicing and removing, weighing and measuring, sectioning off samples for the lab.

"This guy was disgustingly healthy. Arteries clean as whistles. Great lungs, great heart, good liver," Lee said. "I'm surprised there weren't signs of a fight. Guy this fit isn't likely to let someone shove a lethal weapon down his throat without a struggle."

"Maybe he opened his mouth to let out a few orgasmic howls and she slipped it in," Devlin suggested.

"I'm betting there were two," Letorneau said. "Which would be amazing in a car, even a big, fancy one. But aren't we being awfully disrespectful? Poor guy's dead."

"Disrespectful?" Devlin said. "How about envious? There's something pretty awe-inspiring about a guy so horny he's willing to party with two hookers in his car on a freezing February night."

"Except," Burgess said, "we don't know if he was partying with two hookers. Or any hookers."

"Come on, Joe. You think he put on lipstick and sucked his own nipples?" Devlin said. "Not unless he has a rubber neck. And took out his dick because he thought it needed some air? Maybe you think he chucked that little spear down his own throat, too, and this is a suicide. That'd be one for the books."

"Or whether the party took place in his car," Burgess said quietly. "Let's just see what you turn up." He always tried to reserve judgment. He'd seen plenty of odd things over the years. The truth was often more amazing than anything they could imagine. He looked at Lee. "Could he have done this himself?"

"Not very likely. Takes a fair amount of force to shove something like that right through a man," Lee said. "Still, people have killed themselves in some pretty strange ways. You have any reason to think he might have?"

"Not yet. He had a beautiful young wife and a brand-new baby. Loved his work. Loved the money even more."

"Well, Joseph me lad," Lee said, "it'll keep your life interesting, unless you drop dead from a heart attack from long hours, bad habits and lousy food. Not, mind you, that I'm being critical. A man's gotta do what a man's gotta do, right? Exercise is for other guys." He waved his bloody glove over the body. "Look where it got him." He dictated some more, set the stomach in a pan and picked up a scalpel. "Let's see what the guy had been eating, shall we?"

"Could a woman have done it?" Burgess interrupted.

"A strong one or one who was sufficiently angry. Why not? Increasingly, murder's an equal opportunity crime." Lee jerked his chin toward Dani. "Someone want to take her outside?"

Wink put an arm around her and walked her out, returning a minute later to give them the thumbs up. "Dizzy," he said. "Gets so into it she forgets to eat. She'll be okay."

"Then let's finish this thing," Lee said. "Dr. Pleasant hated to be kept waiting."

Lee's breezy style made autopsies easier for some people. Burgess liked him well enough, especially since he was such a good witness, but he remembered his first ME. Dr. Geller had had such a reverence for the process and for the dead. He'd begun every autopsy with a prayer for the soul of the departed and explained the procedure as he went along as though the deceased were still listening. Geller had taught him a lot about death and dying, about the human body and the stories it could tell. Burgess imagined Geller here, and wondered what he might say. He would have looked at the immaculately maintained body, the expensively cut hair and buffed nails, and at the gaudy lipstick-marked genitals and nipples, and he would have known important things about Pleasant—how he'd lived and why he died.

Lee picked up his scalpel and opened the stomach, filling the air with the unmistakable sour scent of stomach acid. He peered in and started to laugh. "Too bad Letorneau left," he said. "Be a good one to start her on. It's yours, Wink. Two guesses where the deceased ate his last meal, and the first doesn't count."

It looked like the man had eaten dog food. "I can't believe it," Burgess said. "A guy like this at a place like that?" There was a pizza place in Portland, Salerno's, put these weird little balls of meat on their pizza, meat that never seemed to get chewed and didn't break down in the stomach. "Not the first time we've seen this, is it, Wink?"

Behind his mask, Devlin yawned. "Man, I'm tired," he said. "By the time we got back from the scene, I was so cold I thought I'd never warm up. A twenty-minute shower barely took the edge off."

"Know what you mean," Burgess agreed. "I didn't even get the shower."

"We can tell," Lee said.

Dani quietly came back in.

"Stomach contents so undigested you could put that mystery meat back on a pizza and serve it again," Lee continued. "What does that tell us?"

Dani made a gagging sound.

"Didn't live long after he ate," Devlin said brightly.

"Exactly. So we proceed. And you now have the challenging task of finding out when he ate that pizza."

"Lucky me."

The autopsy finished, Lee whipping organs in and out of the body with the speed and dexterity of a carny working the shell game, deftly collecting a sample of the stomach contents to be sent off for toxicology analysis, then putting everything back where he'd found it, like a well-behaved child putting his toys away. He left the body nice and neat for his assistant to stitch up.

They stepped out into the hall and Burgess closed his eyes, trying to will away the dull pounding at the base of his skull that was his body's way of signaling exhaustion. He couldn't take a break now. The job was just beginning, the list of questions growing a hell of a lot faster than the list of answers. He pushed his sluggish arms into his coat, already moving on. He'd begin with some calls from the car. By now, officers with pictures of Pleasant should have canvassed the area where the car was found, and another detective would have started talking to Portland's better known ladies of the night.

Ahead of him, Wink was going through the door, lugging a box with Pleasant's clothes in it, a bulging briefcase full of evidence dangling from his hand. Hours and hours of painstaking work. But the frown on Wink's face was not anticipation of all those hours. Wink loved his work. Wink was worried about Dani. He paused in the doorway. "She needs to rest, Joe. Otherwise, she'll make herself sick and I'll be stuck doing this alone." Apologizing in advance for the delay in processing the evidence. Knowing how much they needed information.

"Sure," Burgess agreed. Living people took priority. It was good to take care of your people. Stop caring and you got like Captain Cote, who viewed his fellow cops as job descriptions and badge numbers. Cote, who was waiting to hold an audience with Burgess's particular detective slot. Probably expecting him to arrive with the whole case solved. Cote, though he'd been a detective himself, expected the cop shop to run like a TV show, with cases neatly solved in an hour.

At a minimum, this was a miniseries. And that was if they got a lot of lucky breaks. Otherwise, the series would run until a solution, or bad ratings, ended it. So far, they'd gotten no breaks. Maybe rounding up some ladies of the night would bring one. And wouldn't Cote love it when the station filled up with whores.

CHAPTER FIVE

On the way back, it started spitting snow, harsh, icy granules that bounced against the window. Clouds of it swept across the open fields and onto the wide gray pavement, where it danced and twirled like smoke. The empty road suited him fine. He was glad to be alone with his thoughts. You couldn't be a cop almost thirty years and not develop some intuition. Here his intuition told him that nothing was going to be simple. This case was going to be a big, ugly bitch.

On the surface, it was a tawdry little sex crime. Oversexed doc does a ménage à trois with a couple of hookers, gets rolled for his wallet and stabbed to death. That's what the lipstick, rope marks and missing wallet all said. But that scenario was too obvious, too clearly what someone wanted them to think. Sure, Pleasant's wife said her husband had women service him in his car. Aucoin had seen the car cruising for girls and parked in the same place before. But if Pleasant had been partying with hookers who'd tied him up, it hadn't been in the car. Not even the fit and athletic doctor could have managed that. So whatever had taken place in the car looked like dessert. And why was he out so late?

Pleasant, while admittedly a risk-taker, had valued his professional reputation and income, his lovely wife and home and newborn son. And, as she'd said, he thought he had his wife fooled. So Burgess still had questions. If Pleasant wanted his wife to believe he was working, he wouldn't stay out until midnight. Why hadn't he fought back? He was a strong, athletic guy. Burgess needed to ask Lee how much maneuvering space it took to shove that thing through Pleasant's head. Curious what toxicology would show. If someone had drugged Pleasant, that showed planning rather than the opportunistic act of a hooker or her pimp.

Burgess shifted on the seat, working the stiffness out, trying to wake himself up. Pretending he didn't need the rest he wasn't going to get. In any homicide, major work needed to be done right away, building that picture of the victim, his life and habits, his last days. Interviews and record checks and a canvass of the crime scene area. That was the big picture. It was built of a million small details, each requiring care and attention, accumulated and recorded by officers working as a team.

Another piece of it was taking care of the family, in this case a delicate balance between being supportive liaison and suspicious cop. He had to call Jen Kelly to tell her the wallet was missing. That the body would be released this afternoon and she could arrange to have it picked up. He hated making these calls; hated the pain and suffering he could feel, even over the phone. But it was an important part of the job.

The desk sergeant stopped him. "Captain Cote wanted to know the minute you came in. I'll tell him you're here." He spoke briefly into the phone, then lowered his voice, fishing for details. "I hear the victim was head-to-toe with lipstick kisses. Man. Fat cat doc with a big house in Cape Elizabeth and a beautiful wife. Some people don't know when they've got it good."

Burgess just grunted and went to see Cote. He could already write the script. Your victim's some street kid or scumbag drug dealer, you can rattle any cage you want.

Your victim's a prominent citizen and somebody's sure to know somebody, who'll call your boss and beg you to keep things quiet. Dr. Kenneth Bailey wasn't the exception—he was the rule. It was hard to investigate a murder among the rich. They were less likely to gossip in bars or brag to their friends and more likely to call their lawyers. Language wasn't used in ignorance, but for obfuscation, as a tool and a defense. They were also less familiar with the criminal justice system, considered normal police procedure harassment. Crime was something that happened to "them."

Burgess rubbed the back of his neck and thought about sandwiches. Thick, oily subs dripping with onions and peppers, crammed with artery-clogging cheeses and slices of salami with crunchy, breathtaking bits of black peppercorn. Maybe he should forget dead docs and VIPs, become a food writer. Review cop restaurants. Decent coffee.

Without knocking, he walked into Cote's office, dropped his bulk into a chair and folded his arms, fully aware the posture was defensive. Just looking at the man gave him heartburn. Cote had been born ambitious, probably shaken hands with all the important people in the delivery room while his mother lay exhausted and ignored. His shirts were always starched, his brass and leather polished. He never needed a haircut or a shave, had breath fresh as daisies. His fatal flaw was that he had been a cop at many levels but he couldn't remember what a cop's life was like.

"How are you, Joe?" Cote forced a sickly smile as he aligned a stack of papers.

"Beat."

"This looks like a tough one."

"It is."

"Sensitive, too. I've had calls from the AG's office and the mayor's office."

Burgess wondered why the governor hadn't called. Dr. Bailey and the governor were great pals. They did some sports thing together—hunting, fishing, sailing, he couldn't recall. It had been in the paper.

Cote cleared his throat. "It looks like there are going to be some . . . sordid details . . . concerning the victim. We've been asked to keep that out of the press. To be as discreet as possible."

Cote loved giving orders, but if he was going to put up barriers to this investigation, he was going to have to define them. Burgess's job was to solve the crime; he didn't give a rat's patootie about the PR implications of his acts. That's why Cote, slicker, less experienced, and more political, was sitting on that side of the desk. Cote was a good test-taker. Superb ass-kisser. Lousy cop.

"Paul, this is a homicide. Guy patronized hookers, we've got to talk to hookers. Guy was a doctor. To get a handle on his schedule, his character, his habits—make sure this is what it seems and not work-related—we've got to talk to doctors. What is it you do, or don't, want me doing?"

His shoulder was itchy again. He shifted in his chair, twitching to see if he could ease the itch. A shower would help. He wasn't an aesthetically pleasing creature like Pleasant. He was a big, hairy bull of a man and his hide needed tending. At this point, that shower looked far off. He sighed and twitched more violently. Cote jumped, the pencil flying out of his hand. Proof that you didn't have to go ballistic often to get a reputation.

Burgess had only seriously lost it once. Only dragged one superior officer over his desk and slammed him up against the wall, but that had been Cote. Two years later, people shifted nervously if he made sudden moves. He still regretted the case that had driven him over the edge, regret he'd carry to his grave. Cote's mishandling of the essential details of the Kristin Marks case had resulted in the child's murderer getting away with a laughably light sentence. Cote continued to shrug it off. Burgess still seethed.

Searching for composure, Cote opened his drawer, got a new pencil, then tented his hands and leaned back in his chair. "Dr. Bailey was a bit . . . offended . . . by some of the questions you asked this morning. He found your manner accusatory and belligerent."

"And I was on my best behavior, too." He wasn't making this easy for Cote. In the wastebasket, he could see the remains of lunch. A brown paper bag, neatly folded, the paper that had held a sandwich carefully folded on top of it. His own stomach was empty.

"Use your common sense, Joe. Use some tact. You have to handle these people differently. Less aggressively . . . they're not used to—"

"You can't mean that, Paul. Bailey wanted to tell me they were one big, happy family. That Dr. Pleasant was a brilliant, hard-working practitioner and jovial, well-liked colleague who had a lovely wife and family in Cape Elizabeth. That being said, he wanted me to go home without learning a damned thing about the victim. How, exactly, was that supposed to help our investigation?"

"You stepped on his toes, Joe."

"I didn't put my weight down. And only after he'd rebuffed a couple of polite questions. I didn't go there to make nice. I went to learn about a murder victim."

"You know what I'm saying. You can't go in there and strong-arm these people. You have to be tactful."

Cote paused for effect, but what effect Burgess didn't know. Waiting for the words to sink in? Did Cote think he was some impermeable soil, thick with clay and slow to percolate?

Finally, Cote sighed and said, "Report to me daily. I want to know everything that's happening. I'll handle the press."

"Have I ever leaked anything to the media?"

Cote shook his head.

"Ever let some reporter follow me around?"

Another shake. No one could say Burgess had a reputation as anything but tight-lipped and cautious.

"Are you saying I should let someone get away with murder to avoid hurting feelings? That preventing embarrassment has higher priority than solving crime?"

"You know I'm not saying that. Just use a little tact."

"How do I tactfully ask about his whoring habits or deficiencies in his medical practice?" Cote didn't answer. "You want to give the case to someone else?"

Cote shook his head. "We want this cleared up fast—people in that neighborhood and at the hospitals are already pretty antsy—and you're the best, Joe."

Cote, who hated his guts, really believed that? More likely, it was what the chief believed and Cote was an excellent toady. Burgess was heading for the door when Cote said, "This is bigger than you think, Joe. You know who Jen Kelly is? Edward Bigelow Shaw's daughter."

Bigelow was old name money. Burgess thought of the ratty old pickup. Jen Kelly saying, "Call my father" and giving him Jack Kelly's phone number, which he'd carefully written in his book. "She said her father was named Jack Kelly."

Cote's gloating look said "dumb shit Munjoy Hill Irish." Burgess dropped his gaze to veil the answering "mill-town, sister-fucking, brown-nosed Canuck asshole."

"Shaw's first wife, Clara Casey Shaw, left him when Jen was about six," Cote said. "There was a nasty divorce. She remarried a man named Jack Kelly. When she was a teen-ager, Jen started calling herself Kelly. But she's Ted's daughter. And you know what that means."

Of course he did. But genuflecting was hard with a bad knee, and what mattered was what people had done and why they'd done it, not who their rich fathers were. "What does that mean, captain?"

Cote frowned. "I have to spell this out for you? It means we do our best not to embarrass her or her father. It means you treat that poor widow with kid gloves."

"So if it turns out that he was killed partying with a pair of hookers who rolled him and stabbed him, I should pretty it up so that he actually got those lipstick kisses all over his nipples and his crank at a Salvation Army benefit and then accidentally fell on his fork?"

"You know what to do."

"What if Jen Kelly did it? Got sick of his partying and put an end to it once and for all? Did it herself or hired someone to do it. Wouldn't be the first time a pissed-off wife took a swipe at her philandering husband."

Cote ostentatiously opened a notebook and began studying the contents. Burgess, thus dismissed, left the office, wondering at Cote's fascination with the City of Portland emergency evacuation plan. No matter how badly he handled this, or how many sensitive docs and hookers he offended, he wasn't likely to cause a mass exodus from the city. Both the hooker and rich folks populations were small.

Kyle looked up from his desk with a quick, spare grin. "You been reamed?"

"Dickhead doesn't know the first thing about reaming. He probably thinks it has something to do with stacks of paper." Burgess didn't like to take out his temper on the people around him, but boy, Cote pissed him off! Jerk ought to know better than to give an etiquette lesson to an exhausted cop. "I'm going to the can. Get everybody together and let's go over this thing. Sort out where we are and where we're going."

"Right." No questions. No delay. If he cloned Kyle, they'd have this done in a day.

He met Remy Aucoin coming out of the men's room. "Aucoin!" He thought the kid was going to faint. "Got a few more questions for you. Come by in half an hour. And if you want to put a smile on an old man's face, you'll bring a large Italian sub with everything and a Diet Dr Pepper."

He could almost hear the sigh of relief. Kid probably thought he'd be rescued by a call and never have to face the music. Should know better. Not many got away from Joe Burgess. Correction. He brought them in. After that, it was up to the legal system. He'd seen justice twisted up so badly it was no wonder the lady with the scales wore a blindfold. More than once, he'd gone to the graveyard to apologize to his dead. One, in particular, he visited often, standing with his hand on the small, cold stone, feeling the black rage and helplessness coming over him again. Then he'd turn and walk away, before it swallowed him up.

CHAPTER SIX

They looked like they were auditioning for a "Send this boy to camp" poster, except for Dani, who could be adopted for just pennies a day. There were seven of them in the room. Lt. Vince Melia, head of the criminal investigation division, Sgt. Berman from patrol, who was coordinating the house-to-house, Burgess, Terry Kyle and Stan Perry from personal crimes, Devlin and Dani from forensics. Melia was the boss, but he let Burgess run the show. The others drooped wearily over their papers.

"Anything from the canvass?" Burgess asked.

"Got a woman a few blocks away who saw someone walking down her street a little after midnight. Not someone she recognized from the neighborhood. She thought it was strange for anyone to be out walking in weather like that, so it stuck with her," Berman said.

"Male or female?"

"Person's all she said. But maybe if we talk to her . . ."

"Stan, can you check it out?" Berman gave Perry the information. "Nothing else?" Burgess asked.

Berman shrugged. "Whole neighborhood claims to have been in bed by ten. Lotta places, no one was home. I've got officers going by later. Interrupt their dinners. Good way to get cooperation."

"You check with the city, see if there were any snowplows or sanding trucks or repair crews out?"

"Nada. You wanna kill someone, middle of the night in

February's a hell of a good time to pick."

"Dani? Wink?"

"We've barely begun, Joe," she said. "Sorry. I thought we'd get back from Augusta and dive right in. I didn't expect—"

"See who you can get to help out. Pull people from other things if you need to."

Dani started another apology but Wink cut her off. "Looks like we've got hairs from at least six different women from the car, maybe more. There were some blonde ones wrapped around his fingers, long ones, and on the buttons of his shirt. A couple curly black ones on his overcoat. I told you, we got that pubic hair from his mouth. Haven't had time to go through the pubic combings, head combings, and, in this case, chest hair combings. We might find something. Dani and Boone have just started going over the clothes, looks like we may get some good fibers."

"What about prints?"

"Fumed the inside this morning, got enough prints to keep us busy for a month. Boone's started processing some of those." Wink passed a sheet of paper across the table. "Some of your favorite ladies of the night have been guests in that car."

Burgess scanned the list. "Leave Alana Black to me. She'd take offense if anyone else came to get her." He passed the list to Berman. "Have your guys start bringing them in. Purely voluntary, of course. Just asking them to do their civic duty."

Berman read it and grinned. "Gonna be like Old Home Week. If you don't need me any more, I'll get on this."

Melia sighed. "I give it an hour, and it's gonna be worse than a room full of cats around here. You got anything solid yet?"

"I don't even have something squishy, Vince. Looks like at some point in the evening he was tied up and double teamed, if the two shades of lipstick prove to be different ladies. Wallet's missing. I'm hoping one of these ladies was there, can tell us where it happened. But he was killed in the car."

"Prints on the weapon?" Melia asked.

"Too rough."

"Anything off the money?" Burgess asked.

Devlin stared at him. "Money?"

Burgess pulled out the preliminary sketch and pointed to the crumpled bills on the passenger seat. "This money."

"I didn't bag it. Dani?"

"Not me."

"Well, someone must have. Track it down," Burgess said. "It must be somewhere." This was bad, stuff disappearing already. Nothing pushed his buttons like missing evidence. "Okay." He slapped his palms down on the table, watched 'em all jump. "Wink, you and Dani have plenty to do. Keep me posted as you go. Terry, you start talking with the ladies. As soon as he's done with our witness, Stan will help." He gave them copies of Pleasant's picture. "Ask if they know this guy. Terry, see if the paper's got an archive photo of Jennifer Kelly." He answered their puzzled looks. "Pleasant's wife. Long blonde hair and an unfaithful husband."

"And Ted Shaw's daughter," Melia added. "So we don't have to tell you how sensitive this is."

"You sound like Cote," Burgess said.

"I sound like a realist."

"Shoot," Wink said. "Does this mean I'll have to practice my curtsy?"

"We'll keep you out of sight," Melia growled. Wink sketched a salute, waiting for Dani's slower rise from her chair. "Letorneau, Wink . . . no heroics, okay? Give us what you can, then get some rest. We're in this for the long haul. Tomorrow, the next day. Can't have you sick."

When everyone had gone, Melia said, "So what do you think, Joe?"

"Gonna be a bitch, Vince. Not just the politics. It feels planned."

"Planned how?"

"My gut says this isn't about sex or money. Not just sex and money." He hunched his shoulders forward. It was too soon for this, but Melia was waiting, and Melia was his kind of cop—a careful, observant detective who did things by the book but could read between the lines. Melia understood about gut instincts like Cote never would. The real world was messy. You learned to read it by being in it, not by sitting behind a desk and studying numbers.

"I've only talked with two very guarded people, his wife and his boss, and already I know Pleasant was a self-absorbed, arrogant, ambitious, insensitive and greedy man whose patients were at the most critical points in their lives. His wife's home with a new baby and he's out screwing around. I bet I don't find anyone who liked him."

"You don't kill because someone's miserable to work with. Money and sex aren't enough?"

"They can be. But whose money? And whose nose was out of joint? Cote's talking about stepping on toes. So, whose toes was Pleasant stepping on? I'm talking gut, Vince. It feels deliberate."

"But the hookers are our window?"

"Right. But our window on to what?"

"You'll find out." Melia shoved back his chair. "Callahan's your AAG. Keep me in the loop."

"That's what Cote said, too."

Melia rolled his eyes. "Like Wink said. Practice your curtsy."

"I've got a bum knee."

"You've got a bum attitude."

"Appreciate the support."

Remy Aucoin waited outside the door, holding a greasy brown bag. Kid might grow into a good cop yet.

"Sit down," Burgess said, taking the bag. "Not Salerno's, right?" He grabbed a fistful of napkins from his drawer, unwrapped the sub, and took a bite. Good as a shot of morphine. He could feel the throbbing in his head subside. Mumbled, "Thanks," around a mouthful. His mother would have been scandalized. Controlling himself, he set the sub down and popped the top on the can. Good way to ruin your digestion—bad food on an erratic schedule, eaten too fast. Part of the cop's life, just like the long, dull patches interrupted by adrenaline surges. It was why cops wore out quickly. "How long you been on late out?"

"A month, sir."

"And before that?"

"Early out."

"You've seen Pleasant's car before?" Aucoin nodded. "Late, like last night?"

The boy shook his head. "Not since I got on the later shift. I used to see him around eight or nine, sometimes earlier. He'd roll up with some girl. Her head would stay down a while. Then he'd drive away."

"How often?"

"Sometimes once a week. Sometimes twice. Sometimes not at all."

"You're driving by in a marked cruiser and that doesn't bother him?"

Aucoin fiddled with his belt, trying to settle it more comfortably on his hips. He was tall and lean like his Uncle Guy. Nothing to cushion the weight. Even with the lighter web belt, all that equipment was heavy. No hips. No ass. Not a problem

Burgess had ever had. "Maybe he had his eyes shut."

Maybe he had an arrangement with the cops. Maybe he expected to be left alone. Aucoin didn't seem nervous enough for that to be the case, but it happened. "No complaints from the neighborhood?"

Aucoin shrugged. "He was discreet."

"Guy in a Mercedes was getting a blow job under my window, couple times a week, I wouldn't think that was discreet. Lot of people park there for sex?"

"Teenagers sometimes. When the weather's warm."

"That's it? It's not a spot the girls are using?"

Aucoin shook his head. "Not to my knowledge, sir."

"You knew who he was," Burgess said.

"Yeah." Aucoin shifted nervously and eyed the door.

"How?"

"License plate."

Burgess shook his head. The uncles should teach the kid to be a better liar. "Car's registered to the business. You call the plate in, that's what you would have gotten back."

Aucoin's face flamed red. Another thing to learn. Cops don't blush. Feel what you feel, but keep it off your face. The public's watching. You don't let 'em inside, or they'll poke you full of holes. Cop lets people get to him and he ends up with a soul like Swiss cheese. Burgess had a few holes himself. Most of it, he'd worked 'til it was tough as tanned leather, but there were those thin spots.

Aucoin shifted his belt again. "I followed him one night. Couple months ago."

"You left your shift and drove to Cape Elizabeth?"

Aucoin's head came up, pride warring with deference. Pride won. "No, sir! I'd never . . . I . . . on a day off. I waited until he dropped the girl, then followed him home."

"Why?"

"Just curious. It was odd, what he did. Most guys, they picked a girl up, they'd drive around the corner, park, get it done, and drop her off. Or else find someplace real private. He always came back to the same spot."

"Maybe he liked the view. Same girl?"

"Different girls."

"Recognize any of them?"

"A couple. Little dark-haired girl. Young blonde named Candy. Alana Black. Lotta times Alana Black." He said her name with reverence.

Burgess understood. He was going to be talking to Alana pretty soon. It might be impossible for a man to talk to Alana without a physical reaction. A heterosexual man. Even cops, and they were used to having tits and asses and other female anatomy shoved in their faces. Kyle, who was modest, put his coat over his lap. Burgess figured what the hell, if he stood up when Alana came into the room, at least it proved he was still alive. A polite cock, a bum knee, and a pounding in the back of his head. He had a hell of a physical repertoire. If he could fly, he'd be Superman.

"Notice anything else about Dr. Pleasant? Other than his fondness for girls?"

"He got a lot of phone calls."

"*In medias res?* In the middle of things?" Aucoin nodded. "And he took them?"

"He was a doctor."

"Bummer, huh, having a radiological emergency in the middle of a blow job. Do yourself a favor, Aucoin?" The kid was holding his breath. "Next time, break the window. And watch where you're walking." Aucoin swallowed. Nodded.

"One more thing. You think someone's in a car getting a blow job? Turn on your lights and knock on the window. Not your job to make it easy for them. You can go. Thanks for the sub." He didn't offer to pay for it. He grabbed another bite, picked up the phone, and called Rita Callahan in the attorney general's office.

"It's Joe Burgess, Portland PD, the Pleasant case. Can you get me a subpoena for Pleasant's car phone records?"

"Sure. Anything else I can do for you, detective?" A voice like Brillo on a screen.

"I may need his office phones as well. Depending on their level of cooperation. I'm betting they scream patient confidentiality. Hell, I probably need his financial records, too. Bank, accountant, credit card. You name it. Guy had an expensive lifestyle and an ex-wife nagging him about support. I'd like to see the whole picture."

"Why don't I put them on the list, save us all some time."

"Sure. He had offices in Auburn, Damariscotta and Portland. Betty Ling was his appointments secretary. She can probably give you addresses. I've got his card here." He read her the info.

"I'm on it," she said, and disconnected. At least she wasn't big on small talk. Some AAGs, especially the new ones, were into trying to make connections. Fine in an ideal world, but this was the world of life gone wrong. He didn't have the time or the interest in making new connections. He liked the idea of disconnections. The night shift. Solitude.

He found the number and called Jen Kelly. A man's voice answered. Strong Maine accent. Easy, with a slight twang. In a longer sentence, the voice would have dropped to a mumble, the words being swallowed up. He asked for Jen.

"She's feedin' the baby right now. Can I take a message?"

"This is Detective Burgess, Portland police. Jack Kelly?"

"Ayuh." Half-swallowed. He could see the man nodding. In 'Nam, as a tough nineteen-year-old, hearing Maine in another man's voice could bring tears to his eyes.

"Two things, Mr. Kelly. First, can you tell her that her husband's wallet is missing, probably stolen. She needs to notify his credit card companies and I need a list of the card numbers so I can see if anyone's using them. I know this is a difficult time for her, but the sooner we can get that, the better. If she calls when it's ready, I can have someone swing by and pick it up." He heard the scratch of pencil on paper. Waited to let Kelly get it down. He liked it that Jen Kelly's father was humble enough to need to write things down. Lots of people were too arrogant to bother and too scattered to remember later. "And the medical examiner's office will release the body this afternoon. She can arrange to have a funeral home collect him."

He gave his own number and the ME's number, and disconnected, a little disappointed at not having spoken to her. The memory of her face, the vulnerability of that twist-tie in her hair, the small bare breast, all lingered in his mind. Jen Kelly had a story and it looked to be a complicated one. He hoped it wouldn't lead where he thought it might. He took a few more bites of sandwich, but now that the edge was off his hunger, weariness and work had shoved it aside. Hercules might have cleaned the stable by diverting a river through it, but Burgess had found you missed a lot that way. Stand there and keep shoveling. It was stinking, hard work, and it hurt your back, but that was the way to get to the bottom of things. He leaned back in his chair and closed his eyes.

CHAPTER SEVEN

Alana Black wasn't surprised to find him on her doorstep. "Heard you guys were doing a sweep," she said. She waved an arm toward the kitchen. "I could make coffee, unless you'd like something stronger."

"Coffee's fine."

He stepped in, smiling. She'd positioned herself so he couldn't get past without brushing against her. "After you," he said.

"Party pooper."

"Saving myself for marriage," he said.

He followed her into the kitchen and put his coat over the back of a chair. Alana stuck a filter in her coffee maker and spooned in some coffee. Daylight began and ended today in the kitchens of lovely women making coffee. But there the similarity ended. If Jen's had a theme, it was glossy or sterile. Alana's was shabby kitsch. Big-eyed animal magnets covered the refrigerator. On top lodged a cluster of mangy bears. A row of tiny bears lined the windowsill by the sink. Alana's hair was jet black and wildly curly gypsy hair. And while Jen's pale skin, cheekbones and baby-fine hair personified the WASP princess, Alana's mixed heritage had given her tawny skin, full lips, and dark, seductive eyes. Jen had small, pink-tipped breasts with a tracing of blue veins; Alana's were high, proud melons with jutting brown nipples.

He wasn't an ass man or a tit man or leg man. Mostly, he was a celibate man. Not that he didn't notice or desire.

66

It was just that in a society where lack of impulse control ran rampant, he had too much. Except for occasional explosions of temper, he kept himself locked down. From his earliest years he'd been an observer. Observed his father beating his mother and his mother's silent, stoic grief. Observed the ugliness of what people did to each other. Learned to shift his eyes and pack his feelings down.

"You never come see me, Joe," she pouted, swishing her hips.

Despite the weather, she wore a wisp of low-slung black vinyl and an abbreviated tank top cut so low you could have mailed letters in her cleavage. A faint suggestion of dark hair feathered her stomach below the gleaming silver navel stud. She had skinny little girl arms and legs and a full, voluptuous ass. When she stood on tiptoe to reach in the cupboard, he was treated to the sight of most of it. If she was wearing any underwear at all, it was only a thong. He'd heard a guy describing how she gave a blow job once. He sometimes woke up thinking about it.

She flicked her tongue at him. "Should see your face right now, copman. You know you want it."

"I don't have to have everything I admire," he said. "You taking care of yourself?" Alana couldn't be rushed.

"I do my best, keep away from drinking and drugs and men who want to mess with my mind." She ducked her head in a self-deprecating way. "Mostly. Try to keep some money in the bank. Things have been slow, lotta guys tapped out after the holidays. Bad weather for business. I'm too old to be hanging out on street corners."

She was twenty-two. Senior citizen in the hooker business. "Especially dressed like that."

"Hey. I wear a coat. You think I'm a moron or somethin'?"

"I think you're divine. But does it cover your ass?"

She set coffee mugs on the table with a clink. Bent to get milk from the refrigerator with a grin back at him over her shoulder. "Maybe in your business, you worry about covering your ass. I worry about showing mine."

"Hard damned place to get frostbite, that's all."

She burst out laughing. "I wish you'd come around more. Not many people who can make me laugh. Hey, I'm moving up in the world. Got a beeper and an answering service. Don't have to go out there and freeze my ass." She shot him a sideways glance, daring him to disapprove. "You don't look like you're taking care of yourself."

"I try. Got some money in the bank. Can't seem to stay away from people who drink and do drugs and want to mess with my head, though."

"Yeah, I wouldn't wanna work in no cop shop. Whew! Too much testosterone. Even the women got too much testosterone." She sketched a mustache on her upper lip. "You've got a hard-worn look, man. I mean, I find it sort of attractive, a guy who shows the mileage, but you're never going to get yourself a wife, you go around needing a shower and shave, hair sticking out like that, shoulders hunched like a grouchy old bear. Woman wants a man who takes some pride in himself."

"Thought she wanted a man with bucks in his wallet and an itch to scratch."

She poured his coffee and sat down across from him, holding a small white bear. "That, too, Joe. But any woman wants to be wanted—my kind or the marry and settle down kind. So how come you won't let me . . . you know . . . cheer you up a little?"

"Just seeing you cheers me up."

"Don't give me that moose crap. You're here on business, aren't you."

"My life. My business. No difference. Tell me about the doc with the Mercedes who got killed last night."

Not looking at him, she stroked the bear's head. "He was a simple man. Pick up a girl, drive her to his favorite spot, open his shirt, unzip his pants, and get blown. He was clean. Didn't ask for weird shit. Paid cash up front and never asked for free seconds. Closest he came to kinky was liking to have his nipples sucked. I can handle that. It's kind of sweet, actually. Not that he was sweet."

She dropped the bear and popped out of her chair. "How's your coffee? Want me to warm it up?"

"It's fine. What do you mean he wasn't sweet?"

Sitting again she bent forward from the waist and rested her forehead on her knees, a sudden, graceful move that showed off her amazing agility. She danced at a club sometimes. He'd never gone to see her. She swept her hair forward, covering her face, massaging the back of her neck. "I've got this headache," she said. "You ever get headaches?"

He knew this game, verbal hide and seek, but he wasn't in the mood for games. After a moment, she sat up, giving him an irritated look. "I mean, Mr. Can't-be-distracted, that he never showed any kindness or interest, or even any sign I was human. Lots of guys try to make conversation. They're nervous and shit, so they chatter. Or they don't say much, but what they do say, it's a little like flirting. Like how pretty I am and stuff? Or how they've never done this before and they're nervous and I have to tell 'em they'll do fine, they're gonna love it. But he didn't talk much, just confirmed the price for what he wanted."

She picked up the bear and caressed it nervously. Burgess was curious. It was a dangerous business, but there wasn't much that spooked Alana.

"There was something cold there," she continued. "Like

he needed a woman to do him but she didn't really exist. She was just a mouth, some hands. People didn't matter to him, which was weird 'cuz he was a doctor, you know? So even though he was easy, I didn't like doing him." She raised her eyes to his, eyes that had seen so much they should have been jaded, but they were only puzzled. "I understand need. I understand horny. Most men are pretty simple. I didn't understand him."

"He was always like that?" She nodded. "Always one girl, or sometimes two?"

"One."

"Any idea who he was partying with last night?"

She dropped the bear. "I know something about it."

Probably a lot, if he was reading her right. This hesitation and slow divulging was part of the game, a kind of foreplay between them. They had to make it good because foreplay was all there ever was. But today he was so damned tired. Like an old married man. Not tonight, honey, got a headache. "You going to tell me or am I supposed to beg?" Trying to ignore the way her right forefinger and thumb caressed her left thumb.

"Take it easy, Joe. I'm thinking. I know you don't believe I can, but I'm doin' it."

"Come on, Alana, either you know or you don't."

She gave him a slant-wise look with her gorgeous eyes and made a tut-tut sound with her tongue. "Don't be a booby, Joe. I gotta live with these people. I can't just sit here and dish out everything I know, not with them already thinkin' I'm your snitch, if not your lady friend. I'm trying to think how to do this."

He rubbed the back of his neck wearily. "Sorry."

Her face lit up. "You're the only guy I know ever says he's sorry."

"Look. Alana. I'd love to sit and gossip over coffee, but I'm beat and I've got a million things to do before I get some rest, so can you please hurry up?" A giant vise was squeezing the base of his neck.

"Oh, hell, Joe. Sure. Anything for you. You know that new girl, popped up a couple months ago, young kid with shiny black hair, kind of bouncy, like she's still a cheerleader or something? Name's Lulu?" He nodded. Rubbed. Couldn't ease the pain at all. "Well, her pimp set it up. I don't know who the other girl was. Somebody he recruited. Lovely blonde bitch who could put all the rest of us out of business."

Cold day in hell, he thought. "You know whether Pleasant asked for it or whether this girl, Lulu, suggested it? She was the other girl?"

"He asked, is what I heard, but that might not be true." Ignoring his second question, she came around the table and pushed his hands away. "Here. Let me do that. You want something? Advil? Aspirin? Tylenol? Demerol? Tylenol with codeine?" Her fingers dug into his shoulder muscles, strong, hard fingers, finding the tension and pressing it out. Traveling up his neck and massaging the muscles at the base of his skull, up into his hair where the skin felt tight. "Take off your sweater and unbutton your shirt," she ordered. "I can't do anything through all these clothes."

"I'm fine."

She backed away, leaving him hungry for those searching fingers. "Sheesh, Joe. You're so far from fine I can't even measure the distance. Not that I was ever much good at math. Here's the deal. You come in the bedroom, lie down and let me do something about that headache, and I'll talk to you. Otherwise . . ." She put the heels of her hands to-

71

gether, open like a V, then snapped them shut. "I clam up."
When he didn't respond, she said, "You can keep your
pants on. Protect your virtue. Saving yourself for marriage.
Sheesh. Someday you're going to take some lady to bed and
get out six years later."

"We can talk here."

"Then you'll be talking to yourself."

"Alana. You know I can't—"

"Can't what, copman? Let a friend give you a backrub?"
She left the room.

She'd cooperate if he'd just play her game. Reluctantly, he
heaved himself up and followed her into the bedroom. She'd
thrown a pink scarf over the lampshade and was lighting a
scented candle. "Jesus, Alana, it's only a headache."

She handed him Advil and a glass of water. "Take two."
He did as he was told. A rarity. Then she stripped off his
sweater, unbuttoned his shirt and helped him pull it off.
"You keeping your gun?" He nodded. "Suit yourself. You
always do. Lie down on your stomach. Here. Let me get
these pillows out of the way." The bed was piled with frilly
pillows, the whole room pink and girlish. Monuments to a
girlhood she'd never had.

She straddled his body, the warmth of her bare thighs
against him. There was a gurgling and the smack of palms
rubbing together. "Oh, Jesus, Alana. Not massage oil."

"Shut up." He felt the heat of her hands and the icy tang
of mint on his skin. Her hands spreading and smoothing,
kneading his muscles, working his back up along the edges of
his shoulder blades, hurting him as they pulled the soreness
out. Working and reworking the hard spots until he actually
groaned. She slapped his shoulder lightly. "Good. Let it go,
Joe."

"Talk to me."

"Not yet." Her fingers walked up his neck and tangled themselves in his hair, finding all those tight, tight scalp muscles and soothing them, then moved down his back, working out from his spine across the bands of muscle, traveling down to his lower back. Kneading it, pressing it, soothing it. He wanted this to go on forever. Didn't have forever. A dead man was calling.

Suddenly her hands stopped. "You're thinking again."

"You can feel it?" He slid away from her, rolled onto his back, plumped up some pillows, and leaned against the head of the bed. He felt surprised and blessed. "You're good," he said. "Very, very good. This is what you should do for a living."

"Oh, I'm definitely in the therapeutic relaxation business."

"You know what I mean." She sat a few feet away, cross-legged on the bed, her hands resting on her knees, looking at him. The soft pink light suited her. Her skin glowed, her eyes glowed, she looked soft and mysterious beneath that cloud of hair.

"Penny for your thoughts," she said.

"How beautiful you are. But I came here for information."

"Bullshit. You came here to get onto the soul train," she said. "To plug into the closest thing to a life you got, which is me. You want information, you coulda brought me in like the other girls. You came here to check up on me, because you think you're my daddy, which you aren't even close to. For starters, 'cuz you never beat on me and you never fuck me. You came here to do battle with temptation because you're just a big Catholic prick who thinks he's got life locked down but sometimes just has to let something out of a cage to see if he can tame it."

"About the dead doctor," he said.

She turned her back on him. "There's this pimp. Scary,

mean son-of-a-bitch named O'Leary. Got a place near the bus station. That's good for business. They went there. Pleasant wanted to be tied up. Watch a little lesbo love. The whole nine yards." She shrugged. "I don't know. Not what I would have expected. The guy was so cold and clinical. Like, this was MTV and he's the education channel. Unless he's sci-fi."

"This O'Leary. He got a first name?" She shrugged. Knew and wasn't telling. He wondered why. "Far as you know, Pleasant's always done it in the car?"

"Couple times in the summer, when there were lots of tourists out, he'd go with girls to their places. He was here once."

Burgess knew he was sitting on a hooker's bed but it felt funny, like being in bed with his victim. He started to get up, thinking it would be better in the kitchen. Get some nice, clinical distance.

"Sit down," she said. "I'm not done. How's your head?"

"I think I'll live."

"Coming from you, that's high praise. I don't know. Being inside had a strange effect on him. I'd been with him in his car maybe five, six times, and it was always the same. Short, simple, clinical. When he was here he wanted to get more adventurous." She didn't elaborate and he didn't ask.

"What else did you hear about the party at O'Leary's?" Alana looked away. "What? Come on. Talk to me. What?"

Her eyes swept back, moving slowly down his body. There was more intimacy in her glance than in some twenty-year marriages. He felt a ridiculous urge to cover himself, even though her hands had just been all over him. Even though she did men's bodies for a living. "Dumb ass," she said. "You've got nothing to hide. You're one of those guys who look better with their clothes off."

"What is it," he demanded, "that you're trying so hard not to tell me?"

She pouted, thrusting out her lip and folding her arms. "What makes you think I'm not telling you something?"

"Almost thirty years on the job."

"It's like I told you before. I have to live here. On the street. With these people. So I just don't know—"

"Alana, a man is dead."

"Maybe he deserved to be."

"People might say that about you. Say 'Oh, it's no loss, she was nothing but a hooker.' I don't make those judgments. In my book, death matters. No one gets to appoint him or herself executioner. So?"

"You'd miss me. You'd think I was a loss, wouldn't you, Joe?"

"Of course I would." He studied her tense posture, the evasive eyes. "What are you holding back?"

She lowered her eyes and took a deep breath. "This is just street gossip, Joe. I don't know anything. I don't even know names, though probably I heard some of it from Lulu."

"Heard what?"

She flung it at him the way you'd throw a stick to a dog to make it go away. "That people got drugs from Dr. Pleasant."

"Talk to me," he said.

She stood looking out at a view which was the side of another brick building. "Nothing to tell," she said. "I just heard people got drugs from him . . . or through him . . . that's all. You know me. I don't do drugs, don't want to get close to the people who do. It's the quickest way to hell I can think of, and I'm trying to put hell behind me."

"Remember who you heard it from?"

She shrugged, her back still toward him. "No."

"Who I should talk to?" Silence. "What drugs?"

"Painkillers. Oxycontin." Silence again, then, exploding, "Jesus, Joe, we're talking bad people here. You don't care what happens to me if it will help solve your murder."

"Alana . . ."

"Just leave, will you. Go sweat some of the others. You're good at getting people to talk. Find that big prick, O'Leary, and sweat him."

"And leave you in peace, right?"

"Right. I've got a living to make. Unless you want to shuck the rest of those clothes and let me show you how it feels with a real woman."

"As opposed to what?"

"Your hand," she snapped, turning away from the window. "Go bother someone else. Rhianne. Or that old hag, Polly. She knows more about drugs than the rest of us put together. Or find that mystery woman and ask her what happened. You ask me . . . and, yes, copman, I know you didn't . . . she's the key to this. Your mystery lady. I may be the best, but I'm not the only girl in this city."

"How am I going to find her? You got any ideas?" But Alana was in one of her snits. "Mind if I use your phone?"

"Would you care?"

He picked up his shirt and pulled it on, buttoning it with one hand while he dialed Kyle with the other. "You pick up a cute little black-haired number named Lulu?" Kyle made an affirmative sound. "What about her pimp, guy named O'Leary?"

"Kevin O'Leary? No. You want us to?"

"If you can. And hold her until I get there. Maybe she knows about the party with Pleasant last night. Alana says O'Leary set it up. How's it going?"

76

"Vince was right. It is like a roomful of cats around here."

"Getting anything?"

"Got offered a year's worth of blow jobs."

"With respect to our late doctor."

"He was well known. Nothing about last night, though. You coming in?"

"On my way." He put on his sweater. Alana was still at the window. "Hey," he said, "I'm going. Thanks for the massage."

"I'm still waiting for the day you say you're coming." She didn't turn around. "You know, Joe. I met somebody once who says she had sex with you. She's a burned-out old hag now, so it must have been a long time ago. But I can't help wondering. Why her and not me?"

This was the heart of the matter. Why she'd been so difficult. Not that Alana was ever easy. He shrugged on his jacket and left, crunching down the empty street through the gray cloud of his own breath. He got into his cold, dark car and sat, not turning on the engine. He wanted to be cold right now. It took time to get over being that close to Alana. Alana, who thought he was messing with her mind while she was messing with his.

She was right about the sex. It had been a long time ago, his first year on the job, but it was the kind of mistake that could come around someday and bite you on the ass. He was just back from Vietnam. Still having nightmares. Night sweats. He could go to the range, gunshots all around, and be cool, but a random shot in the night, a firecracker, a car backfiring, and he'd be face down on the pavement, shaking.

Just a brand-new baby cop, doing a door-to-door about a barroom brawl that had spilled into the street and left someone dead. A steamy summer night, full of noise and food smells, people bringing their hibachis out on the sidewalk. He remembered radios blaring "Summer in the City," long-haired girls in tank tops and cut-offs, guys without shirts. Bare skin, musk and incense everywhere.

He'd been hot in his dark uniform, sweat-soaked and nervous, the weight of his gun belt chafing his hips and making his back ache, moving through the crowds, asking his questions, getting called names, trying to keep his temper. Learning how it was to be a cop in America after Kent State, the Chicago convention, Kennedy, King and the riots. He'd knock on a door, get cussed out, ask his questions, go to another and do it all again. His head was pounding, his shirt slimy with the acrid fug of his own sweat. His feet hurt and another long block and hours of his shift stretched ahead of him. Hours of taunts and dirty looks and being called a pig.

He knocked on another door—it could have been his twentieth or his hundredth—bracing himself for the stares and the resistance, and found himself looking down at a diminutive blonde in a blue-flowered dress. Waves of cool air spilled out around her. Her lips were soft pink, her blue eyes rimmed with liner, hair to her waist. She smelled like roses. "Close the door," she said. "I've got air conditioning."

Just as he was shutting the door, something exploded in the street below. He yelled, "Get down!" and threw himself to the floor, grabbing her and taking her with him. He landed on top of her, panting and shaking. Instead of protesting, she put her arms around him, stroking his sweaty hair and his sweaty back, murmuring soothing things. Then she pulled his face to hers and kissed him. He let himself take the comfort there that he desperately wanted. He'd never done it again.

The phone rang. Kyle. "You bringing Alana in?"

"Why?"

"Lulu just coughed up the gem that Alana was one of two girls partying with Pleasant last night."

"Fuck!" Burgess said. That explained why she knew so much.

"Aw, jeez, Joe," Kyle said in mock sympathy. "Don't tell me you were just lied to by a whore?"

"Screw you, Terry."

"Ain't nobody screwing either of us, Joe, despite the company we keep. At least, not in any way we'd find pleasant. Only one who gets happily screwed is Stan. Want me to come get her?"

"Meaning I'm too pissed to be civil? Don't worry about it. I don't think civil's the right approach, anyway."

"Not feeling fond of the lady?"

"Not right now."

He got out, slamming the door, and crunched back down the empty street. Banged on her door. When she opened it, he said, "Did you think I wouldn't find out?" She had the grace to look embarrassed.

"Get your coat," he said. "We're going for a ride."

CHAPTER EIGHT

He drove through the gray-black evening back to the station, Alana silent and tight-lipped beside him, steeling himself for the clamor waiting inside. The benches along the corridor held a ragtag collection of Portland's ladies of the night, arguing, sitting sullenly, or loudly voicing their objections to being kept from their work. They greeted Alana with catcalls and whistles and remarks about him. Alana just stuck her chin out and ignored them. She'd been right about not covering her ass. What she called a coat was a waist-length fake shearling in baby blue. Below it, there were just a few hand-breadths of black vinyl and some absurdly high black boots.

Kyle, looking henpecked and worn, took charge of her. "Let her cool her heels a while," Burgess said. Kyle nodded and led her away. Burgess flung himself into his chair, shoved the pink message slips into a pile, and started reading them.

Stan Perry, looking disgustingly fit and energetic, drifted past. "Patrol stopped by O'Leary's. Nobody home. Neighbor says he left in a hurry this morning and hasn't been back."

"You run a check on him?"

"We're working on it."

"So Lulu says Pleasant was partying at O'Leary's place? Get a warrant and you and Kyle can take some crime scene people over there."

Perry nodded. "Will do. Partying with Alana and some

80

gorgeous blonde babe. I think Lulu's pert little nose is out of joint because she wasn't invited."

"She say why she wasn't?"

"Her tits are too small."

"That's one thing we don't need to worry about."

Perry grinned. "Maybe you don't. I worry about it all the time. Where I'm going to get my hands on a pair of nice big tits."

Burgess rolled his eyes. "Go back to uniform. That's what excites the girls. Not us. What do we know about the blonde?"

"Fuck all. No one's ever seen her around before. Be just as happy if they never do again. Lulu says she's a looker. A hooker who's a looker."

Burgess went back to the messages, giving himself a few minutes to calm down. Some detective he was, letting himself get conned like that.

"I'm getting me and Kyle pizza. You want some?"

"Anything but Hawaiian or anchovy. I can't stand hot ham and pineapple."

"Fine with me. How long you been up, Joe?"

"I've lost track." Perry wandered off and he looked down at the messages. Top one was from Mr. VIP himself, Ted Shaw. Shoot. He'd been too busy getting a backrub from a whore to practice his curtsy. He reached for the phone.

Shaw answered himself. "I appreciate the call, detective. I'm sure you know what I called about. I'm concerned for my daughter, about how all this is handled. It's a difficult time for her. I was hoping you could come by, we could discuss the situation." He had a big, self-satisfied voice, used to getting what it asked for, expecting its booming, genial tones to get a positive response.

"Mr. Shaw, we're in the first twenty-four hours of an investigation."

"Ted," the voice boomed. "Please. Call me Ted."

He didn't want to be on a first-name basis with this man. "Mr. Shaw," he repeated, "I'm sure we can find some time tomorrow to meet." Cote's voice in his ear. Be tactful.

"I have a very busy day tomorrow, detective. Tonight is better. I won't take up much of your time."

He thumbed through the messages. The next was from Jack Kelly. The credit card list was ready. He'd pick it up himself, ask Jen some questions that shouldn't wait. It was almost seven. He could be there by eight, eight-thirty, depending on Alana. "I'm sorry, Mr. Shaw—"

"Tonight." Shaw swatted away Burgess's words and began reeling off directions.

"Hold on," Burgess said. His headache was coming back, but it was nothing compared to the one he'd get listening to Cote's prune-faced whine if Shaw complained they weren't being cooperative. He grabbed a pencil. "It'll be late. Ten, maybe even eleven. I'm tied up 'til then."

"No problem. Whenever you can get here." Mollified now that he was getting his way. Shaw repeated the directions and hung up with neither good-bye nor thank-you. Perhaps manners were for his peers or perhaps the corrosive effect of a lifetime of people saying "yes." Adults could be spoiled as easily as kids and wore it with even less grace.

He found Jack Kelly's message and called. Kelly answered. "Mr. Kelly? It's Sergeant Burgess again. I was hoping I could swing by in an hour or so and get that information?" Kelly made an affirmative noise. "I'd also like to speak with your daughter, if you think she's up to it?"

"Jen's in a bad way," Kelly said. "Maybe it would help her to talk about it. I don't know. But listen, you've got to be gentle with her. She's always been real sensitive."

What'd the guy think, that Burgess was a raging bull who

was going to sweat her under the lights? But that was exhaustion talking. Peel it aside and he was pleased she had someone with her who was protective.

"Yeah. Okay." A man of few words.

Burgess flipped open his notebook and found Janet Pleasant's number. Once he was down there, he might as well make it a two-fer. Three-fer, counting Shaw. His fingers stabbed bluntly at the buttons. While he waited for an answer, he closed his eyes, hoping they'd open again. It wouldn't be good if she answered and got a snore on his end. A woman's voice said, "Hello?"

"Janet Pleasant?"

"Yes?"

"Detective Burgess, Portland police. I need to ask you some questions." Silence, except for an indrawn breath. "I'd like to come by your house, please. This evening."

"Oh. No . . . I don't think so . . . Mackenzie's already upset. I'm upset. I don't think we're in any shape to . . . to . . . well, to be interrogated right now. We don't want to talk about it. Maybe another time. In a few days . . ."

He felt her retreat. In a second, she'd hang up and if he called back, she wouldn't answer. "Mrs. Pleasant, in an investigation like this, time is critical. I know this is difficult for you. I wouldn't ask if it weren't important." Tighten the screws, quickly. "If you'd prefer, I could have someone pick you up and bring you here."

"Pick me up! Bring me to a police station? Surely that's not necessary. I couldn't find a sitter on such short notice. Can't leave Mackenzie at a time like this . . ." He heard the sharp intake of breath, felt her weighing her words. "You have no idea how hard this is for us."

"Actually, Mrs. Pleasant, I do. I can send an officer—"

"Didn't you say you could come here?"

"I could be there around nine."

She sighed. Exasperated. She'd wanted a negotiation and she'd wanted to win, but he hadn't given her a chance. It mean she'd be mad at him from the get go. No big deal. In this business, you couldn't please all of the people all of the time. Often couldn't please anyone any of the time. He'd pretty much gotten over his need to be loved. "If you could give me directions?" She spat them out in an angry voice. In the background, a child cried.

"I appreciate the cooperation," he said.

"This really isn't necessary." She put down the phone.

What was necessary? Why bother solving crimes at all? Real crime was intrusive. Nasty. No one cared except the victims, and there were so few of them. Surely other people shouldn't have to be burdened with this crap. Wouldn't it be better to sweep it under the rug, a nice, tidy unsolved crime so no one would have to talk about unsavory things like sex and hookers and drugs and undigested pizza? Whole goddamned society wanted violence for entertainment and didn't want to be bothered when it spilled over into real life.

He shoved back his chair, grabbed Kyle, and went to see Alana. She was making productive use of the delay. She'd shed the ridiculous coat and her boots, and had her foot up on the table, painting her toenails. She didn't bother pulling down her skirt. She just grinned at Kyle and waved the little brush with its blob of shiny red goo. "He's mad at me, isn't he?"

"He's not big on liars," Kyle said, settling into a chair and switching on the tape.

"I never lied," she said.

Burgess identified them all for the tape and said, "Tell us about last night."

"That ass-wipe O'Leary," she began.

"Hold on. Who's O'Leary?"

"You're a cop and you don't know?"

"I'm asking you, Alana."

"He's a fuckin' pimp."

"Your pimp?"

"I don't use a pimp, Joe. You know that." He waited. "Well, you know. Business has been slow. He called with an offer I couldn't refuse. Said Pleasant wanted to party and had asked for me. As O'Leary put it, the black girl with the big tits." She leaned back and stuck out her chest. "Me, right?"

"Last night the first time at O'Leary's?" She shook her head. "Tell me about it."

She gave a little bare-shouldered shrug. "What's to tell? It was a cold night for sitting in a car. O'Leary suggested a special party and Pleasant went for it. O'Leary picked me and this other girl up at Dunkin' Donuts and we met Pleasant at O'Leary's. I've never seen this girl before, but man, she was nice. Don't mind if I never see her again. Hardly enough business for us girls as it is."

"You didn't know her?" Kyle asked.

Alana gave him the slant-eyed look, showed him the pink tip of her tongue. "Didn't I just say that?"

"How did O'Leary find her?"

She switched feet and started on new toes, caught Kyle's stare and flicked her tongue at him again. "Anytime you want, Terry. You just call me."

Kyle shrugged. "I'm broke, Alana."

She spread her knees. "I'll give you the special police rate."

Kyle looked away.

"How did O'Leary find her," Burgess repeated.

"Shit, Joe, I don't know. O'Leary doesn't confide in me. It's business. I start asking why he's doin' somethin', he's gonna hurt me."

"So you're scared of him?"

Her head came up, defiant, then she seemed to fold in on herself a little. "Yeah."

"Tell me more about this party. What time did it start?"

"Pleasant showed up about eight, eight-thirty. We fooled around. Drank some wine. They did some dope. Usually he was a cold fish. Last night he was really into partying. He wanted to be all over us, wanted us all over him. He wanted to watch O'Leary do her while he did me. O'Leary musta got some great video!"

She put her hand over her mouth. "Oh, shit! He's gonna kill me!"

"O'Leary taped it?" No answer. He wanted to know more about the tape. Made a note to come back to it. "Who suggested tying him up?"

"He did. He was very particular, though. He said nothing that would leave any marks, so his wife wouldn't find out. He always wore a ring."

"He said that, about his wife?" She nodded. "What did you tie him with?"

"These fancy gold curtain ties O'Leary had."

"This other girl. What was her name?"

She shook the polish, the little metal bead clinking. "I don't know."

"Come on, Alana. You know."

"You got anything to eat? I'm starved."

"Yeah, you look real malnourished. Sooner you answer my questions, the sooner you can go get something."

"You mad at me, Joe?" She looked at Kyle. "You got a little something a poor hungry girl could eat?" Flicked her tongue again. Kyle colored. "Fuckin' O'Leary didn't pay me yet. I don't get out there and peddle my ass, I don't eat."

"Thought you'd gone upscale, had a beeper service now," Burgess said, grabbing her purse and turning it upside down. Makeup. Comb and brush. Condoms. Toothpaste. Toothbrush. Breath spray. A half-pint of Southern Comfort. A tube of K-Y Jelly. Chewing gum. A granola bar. A package of Lifesavers. Keys. Business cards. A wallet. He opened the wallet and counted the money. She had more than $600.00. "You've got more money when you're broke than I do when I'm rich," he said.

"You got no right." She set down the polish and started putting her stuff away.

"So tell me about this party. What time did it break up?"

"Eleven, maybe. Then he left with that bitch—"

"Remembered her name yet?"

"Karen." She spat out the word. "Her name was Karen."

"You ever see Karen before?" She shook her head. "What did she look like?"

"Her hair was this crazy blonde color, all these streaks of light and dark, like a bad foil job done on purpose, and she had cheekbones and huge blue eyes and real nice tits and long legs. Like something from Hollywood. After we've done all this stuff, after *I've* done all this stuff, he asks if she'll come with him for a pizza. Like we hadn't just had a three-way and I wasn't the one who'd made it all happen 'cuz she didn't know shit. Like he'd just met her around the fuckin' campus and was askin' for a date!"

"Then what happened?"

"They left. O'Leary followed them out and got the money, then took me home. End of story." She shook the polish again.

"Was O'Leary in the habit of photographing you at work?"

She shrugged. "Sometimes."

"What'd he do with the pictures?"

She narrowed her eyes and tossed her hair, looking like a sullen brat. He was getting real tired of her attitude. "Like I said, O'Leary didn't tell me."

"You never discussed it?" She ignored the question. He'd have to ask O'Leary. "Where'd they go for pizza?"

"Salerno's. If I hadn't heard he was stabbed, I'd of thought he died from food poisoning. She suggested it, he said sure. By that time, they're looking into each other's eyes like fuckin' Tom Hanks and Meg Ryan."

"In what movie, 'You've Got Tail'? Tell me more about your party."

"What's to tell? There was a lot of fucking and sucking and then he left."

"For starters, tell me more about the girl. Height, weight, age. Why you disliked her so much."

She looked cold, sitting there with her shoulders hunched and her arms wrapped around herself. It was February in Maine and she was mostly naked. "I don't know what you want, Joe. Maybe you could ask me questions."

"Are you cold?" She didn't answer. "Questions, huh? Okay, Alana." He pushed back his chair, a sudden, noisy action designed to scare her. "I'll be right back."

He got the Goodwill sweater from his bottom drawer—Alana wasn't the first underdressed young woman he'd interviewed—and stopped by the coffee room for a cup of cocoa. He set the cup and sweater in front of her. "Brought you some cocoa."

She looked warily at his face. "This mean you're not mad anymore?"

"I'm still mad. Tell me about the girl. Was she tall or short?"

"Tall. Well, taller than I am. Maybe five-seven?"

"How old?"

"My age, maybe? I'm not much good at age." She grabbed the sweater and put it on. The pale pink mohair made her look lovely and sweet. Neither lovely nor sweet did anything for him right now.

"Build?"

She considered. "Regular. Her hands and feet weren't small. I remember thinking 'strong' when I looked at her. She had a great body, but it wasn't soft. You could see muscles in her arms." She plucked at the mohair. "Like she wasn't the kind of person who'd wear this. Sexy but not girly."

"You've never seen her before?"

She shook her head. "A girl like that, you'd notice."

"Where'd O'Leary find her?" She huddled in the sweater, visibly considering possible answers. Simply telling the truth was too easy. Alana was a game player and her game was working all the angles. Getting along with the cops, the other girls, the pimps, the dangers of life on the street. He'd been fighting his urge to rescue girls like this almost as long as he'd been a cop. It was like trying to herd squirrels. Lot of young cops tried it until they got their hearts broken, developed calluses, learned to conserve compassion. Otherwise the job was an emotional hemorrhage.

"Where did—"

"Mr. Persistence," she said. "He found girls lots of places. Bus station. Donut place. On the streets."

"That where he found Karen?"

"If that's her name."

"You said—"

"Who the hell do you think you are? I'm tired. I don't want to do this right now."

"Roto-Rooter man," he said. "Trying to work my way through the shit, get the truth flowing. Why do you think that's not her name?"

Alana's shoulder shift was the physical equivalent of *duh!* "Because when I called her that, she looked blank, like she didn't know who I was talking to." She grabbed the mug of cocoa, watching him cautiously. Afraid he was going to take it back? She knew how he was when he was pissed.

"You have no idea how O'Leary found this girl?"

"I think she found him." He raised his eyebrows. "He said," Alana mumbled defensively, "that she left a message on his machine. Said he wished it was always this easy."

"Last night, she seem to know what she was doing?"

The cocoa stopped in midair. "No. She didn't. I mean, she dressed like she meant business. She had the push-up bra and the low-cut dress, but she was wearing panty hose. I mean, please, you wanna wear stockings, wear thigh-highs or a garter belt. But I just thought she was a dumbass newcomer. And she was a snob. Like we're both fucking these guys but I'm just a black whore and she's something special?"

She leaned forward confidentially. "When we were doing each other, I had to tell her what to do. But there's some girls who haven't done that, so I didn't think much of it. I also had to tell that asshole O'Leary to use a rubber. She wasn't going to make him. Screw her, she can take all the risks she wants. But he'll stick it in anything and I didn't want to get some disease."

"Who is this Kevin O'Leary?" No answer. He raised his voice. "Who is Kevin O'Leary?"

She shrugged, as if he were asking about a stranger. "Bad news," she said. She got that nervous look again.

"About O'Leary . . . Does he often make videos of girls with customers?"

She nodded. "He films Lulu all the time."

"What does he do with the tapes?"

"How the hell should I know? I told you. I didn't ask questions."

Alana the fearless was afraid of Kevin O'Leary. He repeated the question. Looked at his watch, elaborately casual. "I've got all night, how 'bout you, Terry?"

Kyle nodded. "I'm enjoying the scenery."

"Oh, fuck you both." She folded her arms and turned her back.

"Let me explain something," he said. "In case maybe you've forgotten this. You know stuff. I'm a cop investigating a murder. I ask you questions. What I want you to do is answer as best you can, without swearing or lying or flirting or flouncing, okay? I'm not interested in what's between your legs, just what's between your ears." He raised his voice. "When I don't get enough sleep, I get real cranky. So just answer the goddamned questions and save your games for someone else."

He slapped his palms on the table, and leaned toward her like a hungry bear studying a morsel. "Tell me about O'Leary and the videotapes."

She cringed back against her chair. "I think he sells them."

"To whom?"

"Guys who are in them, I guess."

"Before he sells them, does he keep them in the apartment?"

"How should I . . ." she began. Burgess shifted angrily. "He hides them. Bragged that he had a great hiding place where no one would ever look." Her hand crept across the table and grabbed his. "I can't talk to you about this, Joe. Don't you see? He'll kill me."

Her hand was icy. He thought about getting her a blanket, then thought better of it. If she wanted to act like a difficult whore, he was going to treat her like one. He disengaged his hand and pushed away from the table. "Why will O'Leary kill you?"

"O'Leary's a pig." She tossed her hair. "He hurts girls. Sometimes hurts them real bad. He's always trying to fuck me. He's rough and dirty and he hurts me. Tries to make me cry and beg him to stop. Like I said. A pig. He wants me to work for him. I'm trying not to . . ." Her gaze swept the room, avoiding their faces, humiliated by the admission she was about to make. "But he scares me so bad, Joe, I do stuff for him sometimes, to, like, keep him happy."

"Like the tapes?" She nodded. "How does he sell the tapes?"

"I don't know. I only know about the hiding place 'cuz he was bragging."

"He was taping you and selling it and not giving you a piece of the action?"

She forced a smile, trying to get her bravado back. "I was The Piece of the action."

"Seems like you got screwed for money, then screwed out of more money."

"So maybe you wanna be my business manager?"

"What's O'Leary look like?"

"Ugly. He's got this big head, like the guy in the Peanuts cartoons, with stick-out ears, and he shaves it, so his skull is all pink and he's got a nose like a pig's snout. He's got a big potbelly and no ass, so his pants always look like they're falling off. His hands are real rough, and he's missing the tip of one little finger. One of his front teeth's broken."

"Any idea where I might find him?"

"If he's not at his place? His mother's up in Rockland. I don't know if her name's O'Leary, though. Sometimes he's there." She slumped wearily in her chair. "Can I go home now? Please? I've tried to cooperate."

"Terry'll find someone to take you home." He turned off the tape and pushed his chair back. "Jesus, Alana, I sure hope you fuck better than you cooperate."

"You bet I do," she said, "but you'll never know, will you, copman?"

He went out, closing the door behind him, and found Perry. "Stan, you get anything from that witness? The one who saw someone walking away?"

"She doesn't know if it was male or female, just a dark figure on the sidewalk. Whoever it was got into a car that was parked down the block and drove away."

"She was sure it was a car?"

Perry slapped a mocking hand against his forehead. "That was dumb. She said car, I wrote down car, didn't ask a follow-up question. How'd it go with Alana?"

"We're getting there. She says Pleasant left with the other woman—someone she's never seen before—to go to Salerno's, and that Pleasant seemed very smitten. She also says that O'Leary videotaped the evening's festivities."

"Melia's working on that warrant. You want pizza?" Burgess glanced down at the pizza, saw Dr. Lee's shiny scalpel slicing into Pleasant's stomach, and felt his own stomach turn. "Think I'll pass," he said. "Gotta go see some people about a dead doc."

93

CHAPTER NINE

He got a fresh radio and shrugged into his coat. Found Perry and Kyle and Alana finishing the pizza. He nodded at Alana, not liking the easy familiarity of the scene, then motioned for his detectives to step away. "I'm going to pick up some stuff from Jen Kelly, see Pleasant's ex-wife, and pay a duty call on Ted Shaw. You guys can finish up with the ladies—ask what they know about Kevin O'Leary. Keep an ear open for anything about Pleasant and drugs. O'Leary and drugs. O'Leary videotaping sex parties. About the mystery blonde, Karen, who was partying with Pleasant and Alana last night. Then see what you find at O'Leary's place. And Stan?"

Perry cocked his pen and waited.

"Give Vince the heads up on the drug angle. Alana says word on the street was Pleasant was a source for Oxycontin. You okay with finishing up here, then doing O'Leary's place?"

Perry nodded. Still eager. "Assuming Vince can find a judge. Hell of a good thing none of us needs sleep, ain't it?"

Burgess went in the locker room and got out his razor. If the man glaring back from the mirror paused on a street corner, the cops would pick him up as a vagrant. Sighing, he mowed his chin, combed his hair, brushed his teeth, and threw cold water on his face. He looked so much better he considered giving this all up for modeling.

Jack Kelly answered the door, one hand on the knob, the other holding the baby, barring the doorway until Burgess

identified himself. Kelly was a block of a man, 1
than five feet, eight inches and an easy 200 pounds,
impression he gave was not of fat but of mass. His
graying hair had receded from his forehead. He had t..ick,
aggressive eyebrows, a wide and friendly face.

"Have to be careful, detective," he explained. "We've
had a lot of people ringing the doorbell today. Jen doesn't
need that." He jerked his head toward the living room.
"She's in there. Lying down. I'm a little worried about
her." He beckoned Burgess into the kitchen. "Sorry. I
didn't want her to hear, and Jen's always had ears like a . . .
like a . . . hell. I don't know. Doesn't miss much, that's all."

Kelly settled the baby into a plastic seat on the counter,
tucking the blankets carefully around it, the infant tiny in
Kelly's big hands. "You want a sandwich or something? I
was about to have one. We've got tuna or turkey or ham
and cheese subs. I brought 'em myself. Jen doesn't eat and
Steve, he was so fussy, it had to be all-natural, low-fat, low-
cholesterol, absolutely fresh. She spent half her life finding
food to please him."

"Tuna sounds good."

"Milk? Beer? Coffee? I brought the beer, too." He unwrapped two sandwiches and put them on plates. "Take a
load off, detective."

Burgess was glad to. He'd been at this so long his eyes
ached and he was beginning to feel light-headed. He put his
coat over the back of the same chair he'd sat in twelve hours
ago. Jack Kelly put the sandwich in front of him, along with
a cup of coffee he hadn't asked for, and sat down across
from him.

"I'm worried about Jen," he repeated, leaning forward
confidentially. "She seems unconcerned. Indifferent. She's
always been quiet, but this is something else."

"Shock," Burgess said. "She was already worn out—pregnancy, the baby, her suspicions about her husband. I don't know how resilient she is but people need time."

Kelly passed him some papers. "Here's that list you wanted."

Burgess scanned the sheets, noting the neat, precise handwriting and the careful inclusion of details. Pleasant had carried a lot of credit cards. "Mr. Kelly, tell me about your son-in-law."

"He wasn't really my son-in-law."

"Jen calls you her father. You're the one she wanted in a crisis. That means you had an ongoing relationship with her and her husband."

"You'd think so," Kelly grunted. "I don't think Stephen had relationships with people. He was so eager when he was courting Jen, so desperate to capture her, to marry her, but I don't think it was ever Jennifer the person he wanted. It was Jennifer the possession. Unless it was Jennifer, Ted Shaw's daughter, and access to Ted's money. I tried to warn her. Should have known better. She's got her mother's romantic streak. These women fall in love, you can't do a damned thing about it."

"That what happened when her mother fell in love with you?"

Kelly's smile was shy. Pleased. "You might say that."

"But her mother isn't here. You are."

"Clara would be. She was devoted to her daughter." He shook his head. "My wife's dead, detective. I'm the only parent Jen has." He hesitated. "Well, you know that's not true. I'm the only active parent Jen has." He slapped his chest with two big palms, a loud sound. In its plastic nest, the baby shifted, made a sound. Kelly watched until it settled down. "I'm just a dumb, working-class guy who cares about her. I'm the father who read her stories and taught her to ride a bike and went to her soccer games. Down the road a piece is the guy who was her wallet, who believes biology is destiny. She goes by Kelly but legally she's Jennifer Shaw."

"Her wallet?"

"Shaw's always been too busy to bother with Jen but she is his only child. He cares how she's turned out. How well she lives. It was important that she go to the right schools, know the right kids, live the right life. When she broke her leg, he was too busy to visit, but she had the best doctors and the biggest bouquets."

"You sound bitter."

"Only on her behalf. It was good for me that Ted didn't want a hand in the day-to-day rearing of his kid. It let me have a relationship with her without a tug-of-war."

Jen had been luckier than she'd probably ever know. Half his cases these days came from broken homes and re-constituted families. Ex-husbands stalking, assaulting and killing their wives or their wives' new boyfriends. Boy-friends and second husbands beating and molesting the children. Stepsons beating up their stepmothers. His sisters always asked why he'd never married. Partly, he'd been so busy and ambitious he'd never found the right girl, one who'd put up with his crazy hours, his passion for the job. Partly, he saw so much of the dark side. Couldn't imagine how a woman could live with that. Live with him living with that.

"You wanted to know about Stephen?" Kelly smiled his shy smile again. "Ever see a movie called *The Manchurian Candidate*?" Burgess nodded. "Well, you ask about him and I find myself nodding and saying Stephen Pleasant was the nicest, kindest . . . then I say, 'Wait a minute, Jack.' Steve was so good at presentation. He was so superficially great, genial, polished, just so damned slick. It wasn't until you got away and took a hard look that you realized it was all packaging."

Who was Jack Kelly? He looked like a stevedore, talked like a shrink. But Burgess knew, start making assumptions about people based on appearance and you missed a lot. People surprised you. Sometimes the surprises were pleasant. "Was he unkind to Jen?"

"I thought so. But I'm not sure she knew it, until she found out about the other women. Jen's so young, detective. She hadn't had a lot of experience before Stephen. She didn't know how she was entitled to be treated. She didn't know what to expect or how to negotiate it for herself. Steve was there after her mother died, offering what she saw as security, comfort. Jen's a natural caretaker." His smile was ironic now. "She thought getting to wait on Steve, trying to satisfy his whims, was a privilege. And Shaw was pleased at her marrying an up-and-coming doctor, even if he was divorced."

"How did she learn about the other women?"

Kelly took a deep breath, held it, slowly let it out. "I told her."

"Why?" Burgess asked. "How did you find out?"

"She asked me to. She called me up one day, she was about six months pregnant then, and . . ." He eyed Burgess across the table, the beady eye of a father assessing a date. "Understand this. Jen's not an emotional girl. She's not given to firestorms and sulks. And she was sobbing so hard I thought she must have lost the baby. I went right over. She met me at the door, threw herself into my arms, and said, 'Daddy, I think Stephen is seeing another woman.' " His eyes stayed on Burgess's face. "A girl like Jen, so naïve and so trusting, she thought it had to be her fault. Some way she'd failed."

Kelly got himself another beer. "Want more coffee?"

"I want the rest of the story."

"Right. Sorry. It was the usual thing. He stayed out late. Came home smelling of perfume. Seemed less interested in sex. She thought it was because she was pregnant and unappealing. Detective, you've seen Jennifer. If anything, pregnant she was even prettier. I told her I'd see what I could find out. So I followed him. What the hell, I'm a widower, what else do I have to do with my nights? I saw where he went and what he did."

"You confront him?"

Kelly gave him a level look. "You were her father, what would you have done?"

"What did you do?"

"Went to his office. I walked in, closed the door, told him I knew what he was doing and he'd better knock it off or he was going to ruin his marriage and break his wife's heart. He said he loved Jen and didn't want to hurt her, but sometimes he needed more sex than he got at home. Said it wasn't going to be easy to stop but he'd try. He begged me not to tell Jen. I agreed, but I didn't trust him. I kept following, he kept doing it. No change. No difference." The big hand gripping the bottle was dangerously close to breaking it.

"So you told Jen?"

"I didn't want to. Didn't see how it helped. But it was her life and with conduct so risky, he might have been exposing her to things. I decided she ought to know."

"How'd she take it?"

"How do you think? She looked stricken, like I'd used my fist instead of words. Then she folded her arms over her stomach, sighed, and said she'd have to think about what to do." The baby murmured and shifted and Kelly's grip relaxed.

"Did you kill your son-in-law, Mr. Kelly?"

Kelly didn't seem offended by the question. "I thought about it." He planted his big hands on the table and pushed himself up, meeting Burgess's eyes. "Someone else got there first. I suppose I ought to be sorry about the waste of a talented physician, but I'm not. He was ruining her life, that little boy's life. He would have ended in disgrace soon enough."

"What does that mean?"

Kelly shrugged. "You're the detective."

"You think your daughter killed her husband?"

Kelly shook his head vehemently. "No way. Jen's a gentle girl and a hopelessly forgiving one. She would have given him a hundred warnings and a hundred chances. Despite how he treated her, see, she still loved him. But if Ted knew?" Kelly's shrug was eloquent.

"Was your daughter home last night?" Kelly didn't answer. "I need to talk to her," Burgess said. He put on his jacket, picked up his papers and notebook, and followed Kelly into the living room. She lay on a big white sofa, covered with a blue blanket, curled up on her side, long hair draped over the cushion. Sound asleep, she looked about twelve. "I'll come back," he said. "Thanks for the sandwich."

They all needed sleep. He hefted himself onto the seat, turned on the engine, and punched the buttons for the tape player. After a scattering of applause, Emmylou Harris began to sing "Love Hurts."

"You can say that again, Emmylou," he grunted. "Love hurts and everybody lies." He jammed the Explorer into gear, maneuvered around Jack Kelly's truck, and crunched away down the drive.

CHAPTER TEN

From Jen Kelly's description and the voice on the phone, he'd expected Janet Pleasant to be a greedy and well-tailored Talbots shrew. He was surprised by the woman who answered the door. She was taller than Pleasant had been, and her dark hair was hennaed, punk-short, and spiked. She probably outweighed Pleasant, too. The black leggings and turtleneck did nothing to disguise her body, which was full-breasted, wide-hipped and comfortable. She wore an expensive silver and turquoise necklace, Native American, and heavy silver earrings.

"Detective Burgess?" He nodded. As he followed her inside, he had an odd vision of his day as a series of rear views. Jen's small, tight, girlish behind. Alana's voluptuous one. Now Janet Pleasant's nice womanly one. He could be a Fuller Brush salesman. You hear the one about the traveling detective and the victim's wives?

She led him into a small room—the sort people called a "den"—and asked him to sit. She paused at the door, listened carefully, and closed it quietly behind her. "Mackenzie's having a hard time with this," she explained. "Despite his flaws, she loved her father. She's only seven. I wouldn't have thought . . ." She didn't finish. "I think she's finally settled."

She got right down to business, settling herself on a small flowered sofa and curling her legs beneath her. "What did you want to know?"

"What was your relationship with your ex-husband?"

"Divorced."

101

"But you stayed in touch, because of your daughter, Mackenzie?" She nodded. "What kind of contact did you still have, Mrs. Pleasant?"

"Every third weekend, Mackenzie would stay with Stephen and Jennifer. Occasionally he would see her more often, but that was rare. Stephen was busy; Jennifer was preoccupied with her pregnancy and renovating their house."

"Mackenzie had a good relationship with her father and his wife?" She nodded, not giving him anything he didn't ask for. "How did she get to her father's house?"

"I dropped her off after school on Friday. Jennifer drove her back on Sunday."

"Who initiated the divorce?"

"What does that have to do with anything?"

"If you could just answer the question?"

"I did. It was a no-fault divorce. We had grown apart."

"So it was an amicable divorce?"

"I didn't say that." She sighed. "Do we have to do this, detective?" When he didn't respond, she answered her own question. "I guess you need to know about him. It's just . . ." She hesitated. "I'm so much happier when I don't have to think about him. I suppose . . . I mean, I know. Right now, what makes me happy doesn't matter."

"Please tell me about your divorce, Mrs. Pleasant."

"I met Stephen when he was in medical school. I was an art teacher. We met through a mutual friend. I was attracted to those clean good looks. He appealed to the artist in me. I wanted to draw him, to photograph him. I wanted to run my hands over those bones—his nose, his chin, that proud forehead." She touched her necklace, rubbing her fingers slowly over the smooth turquoise stones. "In the spirit of frankness—I assume you do want me to be frank—I should say that I wanted to run my hands all over him. Stephen had a finely made and aesthetically appealing body. It was his soul, or lack of it, that finally turned me off."

Burgess raised his eyebrows curiously, waiting for her to continue. Instead, she crossed the room, picked a photograph off the desk, and handed it to him. "Our wedding picture. Every time I put it away, Mackenzie has a fit. I think she still hopes . . . hoped . . . we'd get back together."

He could see what she meant. The younger Stephen Pleasant had had an appealing face. So had she. Longer hair back then, dark and shaggy and cut into layers that framed her face and accented her eyes. The two of them, frozen for all time in a moment of beautiful youth and happiness. Somewhere along the line, it had crashed and burned. "Your husband changed?"

"I'm not sure he did." She shrugged. "It may only be that my view of him changed, that what I thought was passion was ambition. What I took for compassion for his patients and a desire to save lives was really a driving need to be admired, to be the best. Success not so much on behalf of people as through them. He needed his patients to be dependent and grateful, to respect him. He didn't understand that he also needed to respect them. Gradual erosion ended our marriage, detective, not some big blowup. We started out so young and naïve. At least, I was young and naïve. Much like poor, befuddled Jennifer."

She laced her hands behind her head and gave an unselfconscious stretch, like a cat waking up, arching her back and pressing her chest toward him. It wasn't a sexual gesture. He knew when a woman was trying to attract him. Janet Pleasant was merely stiff and tired. One of those rare women who are comfortable in their bodies.

"Jen Kelly said your relationship with your ex-husband was unfriendly."

"I'll bet she did. Poor Jen thinks part of her job is to protect him and make his life run smoothly, because he's such an important, hard-working doctor. She would have gotten over it. Under that schoolgirl veneer lurks the heart of a proud and passionate woman." She coughed. "Excuse the purple prose. It's just that she's so pitiful and I can't stand women who let themselves be made pitiful. He was making such a fool of her."

"What do you mean?"

She gave him a thin smile. "Didn't you tell me the first hours are critical? He's been dead close to twenty-four hours by now. Surely you've learned something about him."

"That's why I'm here."

"I'm being bitchy, aren't I? That's what Jennifer really told you. That I'm a bitch and a shrew who fought with Stephen all the time and threatened to kill him." Again that thin smile. He suspected she had a warmer smile she used on other occasions.

"Are you a bitch and shrew? Did you threaten to kill him?"

"No, except where Stephen was concerned. And yes, I did once say, before witnesses, that if only he were dead, I could collect the insurance and then I wouldn't have to worry about always fighting him for support. I'm sure I'm not the first woman who found her ex-husband's inattention to his financial obligations infuriating. Nor the first to announce in exasperation a desire to kill him." She held out her hands, wrists together. "You want to throw cuffs on and lock me up?"

She was good at this. Sharp. Fun, if you liked verbal tennis, but he was too tired to run after her serves. "Please, Mrs. Pleasant. I've been up since yesterday morning. Can we just talk straight and get this over with?" He thought that underneath it all, despite the bitterness, she was shocked by the death and wanted to talk.

Her shoulders slumped. "I'm sorry," she said. "I've been so mad at him for so long. I shouldn't make it your problem. Yes, Stephen and I had an acrimonious divorce. Not because he opposed the divorce—he already had his eye on Jennifer by then—but because of his pathological affinity for the goddamned buck. He made good money. I asked for a reasonable amount of support. I was not greedy but I was not going to let him cheat Mackenzie at the expense of any new family he might engender. I'm willing to work. I do work. But art teachers don't make a lot of money. Stephen and his lawyers fought me for every cent, every scrap. By the time we were done, I *could* have killed him. Without hesitation or remorse."

She leaned toward him confidentially. "Do you have children?" He shook his head. "Well, children change things. When you have kids, divorce isn't the end, it's the beginning of a different relationship. If it had been just me, I could have walked away, good riddance to him, but Mackenzie has . . . had . . . rights and interests separate from mine. I couldn't kill Stephen because she's his child and she loves . . . she loved him. But because of her, we had an ongoing relationship which took the form of my fighting for every cent he owed us. I had to suck down my anxiety about the mortgage and her tuition and whether I could keep the car running, put on a bright smile, and chat merrily about her daddy."

She sighed. "Yes, it made me bitter. I think he genuinely lacked the capacity to be fair or generous. No matter how much he had, he wanted more and wasn't scrupulous about what he had to do to get it."

She massaged her cheeks, as though the memory of

those false smiles made them ache. "I'm sorry he's dead, because my little girl is hurt by it, and I love my daughter more than anything. At the same time, I feel like someone has lifted a huge weight from me. I'm what Mackenzie calls 'happy-sad.' "

She anticipated his next question. "Yes. He was insured. The divorce settlement required him to carry a policy with Mackenzie as the beneficiary. And given his rather casual attitude toward bills, the cost was included in the child support and I paid the premium." She watched him write that down, then asked, "Do you have any idea who killed him?"

"I was hoping you might." It was pleasant in the little room. The furniture was comfortable, the paintings soothing. Everything was in soft, hushed tones, like a room speaking in a whisper. It was warm and so quiet the only sound was her breathing. He was grateful for the warmth—those frigid hours at the crime scene were still very much with him—but it made him long for sleep and he still had Ted Shaw on his dance card.

She shrugged, a big gesture, not the subdued, musclebound one most people used. "I don't know. Except that bankers are too dull to be killers, I'd suggest you look at his creditors. Or anyone he owed money. He always pled poverty as the excuse for being late with his support. And he was arrogant about his right to be irresponsible. Other than that? It could have been anyone. He was so terribly selfish and unkind."

She fingered the necklace again. Caught his look. "My power necklace," she said. "I got it to celebrate the divorce. I needed courage to face you."

He'd been rough on the phone. But necessarily rough, or she wouldn't have agreed to see him. It was one of the facts of his life, that violence—assaults, rapes, murder—was never easy on the people who had to talk about it. "I don't bite," he said. "I think there was something else you wanted to say?"

"For your suspect list. What about Ted Shaw? Stephen married Jen for her money. Maybe Shaw got sick of dishing it out, given Stephen's sordid habit of visiting hookers."

"Did he do that while he was married to you?"

"Come on, detective. You think he left a saggy-baggy woman like me, married that young beauty, and suddenly was driven to hookers? Neither the little princess, nor I, nor any normal woman was enough for Stephen. It wasn't about normal. We had a good time in bed. For all I know, Stephen and Jen did, too. It was about power. Being larger than life, with larger-than-life needs. Being serviced with no need for reciprocity."

"Did Jen Kelly know about her husband's sexual proclivities?"

"Proclivities?" She shrugged. "Depends on what you mean by 'know.' I tried to tell her what she was getting into. Fairly explicitly. That's one of the reasons she hates me. I told her what he was like and she called me a bitch and a dirty liar. Said I was being horrible because he'd divorced me and wanted to marry her. But she had to believe that, didn't she?"

"You're awfully generous."

"I don't have any animosity toward Jen. I feel sorry for her."

"It didn't bother you that she had a big house and the money to redo it while you were struggling to make ends meet?"

"It bothered me. But most of that money came from Ted Shaw, and he doesn't owe me a thing."

He tried to think how to word his last two questions. "Did

your ex-husband ever have trouble with angry patients?"

"Not that I knew of. But he probably should have."

"Were you ever aware of him prescribing unnecessary drugs or giving drugs or drug samples to anyone other than his regular patients?"

She hesitated. "I sometimes wondered . . ." then shook her head. He was about to ask a follow-up question when a voice called, "Mommy." A pause. Called again, and after the second call, quickly ascended into an hysterical wail.

"I've got to go to her," Janet Pleasant said. "You mind letting yourself out?"

"Not at all. Thank you for your cooperation. If I have more questions . . ."

"Then I'm sure you'll ask them, detective. You don't strike me as a shrinking violet." She hurried out of the room and a second later he heard her calling to the child as her feet clattered up the stairs. She could have done it. She was strong and angry and stood to gain by Pleasant's death. He took another look at the wedding picture, set it back on the desk, and left.

CHAPTER ELEVEN

Investigating a crime was a lot like painting by numbers. Fill in enough spaces with blotches of the right color and gradually a crude picture emerged. So far, he'd gotten a fair picture of Pleasant, but the killer remained a dark blur. The bloodhound in him wanted to keep going, but he'd reached the point where he was almost past being useful. He only had to make it through Ted Shaw and he could crash.

He pushed the bizarre crime scene and Pleasant's grotesque face away by pulling up questions he came back to often. What was a cop, anyway? Why would someone choose a job where you were simultaneously desperately needed and detested? Why be the one who got to see so many others, good and bad, at their worst? And what was a detective? Was he like a net, scooping up great gobs of material and then sorting through it? Like a filter through which information poured, trapping only the needed stuff? Or like flypaper, to which the perpetrator would eventually be drawn and stick? And the hardest question—if he couldn't prevent pain and sorrow for good people and those he loved, couldn't always bring wrongdoers to justice, was it worth it?

These answerless ponderings carried him to his destination. Shaw's house, a great stucco and timber pile big enough to shelter scores of Portland's homeless, was reached by a winding driveway, sheltered from the prying eyes of the great unwashed by a grove of hemlocks. The nine-foot, carved oak doors towered above him as if to remind him of his insignificance. He parked and forced his whiny knee up the steps. Even in the damp and cold of winter, the brass knobs were freshly polished. He rang the bell and waited as cold sneaked around his ankles, crept down his neck, nuzzled his ears. Nothing happened. He rang the bell again.

The wind blew in his open coat and stole his body heat. Last night, he'd been so cold when they finished he hadn't stopped shivering for an hour. Now it was happening again. He zipped his coat but the cold had done its job. He stood hunched on the porch, hands plunged deep in his pockets, feeling the desolation of the night, the weight of his tired body, the spacey moodiness that hits when you're thirty-six hours out. Waiting dumb as a dog because changing course took decision.

Either Shaw had given up on him and gone to bed, or he'd been killed, too, and couldn't answer the door. Burgess fervently hoped it wasn't the latter. Once he might have welcomed the challenging complexity of two interwoven investigations. Now he longed for simplicity. He scribbled, "Sorry I missed you. Please call me," on the back of his card and was bending to shove it under the door when it opened.

Ted Shaw, silver-haired, aristocratic, and at least two sheets to the wind, stood swaying in the doorway, a heavy crystal glass filled with golden brown liquid in his hand. "Dee . . . tec . . . tive. Excuse me. I was out back in the . . . kitchen." He swung the glass in a welcoming arc. "Please come in." Burgess stepped into a dark hall from which he gleaned only an impression of shiny floors and a high ceiling before his host conducted him into a dark-paneled, book-lined room with a crackling fire flanked by two leather wing chairs. English library stage set. The hand with the glass waved toward the chairs. "Sit down. You want a drink?"

"No, thank you, sir. I'm working." Hell, another minute and he would have been gone instead of stepping out on the verbal dance floor with a self-important and belligerent drunk. Ted Shaw was handsome in a Hathaway-shirt-ad way. From a distance, the craggy features, still-dark brows, and slim body were extremely photogenic. Up close—which he couldn't avoid because Shaw kept swaying into his air space—he could see the broken capillaries, sagging skin, the effects of an alcoholic's poor nutrition.

As Burgess moved toward the chair, Shaw gave him a friendly cuff on the shoulder. "You don't have to stand on ceremony with me, dee . . . tec . . . tive. Not like I'm going to tell anyone, is it? Have a drink. I hate to drink alone." His grin was genial, his balance a bubble off plumb.

Burgess shook his head. Good liquor by a warm fire was enticing, but there were too many reasons not to. He knew Shaw wasn't his friend and wouldn't hesitate to cause him trouble. He also knew that if he had a drink, he'd never get out of the chair. He pulled out his notebook and sat, not expecting much, knowing he had to try. "Now then, sir," he said, clicking his pen loudly, "what was it you wanted to see me about?"

Shaw landed heavily in the opposite chair, picked up his drink from a delicate piecrust table, and drew off the first inch. "Single malt," he said. "Delicious." He held up the glass and watched the facets catch the firelight. "Sure you won't?"

"I appreciate the offer but I haven't slept since yesterday morning and I'm trying to get home to bed," Burgess said. "Can you tell me what you wanted?"

Shaw tried to focus. "I'm worried about my daughter,

about how this whole business will affect her. She's recently had a child, you know. Difficult birth. Cesarean. She's barely gotten back on her feet. And now this. As a father, I'm anxious to protect her." He slumped back in his chair, apparently satisfied he'd made himself clear.

Burgess waited for a specific request. When nothing happened, he said, "What is it you want from me?" Probably too blunt to meet Cote's standards of tact, but he was too tired for finesse.

"I want you to keep her husband's ridiculous sexual shenanigans out of the paper, son. That's what I want." He swung his glass for emphasis, sending a wave of Scotch into his lap. He didn't seem to notice.

"Mr. Shaw, we have no control over what the papers print. All we control is the information we give out, which, I assure you, will be as circumspect as possible."

"My son-in-law . . ." The words were barely distinguishable. ". . . was a philandering ass. Cost me plenty. Thash no reashon Jennifer should be . . ."

Burgess thought the last word was "embarrassed." This was a colossal waste of time and now it would be a challenge to get out without a fight. The red face and fist clenching the glass said the genial drunk was rapidly deteriorating into belligerent drunk. Burgess knew Shaw's reputation. He got to his feet. "Sir, I apologize. It's too late and we're both too tired for this. Let me call you in the morning . . ."

"Sit down," Shaw bellowed, standing up himself. Except, his tongue being thick and slippery, he didn't say "sit." "I want you to listen to me." He covered the distance to Burgess with two unsteady steps and poked him in the chest. "Lissen. You find whoever killed that boy, and find him fast. Put as many resources as you have on it. None of this waiting for some damned test or other. I don't want this paraded through the papers day after day, reporters camped out on Jen's front steps, poor girl having to read about her husband's misbehavior in ugly detail. You go arrest somebody. Some whore. Pimp. If it turns out the fool's gotten into any more of those financial messes, I'll pay. No reason for any embarrassing stuff to come out. You come to me, I'll take care of it. Unnerstand? Bailed him out before, I can do it again."

Burgess was glad he hadn't taken his coat off. He took a couple steps toward the door and turned. "I'm going right back to work now, sir. And I promise you, we'll get this wrapped up as fast as we can."

"Good!" Shaw tipped up his glass and drained it. "I knew you'd unnerstand, once we'd talked man-to-man. Supervisor wasn't so sure, but I told him, just send the boy to me. I'll make him unnerstand." He took a few unsteady steps forward, peering into Burgess's face. "You do unnerstand, don't you? How important, keep this stuff quiet?"

He had to get out before he got stuck in a conversational loop that could last for hours. Shaw had admitted knowledge of Pleasant's sexual shenanigans, and made some intriguing remarks about Pleasant's financial scrapes, but this was not the time for questions. "I think I do, sir," he agreed, heading for the door. Shaw stood swaying in the study entrance, a shadowy figure back-lit by the fire like those dapper black silhouettes people put in their yards.

Burgess closed the heavy oak door and limped down the steps, his knee hurting like hell. He heard his doctor's voice, "You've got to do your exercises every day. If you don't, it's going to hurt." Well, the doc was right. Doc also rode him about his weight, like he didn't know his knee would feel better if he lost some. So in his next life he'd be

113

a fitness king. A gym rat. In this life, he couldn't even find time to sleep.

He slammed the car door and paused in the icy darkness, tipping his head back and closing his eyes. He could go to sleep right here. Go to sleep and freeze to death—another body the cops would be called out on. At least it wouldn't be his problem. He pressed his tired arm forward and started the car, driving slowly out onto the empty road.

Partway back, his phone rang and Stan Perry's voice was with him in the car. "Joe? We're at O'Leary's place. Been waiting for the fire department to clear out. Looks like someone wanted to be sure we didn't find anything."

"They succeed?"

"Not entirely. We could use some help sorting through the rubble."

"I'm on my way."

Eat healthy food. Get plenty of rest. And exercise. Just who the hell did doctors think could do that? He'd been awake so long it felt like his eyelids were lined with sandpaper.

He nosed into a tight space behind Stan's car, shoved the Explorer into park, and grabbed gloves and evidence bags from the back seat. Two fire trucks were still parked in front of the building—Portland's history of catastrophic fires had left a bit of a paranoid legacy. Despite the cold and the late hour, a small crowd clustered behind the yellow tape, trying to get the officer controlling the scene to tell them what had happened. He identified himself, slipped under the tape, and went inside. Climbing the stairs, he was assailed by acrid smoke and chemical smells.

Stan came out on the landing and gestured him into the room with one gloved hand. "Looks like they piled everything on the bed and set it on fire."

"They?"

"He. She. It. The perpetrator."

"We know it was set?"

"Gasoline. Can't you smell it? Fire department's going to have their arson guys in tomorrow. They're pissed as hell we want to take stuff."

If he'd been the fire department, he'd have been pissed, too, but if they waited until after the arson investigation, vital evidence might be lost. Might end up in *their* evidence bags instead.

"Anyone see anything? Like who set it?"

Perry shook his head. "See no evil, hear no evil, speak no evil."

"Meaning they're all shit scared of O'Leary?"

"Got it in one."

"Where's Terry?"

"In the bathroom, sifting through the trash and bagging condom wrappers."

He looked around. Wink was carefully putting something that looked like the charred remnants of a bedspread into a paper bag, moving with the ponderous slowness of exhaustion. Where he'd absently swiped at it, his pale skin was streaked black.

Burgess pulled on gloves. "Where do you want me to start?"

"Wink and I have this room. You got the kitchen."

He sloshed across the soggy carpet to the kitchen. Although the fire had been confined to the bedroom, everything here, even the light fixture, was coated with oily black grime. It didn't look good for fingerprints. There were some glasses in the sink but they were black. He moved the top layer of trash and bagged bottles and fast-food wrappers. On the counter was a blinking answering machine. He bagged the machine. Plucked a few more likely bits from the trash and bagged them, too.

He lugged his treasures into the bedroom, found Perry and Wink finishing up and Kyle coming out of the bathroom. "You guys ready to call it a night?"

"Twenty-four hours ago," Devlin said.

Burgess looked around for something to load their evidence in, settled for a plastic milk crate. "Let's drop this stuff at the lab and go get some sleep."

"Sleep?" Perry said. "What's that?"

"Something civilians do," Wink said sourly, staring down at his filthy shoes. "Jeez, I hate fires. My shoes are wrecked, my clothes are wrecked."

"Your disposition's wrecked." Burgess lifted the crate, watching Kyle, stiff and skeletally thin, heading for the stairs. "I'll have patrol drop this off. You guys go home."

Burgess followed them down the stairs and out past the crowd. With their slumped shoulders and dirty clothes, they looked more like perpetrators than investigators. He watched them fumble with their keys, load their tired bodies into their cars, and drive off in clouds of exhaust. He took one last look at the second floor. Tomorrow they'd have to get the drug people involved. What had O'Leary been so worried about that he'd torched his own place, if O'Leary had done it. And where the hell had he gone?

Chapter Twelve

He left his blackened shoes by the door, dropped his jacket and tie beside them to go to the cleaners, and made his way across the cold apartment. The bathroom was warmer. He dropped the rest of his clothes in the hamper, showered, set the alarm for seven, and fell into bed. He'd slept five hours when his alarm clock exploded like the Day of Judgment. He dragged an eye open, stared blearily at the gray morning, and decided to give himself another half hour.

Ten minutes later, the phone rang. Captain Cote, dispensing with civilities like hello or good morning, burst out of the receiver. "Where the hell are you?"

"In bed. Asleep."

"O'Leary's apartment," Cote said. "The fire chief's furious that you were messing with their crime scene."

He lay back down, phone to his ear, and counted to ten as he deleted the expletives from his reply. "It was our scene first. It's where Pleasant was partying the night he was killed. We're looking for anything that'll help us find O'Leary or that second girl. We pulled the warrant before the fire." Cote knew this, should have told the fire department. Sometimes he wondered whose side the guy was on.

"How come I haven't got any reports from you?" Cote continued. "How am I supposed to stay on top of things?"

"Because I've been out interviewing people."

"Then get your ass down here and write them."

"My ass was just working on its fifth hour of sleep in two days. We were up 'til two, working O'Leary's place." God,

117

he hated starting out with a headache. Not that Cote'd care if he had limbs dropping off or was in a body cast. Cote was the new breed of rank—all about management techniques and procedures, solve rates and stats, willing to leave his cops hanging in the wind. Burgess was a by-the-book cop, but he knew sometimes rules were a poor fit and good cops needed some slack. A lot of the job was about judgment.

Ignoring everything he'd said, Cote snapped, "See me as soon as you get in."

Right. As long as you get your beauty sleep, asshole. Burgess cradled the phone and lay back down, but Cote had murdered sleep. Now that the case was oozing back into his brain, he might as well get up and go to work.

He pulled on socks and underwear, and shaved, hearing Alana's voice. "Dumb ass." So he was one of those guys who looked better without their clothes. He wondered if the guys at the station would agree. If naked interrogation would get better results. Guy in the mirror didn't look like he'd give the Calvin Klein models any competition. He dressed, grabbed some painkillers for his knee, found dry shoes, and left.

It was warmer, but the lead gray sky promised snow by noon. He liked snow, but when he had to drive around talking to people it was a huge pain, slowing things to a snail's pace. Tragically, it looked like his New Year's diet was going to be postponed again. He couldn't do eighteen-hour days on veggies and sprouts. Breakfast would be courtesy of the golden arches. Cop cuisine. Drive through, bag a coffee and a bagel sandwich, gulp it down at his desk.

He hoped, as cops always did in a hard case, that something had broken open while he slept, knowing that it was a false hope.

Stan and Terry weren't in. Neither was Wink, but Dani

had left a message that she had something to show him. He scarfed down his breakfast, and went to the lab. Found Dani bent over a microscope. "Got something for me?" he asked.

"I've got a lovely footprint." She carefully lifted a cardboard box. Underneath was a shoe impression cast in dental stone. "Found it beside the passenger door." Her smile was hopeful. "Is it yours? It's not Aucoin's and you guys got the scene sealed off before anyone else could muck it up." He shook his head and the smile faded. "What's the matter? I thought you'd be pleased."

"Looks like a man's foot," he said.

"Man's size eleven. Reebok. That a problem?"

"I was thinking our killer could be a woman."

"Maybe she has big feet."

"Maybe. But our witness says she was wearing very high heels."

"Oh," she said. "FMPs."

"Which are?"

"Fuck me pumps. Shoes with heels so high you have to stick out your chest and ass to stay balanced. They're supposed to make the legs look good. Or so I'm told." She looked at her own feet, in sensible shoes at the ends of her blue jumpsuit-clad legs, smiled her sweet smile and got back to business. "I haven't gone over the photographs yet. There were some other prints—your FMPs. Nothing I could get a cast of, though. The working conditions were less than optimal, if you get my drift." She picked up a stack of pictures from her desk and held them out. "You can look through these, but don't expect much. Heels that high just punch little holes in the snow. And don't mix them up or I'll stab you myself. I'm not feeling sunny."

At his raised eyebrows, she explained. "Had a visit from

Captain Cote, who was visibly and audibly disappointed that I don't have as many arms as Shiva or move as fast as Superman. He couldn't understand why Wink wasn't here. You sure he was ever a cop?"

"I'm not even sure he's human."

"Hey, I heard that." Wink set down a bag of take-out and a coffee and pulled off his jacket, then handed Dani a muffin. The sagging shoulders and weary tread echoed the way Burgess felt. "Hope you weren't talking about me," Wink said.

"Cote," Dani said. "You got a magnifying glass for Joe?"

"Why? He looking for clues?"

"More like a hooker in a haystack. You really think it was a woman?" she asked.

Burgess took the magnifying glass, snapped on a bright light, and started looking at the pictures. "It could have been. Witness says the other woman who was partying with Pleasant—the one he left with—wasn't one of O'Leary's regular girls, but someone who came looking for him. Why would a classy hooker go looking for a sleazy pimp?"

"Classy hooker in Portland, Maine?" Wink said. "City really is going upscale."

Burgess nodded. "Slim, blonde and gorgeous, if Alana's telling the truth."

Wink pried the top off his coffee, unwrapped a bagel oozing with cream cheese and bit into it. "People wonder how we can eat in the midst of all this blood and guts. Hell, if I can't sleep, I've got to eat. Have to have something to keep me going. You getting any closer, Joe?"

"Not yet. You ever strip wallpaper off an old house? You've got a layer of cowboys and Indians, and beneath that some pink thing with trailing ribbons and beneath that old blue flowers, all the way back to the old horsehair plaster, and in those layers is the story of the house. Pleasant's life is like that. Work life. Family life. Secret life. Maybe secret lives. All layers of the same man. Somewhere in one of those layers, one of those patterns, is the answer. But which layer? It's hard to get a handle on him."

Dani gave him an odd look. "That was so poetic, Joe."

Poetic, phooey. He'd let his guard down, a side effect of too little sleep. Last thing he wanted was to be considered poetic. He was here to do a job. He shrugged and bent to look at the photos again, going through them one by one, looking for signs of other footprints. Kept coming back to the same one. He handed it to Dani, pointing at some small depressions in the snow. "Did you mean these?"

She took the picture and the magnifying glass. "Yup, those are your footprints. High heels. Really high heels. So that'll be your hooker. I've got some close-ups but they're not processed yet." She handed the picture back, embarrassed. "Sorry they're not ready. But they didn't photograph well with all the blowing snow. Don't look like much more than rabbit tracks. We were lucky to get that one good cast of the man's shoe."

"Let me know when they're ready," he said. "And keep on with the rest of this stuff. No telling what may be important."

"We found the money," she said. "Boone's working on it." She nodded at a big, hulking man hunched over a terminal. "Boone hates us all right now, don't you, Boone?" The man gave no sign he'd heard.

"Thanks, Dani." He wanted to get out and talk to people, find the one who'd say something that would open this up. Say it or not say it. Eyes and body told a lot, too. But first, he had to write reports, meet with his team, go see Cote. The man was probably pissed because he hadn't genuflected upon arrival. As if bureaucracy took precedence over solving crime. He found Perry and Kyle and Berman and called them into the conference room, frustration sitting as tangible as a fifth person in the room.

He reported Alana's observations: that the mystery woman, Karen, might have contacted O'Leary; that she didn't seem to have much experience and might not even be named Karen; that O'Leary videotaped sexual encounters at his apartment and might have been blackmailing johns. Burgess also told them about the two sets of footprints.

Kyle handed around a mug shot. "Lucas Brown."

Burgess looked at it curiously. "Lucas Brown?"

"Aka Kevin O'Leary. Drug guys are very familiar with him. Sheet as long as my arm. Drugs, extortion, simple assault, gross sexual assault—three rapes where the complainant refused to go forward, plus one as a juvie. Been doing time down in Massachusetts. Back on the street maybe six months. New name. Fresh start."

He'd wondered how someone like O'Leary had gotten under their radar. Now he understood. Lucas Brown was a known, and ugly, quantity. He handed around copies of Jen Kelly's list. "We need to check on Pleasant's credit cards. Probably all his financial records. Look for cash deposits that might support the drug sales angle. Both his father-in-law and ex-wife said Pleasant had financial problems. Find his accountant. Also, phone records. Stan, see if Rita Callahan's gotten the subpoenas we need. And Terry? Put your devious mind to work on how Pleasant might have gotten his hands on drugs to sell."

"Cancer doc, right?" Kyle raised an eyebrow. "Which means pain management. Oxycontin's a great little money maker. I'll see what the drug guys know."

Berman cleared his throat. "On the house-to-house. One guy says he saw a big man in a dark coat sneaking through the bushes, but between the blowing snow and the weather warming up, we've got no prints. He has to get up a lot. Prostate. Says he's seen Pleasant's car there before. Never this late." He held out a sheaf of papers. "Otherwise, we got squat."

"Went by Salerno's," Kyle said. "But it was the day shift and nobody knew anything. Gotta go back at night."

Burgess asked Perry and Kyle to run background checks on Jack Kelly, Janet Pleasant, Jen Kelly and Ted Shaw, then called Pleasant's office and arranged meetings with Betty Ling and Chris Perlin during their lunch breaks. He was writing up yesterday's interviews—blessing the computer jock who'd put report templates up on all the computers—when Cote's secretary called, wondering if Burgess might be free? He didn't expect to be free for the next several weeks, agreed he'd be right up.

"Ted Shaw called, sounding pleased," Cote said. "Says you've promised him a quick arrest and a blackout on publicity."

Burgess shook his head. "I didn't. Couldn't. Man hears what he wants to hear. Drunk as he was, I'm surprised he heard anything."

"I hope comments like that go no farther than this office. Shaw's a very prominent man. Now, tell me about this quick arrest. Are you close?"

Of course Cote hadn't read his reports. He wasn't done writing them. Still. Guy should know if they were close to an arrest, he'd have heard. "I don't even have a suspect yet." It was hot in the office. Be so easy to go to sleep. And boy, would it piss Cote off. "It's gonna take time."

"You need more people on this?"

Like more bodies were the answer. "Devlin could use some help on the forensics, and I could use a good financial person.

We've got phone bills, credit cards, and financial stuff to wade through. Trying to get a handle on the victim's finances."

"The victim was a wealthy physician."

Dani was right. It was hard to believe Cote had ever been a cop. "The victim was a philandering husband who was habitually late with his child support. Maybe video-taped having sex and being blackmailed. He'd been bailed out of some financial scrapes by his father-in-law, may have supplemented his income by supplying drugs to individuals other than his patients. And I haven't met anyone, aside from his wife, who didn't either detest him, disapprove of his habits, or both."

Cote's nose wrinkled like he'd smelled bad cheese. "Not a word of this gets out, understand? And where are your reports? I haven't seen anything since yesterday."

"Since then I've been interviewing people. I was just writing those up."

"Well, get back to it, and stop wasting my time." Cote picked up the phone. "I'll tell Vince to find you some more help. I want this thing cleared up before the press gets wind of all the dirt. And I'm sure I don't have to remind you. All contact with the press goes through this office." Cote looked petulantly down at his immaculate desk, nostrils quivering in frustration. "Chief's really feeling the heat on this one, Joe. Every VIP in the West End's called to express concern. When are you going to get out there and get us something?"

Hadn't Cote just told him to stay in and write reports? He was the primary on this. Cote couldn't investigate his way out of a paper bag. He stood up, towering over his seated superior, and planted his hands on the man's blotter. "This one's going to take time, captain. There won't be a quick arrest."

Cote pushed his chair back. "Just find the hooker who was in the car—"

"I'm not sure she was a hooker."

Cote wasn't listening. He smirked, and Burgess knew what was coming. "Ask your friend Alana Black. I'm sure she'll be happy to tell you."

He didn't like Alana's name in that dirty mind, coming out of that pursed-up, duck's ass mouth, even if she was a lying, manipulative, game-playing whore. Below the prissy veneer was a greedy pubescent boy, wanting to ask what she was like in bed. And anyway, could Cote really believe you could walk out on the street and find anyone you wanted? That sources gave up everything the second a cop crooked his finger? "She's been helpful, Paul, but she doesn't know the girl. No one does."

"Maybe you need to ask her again." Cote licked his lips.

He wanted to slap Cote's flabby face and tell him get real, but Cote had rank, and the two of them had history. "I *need* to write reports, then interview Pleasant's office staff. I'll send up copies when I'm done."

Cote waited until he'd reached the door. "Try to stay away from the widow, Joe, and tread lightly over at Maine Med. These people aren't used to being bothered by the police. And give my love to Alana." He cupped his hands like he was fondling breasts.

Bothered by the police? Burgess flew down the stairs, fuming. He shouldn't let Cote get to him. Cote wanted him to lose it.

Staring at the screen, trying to write reports, what he saw was Kristin Marks, only nine when she was kidnapped, assaulted, strangled and dumped in a landfill.

The man had been easy to find—a twenty-three-year-old college student with a history of assaulting little girls. In the beginning, there had been plenty of evidence. Though his deviant history had taught him to use a condom, he'd left semen on Kristin's underwear. An eyewitness had seen him dragging the child into his car. Kristin's hair and fibers from her clothes were found in the car, fibers from the car found on her body.

Then the thing had begun to unravel. The perpetrator was the youngest son of a Superior Court judge, represented by the best criminal lawyer in town. Evidence began to disappear. The underpants vanished from the lab. The eyewitness left the state with no forwarding address. And the court declared a fatal flaw in the search warrant issued for the suspect's car, tainting all the evidence that had been collected.

From the moment he'd stood in that landfill, staring down at her pitiful little body, Burgess had worked the case day and night. For weeks he'd slept as little as humanly possible, following leads, checking and rechecking, doing everything he could to find Kristin's killer. Once the killer had been found, he'd continued to gather evidence, determined the man wouldn't walk away again with only a slap on the wrist.

He'd been like one man trying to bail the sea. They'd been understaffed at the time, and the case was a political hot potato, so he'd worked it virtually alone. Like a bloodhound, he found things no one expected him to find, brought them in, and watched them vanish like smoke. Lead after lead. Witness after witness. He would bring things in, and Cote, who'd had Vince Melia's job then, head of the investigations division, would tell him not to waste his time. Burgess would say a polite version of "fuck you," and go look some more, haunted by his vision of the body. Of her parents' faces. Of a small photo he carried of

Kristin making her first communion, lovely as an angel in her white dress.

He lost thirty pounds. He lost his voice. He shambled about with a ghastly stare that scared people into cooperating, drank coffee until his hands shook like a drunk with DTs. And everything he found was lost, stolen, pissed away, or swallowed up by the justice system. Injustice system.

It ended the day Cote called him in and explained about the invalid warrant. A warrant Cote had obtained. Cote explained further that, because of this lost evidence, the DA had agreed to a plea bargain. Involuntary manslaughter and an alternative sentence of treatment in a private facility for sex offenders until the doctors determined he was fit to rejoin society. Burgess had yelled, "She deserves better," and grabbed Cote by the throat. It had taken four officers to pull him off. Four officers, four nightsticks, pepper spray and a pair of handcuffs.

At that point, he'd entered into what his doctors called a "dissociative state." Most of the story he'd gotten later from Kyle. He remembered being dragged into the chief's office and dumped into a chair, his face so battered he could barely open his eyes, but he couldn't have seen much. He was still blinded from the pepper spray. His shoulder was dislocated, and, with his hands cuffed, he must have been in excruciating pain, but all he could feel was rage.

Tears from his eyes, blood and mucus from his broken nose, and blood and saliva from his battered mouth ran down his face. There were pains in his chest where they'd broken two ribs, but the real pain was from fury and horrible grief. What hurt was the profound immorality of the way justice for Kristin's life was traded away because it was expedient. Because people had screwed up.

The chief's voice had been a steady drone in the background, like a small plane on a summer day, buzzing around but not penetrating the bands of red anger and black despair that surrounded him like the rings of Saturn. The first voice he heard was Kyle's. A Kyle unlike the self-contained detective he'd worked with for years, bursting into the room and blazing with a machine-gun fire of angry words. Maybe the words penetrated because he'd rarely heard Kyle's voice raised in anger. A few simple sentences. "What the hell is going on here? If he were a suspect, he'd be on his way to the hospital, and you don't even wipe his face? Who's got a key for these cuffs?"

There was a mumbled response, like a church congregation, as the cuffs were taken off. Kyle wiped his face, discovered the extent of his injuries. And then a few more indelible sentences. "This is a disgrace on the department. No one speaks to this man again without a lawyer and a representative of the police union present. I'm taking him to the hospital."

Like Kennedy after Chappaquiddick, they kept him sedated while they figured out what to do. His lawyers and friends battled to save his career while he lay deep in a chemical-induced trance. Then, as the anger faded into exhaustion, he fell into a deep, natural sleep. He woke on the third day, still almost too exhausted to open his eyes, to find Kyle dozing beside the bed, worn, pallid, and victorious. Thanks to Kyle, he still had a career. Because of Kristin Marks, he wasn't sure he wanted it.

It had been a long road back. Kristin still haunted him, awake or asleep. And that careless starfucker Cote could still push his buttons. But today he had a new victim to attend to. He snapped open his notebook, and began taking out his anger on the keyboard.

Chapter Thirteen

Report writing was an essential part of police work. If he left what he'd learned in his notebook in his unreadable scrawl and got run down by a snowplow, his colleagues would have to start over. By now, it was second nature. The words flowed. But it took time when he could have been interviewing people, searching for the elusive key to this thing. When he printed the last report, he felt like a kid let out of school. He gave the secretary copies for Cote, then grabbed his jacket and left.

He crossed the parking lot under a sky that was spitting snow. By the time he hit the street, the sky wasn't spitting, it was heaving. Great, fluffy white gobs smacked against the windshield and surrounded him with a lace-curtain landscape. At the hospital, he parked in his usual spot, nodded to Charlie and went to the cafeteria to meet Betty Ling.

She was waiting by the door, a small, no-nonsense Asian woman with thick, cropped hair and big glasses. She wore a dull green dress, shapeless and too long, low black oxford shoes and a thin black cardigan. The white collar and cuffs on the dress gave it a severity that reminded him of the nuns at school. She was probably only in her mid-thirties, yet he half expected that if his questions displeased her, she'd slap his knuckles with a ruler. Before they'd exchanged a word, he knew she would do her best not to help.

"Do you want to get some lunch?" he asked. "We can talk while we eat."

"That was the point, wasn't it?"

No sense wasting any charm on this woman. Following her through the line, he watched her choose a lunch as dull as her clothes. Tuna on wheat—no veggies or condiments—and a cup of chicken soup. Tea with lemon. He'd eaten here a lot. The food was adequate. He chose beef stew and biscuits, pie and coffee. She chose a spot far from anyone else and laid out her lunch as precisely as if she were setting the table for company.

He shucked off his jacket and got out his notebook. "How long did you work for Dr. Pleasant?"

"Almost eight years."

"So you knew him pretty well?"

"No."

He took her through Pleasant's schedule. The procedures for arranging it. Pleasant's typical day. What Pleasant was like to work with. Who else in the office might be able to tell him about Dr. Pleasant. She doled out answers like an impoverished mother with too little food, not wasting a word.

She didn't know anything about his financial situation or who he associated with. "Who were his friends?" She really couldn't say. "Did Dr. Pleasant ever have any difficulties with patients? Were there patients who might have wanted to cause him harm?"

Her spoon stopped in midair. "Dr. Pleasant was a very competent physician."

"You're not aware of cases where his patients were upset by their treatment?"

"No. None." Speaking to the soup. He thought she hadn't liked Dr. Pleasant very much. Wondered why she'd lie for him.

"What was your relationship with Dr. Pleasant?"

"Professional."

"You didn't exchange pleasantries, stories about your weekends or vacations, never socialized with him?"

"I was an employee, not a friend. I sent presents when his children were born."

"You knew his wives?" She nodded. "Did you have any relationship with them?"

"Janet and Jennifer, Ms. Kelly, were both very pleasant on the telephone, and when they came to the office."

"Did you know Jen Kelly when her mother was a patient?"

Her answer was quick. "Her mother was never Dr. Pleasant's patient."

"Do you know of any lawsuits or complaints against Dr. Pleasant?"

She parked her teacup and wrapped one hand around the other. "I believe you should ask Ms. McFarland. Or the hospital administration." Obviously coached by Dr. Bailey.

"Was Dr. Pleasant in any financial difficulty? Did he ever receive calls from creditors, have problems with his credit cards, anything like that?" She shook her head. "Were you aware of any issues or inquiries concerning Dr. Pleasant's prescriptions or handling of drugs?"

"I really wouldn't know." She stared at her empty tray and his full one, then plucked up her sleeve and checked her watch. "Was there anything else?"

Another helping of nothing? "No. Thank you, Ms. Ling. I appreciate your time." She got up and grabbed her tray, showing more animation than she'd shown in their whole conversation. "Just one thing." She stopped, the tray swinging back toward him involuntarily, like a dowser's wand. "Do you know of any reason someone might have wanted to kill Dr. Pleasant?"

"No! No, of course not. He was a very competent physician."

"Ms. Ling, everyone makes mistakes."

"I have to go," she said. Back, he was sure, to report on the conversation to Dr. Bailey. He wondered how long it would be before Bailey called Cote again and what the complaint would be this time. A detective daring to ask questions?

He sighed for the wasted time and ate his lunch. Then he handed in his tray and went to meet Pleasant's nurse, Chris Perlin. She'd suggested they meet at a coffee shop away from the hospital. He hoped it indicated a desire to speak freely. Anything would be better than Betty Ling.

On his way out, he passed Charlie, the security guard. "You going to be around a while?" he asked. The man nodded. "Mind if I ask you some questions?"

"Why would I?"

"People around here seem mighty close-mouthed about Dr. Pleasant."

"Dr. Unpleasant, you mean."

"See you in about an hour." Burgess climbed into the Explorer and set off.

Chris Perlin was tucking into a huge burger smothered in onions, mushrooms and peppers, which spilled over her hands in oily drips and fell onto her plate. She smiled at him and nodded at the empty seat across from her. When she finished chewing, she set her burger down, wiped her hands carefully, and thrust one across the table. "Sergeant Burgess? Nice to meet you. I'm Chris." Her handshake was firm and confident. "I don't know if I can help," she said, "but fire away."

"I've just been talking to Betty Ling," he said.

"Blood from a stone, right?" She had a fresh, open smile that patients must love, and honey-brown hair in a thick braid down her back. "Don't take it personally. Betty's like that with everybody." She grabbed her burger, then hesitated. "Do you mind if I eat? Once in a blue moon I allow myself one of these cholesterol bombs and I want to savor every greasy morsel while it's hot."

"Go ahead. I was just wishing I had one myself. I ate at the hospital."

"Filling but dull," she said. She cut off a chunk of her burger and passed it to him with a couple of napkins. Burgess didn't say no.

"I'm trying to get to know Dr. Pleasant better. Trying to figure out who might have wanted to kill him and why. I'm hoping you can help."

"I didn't know him well," she said. "Stephen was a snob. He didn't believe in fraternizing with the help."

"You didn't like him?"

"Not very much. He was perfectly polite and a reasonable boss—mostly reasonable, anyway. He could be pretty finicky. The office was congenial. It was a good job for a nurse, especially the way nurses are treated these days. But I didn't like the way he was with patients."

She glanced quickly around, perhaps fearing the long reach of Dr. Bailey. "He had an arrogance, a disinterest in them as human beings, that was hateful. He trivialized their fears and dismissed their questions. Fifteen years ago, when I was a young nurse, lots of doctors were like that. But Stephen wasn't old enough to carry it off, wasn't great enough. He didn't have enough stature to play God. Wait . . ." She waved the burger, sending cheese and onions everywhere, then took a bite and set it down with an embarrassed grin.

"Okay. I'm a carnivorous slob. Now you know everything you need to know about me. I meant that if a doctor is so good, and so dedicated, and incredibly hard-working, maybe he can be forgiven for being impatient with people if he's also saving their lives. But that kind of stature has to be earned, and even then, it should be questioned. Don't get me wrong. He was able, ambitious, and hard-working. Good at the technical side. I just never understood why he'd become a doctor."

"You call him by his first name."

"Well, I don't go in for that me Dr. Pleasant, you Nurse Chris crap."

He nodded, unsurprised. "Sorry. I interrupted you."

She took another bite. "Nurses work more directly with patients. We see their fears, their strength, their confusion. We deal with their families. We have a different picture. But a good doctor has to get some of that. He . . . or she . . . has to give the patient information about what's going on. The patient has to be a part of the team. Stephen treated pieces of them. He looked at people and mentally drew maps on their bodies, always measuring the types of radiation treatment to be delivered, so impatient, hurrying to get on to the next patient, and the next. The trouble was . . ." She finished the burger and licked her fingers. ". . . he wasn't hurrying because he wanted to help as many people as possible. He was hurrying to make more money."

"Did you ever hear or observe anything which suggested he had money problems?"

"Other than visits from Janet?" He nodded. "Betty would know. Never tell, though. She's a nineteenth-century soul. The only Asian Victorian you'll ever meet. Just what I said. Trying to see as many patients as possible."

"And people who hurry make mistakes."

Her frank blue eyes met his. "You didn't hear that from me." She hesitated. "I have a job I like. You've met Ken Bailey, right? So I probably don't have to tell you, if Ken Bailey thinks I've said anything detrimental to the practice, that's it for me."

"And talking honestly about Stephen Pleasant is detrimental to the practice?" She nodded. "But you're here, talking to me. Really talking, not just giving me the party line."

"I'm a nurse, okay? My job is helping sick people get well. It's about healing. I don't believe in killing people, even disagreeable ones, to solve problems."

"So maybe there were some patients who got careless treatment from Dr. Pleasant, and maybe they were mad about it, but you aren't going to tell me, is that it?"

"That's it." Her bright warmth faded. "I thought he was killed by a prostitute, someone trying to rob him. You don't really think it could have been a patient?"

Cops ask questions. They don't answer them. "At this stage, I have to look at everything," he said. "What if it was a patient or a patient's relative? If you won't help, how would I find them?"

"Patient records?" She shrugged. "But for that you'd need an oncologist and a radiologist, wouldn't you? You could see who's complained to the hospital, or written to the practice, complaining, couldn't you? Talk to Martha McFarland. What about the Board of Registration in Medicine?"

"A man's been killed," he said, "leaving a wife and a tiny baby who'll never know his father. If you know anything that might help catch the killer, you should tell me."

She shifted uncomfortably on her chair. "Why me? Why not ask his wife? His partners? His friends? They knew him better than I did."

"Party line," he said.

Chris Perlin looked miserable. "I don't know. Let me think about this, okay? I'm no coward but I've got a living to make. Rent to pay. You know how it is."

He did. Although everyone supposedly had an obligation,

and an interest, in promoting justice, he often talked to witnesses who walked a fine line between their loyalties. Like Alana Black. She knew far more than she'd told him, but she was trying to balance her loyalty to him with the necessity to get along on the street. For that matter, Ted Shaw and Ken Bailey obviously knew more than they were saying, yet felt no obligation to cooperate. The cop's lot. As though they'd said, You want to be a detective, son? Fine, we'll put out one eye and tie your hands behind your back. Now go serve and protect.

"Detective?"

He looked at her, startled, something in her tone making him wary. It wasn't like him to drift off like this. Was he getting too old to run on minimal sleep?

"I remember you," she said. "Couple years ago. Talk about people who got mad at him. I thought you were going to tear him apart. You probably would have if your mother . . . it was your mother, wasn't it? A frail, sweet-faced lady with tremendous dignity, hauling on your arm and trying to get you out while you're yelling, 'A year! A whole goddamned year! You let her go a year without treatment because you misread your own goddamned X-ray!' "

She pushed her plate of fries toward him and poured a pool of ketchup. "Help yourself. I'll never eat all these. If they knew, would they still let you work on the case?"

He turned away from her to watch the snow. This was getting way too personal. "I told them. They said it was fine. I only met him that once. Hell," he said, trying to diffuse it, "if I didn't work cases where I'd met people, I couldn't work in this town."

"Met? Is that what you told them?" She changed the subject. "It's pretty, isn't it, the snow? I don't mind it when it comes down all soft and fluffy like this. I just don't like ice." When he didn't respond, she said, "In case you're worrying, I won't tell."

"Why?"

"Because I think we share an old-fashioned notion of right and wrong. Even when the system doesn't work very well."

"Sometimes I wonder," he said.

"Me, too. I've wanted to turn off patients with no quality of life, whose families were keeping them alive when they were in agony and wanted to die. I've wanted to take a scalpel to the father of a severely abused child who'll spend life as a vegetable because Daddy lost his temper, but I always come back to the same thing—that I'm not qualified to play God. If we all decide we've got that power, everything falls apart."

She reached across the table and took his hand. He didn't pull away. They sat, oblivious to the noise and people around them, watching the snow fall. Finally, he said, "I've got to go. Got more people to see. You'll think about what we discussed?"

"I will."

"Thank you," he said, reluctantly withdrawing his hand.

"For what?"

Burgess smiled. "Being," he said.

Chapter Fourteen

He drove back through thickening snow, found the security guard in the hospital lobby. He thought when he finished here, he'd pay an unannounced visit to Jen Kelly. "Coffee break?" he suggested.

"If anyone's looking for me," Charlie told the receptionist, "I'm in the cafeteria."

Charlie pointed to an empty table by the window. "Why don't you grab that one. I'm having coffee. You want something?"

He did. He wanted a clue. He wanted the truth, the whole truth, and nothing but the truth. He wanted his knee to stop hurting. Wanted to put this homicide, and himself, to bed. "Diet Coke?" Charlie made a face and walked away. Burgess sat by the window, looking through streaky glass at the falling snow, allowing himself a recreational minute to think about Chris Perlin.

Charlie arrived with the drinks and three donuts. "This time of day, I need sugar."

"One of those donuts isn't for me?"

"Sure, one's for you. Not 'cuz you're a cop. I just hate to sin alone. So . . ." He tore open two packages of sugar and poured them into his coffee. "You want to know about Dr. Unpleasant, huh. Ask any of the nurses who've worked with him. For him. They'll all tell you. Guy was a son-of-a-bitch. Treated everyone like dirt, except other doctors. I used to wonder what makes a guy like that? Toilet trained too early or maybe his daddy beat him, or he grew up eating out of garbage cans? That place you park? He thought it was his private spot. He'd fling me the keys, say, 'I'll only be a minute, Chuck. Move it if you have to,' and not come back for hours. Like I was a doorman."

"You didn't like him."

"I ever tell you how much I hate being called 'Chuck'?"

"So you killed him."

"There were moments, but if I killed him, I'd lose my job, and my wife, she'd be real upset. Know what I mean? Not like he's the only arrogant asshole around here. You learn to live with it. Start killing people 'cuz they're assholes, pretty soon the pile of bodies is sky high. There's good people, too. There are nurses around here who are saints."

Burgess sipped the Coke, shuddering at the nasty chemical taste. His first sergeant, back when he was on patrol, had taught him not to overlook the invisible people—store clerks, gas jockeys, street people, security—advice that had paid off hundreds of times. "Give me something, Charlie."

Charlie tore a donut in half, then in half again, and shoved a quarter into his mouth. "About a month ago, I saw this guy, sitting in a car in the parking lot, watching the door. Not so unusual. Guys sit over there while their wives and girlfriends come visit. Better to sit in a cold car than look at a sick person, much less talk to them. Strange thing was, when Dr. Pleasant left, this guy followed. And a week later, I saw him again."

"Just those two times?"

"Saw him again last week."

"Get a good look at him?"

Charlie shook his head. "It was night. Light's not that good."

"Thought you worked the day shift."

"Sometimes I do double shifts, covering for other guys. Saving for retirement."

"So there might have been other times?" Charlie nodded. "What was he driving?"

"Pickup. Big old beat-up thing. Some dark color. Black or green? GMC, I think."

"License plate?" The guard shook his head. "What can you tell me about him?"

"Not much. I had the impression he was big. Beard. Mustache. Wore a bandanna, like Willie Nelson. Pretty good driver."

"What makes you say that?"

"One night it was damned slippery. Pleasant's Mercedes was all over the place. This guy wasn't. When I went home, it was like ice skating. He knew what he was doing."

"Pleasant ever notice?"

"He left here, he had his mind on nooky, know what I mean?"

"Everyone knew about that?"

"People who were observant. He wasn't very discreet." Charlie's head bobbed. "I felt sorry for his wife. Nice kid. She tried to keep him straight. Used to come meet him after work. Then she just stopped coming. I always wondered what happened. Maybe the pregnancy. She always seemed worn-out."

"You ever see them fight?"

"Not really. Once or twice she was crying and he seemed angry. That's all."

"Anything else?"

"Last week the guy in the truck had someone with him." The guard ate another chunk of donut. "Aren't you gonna eat yours?"

"Someone with him?" Charlie was enjoying this and

didn't want to be rushed. Burgess picked up his donut and bit off a chunk. Crisp on the outside, greasy inside. Just the way he liked 'em. He chewed and waited.

"A girl. Blonde. Long hair. When Pleasant came out, the man pointed him out to the girl. She nodded. When Pleasant drove away, they followed."

"Charlie, don't tell anybody about this, okay? You may have seen the killers."

The guard's homely face crinkled up in a grin. "You mean it?"

"I mean it. You're pretty observant. I wonder if any of the other guards, the regular night guys, noticed the man in the truck."

"Guess you'll have to ask them." Charlie shrugged. "No one ever mentioned it to me, but then, I never mentioned it to anyone either. So who knows?"

"Notice anything else unusual about Dr. Pleasant?"

"Other than that he used to leave around eight, come back a little later, run in, and rush out fifteen minutes later, with wet hair?" Charlie paused. "Washing off hookers!"

"Anything else?"

"You're greedy, detective."

"Have to be. Never know what might turn out to be important."

"You're right there. Let's see." Charlie ate the last donut as he considered.

How could a man who led an essentially sedentary life and feasted on donuts stay thin? Metabolism and genetics. Charlie was meant to be a skinny, pale-skinned, red-haired banty rooster of a man. Burgess was meant to be a beefy hulk. His father, the violent drunk, had been a beefy hulk. So had his uncles. And his grandfather. He had no sons, so the beef stopped here.

"One night I spotted this guy in the parking lot, hanging around the Mercedes . . ." Most of his life, Charlie was invisible, now he was enjoying the spotlight. "I went over to ask him his business, show a little badge, and he tells me to screw off, he's waiting for Dr. Pleasant and it's okay. This guy is all attitude. But he doesn't look like Dr. Pleasant's type, you get me? He's got a shaved head, leather jacket, tattoos. So I say suit yourself but I'll be watching, and I go back inside."

He looked sadly at the empty tray. "Then Pleasant comes out, goes up to this guy, and damned if they don't get in the car and drive away. You coulda knocked me over with a straw. Normally, Pleasant wouldn't give someone like that the time of day."

"This bald guy. Tall or short? Fat? Thin? How old?"

"Medium tall. Thirties. Beer gut." Charlie fingered his chin. "Big jaw. Stuck-out ears and a broken front tooth. Lotta prison muscle."

Kevin O'Leary. "Only time you saw this guy?" The guard nodded. "You're doing great," Burgess said. "Got anything else in that bag of tricks?"

"Only other things were the sad things. An old man once, came up to Dr. Pleasant, tried to grab his arm, and he's saying, 'You killed my wife. You know that. You killed my wife.' Pleasant just shook him off and walked away. Couple times, I saw stuff like that. But you see that here. This can be a pretty sad place. You know it yourself."

Burgess nodded. "Thanks, Charlie. You've been a big help. I'll come back, show you some pictures, see if there's anyone you recognize."

"Anytime." The guard consulted his watch. "Guess I'd better get back to work. Keep my eyes open. Who knows what I might spot? I've got ten minutes."

They passed a frowning Ken Bailey in the hallway, the frown following them until they were out of sight. Charlie took up his post near the door, Burgess went out into the swirling snow. He called Perry and Kyle, told them about the man in the truck and Pleasant's meeting with O'Leary. Passed on Chris Perlin's suggestion about checking with the medical board. Said he was on his way to see Jen Kelly, he'd call in when he was through. He urged them to get some rest, though he doubted they would.

It was only four, but daylight had been swallowed up by the dark sky and the snow. Street lights were lit. Cars slowed by the blinding white crept up to traffic lights and stop signs and fishtailed around corners. Pedestrians ducked their heads and hugged their coats around their chins, struggling against a rising wind. No namby-pamby flurry, this was a real snowstorm, the kind of day the Explorer was made for.

He crossed the Million Dollar Bridge in a world so white it hurt, the big metal girders folding around him like a gray skeleton coated with white cotton. Then he was back on the streets, among the cars and lights and half-hidden buildings. He bent low over the wheel, peering through the bright needles. By the time he turned in at Jen Kelly's house, the road was a smooth white blanket with no tracks at all. Her father's truck was still there, surrounded by undisturbed snow. Burgess pulled in behind it.

His steps were soundless, his feet disappearing as he walked to the door, the world engulfed in the peculiar silence of a snowstorm. He reached out a gloved hand and punched the bell. Falling snow tickled his face, piled up on his lashes and clung to his hair. He rang again. Little piles grew on his shoulders. Snow sneaked in the front of his jacket and began to melt. He watched the clouds of his breath and wondered what was happening on the other side of the door.

When it opened, Jack Kelly filled the space, glaring up at him belligerently. "Haven't you got anyone else to bother, detective?"

Last night, Kelly had been eager for him to talk to Jen. One problem with letting time slip by. Families quickly circled the wagons and wanted the cops to go away. He blinked the snow off his lashes. "May I come in?"

"She doesn't need this right now."

"I'll be as gentle as I can, Mr. Kelly, but I need to talk to Jen."

"Daddy, who is it?"

"It's that detective. Burgess."

"Let him in, then. There's a blizzard out there. Maybe he'd like some coffee?"

He'd like a heater. His ears and neck were freezing because he'd left his hat in the car. A heater and a bottle of aspirin and twelve hours' sleep. His arms and shoulders ached from holding the car on the road, and his eyes stung from peering through the snow. He was ready to sweep Kelly aside.

Jen Kelly, holding the baby, appeared behind her father. "Come in, detective. I suppose this is neither rain nor snow?"

"That's the post office." He stepped past Kelly, who'd moved a grudging few inches to let him pass. He ran a hand over his head, sending clods of snow cascading onto the polished wood.

"Come in the kitchen," she said. "You can't hurt that floor." The room was dark and gloomy without the sunlight pouring in. Beyond the windows there was no view, no lights, just blackness. "You want coffee?"

He shook his head. Too much sitting, too much food, too much coffee. "I'd do tea," he said.

"Two for tea and tea for two," she said. "Daddy, you want anything?" Kelly just stood in the doorway, arms folded, looking stubborn and unfriendly. "And please don't pick a fight. I don't need any more discord around me. Take off your coat, detective, and hang it on one of those pegs. You're making a puddle on my floor."

Feeling like a chastened two-year-old, he slipped off his coat and hung it as directed. A huge register in the floor sent up a wave of heat. He stood a moment, holding his hands in the warmth.

She looked like she could use a month in bed. Beneath her eyes were deep purple bruises, and the skin drawn tightly over her bones was pale and dry. Her unwashed hair was pulled into a thin braid. She wore yesterday's shirt. Seemed too young and frail to have borne a child and lost a husband. "Stay there if you want," she said. "You look cold."

He didn't like taking kindnesses from people he was unsure of, but he was a practical man. He was cold and wet. Insisting on remaining so did no one any good. He used his handkerchief to dry his face and hair.

"Better?" she asked. "Here, Daddy. You hold Stevie. I'll make some tea."

Kelly took the baby and was transformed from pugilistic anger to a kind of smiling wonder. His daughter nuzzled his shoulder with her chin and then leaned over to kiss his cheek. "Softie."

"I think he needs changing," Kelly said. He carried the baby out of the room.

"He thinks it's all his fault. That he should have kept me from marrying Stephen."

"Could he have stopped you?"

"Of course not. Doesn't keep him from blaming himself, though." She filled the kettle, put it on the stove, and dropped into a chair, her head in her hands.

"How are you?"

"Stunned. It's so unreal. I don't know what to feel. I don't think I believe it yet."

"I need to ask a few more questions."

She didn't look up. "What?"

"About financial stuff. I was talking with your father last night. Ted Shaw. He said he'd bailed your husband out of some financial scrape. What was he talking about?"

She stiffened, her eyes going to the viewless window. "Why didn't you ask him?"

"Because he was . . ." Burgess searched for a neutral word.

"Drunk?" she suggested.

"Well on his way."

Her forced smile was painful to watch. "It was no big deal, detective. Stephen . . . we . . . just got a little overextended, with the house and the business expanding and buying the cars and support for Janet and Mackenzie. He was embarrassed about it, but Stephen had to ask Ted for a small loan. He was going to pay it back."

She never could have betrayed her husband the way Pleasant had betrayed her. She was too bad a liar. "Did they make a written record of the loan?" She shook her head. "Otherwise, your finances are stable?"

She looked over at him, scared blue eyes and trembling lips. "As far as I know. Stephen took care of all of that. I was . . . I've been . . . it was a difficult pregnancy. I'm afraid I was concentrating on not losing the baby and not much else."

"I'm glad things worked out," he said, and then, "I need to know about your finances, where you had accounts, who your accountant is, things like that."

She stayed where she was, slumped at the table, massaging her forehead with unsteady fingers. "If I take you to his study, can you find those things yourself? Stephen was very neat. There's a copy machine. Help yourself. We've got nothing to hide."

She wanted him to leave before she broke down completely. He wasn't ready to go. "Was your father, Ted Shaw, aware of your husband's infidelity?"

"Infidelity?" Her blue eyes widened. "You mean those women?" Her hand flew to her lips, pressing against them as she tried to read the right answer off his face. "I don't know," she said. "I don't think so."

"Ms. Kelly, were you aware of anyone threatening your husband? Did he ever get phone calls or letters that made him unusually nervous or distracted?" She shook her head. "Did he ever worry that he was being followed?"

She shook her head again. "What are you suggesting?"

"Were you ever aware of any angry patients contacting him or bothering him?"

Her head came up and tear-filled eyes pleaded with him to stop. "No. No. Of course not," she said. "You're being ridiculous. Stephen was a good doctor. Patients liked him."

"Were there any malpractice suits against him that you were aware of?"

"None that I've ever heard of. You'd have to talk to Martha McFarland."

"Did your husband ever abuse drugs?" She didn't answer. "Have you ever heard him mention someone named Kevin O'Leary?" She shook her head, avoiding his eyes. "Any phone calls from someone called Kevin? Any calls he didn't want you to overhear?"

"No. No. No! Detective Burgess, please! I loved my husband. How do you think I feel, having you asking these questions with all the ugly things they suggest? It's bad enough to think he was killed in his car by some prostitute. Why aren't you satisfied with that? Why do you keep trying to dig up more dirt?" She turned away from him, covering her face. "Is it too much to want a few days to get used to all this . . . a few days with my good memories of Stephen, before you try and rip everything to shreds?"

She pointed toward the door. "Stephen's study. Turn left, go down the hall and it's the last door on the right." When he didn't move, she came over to him, grabbed the front of his shirt, and stared up into his face. Close enough to see her eyelids flutter, the pale blue veins at her temples, the tender, slightly chapped lips. "Why are you doing this?" she said. "Haven't I been hurt enough?"

"I'm not trying to make things worse for you, Ms. Kelly. Truly. I'm trying to find a killer. You're my best source of information, and time matters. I'm sorry I have to do this."

"Are you sorry? I wonder."

"And I wonder why you keep evading me, Ms. Kelly, if you want his killer caught. No one knew your husband better than you. It's harsh, I know, but it's true—try to protect his privacy and you end up protecting his killer. Why would you want to do that?"

She dropped back onto a chair, blinking her teary eyes. "I'm not evading—"

"You are." It came out fiercer than he'd meant. It wasn't easy not to think with his dick. She was a lovely woman, sad, weary, and staring at him with hopeful eyes while she asked how he could be so cruel in that husky, whispering voice. She smelled of baby powder and fresh, clean soap.

148

But even if Burgess the horny bastard wanted to feed her cookies and milk and take her to bed, Burgess the cop wanted truth. "Look," he said, "you lived with him . . . saw things . . . heard things . . ."

"I don't know what you're talking about." Angry now, not pleading. Chin up, back straight. Ted Shaw's daughter. "I'd like you to go now, detective. Leave us alone."

His phone rang, Kyle's tired voice rasping in his ear. "Joe? You there?"

"What's up?"

"Alana called a few minutes ago, really spooked. She says something's happened and she's afraid to go home. She'll be at the Dunkin' Donuts until you come and get her. Says she has to talk to you about Pleasant . . . or O'Leary. I don't know. She was too upset to make sense."

"I'm in the middle of something. Can you swing by and—"

"She won't talk to anyone else, Joe. I wouldn't have bothered you, but you know she's not afraid of anything. And she's scared. Damned scared."

He looked at Jen Kelly, crying quietly at the table. She was hiding things and he didn't know why, but pushing would be futile. She wasn't as soft as she appeared. The tears might be genuine, but so was the rod-straight back and the reassertion of attitude. What he'd done already was gonna get Cote on his ass faster than flies on a corpse. He'd bet money the minute he was out the door, she'd be on the phone to her daddy the wallet.

"It's gonna take me a while. Get someone down there to baby-sit."

"Done deal, Joe."

He didn't feel like rushing back through this damned storm to try and pry stuff out of Alana. That's how it would be. She was such a confirmed game player, she couldn't help herself. Maybe Jen Kelly was, too. Irritation with being stuck between bad choices bothered him like an unscratched itch. He grabbed his jacket off the hook, pausing a few seconds on the heat. Across the room, too late for him, the kettle cleared its throat and began to sing.

CHAPTER FIFTEEN

It was like driving into a ball of cotton, sky, buildings, ground, all the same fluffy white, no divisions where things began or ended, the occasional ghostly tree or telephone pole his only guides. The snow-plastered stop signs were giant lollipops, streetlights only a faint glow. The concentration hurt his eyes and made his head throb, but he liked the solitude. It was his kind of world, something pure and natural you had to take on its own terms. Men thought they were masters of the universe, but weather won every time. Even when it was an incredible pain in the ass, part of him cheered it on.

Eventually he got behind a plow, the stroboscopic yellow lights giving him something to follow. He wondered how the plow's driver could find the road. Maybe they were simply plowing a path through yards and buildings, crushing all beneath the huge blades. There was something massive and elemental about a snowplow, thrumming relentlessly through the dark, sending out twelve-foot waves of snow, like the wings of enormous angels, the driver safe and warm in his cab high above the earth.

Normally Burgess would use this time to sort through the case, plan his next moves. Tonight driving took too much effort. The best he could do was the gut test. What felt right. What felt wrong. Whose lies were closer to the truth. He knew he hadn't gotten the truth from Jen Kelly from the start, but his gut said most of her lies didn't matter. She was protecting herself as a girl who'd made a

151

wrong choice and didn't want her face rubbed in it, the self of a wife and mother who needed some dignity and privacy in a matter both vulgar and public. Occasionally, his gut was wrong. He had to be careful of the obvious assumptions—that she was too young and inexperienced to plot a crime like this. That beautiful rich girls and young mothers didn't kill their husbands. Everyone was a potential killer, given the right provocation.

It was nearly an hour before he spotted the garish pink and orange and brown, softened tonight by the snow. He pulled into the Dunkin' Donuts lot, slammed his car into park, and killed the engine, working his stiff shoulders under his coat, postponing the moment he'd have to face Alana. Never easy, tonight she'd be worse, demanding patience and reassurance while jangled nerves made her desperately seductive. She'd regard the hour it had taken him to get here as disrespect. Alana was like cotton candy—tempting and delicious until you got close and were entangled in a sticky mess.

He waded through the snow to the door. She was at the counter, slouched over her coffee. When she saw him, she flounced and turned away. So damned childish sometimes he wanted to give her a good spanking. At least she'd dressed sensibly. When she turned back, her frown became a cautious smile. "Joe. You came."

He slid onto the stool beside her. "Yeah. So what's up?"

She looked around the nearly empty room. "We can't talk here."

"Alana, there's a blizzard outside."

"I don't care. I'm not talking where anyone might overhear us."

"I'm too tired for games, Alana. I just drove a goddamned hour through a snowstorm to get here. If you've got something to say, spit it out."

"You do look tired." She lowered her voice. "Some-body's after me, Joe. You've got to take me with you."

"I can't do that."

"I don't dare go home. He knows where I live. I don't know his name." She fidgeted with the strings of her hood. "This guy . . ."

"This guy got something to do with the Pleasant thing?"

Her smile was coy. "Maybe I'll tell you when we get to your place."

"Just tell me, Alana. Please." His clothes were heavy and damp. His stinging eyes wanted to close. He let the lids fall and rested them. Better not to look at her anyway. "I'm a cop," he said. "You're a hooker. I'll take you somewhere else if you want. You got a friend you could stay with?" They'd been doing this dance so long, she should know when she could push and when she couldn't.

She slid off her stool, her feet slamming loudly on the tile. "Yeah. I'll have to call. See if she's home." Furious at not getting her way after cooling her heels so long. Taking it out on him because she was scared. "She's up in Bruns-wick, you know."

Twenty minutes on a clear day, easily an hour tonight. A grueling hour up, another hour back. "Don't you have . . ." he began, but she wasn't listening.

She stomped off to use the pay phone, stomped back, her hands on her hips. "She says okay, copman. We can talk in the car."

She'd chosen Brunswick hoping he'd give in and take her to his place. He was too burned out not to find it tempting, but he wasn't getting sucked into that game. He waved a heavy arm toward the door. "After you."

She stopped outside, staring in amazement, her bad

mood vanishing. "Jesus! I've never seen it snow so hard. Do you own a sled?"

"I own a bed. Which I want to be in as soon as possible. You want a pal to play in the snow, little girl, find somebody else."

"Party pooper." She tossed her hair, striding toward the car. He was unlocking her door when he registered the movement. That faint sixth sense that keeps cops alive. He dove sideways, the blow aimed at his head striking his upper arm instead. His right hand went for his gun, getting the holster unsnapped just as the man's second blow hit with an explosion of pain and a great gush of blood. He went down on his knees, still fumbling for the gun, ducking a third blow that grazed his cheek. His only impression of his attacker that it was a big man in a dark coat.

"Let me go! Let me go! Joe! Help!" Alana was screaming, struggling with someone. Less than ten feet away, they were already disappearing into the falling snow.

He clawed his way up the side of the car, clinging to the handle, his left arm hanging numb and useless. Upright, there was a whirling sensation as much inside his head as from the storm. He got the gun out, focusing on Alana and her assailant, struggling and swearing behind the opaque curtain of snow, but the blood poured into his eyes and he couldn't sight well enough for a safe shot. No crisp black silhouettes with neat white centers. Nothing crisp or neat, though the world was black and white.

Spots dancing in his eyes, he struggled toward them, swaying like a poleaxed steer. Where the hell was the babysitter he'd requested? Given up and gone home? Then a voice yelled, "Freeze! Police." The man holding Alana gave her a shove that sent her sprawling and disappeared into the swirling snow, another figure after him, calling a second warning. "Police officer. Freeze." Remy Aucoin crossed his small field of vision and disappeared into darkness. Alana pushed herself up and came toward him.

He put his gun away, fumbled the radio off his belt, called in the code for an officer needing assistance. Trying not to fall on his face. His left arm hung useless. Blood poured from his throbbing head. Then Alana was there, propping him up, pulling the radio from his hand.

"Can you hear me?" she asked. No codes. No subtlety. Just a terrified woman's voice. "It's Joe Burgess. Someone hit him in the head and he's bleeding something awful. There's another cop here, took off after the guy. We're down at the Dunkin' Donuts and we need help. Can you hear me?"

"Yes, ma'am. Which Dunkin' Donuts?" The voice calm and reassuring. Dispatch sat in a darkened room. It was peaceful and soothing and didn't distract them from their terminals and their consoles. Alana gasped out their location. "Help is on the way, ma'am. Is Sergeant Burgess conscious?"

"Sort of," she said, "if moaning like a sick cat means conscious."

He'd never live that down. The day he retired they'd still be looking at him and thinking "sick cat." He pushed away from her and grabbed the radio. "This is Burgess," he said. "I'm okay. Going over to the hospital for some stitches. Aucoin needs backup. Tell Medcu to stay home."

"We have officers en route."

"Good." He put the radio away and leaned back against the car, his face tilted toward the sky and the icy bite of the snow, sucking in air and trying to clear his head. Warm blood dripped down his neck. He cradled his left arm with his right, cushioning pain as fierce as a toothache, readying himself to get back in the car and drive. Alana stood quietly beside him, silent except for the occasional sob.

"You okay?" he grunted.

"I . . . he . . . I don't know." She moved closer. "I told you there was this guy . . ."

Oughta ask what guy, but he couldn't focus on anything beyond his pounding head. "Hold that thought," he told her.

Time passed, the world around them empty and still as the relentless snow turned them into ghosts. It was a slow-motion emergency, help coming with the speed of a different age, trudging and ponderous, cops slewing into the parking lot in a noisy red, white and blue confusion. Kyle materialized, pulled enough information from him to sort it out, and put them all to work.

"Joe, I need your car keys."

He fumbled through his pockets before remembering they were still in the door. Kyle helped him in. "Wait," Alana said. "I'm coming with you."

"Guy who hit me was waiting for her." Burgess tried to keep his bloody head away from the seat. Nobody wants to ride with the smell of his own blood. There was a plastic bag in the back. "Grab that bag, Ter, would you? The seat?" Then they were backing up, making him vaguely seasick. As they lurched forward and headed onto the street, the car slithering through the ruts and ridges, it got so bad he had to lower the window and let the wind blow into his face. Better frostbite than being sick in his car.

Alana screamed when she saw him in the light, his face and hands red with blood. Kyle told her to go in the waiting room and shut up. For once, she didn't argue.

"Someone tried to snatch her, Terry," Burgess said. "Roughed her up. Better ask security to keep an eye on her."

"I'll take care of her," Kyle said.

Burgess gave an outline of the attack, then lapsed into a passive state and let the docs do their thing, figuring it was about as much rest as he was going to get. He was examined—probably concussed; stitched—fifteen; and X-rayed—possible minor fracture of the upper arm. No cast. Wear a sling and take it easy. No jogging, no jarring, no heavy lifting. The doctor used the ridiculous word "rest" followed by the equally absurd "take it easy."

The shift commander came and stared at him, asked the doc some questions, reported Aucoin hadn't been able to catch the guy, and patted his shoulder, telling him to take it easy for a few days. That made two votes for taking it easy.

"Easy?" he said. "I'm the primary on a homicide."

Finally, after he'd been poked, prodded, repaired and drugged enough to take the gasping edge off the pain, they left him alone. A large, friendly, middle-aged nurse came in and closed the curtains. "I'm going to clean you up." She went to work with a washcloth and a basin of warm water, getting the dried and sticky blood off his face, his neck and out of his ears. She washed as much as she could out of his hair, off his hands, out from between his fingers, gently as a mother with a small child. It was pleasant to lie there, half dozing, and be ministered to.

As the warm washcloth stroked and soothed, she said, "You're working on Dr. Pleasant's murder, aren't you?" He managed an affirmative sound. "Maybe you should look at drugs being prescribed for terminal, even deceased, cancer patients."

Lassitude fled. "Your name?"

"Margaret Keller. But I'd prefer not to appear in your reports."

"Then why talk to me?" Making no promises about anonymity.

"I never liked him. He was a vile man. I used to wish something bad would happen to him, so he'd know how other people felt. Maybe I'm feeling guilty."

"Wait." He struggled to get his brain on line again. "How do you know?"

"Hospital rumors. That's all. I have to go." She went out, closing the curtain behind her.

No one had said anything about admitting him or letting him go. They'd taken his clothes, put him back together, numbed the pain and abandoned him. He wanted to go home to his own bed, and sleep. Maybe Terry would drive him. And there was still Alana. She'd have to swallow her distrust and talk to someone else. He wasn't hearing confession tonight. It might not fall on deaf ears, but it would fall on a deaf brain.

Slowly, very slowly, he sat up. Not his first head injury. The first time, he'd gotten up off the table like a raging bull and fallen flat on his face. He sat on the edge of the bed and took inventory. Two working feet in wet, heavy boots. Pants. His belt, with gun and cuffs, though his radio was gone. His wallet and his badge. That was important, that he hadn't lost his gun. Losing his gun and moaning like a sick cat, he'd have to go away to the Yukon or the Northwest Territory and live out his days. He was wearing a bloody T-shirt. His left arm bore an enormous reddish-purple bruise and was swollen and puffy. Carefully, he slid his feet toward the floor. Made contact. Stood up. The room rocked a little and settled down. His heartbeat whooshed in his ears.

Someone jerked back the curtain and came in. Young cop with a notebook. Come to take his story. Like he wouldn't be at work in the morning and able to write the report himself. "Sheffield, sir. If I could have a moment." Winced at the blood on his shirt and his ugly arm and pulled out a pen. He saw himself, years and years ago, wearing the same uniform, carrying the same notebook, clicking the same pen. "Sir. Shouldn't you be lying down?"

Go ahead, kid. Make me feel old as the hills. Still, it wasn't a bad idea. If he couldn't leave, he might as well lie down. He hadn't felt tired before. The adrenaline, probably. Now he felt flattened. What his body didn't tell him he heard in his voice, a lethargic recounting of those few intense moments. Then it was over, he was thanked, called "sir" again, and the officer left.

"Ready?" Kyle waved a plastic bag. "Got your meds, pal. Dandy chemical relief."

He did the careful slide off the table again. Kyle picked up the bag of soggy clothes and followed, matching his normal brisk step to Burgess's slow one. If the world moved at 33 rpms, Kyle moved at 45. The car was at the door, already warm, wipers slapping away the snow. Kyle slung the bag into the back seat, waited until he was in, and shut the door like a prom date. He'd done the same thing for Kyle. They'd all done it for each other. Sooner or later, everyone went home hurting.

He hadn't noticed Alana in the back until she leaned forward and said, "Joe. I'm sorry." Like it was her fault.

"You set me up, Alana?"

"How can you even ask?" There was a note in her voice that was rare. Soft, vulnerable, scared. A young girl's voice that recalled how they'd met. Five years ago. Alana a luscious seventeen, the new kid in town. Too hot, too popular, too new at the game to know it was important to keep the other girls on her side. A couple of girls, jealous and angry, got some biker friends of theirs to rape and beat her. They dumped her, naked and bloody, down in the park on a cold November night. He was out looking for a witness when he found her.

The image of her honey-colored body, curled in a fetal position on the frosty ground, was still clear in his mind. Scooping back the hair from her face to look for breath, for a pulse. He'd wrapped her in his coat, carried her to the car, and driven her to the hospital. She'd clung to his hand like a frightened child that day, so hurt and violated, begging him not to leave her among strangers. He'd stayed as long as he could. Gone back to visit. When she was ready to leave but still needed care, he'd taken her to his sister's. Sandy had tried hard to get Alana off the streets. Lost the battle, but Sandy still invited her for holidays, baked a cake on her birthday.

He tipped his head back and rested, so beat it was an effort to breathe, watching the world float by through half-open eyes. Heard her repeat her question, very faintly. Didn't bother to answer. Kyle answered for him. "Leave him alone, Alana. He knows you didn't."

"I couldn't bear it, you know, if he thought . . ."

"He doesn't," Kyle said. "He knows you, remember?" Talking like he wasn't there.

"Don't you think I know that? I just feel bad. I'd never hurt him. It's only that ever since what happened back when I met Joe, I've always tried to keep a balance. Try to give him what he wants and still cover my ass on the street."

"Come on, Alana, you never cover your ass on the street."

Kyle at his most loquacious. Speaking whole sentences. All to comfort a distraught hooker so she wouldn't bother a battered colleague. Better guys were hard to find. He had a million questions for Alana, so many things to tell Kyle. Couldn't summon the energy to do either. He stopped listening to their conversation and drifted.

Chapter Sixteen

He submitted in a dozy haze to having his clothes removed, and fell into bed. He felt her tuck the covers around him and their voices moved away, becoming a background hum as he was sucked down into sleep.

He thought she'd gone until he heard soft footsteps, the sound of covers being pulled down, and she slipped into bed beside him, fitting the curves of her body to his. When he woke, in pain, a few hours later, she was up in a flash and back with pills and water. "Nurse Jane Fuzzy Wuzzy," she muttered, settling back into her place beside him, a hooker who made lit refs to Uncle Wiggily.

He waited for the pills to work, listening to her breathe, thinking how few times in the last years he'd slept beside a woman, felt that alien warmth, the unfamiliar sounds of another person's rest. The hot ache in his arm surged like a fever, his shame at letting himself get ambushed fanning it into an angry sweat. He clenched his teeth and endured the pounding in his head, the sickness and dizziness, thinking that he deserved it. This was his penance for inattention, for letting himself get beat down.

Finally, the medicine kicked in, bringing a gentle lethargy that let him sleep. With the sleep came dreams. He sat beside his mother, holding her swollen, unresponsive hand, watching the electronic read-outs of hope and hopelessness, as she failed in full-screen living color. Doing the death watch, there for her as she'd always been for him. His sisters came and cried and left and came to do it all again, making him the rock for everyone. He'd never cried.

In his dream, he cried with a dream's surrealism. Tears flowed in silver columns down his face, tracing silver stripes down his clothes, pooling at his feet like mercury. In the hospital he'd sat silent. In his dream, he spoke of those magical nights by the window when she taught him to see, of his anger toward his father, his sorrow that her life had given her so little of what she deserved. Said all the things she'd died without hearing.

The dream took on an angry reddish hue that spread until the light was ruddy and thick with it. He gripped that unresponsive hand, infested with tubes and wires, that wrist that now came with a little stopper-cock so they could draw blood like water, and spoke about his anger at Dr. Stephen Pleasant, who had been in too great a hurry to read the X-rays carefully. Who had sent her home healthy while the deadly disease kept growing, let her go a year in pain, a woman who trusted doctors. Who had condemned her to death.

The dream took him, floating like a man on a magic carpet, to the place he always went, awake or asleep. The darkest spot on his soul. He hovered there in the crystalline blue light of a morning just past dawn, looking down on the sprawled white body of little Kristin Marks. Thrown away on a landfill like an empty can, worn shoe, or yesterday's news.

Every cop had them, the cases that wouldn't let go. Kristin was his. Sometimes she came to him alive, running eagerly to show him a drawing or tell him something about school, though he'd never known her alive, and when she got close, he would see the maggots crawling out of her mouth and down her thighs. As he hovered above her defiled body, her eyes flickered open. Soft, shining brown eyes. She looked up at him and tears rolled down her face.

He groped his way out of bed, staggered into the bathroom, and threw up. Kristin lived inside him like a chronic disease, occasionally flaring up in an acute attack of memory and sorrow. He drank some water, splashed some on his face, and went back to bed, hoping the dreams were over. For a while, they were.

When his dreams returned, they were erotic. Ironic and entirely in keeping with his life that he should lie chastely in bed beside the sexiest woman in town, dreaming of sex with imaginary women. When his alarm went off, he moaned and reached for it, found Alana's hand had beaten him to it. She shut it off and moved it out of his reach. "Not this morning, copman," she said. "You need to sleep."

"Gotta get up, kiddo. Work to do." Words thick and slurry, eyelids glued shut. He struggled to sit up.

"No," she said firmly, emphasizing her point by straddling him, sliding her legs down along the outsides of his. Bare skin against bare skin. Her hands on his shoulders pinning him to the mattress. "You're staying right here. Doctor's orders. The streets aren't even plowed and Terry has your car."

"Got to—"

She stopped his words with her mouth. He put a hand on her shoulder to push her off. Her incredibly warm bare shoulder. Ran it down her bare back, along the length of her, as far as it would go, back up again, and down, marveling at her smooth warmth. Even half-asleep, it shook him, a bone-deep shudder of desire. He buried his hand in her hair to keep it off that skin, wanting to feel her breasts against his bare chest. Forgetting she read men's minds for a living, held a Ph.D. in desire from the school of life.

She rolled up his T-shirt and let her nipples slide across

his skin, down over his stomach. He opened his mouth to say "no" and was given a nipple to taste, an experience that had been the stuff of more than one dream. Now, somewhere between dream and reality, he didn't protest when she helped him out of his T-shirt, teasing him with her slowness, tenderly easing it over his bad arm. Nor when she stripped off his underwear and lay on top of him, her hands expertly stroking and guiding. "I've waited five years for you," she whispered. "Don't rush me." Moving him slowly yet surely toward that place he'd been dreaming about. Whispering into his neck, "Let it come, Joe, let it come, Joe, let it come," as he exploded, groaning, gasping, and fell back into the abyss of sleep.

He woke again to the smells of coffee and bacon and voices in the kitchen. Alana and Kyle. He lay listening, unable to summon the energy to move. The assault had laid him low, the drugs made him dizzy and inert, and the sex had drained the last drop of energy out of him. For years, half the department had assumed he was getting this. Snickered and envied him behind his back. Now his position was anything but enviable. Alana was a major player in a case he was working.

The phone rang. He heard Kyle answer, then footsteps. Kyle came in, his hand over the mouthpiece, looking apologetic. "Sorry. It's Cote," he whispered. "He insists."

Burgess struggled up on the pillows and took the phone. "Yes, captain?" His voice sounded thin and weak. Not how he ever wanted to be with Cote.

"Ted Shaw's very upset with you." Cote didn't ask how he was doing, didn't even acknowledge the attack. This wasn't how things were done. An assault on a cop was a big deal. If they didn't close ranks and get tough, it was that much easier for some joker to do it the next time. The public had to know—you touch one cop, you've touched them all. Burgess waited, conserving his strength.

"Are you listening?" Cote asked.

"You heard about last night?"

"That's why I'm calling. Jen Kelly was terribly upset." Exasperation hissed down the line.

"Kind of her. Was it the stitches or the cracked bone or just that I was attacked?"

Cote cleared his throat. "Yes. Right. Of course. How are you, Joe?"

"Hurt."

"How long do you expect to be out?"

Was that hope in Cote's voice that he could find a better yes-man and put him in as primary? Not among Burgess's people. "Until noon."

"Noon today? What's the doctor say?"

"The usual. No heavy lifting. No contact sports. No jogging for six weeks. Be sure and take my medicine. I think that's what he said. I was a little out of it." He must not be too badly off. He could engage in malicious obedience designed to drive Cote crazy without giving him any reason to complain. Burgess was, after all, answering his questions.

"You should take a few days. Let someone else run the investigation."

"Hard to hand it off at this point, I've got reports to write, but I appreciate your concern." Back in your court, asshole. "Shall I stop by when I get in?"

Cote said a frustrated "yes" and disconnected without achieving his purpose. Burgess cradled the phone and closed his eyes. "Did I really say noon, Terry? Am I crazy?"

"No. You just hate his guts. You'd crawl there if you had to, just to stick it to him."

"No way." He sighed. The pillow felt so good and more

sleep looked so tempting. "Just want everyone to know what a tough guy I am."

"They already cringe when you walk by, what more do you want? Oh, looky, here comes your nurse. Breakfast must be ready."

Alana had skewered her hair on top of her head and wore one of his shirts. Devoid of makeup and covered from neck to knee, she looked like somebody's kid sister, complete with little pearl earrings. She smiled sweetly. "How's my patient? Hungry?"

"Worn out," he said.

A smile so big she might as well be wearing a sign that said: "I fucked Joe Burgess."

Kyle looked at him curiously.

"Hope you like bacon and eggs," she said.

"You fix it?"

"No. I can't cook. I called Terry to come fix it. What the hell do you think?" She sat cross-legged on the foot of the bed and let her hair down. "I'm tired, too. You're as restless asleep as you are awake. You talk in your sleep, too." He knew something was coming. Didn't expect what followed. "Who's Kristin?"

Now that she'd gotten what she'd wanted for years, she wanted more. Probably nothing would ever be enough. She was so hungry for love, she'd suck him dry and still want more. He didn't have enough Band-Aids in his own cold heart to patch her together. Kyle looked at them uneasily, wanting to intervene with no idea how. No one mentioned Kristin Marks around Burgess.

He hated violating his privacy like this, but was too tired to deal with the hours of game playing any alternative would produce. "Open the closet," he said.

Looking puzzled, she crossed the room and opened his

closet. She stared at the inside of the door, then silently closed it, her face white. "What the hell . . . Joe . . ."

"That's Kristin."

Her hand went to her mouth. She stared with big, sorry eyes as her legs folded beneath her and she crumpled into a little heap on the floor. She wrapped her arms around her knees, pulled them into her chest, lay her face on them. She made no sound but he knew from the shake of her shoulders that she was crying. "I'm sorry. I'm so, so sorry. I'll never get it right, will I, Joe? Even when I want to help, I hurt you."

"I'll go get that coffee." Terry backed out of the room.

He got out of bed, awkwardly pulled on his underwear, and knelt down beside her. Ignoring the pains in his arm and his head, he drew her against him, feeling the wetness of tears against his chest.

"You should have left me in the park," she said. "I'm nothing but trouble."

He rubbed his stubbly chin against her hair. "Hush. You're talking nonsense."

"I know I can't cure anything that ails you with a good fuck."

"It was good, though."

She threw her arms around his neck and kissed him. "You think you're a cold, hard, locked-up man, Joe, but the weird thing is, all you know how to do is give. You don't know how to take."

"I take plenty. Plenty of shit from scumbags. Liberty from people who don't belong on the streets. Money from the taxpayers. Grief from my sisters and my boss."

She pointed at the closet. "You carry stuff like that around with you, never saying anything to anyone, letting it eat you up inside."

"I said plenty about that at the time. Damned near lost my job."

"Because the guy who did it walked, didn't he, Joe? I remember now."

"He didn't walk, he . . . look, we're not going to talk about this, okay?"

"Sure, Joe. It's something we're both good at anyway. Not talking. Come eat before it gets cold. I really am a pretty good cook."

"Alana . . . about last night?"

She swiped away a tear and gave him a trembling smile. "Don't worry, copman. Your secrets are safe with me."

"Speaking of secrets, what was it you wanted to tell me last night? Before we were so rudely interrupted?" He let her help him into his robe and followed her into the kitchen. Kyle poured three cups of coffee, and Alana told her story.

CHAPTER SEVENTEEN

"A man picked me up one night about a month ago." She made a face. "I know what you guys are thinking. Plenty of men have picked me up in the last month. Just listen, okay? Let me tell this my way. Then you can ask all the questions you want." She pointed with her fork. "And not a word until Joe eats something."

What was it with women wanting to mother him? There wasn't anything needy or boyish about him. He wasn't hungry but he wanted her story, so he ate a piece of bacon. After the first bite, he was famished.

"Okay," she said. "So this guy picks me up and drives me to a big empty parking lot. So far it's perfectly normal, right? I ask him what he wants, to give him a price, and he says, 'I'm not here for sex, okay?' Sure, I think, but I say, 'I've got a living to make, so if you aren't here to do business, please take me back where you found me.' He says, 'Look, I'll pay you, no problem, I just want to ask you some questions.' So I'm thinking this is some newspaper guy, because, like, they do that sometimes, want the point of view of the girl on the street, you know?"

He waved his fork over his empty plate. "This is better than Becky's. Got any more?" Becky's was a waterfront restaurant known for great breakfasts and a clientele ranging from fishermen to bankers.

"Yeah," Kyle seconded. "Got any more?"

She refilled their plates with a knowing smile. She made a man hungry, that was why. Satisfied him and left him

169

hungry. "Was he a reporter?" Burgess asked.

"No. He said he wanted to get close to one of our customers, a guy who was a regular on the street, and could I help him? I didn't know what that was about, drugs maybe? I said, 'Look, mister, if you're looking to deal drugs, don't ask me to help.' That surprised him, like he'd never thought it, and he says, 'Hey, I just want to talk to this guy.' But it was, you know, just too weird. Then I thought maybe he was a cop, so I asked him and he said no way."

She grabbed the coffeepot and filled their cups. "I was curious what he was up to, and everything, but there was like this atmosphere in the truck that spooked me. He was so nervous. I thought maybe this was about drugs and stuff, even if he did say no, and I don't have anything to do with that." Not quite the truth. Alana used occasionally, but she said she didn't deal, and he believed that. "Whatever it was, he was like, so focused on finding this man it creeped me out. I mean, there's lots of ways to find someone, right? Especially a doctor—"

"Hold on," Burgess interrupted. "He was looking for a doctor?"

Alana rolled her eyes. "Isn't that why I called you?"

He tried to recall Kyle's message. "You think it's the same guy who tried to grab you?"

"Joe, will you let me finish? I just wanted to get out of there, so I said I couldn't help him but probably one of the other girls could and to please take me back."

"Did he?" She looked tired. He wondered if she'd stayed awake, watching over him? When she moved, her breasts bounced gently under his shirt. Trying not to look at them was like trying not to stare at the sun during an eclipse.

She shook her head. "Not everyone's a gentleman like you, Joe. Lotta mean people out there. He got really mad, maybe 'cuz he was nervous and I wasn't making things easy. He said, "You could help,' and shoved me out of the truck. And wouldn't it be the one time I wasn't carrying my phone? I had to walk miles in my damned high heels, freezing my ass off, and then business was dead."

"Ever see him again?" Kyle asked.

"Why didn't you tell me about this the other night?" Burgess asked.

She looked from one to the other, confused. "Who's first?" she asked.

"Kyle."

"Yeah, I saw him again. Yesterday afternoon, across from my place. I was wondering what some guy was doing, just standing out there like he's waiting for something. Not even a Portland cab takes that long to come. Hell . . ." She grinned wickedly. "Not even a geriatric takes that long to come. Then I saw his face and I remembered. That's when I called Joe and took a cab over to Dunkin' Donuts. He must have followed me."

"Why didn't you—"

"Oh, gimme a break, Joe. I forgot all about it until I saw him in front of my house. Then, it all came back, that the guy he wanted was a doctor. So I called you. Okay?"

Yeah, right. Alana and her goddamned games. Who knew how long she would have held it back if the guy hadn't spooked her. "What did he look like?"

"What was he driving?" Kyle added.

"What is it with you two?" She checked her watch. "You look like shit, Joe. It's time for your pills and then you should go back to bed, shouldn't he, Terry?"

Kyle stayed diplomatically silent.

She started crumbling her toast. "You think he's connected to what happened to Dr. Pleasant?" When they didn't respond, she said, "Hey, come on. You guys are used to this stuff. It scares me." When they still didn't respond, she went back to shredding her toast. Finally, sighing, she said, "He was real good-looking. A big guy like Joe, strong but not as heavy, like his work was physical. Dark hair, curly, I think. Hard to tell. He wore a bandana. Neat beard, not that little faggoty thing some men wear. He looked, I don't know . . ." She glared, obviously expecting them to laugh. ". . . like a pirate. When I saw him out there yesterday, he was all bundled up. I only recognized him because of the bandana. He had nice eyes, too. That browny-green color, hazel?"

"You noticed a lot for a scared girl who was anxious to get out of there," Kyle said.

"Yeah, so maybe I shoulda been a cop, like you, Terry." She tossed her hair and shot him a challenging look. "Sure as hell wouldn't have worked the other way. Guy as homely as you'd never make it on the street." She regretted it as soon as she'd said it, sliding an apologetic hand up Kyle's arm, leaning in with a breast for emphasis. Kyle's pale face reddened.

"Sorry," she said. "I meant girls in my business have to watch people closely to figure out what they're going to do—whether they're honest, or crazy, or mean, or violent. I can look at a guy's eyes and know he wants to hurt someone. Now this guy, he was scared and determined, but not out to hurt someone. He was . . ." She twisted a piece of hair. "On a mission. And I was in his way. So he pushed me out of the truck and drove off."

Burgess swallowed the pills. He didn't like the way they dulled him down, but the pain in his head made him sick. He couldn't afford to be sick. He was following a faint trail of goddamned crumbs through the great dismal swamp.

Couple days off the job, the animals would eat them, trail would disappear. "Notice anything about the truck?"

She took her time, fiddling with her hair until he wanted to slap her hands. "Like a million other ratty pickups. Dark and dirty and dented, with a cap on the back. He had a gun rack and one of those deodorant trees. Only thing missing was a half-empty six-pack, which guys in trucks usually need to get up their courage. Dog was a nice touch. Guys don't usually bring their dogs along when they come to get blown."

She cast a quick glance at him. "Sorry, Joe." She came around and started massaging his neck. Her hands were rough and jittery.

"How old?"

"Early forties, maybe?"

"You know something about this guy, Joe?" Kyle asked.

"Fill you in when everyone's there," he said. "It ties into something I picked up yesterday." He was eager to dump Alana and sit down with the guys, see if they could make sense of all this. Do that, put more things in motion, then come back here and be alone. Alana in his bed, his closet, his kitchen. He felt too exposed.

"Yeah and when I'm not," she said, her fingers pinching.

He moved away. "Pass me the phone, Terry." He dialed his sister's number. "Sandy? It's Joe." He listened to a small explosion of concern. "Right. Don't believe everything you read in the papers. I know you would have come if your street was plowed. Look, I'm fine, really, but I need a favor." Alana took an audible breath. "Alana's got a guy stalking her, needs to get away for a few days until we can grab him. Can she stay with you?" He covered the mouthpiece. "She wants to know if you eat pot roast."

Alana's fist pounded his shoulder, sending pains down

his arm. He winced. "She says she loves pot roast. She'll even help peel potatoes. You plowed out now? How about half an hour?"

"I'm not a piece of baggage to be picked up and dropped off," Alana exploded. "Someone has to take care of you. You haven't got a clue how to do it yourself."

"Last fifty years were just a fluke," he agreed. "I'm going to work. We'll drop you at Sandy's on the way."

"I don't want to go to Sandy's."

"Well, where *do* you want to go? That friend up in Brunswick? I need you someplace safe where I don't have to worry about you."

"I'm a working girl, Joe."

"You want to get dead, Alana? That guy wasn't hanging out across the street from your house because he wanted to apologize for being rude. I'm getting dressed. Terry, see if you can talk some sense into her."

As she turned her back on them, Terry gave a slight shake of his head and Burgess realized he'd made a mistake, letting her con him into thinking she was okay because she acted okay. Thinking like a john, buying her tough girl act, instead of a cop. He knew better. If he couldn't handle this, he might as well stay home. Dealing with people required attention. Act on assumptions instead, you put yourself and everyone else in danger.

"I could use a little help, Alana, if you don't mind."

She followed him into the bedroom, slapping her feet angrily against the floor. He backed her against the wall and held her there, cupping his good hand around her head, feeling the vibration in her body, the potential explosion of her fear. "Listen to me, Alana. It's going to be all right," he said. "You're going to be all right. I know you were with Pleasant just before he was killed and now someone's after

174

you, but you're going to be all right. Look at me." She pressed her face against his chest. "Alana, please?"

She shook her head. "I can't."

"All right," he said, stroking her hair, slow and steady, taking time he didn't have. "Just listen, then. You'll be safe with Sandy. She cares about you. And I've got a murder to solve, which takes concentration. I can't concentrate if you're in danger."

He felt the shiver of resistance. "I want to stay with you!"

"But I won't be here."

"You can't go to work, Joe. You're hurt."

"I'm stubborn. Like a dog with a stick. Once I get my teeth into something, I don't let go. God, Alana, you know that." Waiting for her to remember what he'd done after he found her in the park. "Is there anybody in this city who'd work harder to make you safe? Who cares more?"

Forcing a patience he didn't have—the day, and the case, were getting old—he asked, "Will you help me get dressed?"

"But Joe . . . I . . ."

He felt that quiver of resistance again. "Take a deep breath." He waited. "And another. That's good." Working it until she was breathing normally again. "Now look at me and say 'I'm going to be okay.' "

"I'm going to be okay," she said. "I'm going to be okay."

Outside was a big, white beautiful mess. Overcast and still too bright for tired eyes, the air filled with the scrape of shovels and plows, muffled moans and curses, the whine of spinning tires, the cries of playing children. Kyle was grim and intent as he navigated the half-plowed streets, Alana silent. Burgess tried a few more questions—did she know any more than she'd told them about people getting drugs from

Pleasant? She didn't. What could she tell him about O'Leary? Not a damned thing. He was sure she knew more, but O'Leary really scared her. He gave up.

They left Alana, angry and sullen, on his sister's doorstep. "You'll be sorry, Joe," she said, shaking her fist. He gritted his teeth and nodded. In complete agreement. He hadn't chosen this because it was a happy job, had he? By the time her parting snowball smashed against the rear window, he'd moved on, already putting Alana's story together with the security guard's, and wondering how to learn more about this guy who'd come looking for Pleasant.

CHAPTER EIGHTEEN

Though the hot conference room made him drowsy, Burgess didn't dare put more coffee in his uneasy stomach. The joys of medicine. What cures one thing usually harms another. There were four of them around the table, himself, Kyle, Perry, and Vince Melia. Captain Cote had been invited and declined. He'd rather bitch than be informed. No one was cheerful or rested. There were no jokes or wisecracks. The mayor and the chief had the press breathing down their necks and were passing it down the food chain. Too many citizens were playing see no evil, hear no evil, speak no evil. From now on, the case would be pure drudgery.

He couldn't stand himself in this tamped-down state. He wanted to take the pipe that had beaten him down and use it on a few people himself. "All right," he said, "let's look at what we've got." He went to the dryboard and wrote:

1. Robbed by a hooker and her accomplice;
2. Angry current/former wife;
3. Stalked by someone/Disgruntled patient?
4. Embarrassing videotape/blackmail gone wrong?
5. Complications from drug dealing;
6. Debts/financial problems.

"Anything else?" Only a chorus of groans. As they shuffled through their notes, a wave of dizziness rocked him. He put a hand on the wall and closed his eyes. Goddammit! How was he supposed to work this if he couldn't even stand up? "Stan, you mind taking over?" He handed over the marker and sat down, weakness doing nothing to improve his mood.

They called things out, attaching what they'd learned to the possible scenarios on the board. Among the surprises—that both Janet Pleasant and Jack Kelly had been arrested, at different times, for assault on Stephen Pleasant. In both cases, the charges had later been dropped.

When they finished, it was like a secondhand jigsaw puzzle. Too many missing pieces.

"Any sign of O'Leary?" Burgess asked.

"Gotta snitch hangs out at the Big Apple, saw him buying gas yesterday morning. Day after our vic bought the farm," Kyle said. "Guy's got even half a brain, he's in Florida by now."

"Half a brain's about what he's got," Perry said, waving a sheaf of papers. "Got a sheet a mile long. Lotta drug stuff, the occasional recreational rape."

One of the few things that worked to their advantage was how many criminals did have only half a brain, Burgess thought.

"Oxycontin?" Kyle asked.

Perry nodded. "Tommy Duggan in Narcotics says he was a reliable source. Natives been getting restless since he disappeared."

"You think this was a drug thing, Joe?" Melia asked hopefully. As head of criminal investigations, the weight of this was on his shoulders and they were sagging a little.

"Why kill the golden goose? Stan, drug guys heard anything that connects Pleasant and drugs?"

Perry shook his head. "Nothing solid. They're shaking some cages."

Burgess shared what he'd learned from the security guard, Charlie, and from Alana. The guy in the pickup.

Pleasant's meeting with someone who fit O'Leary's description. The tip about drugs from the ER nurse. The suggestion they look to disgruntled patients. "No clear winners. So we keep digging. Stan, talk to the Rockland police, see if they have any leads on O'Leary, get an address and find a time to go see his momma. Go by Pleasant's place and get his financial records. His wife said she'd give us access. And expect the cold shoulder. She's decided we're a bunch of mannerless thugs." He gave quick directions.

"Terry, you come to the hospital with me. We've got a list of people to see. Three docs who were Pleasant's friends. The parking lot attendant. Got to get the names of other security guards, other parking lot attendants, their schedules. Talk to the administration. And then there's Pleasant's attorney." He snapped his notebook shut. "Anybody got any ideas where O'Leary might have hidden those videotapes?" He waited. "Think like a scumbag, it just might come to you."

"At the hospital," Melia said. "Kid gloves, okay?"

Burgess pushed back from the table. "Not you, too, Vince."

"Just a part of the food chain, Joe. They bite my ass, I bite yours."

There was a knock on the door and a detective stuck his head in. "Hey, Joe? There's an old lady out here wants to talk about Dr. Pleasant. You got time?"

He always had time for someone who wanted to talk about Pleasant. "Tell her five minutes." He opened his notebook, scribbled a quick list, and gave it to Kyle. "See if these docs can give us some time?"

Melia stayed behind, resting his arms on the back of a chair. He dressed smart and he looked smart, a *GQ* kind of guy with a gun on his belt. His crisp shirt matched his sharp blue eyes. "I should send you home, Joe. Doesn't look like you're gonna make it."

They both knew Melia wasn't sending him anywhere. Not with a jittery city and bigwigs breathing down their necks. "We're playing pin the rap on the bad guy and we might as well be blindfolded, Vince. This case has everything—unhappy wife, angry ex. Hookers. Drugs. Money problems. Maybe blackmail, and a vic nobody liked, including his patients. Hard to pick a winner. But I got my shoulder to the wheel, and if I just keep pushing, it'll move. Besides . . ." He allowed himself a smile. "Gotta let Cote gnaw my ass."

"Let Terry drive you, okay? If you need him for something else, I'll find you a driver. I don't want heroics here. Understood?" Right. Vinnie wanted X-ray vision and for him to leap small buildings in a single bound. "Better go see your old lady. Any senior citizen out on a day like this deserves a medal."

Burgess got slowly to his feet. This must be what it was like to be old—mind racing ahead like always, poor old body dragging behind like an afterthought.

A small, upright woman in a severe navy coat and an ancient hat sat by his desk. "Sergeant Burgess, ma'am. You wanted to see me?"

Her glasses were thick, her face gaunt and wrinkled, but her response was quick. "You're investigating Dr. Pleasant's murder?"

"I am."

"Then it's you I came to see. I'm Maude Libby. My late husband, Oscar, was one of Dr. Pleasant's patients."

He got an address and telephone number. "What did you want to see me about, Mrs. Libby?"

"I read about you in the paper," she said. "You got attacked last night but you're not home in bed, feeling sorry for yourself. My Oscar would have approved of you. Hit Oscar over the head and he would have come to work extra early, just to show they couldn't keep him down." She pulled a crumpled tissue from her coat pocket, took off her glasses, and wiped them. She didn't wipe her eyes, though Burgess saw tears. "I didn't like Dr. Pleasant, though I suppose he was a good enough doctor. He didn't treat people with respect. He treated Oscar like an old dummy."

She touched Burgess's arm, a sign this was important. Women of her generation didn't touch strange men. "My Oscar ran a trucking business nearly fifty years. That's no business for weaklings. He fixed trucks, loaded trucks, drove trucks. Beat up people who tried to steal his trucks. He wasn't the sort of man you patted on the head and told what to do. Seeing him humiliated was one of the hardest parts of watching him die."

She pulled her hand back and set it in her lap, a wrinkled, age-spotted hand with a magnificent diamond ring. "I know you're a busy man and I don't mean to waste your time. I'm telling you this so you'll understand. I'm not usually a vindictive woman. I hope I'm not being one now." She coughed, patted her chest, and said, in a smaller voice, "Could I have some water?"

He couldn't get water with one hand, so he asked one of the other detectives to do it. Where was this going? He'd seen plenty of people with chips on their shoulders, few so open and dignified about it. He gave her the water and waited.

"Oscar died at home on a Thursday morning. That afternoon, Dr. Pleasant stopped at the house to collect Oscar's unused medicine. He said it was donated to an organization that provided medicine for people who couldn't pay. Perhaps I'm making a mountain from a mole-hill, but I didn't believe him. He didn't give me the organization's name. He seemed extremely nervous. Just the week before, when we all knew the end was near, he'd prescribed a batch of new painkillers without explanation. I wondered whether he wanted that medicine for something other than humanitarian purposes."

She reached up and straightened her hat. As she did, her neck lengthened, her chin tilted up, and he had a sudden vision of her fifty years earlier, of the grace and elegance which had attracted Oscar. She noticed the look. Lowered her eyes with a faint smile. "I hope I'm not wronging the man, sergeant, but I have always been a good judge of character."

He got the name and address of her pharmacy, and she agreed to call and okay the release of her husband's prescription records. "If he did it to Oscar," she added, "he may have done it to others. Prescription drugs for the elderly are so expensive and our insurance companies fight constantly to keep from paying. We don't need this nonsense on top of everything else."

While people much closer to the crime were hiding their heads in the sand, Maude Libby had come out on the morning after a snowstorm to tell him this. "Mrs. Libby, I wish more of our citizens were like you."

"So do I," she said.

"How did you get here today?"

She seemed surprised by the question. "I drove, of course."

Fifty years married to a trucker, Maude Libby was probably a hell of a driver. Undaunted by a little snow. "Did you ever drive the trucks?"

"During the war, my sister Edna and I both did. Had the

time of our lives. Then the men came back and needed the jobs, so we went home and had babies. Driving in snow, you know, some of it's experience, a lot is common sense. Something that seems to be sorely lacking these days." She stood up. "I won't keep you. I know you're busy. I'd appreciate knowing what you find out, though."

"I'll let you know. Thank you for taking the time to come in, Mrs. Libby." One more thing he had to ask. "What are you driving these days?"

It was there again, just a touch of pride. "Oscar always thought I should drive cars. He considered them more ladylike. I used to have a Lincoln. Now I drive Oscar's truck." She inclined her head, a very small gesture, and walked away. She'd been a woman men noticed. It had never quite gone away.

He found Kyle making coffee. "Any luck with the docs?"

"Level of cooperation over there is very low today."

"Then we'll just drop in. Sometimes that works better anyway. You ready?"

"Thought I'd get some coffee first. That hospital stuff's pathetic."

"No problem. I've got reports to write."

"One-handed?"

"I've got a choice?" Back at his desk, he called his sister. "Hey, it's Joe. Listen, if you're looking for a project, Alana would be great at massage. Maybe you could find a program she might get into." He listened to Sandy's reflexive complaint about money. "Pay? Who'd you think, the Hooker Rescue League? Of course I will. Well, I guess that's right. I found her so that makes her mine. Meanwhile, you could bake some cookies or boil a chicken to make soup for the invalid."

He started typing. Not doing too badly for a cripple. He

was into his third report when Kyle showed up, and only then remembered that he was supposed to see Cote. Odd how easy it is to forget what we don't want to do. "Give me a minute, Terry. Gotta pop upstairs and see the captain."

Normally, he wouldn't take the elevator up one flight, but today, the slam of his feet hurt his head. Must be time for another pill. Light was painful and he wanted to squeeze his head between his hands and bellow curses. Those were clues. The throbbing in his arm was another. That little crack in the bone felt like dentistry without Novocain.

Cote, on the phone, motioned him into a chair. Burgess lowered himself slowly, tipped his head back, and rested his eyes. He heard a muffled mumble-mumble, some placating phrases about busy man and so sorry, his officers hadn't meant to be rude, and he'd see what he could do. Suddenly, in a louder voice, he heard Cote say, "No, they are not harassing your medical staff. It's standard procedure for detectives to question the victim's friends and co-workers. These aren't interrogations, they're interviews, collecting information about the victim. Of course they'll respect your staff's privacy."

Captain Rigid SOP actually defending cops? His eyes popped open. What was wrong with Cote?

"Sir? I'm not sure I understand your complaint. A serious crime has been committed. It's the duty of every citizen to assist the police."

Burgess stared. It was Cote's head, Cote's voice. "Suppose your wife or child was a victim. Would you want people to refuse to give information because it was inconvenient?" Cote listened, then asked, "Well, how many people have the detectives spoken with?" Burgess held up three fingers. Cote sighed. "Do what you feel you must, but I'm not going to instruct detectives working a homicide to stay away from the victim's workplace or his friends and colleagues. And, doctor, if you think calling the mayor is necessary, that's certainly your right, but why not just cooperate?"

It was so unlike Cote's normal placating and servile attitude toward VIPs. Enlightenment came quickly. The chief, who'd been in the doorway, cleared his throat as he came into the room. "No one wants to be bothered anymore, do they? Hey, Joe," he said. "How are you?"

"Been worse," Burgess said. It was true. His life had been a trail of tears.

"Who was that?" the chief asked.

"Hospital administrator. Complaining our detectives are driving them crazy."

The chief's calm eyes fixed on Burgess. "Are you?"

"I've been there twice, sir. Right after the murder, I interviewed his boss. Yesterday I interviewed his secretary and a security guard. We called just now to set up interviews with three docs who were Pleasant's close friends, and they blew us off."

"Sounds like they got on the horn to this guy right away. Any idea why?"

"Case is ugly. No one wants to be connected with it. Vic was partying with two hookers just before he was killed. The body was found partially undressed. Hooker we've located says the party was videotaped. We've got rumors on the street that the vic might have been peddling classified drugs, including Oxycontin. Vic may have had financial problems. All pretty nasty, and the widow's Ted Shaw's daughter, so he's throwing his weight around, doesn't want to be embarrassed. As for why they're in such a snit over there, I can't tell you, sir. Everything's been SOP."

The chief nodded. "Everyone's in favor of law enforcement as long as it stays away from them. But we don't have one set of rules for the little people, another for the big fish. Go over there and do what you have to do." He headed for the door. "And keep Paul in the loop so he can run interference."

Cote stared coldly over his desk, looking really eager to run interference for Joe Burgess. "You got anything on this yet? Anything?"

"What I told the chief. Bits and pieces."

"Well, go out there and get me something."

Like he'd been hanging around eating donuts and drinking coffee. Like Cote wouldn't have made doing interviews at the hospital impossible if the chief hadn't been listening. Cote was looking at him like he had dung on his shoes. He knew he wasn't pretty today, but he hadn't been pretty before, either. He hadn't even been a pretty baby. He wanted to pound Cote's mean little two-faced head against the wall until the faces blended into one. It was an ugly impulse and he didn't like having it.

He stood up ever so slowly, being careful of his own head. Sketched a salute. "I'm on my way . . . sir." Off to interview the hell out of those whiny suckers. Stomp on every foot he could.

CHAPTER NINETEEN

He always longed for a shower after he'd been in Cote's office. It was an ugly fact of his ugly life that the bastard could wear him down. Like the song says, though, you can't always get what you want. If he couldn't be alone, being with Kyle was the next best thing. He reported on his talk with Maude Libby, Kyle grunted, and they lapsed into silence.

The short trip from Middle Street to Bramhall took forever. The plows had made little progress. Bundled pedestrians shuffled and minced. Cars slithered and tires whined. In the cold, bright light, the city looked like hell, all dirty snow and sandy muck the color of dog turds. Even the normally warm red brick buildings seemed hard-edged and dingy. Was it all in the eye of the beholder? Was it unreasonable to have a jaundiced moment when getting to be lead detective through the accumulating heaps of shit didn't make him feel like Little Mary Sunshine?

After he'd tried to dismember Cote, they'd taken his gun and sent him to a shrink for some anger management and grief counseling. SOP for a cop under stress. After the required meetings, the shrink opined that he'd benefit from some long-term work. He was saved by department regulations, which only asked whether he could perform the job without being a danger to himself or others. The shrink had agreed he could, and Burgess had stuffed his anger and sorrow into emotional footlockers and gone back to work.

Days like this, worn down and mired in death, when he'd had the dreams, it felt like the lids were coming loose.

He needed to get back in balance. Therapy. Prozac. Alcohol. Drugs. Violence. So many solutions to choose from. Some days, when he couldn't avoid thinking how they'd totally failed Kristin, his gun looked too good.

Kyle broke the silence. "Think you're losing it, Joe?"

"Why?"

"You're wearing your 'don't mess with me I'm a crazy fucker' look."

They rode in silence a while, then he said, "I am a crazy fucker."

"I know that." Kyle swerved around a pile of snow extending halfway across the street. "Sweet Jesus," he said. "Doesn't this city know how to plow snow?" He swerved around another pile, grinning. "This is like bumper cars. You want to eat somewhere?"

"Not hungry."

"Got any idea who did it?"

"You saw the board."

"Sure I saw it. I'm asking what does Joe Burgess think?"

"Got two ideas running a dead heat, bunch more right on their heels."

"Wanna share or are you into cherishing the mystery, see if the rest of us peons can figure it out?"

"You think you're a goddamned peon?"

"No."

"You think I think you're a goddamned peon?"

"Get a grip, Joe." Kyle wasn't getting dragged into his bad mood. "Your theory of the case?"

"Theories. Either it was an arranged hit, for which we've got a bunch of candidates, or he was killed by a former patient, or the relative of a former patient, which seems a little far-fetched at this point." He recalled Chris Perlin's reluctant hints on that subject.

"What about rolled by a hooker or her pimp? Too obvious?" Burgess nodded. "Okay, arranged by whom?"

"Pick one. Ted Shaw. Jack Kelly. Pleasant's wife. Or ex-wife. Unless it was Pleasant's partners. Unless it was someone he was dealing drugs with. Or to."

At the hospital, Kyle pulled into Burgess's favorite spot and killed the engine. "Why?"

"To avoid potential embarrassment. Whatever people say, avoiding scandal is a powerful motivation. Look what we know about Pleasant. He went to hookers, which was expensive and dangerous, maybe spinning out of control. His wife knew it, Jack Kelly knew it, Ted Shaw knew it. His partners knew it. Hell, half the hospital knew it."

"But if it was embarrassment, why kill him in such a compromising position?"

"Easiest way to get to him?" Burgess shrugged. "Then there's money. He was in financial trouble. Shaw had bailed him out at least once. He was the star of an incriminating videotape—and we don't know that this was the first. That could be the financial trouble Shaw mentioned. Blackmail. Docs are a lot like cops, the way they cover for each other. So are rich folks. But everyone's got their limits. Maybe he was improving his financial position by selling Oxycontin and his partners knew and couldn't get him to stop. People have killed for a lot less."

"So you don't think it was a woman?"

"Despite Cote demanding I find this mystery woman and arrest her? Don't know, Ter. Got no gut feeling about this one. There's the woman O'Leary brought in, but we've also got Dani's footprint."

Kyle parked at the hospital. "You think maybe someone hired O'Leary to kill Pleasant, and the mystery girl was just the bait?"

"It's a thought."

"Then why not kill Alana? And this mystery girl—you think she's dead?"

"Maybe they tried to whack Alana and we got in their way. Maybe the mystery girl is dead. If I had all the answers, Terry, I wouldn't need you."

"What's our game plan here?"

"We'll start with the docs. Lunch time, we might find them with a bit of free time on their hands. You take Stavros. I'll take Shorter. I'll do the administrator's office, you see Conklin. Then I'll see the parking lot attendant, you get contact info for the other attendants and security guards, and we'll meet back in the lobby."

"This place gives me the creeps."

"To paraphrase Robert Frost, it's the place that, when you have to go there, they have to take you in. And you're usually bleeding."

He found Dr. Shorter in the cafeteria with some other doctors. Burgess pulled up a chair, introduced himself, and asked for a few minutes of the man's time. Shorter looked irritated but he agreed. As the others moved away, Burgess pulled out his notebook, but before he could begin, Shorter said, "What happened to you?"

"Colonel Mustard with a lead pipe in the Dunkin' Donuts parking lot."

"Oh, right. Read about it in the paper."

"I have some questions about Stephen Pleasant."

But Shorter was studying his eyes. "You still have a headache?" he asked. Burgess nodded. "Any dizziness?"

"Slight," Burgess said. "Occasional." Been through this drill before.

"Nausea?"

"Some. Look, doctor, I—"

190

"Detective, what are you trying to prove? You should be in bed. Head injuries aren't something to mess with."

"Appreciate your concern, doctor, but I've got one man dead, another missing, and last night there was the attempted abduction of a witness. I catch a break and maybe next week I can stay in bed."

"Who's missing?"

"Pimp named Kevin O'Leary." Watching Shorter's reaction. He'd hoped for recognition. Got a mixture of regret and distaste.

"So you know about . . . Stephen's problem?" Shorter stood up. "You mind if we talk in my office? This is awfully public."

In the elevator, Burgess refrained from rubbing his head, aware of Shorter's scrutiny, of the way, in the manner of their respective professions, they circled each other like fighters in a ring. Shorter jumped out ahead of him and held the elevator door, making Burgess feel geriatric and cranky. He followed Shorter into his office and dumped himself gratefully into a chair.

Shorter switched on the lamp and leaned forward. "So what can I tell you?" He might be old enough to practice medicine, but he had the downy, unformed look of a prepubescent boy.

"You and Dr. Pleasant were golf buddies?" Shorter nodded. "Other than that, did you socialize together?"

"Some. Dinner parties. Restaurants. Movies. My wife Lauren is friends with Jen."

"Seen from the outside, was it a good marriage?"

"I guess. Jen was kind of fragile. Demanding. She had a lot of trouble with the pregnancy, you know. She was scared, and she's awfully young. It made her short with Stephen sometimes. Lately. Otherwise, things seemed fine."

"How did Dr. Pleasant respond to his wife's demands?"

Shorter shrugged. "I don't know. He was impatient with her. Supercilious. That's how Stephen was. He didn't mean anything by it. Why is his marriage relevant? You can't possibly think Jen killed him."

"Why not?"

Shorter stared. "Well, because she loved him, that's why."

"Do you think she knew about his infidelity?"

"Infidelity?" He seemed to be trying to decide whether quickies with prostitutes constituted infidelity. Burgess decided to help him out. "The hookers he picked up. The women he paid to give him blow jobs in his car."

"I don't know," Shorter said, reddening. "Stephen never mentioned—"

"Would your wife know? You said she was Jen's friend."

Shorter made a quick, defensive gesture. "Look, it's bad enough having to deal with this here in the hospital. I don't want you coming into my home, bothering my wife. That's not necessary. Stephen had a weakness. He indulged that weakness with the wrong woman. She stabbed him. End of story. Find the woman and arrest her. This murder has nothing to do with the hospital or his family or my family. Nothing to do with any of us. You have no right suggesting it does."

If he had a dollar for each time he'd been told he had no right to do things, he'd be retired and rich. Anyway, Shorter was wrong. This murder had everything to do with Pleasant's family. Families. They'd never be the same again. Death, like life, didn't occur in a vacuum. "Dr. Shorter, what kind of medicine do you practice?"

Shorter looked puzzled. "I'm an internist."

"If I came in here and told you how to treat a patient, what would you think?"

"You don't know anything about medicine."

"And you don't know anything about investigating a homicide."

"I watch TV."

"Then you know that the majority of people are killed by someone they know."

"You can't possibly think that Jen—"

"What I think is I should ask the questions and you should answer them."

Shorter pushed back from his desk and stood up. "This is outrageous!"

"So's the willful taking of a human life. Sit down, doctor. I'm not done." Cote would say he was stepping on toes here. But curtsying hurt his knees and he was too tired for patience. "Was Jen Kelly aware of her husband's infidelities?"

Shorter no longer looked pleasantly boyish, but like a spoiled kid who'd been on the wrong end of a fight—his cheeks blotched red, his mouth sulky. "Yes," he said.

"Yes, you know, or yes, she was?"

"Yes, goddammit, she knew! She told Lauren. Then Lauren got on my case to do something. I told Stephen he was being an idiot. He told me to mind my own business. Look, he wasn't my best friend or anything."

"How did Jen Kelly react when she learned about her husband's other women?"

"They weren't other women. It wasn't like he had a relationship with them."

"You're saying she shouldn't have cared?" Shorter shook his head. "So, how did she react?"

"The way any woman would. She was hurt. Angry."

"Do you know whether she communicated this to her husband?"

"No. Well, yes. Maybe. She told Lauren she was going

193

to speak to him. Actually, she told Lauren her father had spoken with Stephen and he'd promised to stop."

"A promise he didn't keep?"

Shorter looked miserable. "No."

There was something behind the "no." "And?"

"Lauren said Jen wasn't going to put up with it. That he would stop humiliating her or it was over between them." Shorter swallowed. "I don't know. Jen's money was very important to Stephen. If Jen told her father . . ." He trailed off. "But I don't see what this has to do with what happened."

Burgess changed the subject. "Did Dr. Pleasant talk to you about his finances, ever mention financial difficulties?"

Shorter ran a distracted hand through his hair. "Jesus, detective. I hope no one ever murders me. I'd hate to have someone pawing through my private life."

"His finances," Burgess repeated.

"He was always complaining about money. Worrying about it. Doctors have a reputation for that, but this was worse. See, Stephen was the one who'd persuaded the practice to expand. In the long run, it would have made them all much richer. But in the short run, there were big expenses setting things up. And he liked to live well, wanted to give Jen a nice house. Janet was always nagging about support. Plus . . ." He tried for a laugh. "I don't suppose a three-hooker-a-week habit came cheap."

"His predilection for hookers was common knowledge? Any idea how his partners reacted to that?"

Shorter glanced at the closed door. "Ken Bailey was furious. I've heard . . . pure rumor, you understand . . . that he'd given Stephen an ultimatum—shape up or ship out. And Pine State's practically the only game in town." He shrugged. "Look, detective. I'm cooperating. I want you to give me your word that you'll stay away from my wife."

He'd never given a promise like that. He went where the story sent him and Lauren Shorter sounded like she could be helpful, but he was supposed to be practicing his curtsy. "The way things look, I see no need to bother your wife. Just a few more questions," he said, "and I'll go." Go? Even getting out of this chair seemed too hard. "Do you know of anyone who might have wanted to harm him?" Shorter shook his head. "Did he ever mention that someone might be following him?"

"Stephen didn't confide in me. He didn't confide in anyone, as far as I know."

"He ever seem nervous or threatened?"

Shorter shook his head. "Stephen was too arrogant to be nervous." He seemed aghast at his own honesty.

"Did you ever hear any rumors or concerns about his misusing controlled drugs?"

The denial was a bit too vehement. Shorter hesitated, then said, "Now it's my turn. What are you taking for your head?" Burgess told him. "Well, I've got something better. The stuff you're using takes too long to kick in and wears off too soon."

He was about to say "no, thanks" when Shorter stopped him. "What did you say earlier? That I shouldn't tell you how to investigate a murder? Well, I do know how to treat pain. You won't make it if you go on like this. Pain saps your energy. I'm going to give you a pill and something for the nausea, and I want you to lie down for fifteen minutes." Burgess started to get up. "Come on, detective. You want to be pig-headed, fine, but it's only fifteen minutes. Isn't it sensible to spend the time if it'll buy you hours?"

Reluctantly, he nodded. Shorter led him down a hall and opened a door. "It's not the Ritz, but it will do. My nurse will bring you what you need." Shorter paused at the door. "In case you're wondering. I don't like being questioned. I bet nobody does, but I do want you to find Stephen's killer. I guess this is my way of helping." He left Burgess admiring the deft way he'd turned the tables.

A nurse knocked and came in. "Detective Burgess? Dr. Shorter asked me to bring you these." After he took the pills, she put a pillow under his head and covered him with a blanket. "I'll be back in fifteen minutes." She turned off the light and he closed his eyes, grateful for the rest.

She came quietly into the room, the open door following her with a spill of light, and stopped a few feet away. "Detective Burgess?" It was a different voice—not the nurse who'd brought his medicine—but a familiar one. The tone tentative and hopeful.

"Nurse Perlin?" He struggled with the blanket, remembering not to sit up too quickly, unwilling to make his head spin and his stomach lurch again.

"Chris," she said. Quickly, she was beside him, assisting the transition with a whiff of subtle perfume and the touch of strong, warm hands. "Nice and easy, now. I can't stay." He heard the faint strain in her voice. "I've got to get back. But I heard you were here and . . . and I've been thinking . . ."

He sat in the gentle darkness, legs dangling off the table, in no rush to rejoin the day. He felt good, the best he'd felt in days. He wanted a minute to savor it, wished she hadn't come in, so he wouldn't have to probe for why she was here. "You were thinking?"

"About what you said at lunch." Her laugh was a warm little self-deprecating sound. "At *my* lunch. Yesterday. I didn't like myself much when I went home last night. I looked in the mirror and all I could think was 'coward.' " Her voice dropped a range, became huskier. The kind of change in a woman's voice that calls forth a physical response. "I see a lot of courage around here, detective, and I didn't like what I was seeing in myself. It seemed cheap, leading you on then saying, 'What? Who me? I can't do that,' and walking away, leaving you frustrated."

"I understood," he said. Could she hear the response in his voice that had everything to do with her and nothing to do with what they were discussing? Did she read voices the way he did? "I see it all the time."

"That's just it. I didn't want to be one of those people you see all the time, the ones who don't help because it's too much trouble, because they don't want to get involved. I don't value people who are too busy or too self-important to care. I believe you are what you do. I wanted to be one of the people you admire. One of the good ones."

She took him by surprise, putting her hands behind his head and gently drawing his face to hers. It was a tender, searching kiss that made him long to put the investigation on hold. "I've been thinking about that since yesterday," she said, slowly pulling her hands away. "I felt a connection between us. I hope it wasn't just my imagination. I hate making a fool of myself." There was a rustle as she thrust an envelope into his hand. "This is the part I had to struggle with."

Before he could speak, she'd gone.

He stayed in the flower-scented darkness a moment longer, collecting himself, then slid off the table, turned on the light, and dumped out the envelope. Copies of letters from patients, from patients' families, complaining about their treatment at the hands of Dr. Pleasant. Bless her. She'd taken a big risk to give him these. Dr. Bailey didn't want Pleasant's failings known, and he was a powerful man.

His cop's gut told him there was something here. Maybe

because Bailey and Pleasant's other associates were so se-
cretive, maybe because Chris Perlin had thought it important enough to take a risk for. Either way, he didn't know
where it would take him. Had someone outside the circle of
colleagues and relatives paid O'Leary or the mysterious
second girl to kill Pleasant? It fit his theory that this wasn't
what it seemed. He shrugged. Another piece for the puzzle.

Using his good hand, he stuffed the letters back into the
envelope and went to find the administrator's office.

There he ran into a brick wall. Marla Leclaire, the direc-
tor's executive assistant, was poised, polite, and as inflex-
ible as Sister Mary Catharine had been. Her chic gray suit
hung off a frame that, if he read her thinning, lusterless hair
and dry skin correctly, had been starved into submission.
Her office was devoid of character. She was sorry she
couldn't help him but rules were rules. Patients and their
families expected confidentiality. The death of a respected
physician was tragic. Shocking. She had known him herself
and was personally distressed, but she wasn't going to answer his questions.

He had the same impulse he'd had with Sister Mary
Catharine, to do something to shock her out of her complacency. "If the hospital gets a complaint about a physician,
how is it handled?" He listened to her explanation of peer
review committees and the hospital board. "At what point
do you decide you've got a problem?"

"I'm sorry. I don't understand the question."

"Well, a dog, say, gets one bite before it's considered a
dangerous animal. How many bites does a doctor get before
he's considered dangerous?"

"I'm afraid it doesn't work like that, detective."

Big surprise. And so it went. A Q&A about as satisfying
as chewing on gristle. He persisted until she snapped,

"What is your problem, detective?"

"My problem? Got a dead man. Like to know who killed him. Do you know anyone who might have wanted to harm Dr. Pleasant?" She didn't answer. "Do you know whether Dr. Pleasant had financial difficulties?" Again no answer. "If I want to see your records, I'll need a subpoena, is that right?" This time, she nodded.

He stood up. "Thank you for your time. And Ms. Leclaire? You might ask yourself, anyone close to you ever gets dead, do you really want people to clam up and not co-operate with the police? You think you're protecting Dr. Pleasant and the hospital, but you know who you're really protecting? The killer. I wonder why you'd want to do that?" He walked out of her office. Take that, Sister Mary Catharine. Thirty-five years later, it still felt good.

He was crossing the lobby to see the parking attendant when a voice called, "Just a minute, detective. I want to know what the hell's going on around here." Just what Burgess had been wondering, but from the look on Dr. Bailey's face, they weren't about to have a meeting of the minds. Bailey's broad face was ruddy, his voice half-strangled with suppressed rage. Dressed for the outside in an expensive shearling coat and a black fur hat, Bailey looked massive and important.

He let Bailey come to him. He felt pretty good right now but it was chemical, and temporary. Conserve scarce energy was still the rule of the day. The doctor quickly closed the gap between them, grabbed Burgess's good arm and practically hauled him off his feet. "Over here, if you please, where there's a little more privacy."

Burgess didn't like to be touched, let alone dragged, but humoring Cote in absentia, he allowed himself to be pulled behind a large potted plant. Bailey was much too close, invading his personal space. He took a step back. Bailey took a compensating step forward. Oh my, doctor. Shall we dance?

"Your superior assured me your investigation would be conducted with the utmost discretion," Bailey said through tight lips. He'd insisted on a more private space, but made no effort to lower his voice. "And now the hospital is crawling with police officers, interrupting busy physicians in the middle of their working days, asking suggestive questions about one of their esteemed colleagues."

There was more, but nothing worth listening to. Burgess tuned out, focusing on demeanor instead. He'd never heard the phrase "esteemed colleague" in everyday speech before. Initially, Bailey had impressed him. Now he wondered why the guy was being such a pompous windbag? Was this true concern for the hospital or did Bailey have something to hide? He waited for a question. Finally, Bailey took a step back, sweeping him with a contemptuous look. "Well?"

"Well what, doctor?"

"What the hell is going on here? Is it necessary to broadcast to everyone that the police have concerns about Stephen's finances? His patient care? His decisions about when and what to prescribe?"

So the questions they were asking had really set their little bells jingling. It was a tight little world, wasn't it? Were they trying to hide something here, or was it simply that Pleasant's death was like a healing wound in the hospital's skin and they saw the police as enemies who kept trying to tear that wound open? It wouldn't be the first time he'd dealt with people who just wanted it to "go away" so they could get on with their lives. His presence was an all-too-vivid reminder something bad had happened.

But this diatribe was way out of proportion. The police

presence was subtle. They weren't going around in uniforms, brandishing badges and smashing people up against walls. "Broadcast? There are only two officers here, both plainclothes detectives. We've conducted discreet interviews with a few people. We haven't discussed the content of those interviews with anyone. What's the problem?"

"The problem is, I told him not to bother us, and here you are!"

He'd tried to stay cool, but now Bailey was stomping on *his* toes. "You think that's how it works, doctor? Anyone who doesn't want to be bothered by a police investigation just calls up the chief and says, 'Make them leave me alone'? Isn't the problem that a man's been murdered, and we need to work together to find out who did it?"

"We know who did it!" Bailey said. "Some hooker. You should be out trying to find her instead of hanging around here, disturbing busy people. I told your boss—"

"Look at me, doctor," he said. "What do you see?"

Bailey's eyes swept him disdainfully. "Overweight, middle-aged cop who doesn't take care of himself, who'd rather hang around here, bothering people, where it's warm and he can drink coffee than go out on the streets and try to solve the crime."

Whereas you take extremely good care of yourself, from your well-cut hair to your polished shoes. "Yeah, I look like hell, don't I? You think I'd be here if I didn't have to? That I dragged myself here today to be a pain in your ass when I could have stayed in bed?"

"Dammit! Your boss said you would be polite and discreet, and here you are standing in my hospital, yelling at me!"

He'd never found doctors particularly rational thinkers, a prejudice Bailey was confirming. He hadn't been yelling.

He'd deliberately kept his voice low. "Dr. Bailey, what would you like me to do?"

"Leave!"

"I have one more person to see. Detective Kyle may be done, or he may not. When we're finished, we'll leave. We will continue to be discreet. We will continue to keep what we learn to ourselves. I hope we won't have to come back, but I make no promises. I'm sorry if this upsets you."

Bailey hadn't been listening. Now he threw up his hands. "This is completely unacceptable. I'm calling your boss again. I want you out of here. I want you stopped!"

"You're spending a hell of a lot of energy trying to keep me away," Burgess said. "Is there something here you don't want me to find?"

"How dare you!" Bailey glared at Burgess. "What the hell is that?" he demanded, trying to snatch the envelope. Burgess kept it out of reach.

"Excuse me, doctor. I have work to do." Burgess tried to step around him. Kyle was maybe ten feet away, watching. He knew Kyle was reading the situation and would read it right.

Instead of getting out of his way, Bailey shoved him backwards. "Hold on," he said. "I'm not finished."

Quickly, Kyle closed the space. He wouldn't interfere unless it was necessary. Burgess felt a swell of anger, a sure sign that his behavior would exceed the limits of Cote's restrictions if he didn't end this quickly. "Take your hands off me," he said coldly, as Kyle moved in beside him.

Bailey didn't move. "Now!" Burgess barked, his hand automatically opening his coat, clearing access to his gun. "Put them down by your sides and back away from me, doctor. I said now!"

Bailey was so startled he did as he was told, though he was already protesting.

Burgess cut him off. "You're done asking questions. It's time to listen. I don't care how you deal with other people. What matters is this. I am a police officer." He spoke slowly and carefully, all his force and attention focused on Bailey. Bailey's eyes were fixed on the hand that rested near the gun. He wore a slightly stupefied look. "There are some very simple rules in this world about dealing with police officers. You don't touch us. You don't push us around. Assaulting an officer is very serious."

Beside him, Kyle had pushed his own jacket back to show the gun on his belt, doing one of the things he did best, casting an air of quiet, powerful authority over the proceedings without saying a word. Burgess watched Bailey's eyes flicker from one to the other, and saw the dawning of what was probably a rare thing for the man—a sense that maybe he'd gotten it wrong. The doctor swallowed and his gaze dropped. Score one for the alpha male. This time. Burgess felt a prickling of the hair on the back of his neck, though, and a sense that, despite the setting and their respective professional affiliations, Bailey wasn't someone he was comfortable turning his back on.

"You ready, Joe?" Kyle asked.

"Yeah." He stepped around Bailey and followed Kyle out, pausing outside the door to suck in some air, trying to bring his anger down to a manageable level. He'd just been shoved around by a belligerent asshole in a public place. He had evidence that Bailey was trying to interfere with an investigation and was intimidating witnesses, and he hadn't even dragged the guy down to the station. Man didn't know when to be grateful. Probably didn't know enough to let it drop, either. By the time he got back, Bailey would have called and Cote would be in a new snit.

Kyle waited until he'd calmed down. "I think we just

saw a side of Dr. Bailey that few people have seen."

"I think he was surprised, too." After a few minutes, his equilibrium restored, Burgess said, "I still need to speak with the attendant."

"Sure thing."

"Can you call Martha McFarland and see if she can make some time for us?"

Burgess set off across the lot. He didn't know what was going on here—a conspiracy of silence or a bunch of different people, acting from different motives, who happened to work in the same place and share a similar disinclination toward cooperation. The guy in the booth better be cooperative. He wasn't in the mood for any more crap. He knocked on the glass and showed his badge. "Sergeant Burgess, Portland police. Investigating the death of Dr. Stephen Pleasant. I need to ask you some questions."

Chapter Twenty

The kid in the booth had a biology textbook open on his lap. He nearly dropped it when Burgess said "police," but he recovered himself, closed it, and tried to look calm. "I don't know anything about that, sir," he said. Despite the spiked hair, a jagged mix of blond and black, and the eyebrow ring, he was clean and polite. Not the attitude many of them affected.

Nice parents, Burgess decided. "Maybe," he said, "maybe not. How long have you worked here?"

"Since September."

"You're a student?"

"Yes, sir. USM."

"You usually work days?"

"No, sir. I go to school days, work evenings. They got stuck today, so I cut class."

Burgess got his name and address. "You ever see a big guy in a battered truck come in here, just sit in the truck watching the hospital, and then drive away without ever going inside? Ever notice anything like that?"

The kid considered. Swallowed. "No, sir, I don't think so. We get a lot of battered trucks. I haven't noticed anything special." He shook his head and looked hopefully down at the book. Student or not, this kid liked the easy answers.

Burgess's feet were getting cold. "You never saw someone like that wait down at the far end of the lot, then drive off when Dr. Pleasant came out?"

The kid swallowed again, then stretched his neck and looked down the lot as if the answer might be there. Nothing but rows of dirty cars and piles of dirty snow. "The guy with the bandana?" he offered.

Burgess nodded. "What did he look like?"

The kid's hand described big curves beside his mouth. Kid's nails were polished black. Probably gave his father heart failure, if his father was still in the house. Now that his nieces were growing up, Burgess understood this stuff better. They might look like painted savages and dress like bums, but they were just regular kids. "Mustache," the kid said. "Big one. Dark."

"Can you tell me anything else about him?"

The kid shrugged. "People come. People go. I try not to look at their faces. Too much bad stuff there."

"Try," Burgess suggested.

"He was a big guy. Strong Maine accent."

"Age?"

"About my dad's age, maybe? Forties?"

"Good. What about the truck?"

"GMC. Cap on the back."

"Anything else?"

"The dog?" Like this was a test and he was hoping to get the answers right.

"Big dog? Little dog?"

"Medium. No special type."

"Anything else?" Burgess tried not to throttle him. Kid's brain was like a Magic 8-Ball—ask a question, then wait for the answer to swim into the window. Shaking wouldn't help. He wanted to do it anyway. Finally the kid said, "Dented right fender?"

"He come often?"

"A few times."

"Except for the dog, he was alone?"

"Once he had someone with him. A girl." The kid's eyes darted nervously over Burgess's shoulder. "Excuse me, sir. Cars?"

Burgess stomped his numb feet impatiently while the kid checked out some cars. "Tell me about the girl."

The kid wrapped his arms around himself. Talking with Burgess let the cold in. "I only got a quick look when they drove in. But she was a babe."

"Care to elaborate?"

"Blonde hair. Gorgeous. You know." The kid made curves with his hands.

"Was she the same age as the guy?"

"I told ya. She was a babe." Women in their forties weren't babes, they were mothers. "Like my age."

"She wasn't wearing a coat?" Kid shook his head. "Was the guy wearing a coat?"

The kid shrugged. "I didn't notice."

Thinking with his pecker. "The guy would drive into the lot, and then?"

"Sit there with the engine running. I figured he was waiting for someone."

"Anyone ever come out and get into the truck?" Negative. "Anyone ever get out and go inside?" Another negative. "He sat and watched, and then what?"

"He'd drive away. He was always in a hurry going out. Used to give me five bucks, no matter how much he owed."

"You figure out why he was driving away?"

"He was following the doctors."

"Which doctors?" Now his ears were freezing. Made him wonder why he'd ever wanted to be a cop. It was a miserable life. Bad hours. Bad pay. Bad dreams. He shifted his shoulders and stomped his feet.

The kid shrugged for the millionth time. Burgess repressed an urge to haul him out of the booth and pound him, knowing it wasn't the kid he wanted to pound, kid was just the next thing that crossed his path. "He followed Mercedes. Couple of the docs have 'em. I thought maybe he was looking to steal one."

"You ever report this to anyone?"

"Not my job, was it?"

"You work the night Pleasant was killed?"

"Yeah. 'Bout froze my ass off."

"Anybody watching him that night, follow him when he left?"

The kid shook his head. "Bandana guy wasn't here that night."

"You happen to notice when Pleasant left?"

"He wasn't in the lot," the kid said unhelpfully. "He never parked here, used to leave his car by the door. Like he was better than everybody else."

"You see him leave?"

"Yeah. But no one followed him except his wife." The hands sketched briefer curves. "Good-lookin' blonde, if you don't mind skinny. She didn't follow exactly."

"What did she do?"

"She was waiting by his car when he came out. She'd been standing there a hell of a long time. Musta frozen her ass off. Not that she had much ass to freeze. She looked so pitiful, standing there . . . she didn't have a hat and the wind was blowing her hair around." The kid traced circles around his head.

Burgess saw Jen Kelly's sad blue eyes, her translucent skin. Pictured that thin hand clutching her coat. Wondered why she'd lied. He looked down the parking lot to the distant hospital door. Could the kid have seen all that? "It's pretty far," he said.

The spiked hair bobbed. "But the lights are bright. And there wasn't much going on. When Dr. Pleasant came out, she went up to him and grabbed his arm. He shook her off. Said something to her. I don't know what it was, but she turned and ran. Ran right across the road without looking, almost got hit. Got into her car and drove right out of the lot without paying. Took the arm clean off."

He touched his forehead, the black fingernails like punctuation marks against the pale skin. The little ring through his eyebrow shivered. "Oh, yeah. Guess I should have remembered that, huh? But my boss told me not to worry about it, said people get upset by things that happen in the hospital, we should be sympathetic. He gave me a twenty, said the family had asked him to apologize, like I was traumatized or something, you know? You ask me, she was the one who was traumatized, pale like a ghost, her hair all wild, tears running down her face. Then he goes and gets killed and she never sees him again."

"You notice a lot," Burgess said. Couldn't organize it or spit it out, but that was no different from a lot of people. Another day, another mood, he'd be grateful for this. "You've seen Pleasant's wife before, waiting for him?"

"Sometimes, back in the fall, she'd be meeting him, like for dinner, I'd guess, because she was all dressed up, but then she'd park and go inside. Last couple months, I haven't seen her at all."

A car behind him honked and the kid jumped a mile. "Excuse me," he said. "I'd better—"

"When did you get the twenty?" Burgess asked.

"Next day."

Burgess muttered thanks through gritted teeth, slogged across the lot, and got in the car. "Get anything?" Kyle asked.

"Terrorists could have been setting up a bazooka and the kid would have sat and watched. Not his job to get involved. It was like pulling teeth, but he did say a couple interesting things. He saw Alana's guy in the truck with the dog, says once the guy had a gorgeous blonde with him. And he saw the Pleasants arguing the night Dr. Pleasant was killed."

"Wouldn't occur to him to come and tell us that, would it? It's the TV generation. Life as entertainment. Attorney McFarland can see us this afternoon. So can we eat, please? My belly button's sticking to my spine."

Kyle got any thinner, he'd vanish, and Burgess needed him. "Whatever you want, Terry. Just give me some heat. My feet are frozen."

"Thought you were the guy always dressed for the weather."

"Alana picked my summer shoes. Where you want to eat?"

"Sportsman's Grill okay?"

A bit heavy on cops, and half the kitchen staff were the usual suspects, but the food was okay. "Fine."

"I admired your restraint with Bailey," Kyle said.

"Don't think I could have taken him with one arm."

"And the sterling admonitions of Captain Cote ringing in your ears."

"Cote's an asshole. Bailey's an asshole. Kid in the parking lot's an asshole." He had a vision of a world populated by hairy pink butts with legs. "You get anything?"

"Tell you over lunch," Kyle grunted, jamming the car into a tight space and turning off the engine. "And whether you're hungry or not, you'd better eat something. In case you haven't noticed, you're in a piss-poor mood."

"You must be a hell of a detective to have figured that out."

Kyle ordered pot roast with mashed potatoes and gravy. Burgess got a bowl of beef barley soup. After the waitress had poured their coffee and left, Kyle sighed. "This thing's clear as mud, isn't it?"

"Not so bad, Ter. The wife's lying, the docs are lying, Alana's lying. If we could find anyone else to talk to, they'd be lying. How'd it go with your guys?"

"One of 'em's still living on Sesame Street. Thinks Pleasant was the nicest guy he ever met. Could hardly bring himself to admit he knew about the hookers. He did, though. And when I asked him about drugs, I thought he'd wet his pants."

"And the other?"

"Clams are more talkative."

"The surgeon, right? What the hell is it with these people?"

"Hey, if we truly understood human nature, we'd hang out shingles and rake in the bucks, instead of getting worn out and nasty peering into the sewers of human lives."

"Thought I was the one in the black mood."

"It's contagious."

"I sure hope not. Bad enough looking in the mirror, seeing all that ugliness coming back at me. Hate to see it spread around the office."

"Alana thinks I'm ugly."

"No, she doesn't. Alana thinks you ought to pay more attention to her. Give her more respect." Truth was, Kyle wasn't bad-looking, just cold-looking. His efficiently short black hair did nothing to soften the sharpness of his face. A lean, bony face with probing gray eyes and a narrow mouth. People complained that Burgess's face was fierce, but it was Kyle whose cold eyes could stop conversation with a look.

"A whore who wants respect? Why not," he said. He arranged a forkful of meat and potatoes. Chewed thoughtfully. "So you finally slept with her. Can you handle it?"

"I've got no choice."

"You know what I mean."

He stared down at his untouched soup, soggy brownish bits floating in a brownish liquid, and saw Dr. Lee's knife slicing through Pleasant's stomach. He pushed the bowl away. "I'm supposed to be the master of self-control and I let it happen. Hell, Terry, I don't know. It's another goddamned albatross around my neck. She'll never keep her mouth shut. Why'd you leave her, anyway?"

"You needed to be taken care of." Kyle looked guilty.

"Oh, I was taken care of."

"I'm sorry. You gonna eat that?"

"Can't even look at it."

"You've got to eat something, Superman. You're flying too close to the earth." Kyle signaled for a waitress, ordered grilled cheese and tuna, fries on the side.

"You're so nurturing," Burgess said.

"Self-interested. I don't want to work this alone and Cote's dying to send you to your room. If I can't help keep your soul together, at least I can help with the body."

"Maybe I belong in my room."

"That's right. The case is a bitch and you're running on two cylinders, so you might as well give up. Sit in your room and stare at pictures of a dead kid, see if you can tie yourself in a couple more knots. Give Bailey and Cote the satisfaction of having sent you packing. Score one for the bad guys."

"Sometimes I wonder if any of it makes any difference."

Kyle leaned in, his voice low and angry. "Get a grip, Joe. Not every case is Kristin Marks."

"I hated that man, Terry."

"Pleasant? I know. I also know it'll only make you work harder to find his killer."

They sat in silence, Kyle because he'd crossed the line, Burgess because Kyle was right. If he was going to let the Kristin Marks fiasco run his life and stop trying because the criminal justice system was fucked up, he should have quit long ago. If he was going to stay, he owed it to Kristin to keep bringing in the bad guys. The sandwich arrived and he ate without tasting it. Around them, people came and went, ordered, talked and ate loudly. A road grader doubling as a plow did a noisy back and forth outside. Someone could have been killed at the next table and he wouldn't have noticed. He was trying to pull himself out of a black lagoon.

Kyle's shoulders slumped. "Where the hell are we going with this?"

"Toward an arrest, I hope," Burgess said. "Death is in the details. While I'm enjoying the company of Attorney McFarland, you want to pop over to the courthouse and see if you can find any lawsuits against the hospital which mention Dr. Pleasant? Or lawsuits against Dr. Pleasant, just in case she isn't forthcoming?" He wasn't optimistic about a lawyer being frank.

"It would be my pleasure. What's in the envelope?"

"Letters from Pleasant's patients." Burgess passed it across the table. "Try not to get grease on them."

Kyle pulled out the letters and started reading. Scanning at first, then becoming absorbed. He didn't even hear the waitress ask if they'd like dessert. Burgess ordered two apple pies with ice cream and more coffee, watching Kyle as he read. Watched him read through one of the letters, then another. Watched him read a letter, then go back and read it again. He read it a third time and looked up.

"Where'd you get these?"

"Pleasant's nurse. Chris Perlin."

"Well, this is it," he said. He shook the letters until they rattled. "Forget the lawyer, in-laws, out-laws, partners. Man who generates this much anger, it's here someplace."

"Stan likes the Oxycontin angle. I kind of like the wife or her father . . . stepfather."

His phone rang. Lt. Melia. "Joe? Got an assault on a clerk at a video store, couple blocks from O'Leary's place. Sounds like it might tie in. You want to follow up?"

"We're on it." He got the address, asked a few questions, and nodded to Kyle. "Guy who fits O'Leary's description went into a video store looking for some tapes he said they were keeping for him. When the clerk said she didn't know what he was talking about, he started beating her up. Ran off when another customer came in."

"Could be a break." Kyle grabbed his jacket. "Sounds like the shitheads are getting squirrelly."

CHAPTER TWENTY-ONE

The clerk was Vietnamese or Cambodian, small as a child and young, with waist-length hair caught in a butterfly barrette. She sat behind the counter on a stool, shielding her face with her hand. There was blood on her gray Gap sweatshirt. A young patrolman was with her, one hand solicitously on her shoulder. His hand was very big and black, the girl's shoulder small and narrow. His other hand held a clump of bloody paper towels.

He looked up when they entered. "Patrol Officer Gabriel Delinsky, sir," he said. "Her name is Mai Phung. Says she's seventeen. Works here after school. I think her nose is broken. She won't let me call an ambulance." He had a calm, easy voice.

The place was littered with spilled candy, an overturned gumball machine, packets of microwave popcorn and scattered videos. Whole shelves of videos had been swept clean, tumbled onto the floor. A smashed phone lay among them.

The girl's dark eyes studied them cautiously. She was pale, but Burgess didn't know whether it was shock or her natural color. As he watched, a tremor ran through her, like the shiver of a horse's hide, and he understood why Delinsky kept a hand on her.

"Can you tell us what happened?"

She moved her head slowly back and forth, eyes wide with fear. She couldn't.

"Sergeant Burgess," he said, "and this is Detective Kyle. We need to ask you some questions." To Delinsky he said, "What did she tell you?"

"Not much. Obviously, she speaks English well enough to get this job, but when she's this scared, it deteriorates. She says . . ." He hesitated. "I'm afraid I haven't written all this down yet, sir. I didn't want to leave her."

Burgess's reputation again. He'd yelled at more than one young cop for not writing things down, so details got left out or lost. "You're doing fine," he said. "Go on."

"She says a big, ugly white guy came in. Excuse me, sir. Those are her words, not mine. A big, ugly guy with tattoos and stuck-out ears . . . ears like cups . . . and he said he'd come to pick up some tapes." The girl made a little moaning sound and Delinsky tightened his steadying hand.

Burgess noticed her jeans were undone and remembered what Alana'd said about O'Leary. "Was she assaulted?"

Delinsky shook his head. "She'd never tell me, sir, but I don't believe so. I think he was trying to, but was interrupted by some customers. Bunch of teenagers. Two of them, two girls, ran across the street and called us, the four guys chased him away." He patted his pocket. "I got their names and addresses. Look, there's not that much more to tell. Let me give it to you quickly, then I'd like to take her over to the hospital."

"No!" the girl cried. "No hospitals. No doctor."

"She's worried about medical bills," Burgess said. "Get the hospital to explain that they have to treat her for free, if she doesn't have any money. So the guy comes in and says he's come to pick up some tapes they kept for him. Did she know what he meant?"

"She's only worked here for a few days. When she asked if they were tapes he'd reserved, he grabbed her and dragged her right over the counter. Screamed at her and swore at her, throwing things, then he started knocking her around, yelling, 'Sun knows.' He was trying to get her pants off when the kids arrived."

"Who's Sun?" Kyle asked.

"The owner."

"Can she do better than big, ugly white guy?" Burgess asked. "I'm a big, ugly white guy." He asked Delinsky, but watched the girl. Caught the glimmer of a smile.

"Bald," she said in a tiny voice. The hand that wasn't shielding her face described girth. "Strong. Fat." The hand swooped out, sculpturing a pregnancy-sized belly in the air, touched her mouth. "He had a broken tooth."

Kyle was prowling around, looking the place over. Standing at a doorway closed by a blue curtain. "What's in here?'

Delinsky grinned. "Thought you were a detective? That's the adult videos."

"Guess I'll check it out." Kyle disappeared through the curtain.

Burgess pulled out the picture of Kevin O'Leary that was folded inside his notebook and handed it to the girl. "This the guy?"

She looked at it, moaned, and closed her eyes, leaning against Delinsky as if she needed his protection, even from a photograph. The young cop steadied her as she shoved the picture toward Burgess. "Yes. That's the man." Her voice was a whisper.

"Thank you," Burgess said. "You've been a big help. Did you notice how he got here? Whether he had a car?"

"A big black car," she whispered. "It waited for him outside."

"Do you mind if we look around?" he asked.

"No. Please. Maybe you find those tapes. Take them away?"

"Has the owner been notified?" Burgess asked.

"Yes, sir. He's supposed to be on his way over." Delinsky pointed to a sheet of paper on the wall. "His name and number are right here."

"You want to take her to the ER, go ahead," Burgess said. "Her family been contacted?"

"She doesn't want to bother them. She says that they'll be scared, and she doesn't want to scare them when she's all right. She wants to know if I'll drive her home."

Burgess shook his head. "Don't take any chances. Take her to the hospital. And stay with her. She trusts you. We'll swing by later, see how she's doing."

Delinsky reached under the counter, grabbed her coat and purse, and helped her into the coat. She was as floppy and loose-jointed as a sleepy child. Delinsky didn't wait to see if she could make it to the car on her own. "If you'd get the door, sir?" he asked, scooping her off her feet, cradling her against his chest in a way that suggested children of his own. Where her sweatshirt rode up, Burgess saw raw, red scrapes on her stomach.

He followed Delinsky out to the cruiser, opened the door, and watched him settle her in the passenger seat, buckle her seatbelt, put his coat over her. "Good job, Delinsky. Looks like this could be O'Leary."

"I thought so, sir, when I heard her story. That's why I called Lt. Melia."

"I'll take the names of those kids. Kyle and I will follow up."

"Your witnesses are four guys, basketball players, and two girls who are cheerleaders. All friends of Mai. They said there was a man in the car, waiting. Couldn't describe the car other than big, dark, and expensive. They say it took off as soon as O'Leary got in. Nearly collided with a truck as it pulled into the street." Delinsky shrugged. "Maybe you can get more out of them, sir." He took out his notebook, copied six names and addresses, and tore out the page.

"Hard to believe, isn't it, sir? She can't be a day over fifteen. It would be like raping a child." Burgess looked away and Delinsky suddenly became very interested in adjusting his belt. "Guess I'll get moving."

Burgess watched the car drive away. That was a good cop. Smart and compassionate. If only he didn't burn out. He turned and went back inside, past the mess by the counter and into the back room. Kyle was kneeling on the floor, gloved, opening and closing video cases, piling the ones he'd checked on the floor beside him. Suddenly he bent forward, slid a bit of shelf aside, and reached into the hollow space, fishing around. Grinning triumphantly, he dragged out a plastic trash bag. "I wonder what's in here?"

He passed it to Burgess, put the other videos away, and got up, dusting the dirt and lint off his knees. "Kevin O'Leary?"

"I'm not wearing gloves," Burgess said. "Can't get 'em on without help. If I ever find that guy with the pipe . . ." He passed the bag back. "Looks like O'Leary. But here's a twist. He came in a big, black car that waited for him. She wasn't too clear, but it sounds like he wasn't driving. We'd better talk to those kids, see what they noticed."

"What about the videos?"

Burgess shrugged wearily. Decisions. Decisions. Would this day never end? He was sick of the sensory stimulus, the voices, faces, stories, the lies and evasions. Tired of twisted fucks who liked to rape children. Soon as this case was over, he was becoming a hermit. "We can save those for later. Get pizza. Sit around and drool."

From the other room, a voice called, "Hello? Hello? Is anybody here?"

They found a small, round Asian man staring sadly at the mess on the floor. "I am the owner," he said, shaking his head in dismay. "I am Sam Sun. What has happened here? The policeman wasn't very clear. Is Mai all right?"

"She's gone to the hospital."

Sam Sun looked at them, and then he sighed. "She is so young and yet she is determined to work. Not like some, for the money to buy things, but to help out her family. Mai is a good girl." He stared at the bag in Kyle's hands. "You are cleaning up? There is no need. I will attend to it. First, I must go to the hospital and see about Mai. She will be frightened. Do you need me for anything before?"

"Yes. The man who attacked Mai was looking for tapes he said you were keeping for him."

Sun's opaque expression was defeated by agitated blinking. "How odd," he said. "We rent tapes to people. We do not store them."

Kyle hefted the bag and dumped the tapes out on the counter. "These videotapes were hidden in the back room. Do you mind if we take them?"

Mr. Sun bowed slightly. "Of course not, if you think they will help. May I see?"

Kyle, who still wore gloves, held out a tape. "Please don't touch it," he said.

Sun looked at the label. "These are not mine. I don't know. I don't know how they came to be here. Now please, if I may, I would like to lock up?"

They explained that a crime scene team needed to take photographs and fingerprints, but that if nothing was disturbed, it could be done when Mr. Sun was finished at the hospital. Burgess gave him the name and number to contact and a receipt for the bag and videotapes.

"Looks like Attorney McFarland will have to wait," Burgess said. "You want to call Vince, tell him what we've got?"

"Maybe Stan can go see McFarland. He might charm the woman. Unlike us."

"Yeah, we scare the hell out of people."

"I'd like to scare a little hell out of Kevin O'Leary."

"I'm with you there. Alana was right. He is a pig. What do you think of Sun? Telling the truth about the tapes?"

Kyle shrugged. "I doubt it. Maybe he got some money from O'Leary to hide them. He isn't above employing fifteen-year-olds, we know that."

"We think that."

Kyle sent Stan Perry off to talk with Pleasant's lawyer, while he called the first name on Delinsky's list and asked if they could come by. It was a girl, nervous and giggling, who agreed they could come and gave directions.

"You want me to take you home first?" Kyle asked. "I can do this."

"Jesus, Terry, I know that." Burgess stared out the window. The snow was already a dirty gray. A gray landscape and gray weather, with a piercing damp that made his bones ache. Marks of violence on children's bodies made his heart ache, made him simmer with unproductive anger. At least anger had given him some energy. "Let's follow this a little, see where it takes us." He hoped it took them to O'Leary. Regretted that he only had one good arm. He was dying to slam that plug-ugly face into something unyielding.

CHAPTER TWENTY-TWO

The six teenage witnesses were bright, helpful, caring and shocked, but an hour in their company brought not much more than Delinsky's succinct one-paragraph summary. They thought the car might be a Lexus or a Mercedes. The truck it had almost collided with was a FedEx van. Weary and unenlightened, he and Kyle drove through the damp, gray dusk back to headquarters.

The station was bright and quiet. The shift change had come and gone, leaving rows of tired radios and flashlights to recharge. Civilian day people were winding down. The phones were resting. Burgess, who'd dozed during the ride, was having trouble getting going again. Sleep was like sex or alcohol—getting a little only made you want more.

His plans to get on to other things were derailed by bureaucratic minutiae. Check in with Melia. Check in with Cote. Check with Andrea Dwyer, the cop who was babysitting Mai Phung. A bit of good news. There had been no rape. Then he had to follow up with Federal Express. See the shift commander and arrange for a door-to-door on the street near the video store. Arrange for a crime scene team. Write reports. Read reports.

Stan Perry came back from his interview with Martha McFarland looking sour, and reported two cases against Pleasant, both settled. No details forthcoming. He hadn't hit it off with the attorney. Burgess, being an experienced detective, deduced this from the comment that she probably ate babies for breakfast. Perry'd been too late for the courthouse, would get on it in the morning. He had a pile of stuff he'd copied at Pleasant's house to go through, but from the number of dunning letters, it looked like a grim financial picture. None of the missing credit cards had been used. The widow had been icy.

"I missed lunch," Perry complained. "And my feet got soaked. Car rolled through a huge puddle and dumped a wall of muddy water on me. Everything's going to have to go to the cleaners. Even my underwear's wet. And my sometimes girlfriend has left three messages complaining that I don't call her. Call her? I don't even have time to brush my teeth." He threw himself into his chair and kicked his desk drawer shut.

"Makes you wonder why you wanted to be a detective, doesn't it?" Burgess said. Pleasant's records could wait for morning. He wanted to sit in a comfortable chair, put his feet up, and eat things that were bad for him. He wanted to open some Jack Daniels and drink himself into oblivion, go somewhere murder victims and needy survivors couldn't find him. He wished he could tell Perry and Kyle to take a break. They were as ragged as he was. But he couldn't. Not 'til they cracked this thing or wore out their leads.

"Hey, Terry," he said, "think you could give me a ride home?"

Kyle hefted the trash bag they'd taken from the video store. "How about we get some take-out and watch six movies."

"Six movies?" Perry said, getting up from his desk and walking over. "Don't you guys need sleep?" He still looked fresh and dewy, despite the sad condition of his stylish suit. Just looking at him gave Burgess heartburn, and he liked Perry. Kid probably didn't creak when he walked.

"Homemade porn, maybe," Kyle said. "O'Leary's private collection. Wanna come?"

"You think I have to ask my mother or something?"

"Girlfriend. If you still have one."

Perry just shrugged. "Last thing I need's a ball and chain who thinks a cop works normal hours. Joe's place, right? It's the only one clean enough for company." Perry shook his head. "What's wrong with us that none of us are married?"

"I was married once," Kyle reminded him. "The PMS queen's enough to put a guy off marriage forever."

"We're social misfits," Burgess suggested. His phone rang. He eyed it warily, wondering what kind of bad news it was bringing. Hoping it wasn't going to be more work. It wasn't likely to be someone calling to confess. He half expected to hear that O'Leary had been found dead. It was a logical step in this chain of violence. Reluctantly, he answered. "Burgess, investigations."

His sister Sandy's voice exploded out of the phone. "Joe, you are such an asshole! I cannot believe it. You slept with her!"

"Not exactly . . ." he began, "it wasn't like that . . ."

"Don't start with me. I'm not some judge or lawyer. Some baby cop who thinks you walk on water. I'm your sister. I know how you work. I let you start talking and you'll convince me the poor kid had a hallucination or something. Look, there's no way to twist this around to make you look good. You've known Alana since she was seventeen. You're like a father to her. And now this!"

He didn't bother to mention that Alana's father had slept with her. It wasn't the right moment. Knowing Sandy, it wasn't the right moment for any kind of remark. She wasn't calling to hear his side, she just wanted to yell at him. "Sandy, look—"

"I don't care what your explanation is! I'm so pissed at you, Joe Burgess."

"I'm getting that impression."

"This isn't funny. You, of all people, should know better. You could ruin your career with something like this. You know she's always been crazy about you. Did you think this would help? That if you did this, she'd get over it? I mean, honestly, Joe, what could you possibly have been thinking?"

He held the phone at an arm's length, letting the angry words pour out. Let her get a little of it out of her system. "Sandy, listen, will you let me get a word in?"

She sighed. "All right."

"It was rape," he said.

"You didn't!"

"Not me. Alana. You ask her. I was drugged, asleep, helpless. She took advantage of me. By the time I was fully conscious, I'd been violated."

"Oh! You! That's disgusting." His sister slammed down the phone.

So much for truth. He wished he hadn't answered. It would take hours of talking to put this right. And it still wouldn't be right. If Sandy would listen to him. At least he knew the value of Alana's promise that his secret was safe with her. Next he'd be reading it on the front page of the *Press Herald*. Maverick cop coercing sex from prostitutes. Honored detective ends distinguished career in disgrace.

"Trouble, Joe?" Kyle asked.

"Sandy. Calling to yell at me about sleeping with Alana."

"Ouch!" Kyle slung his coat over his shoulder. "Ready?"

"Yeah. Let's leave before something else goes wrong."

"Bring the letters, okay? Stan, you coming?"

"I wasn't sure I was invited."

"Oh, we're all for one and one for all around here, aren't we, Joe?"

Rush hour should have been over, but the snow had slowed everything and driving was still a nightmare. On every block a stuck car was being pushed, on every third, a patrol car, light bar flashing, sorted out a fender-bender. Kyle was cool with it. He tuned the radio to NPR. "Love those BBC announcers. Listen to a few reports from the Middle East and India and it puts things in perspective." Confident British voices competed with the hiss of the tires, clods of snow slamming on the undercarriage, the intermittent thunk of wipers. The storm had gone, leaving a clear black sky sparkling with stars. Against the black, the time and temperature sign kept the city informed.

"I've got a feeling," Kyle said. "Somewhere in the stuff we're going to look at tonight there's dynamite."

"Right now, it would take dynamite just to keep my eyes open."

Kyle swung into the restaurant parking lot and pulled into the handicapped space. "You're handicapped," he told Burgess. "Anything special you want?"

"Boneless spareribs. General Gau's chicken."

"Boneless spareribs is an oxymoron," Kyle said, getting out of the car.

The interior cooled off quickly, the chill seeping through his skin and digging into his bones. At least he was alone. To distract himself from his miserable body, he regurgitated what he knew and chewed it over. If Pleasant was being blackmailed because of an incriminating videotape, why put himself in a situation where it might happen again? Had he been killed because he was out-of-control, because if he were bailed out, he'd only get in trouble again? If so, who'd arranged it? His wife? Jack Kelly? Ted Shaw? He liked Ken Bailey for it, but that was because Bailey pissed him off.

If it was a set-up, as the facts suggested, using O'Leary

made sense. He had a record going back to age thirteen. Placed no value on human life. But who'd hired O'Leary?

Then there were the pieces that didn't fit. If Pleasant was killed because of scandalous behavior and embarrassing videotapes, why do it in a way that would be so embarrassing to his family and colleagues? Unless someone had decided to cut him loose? Or they'd decided that embarrassment of that sort was worse than the scandal revelation of his drug sales would cause? If there was anything to the drug angle. Oxycontin was hot on the street. People would pay big bucks to get it. And Pleasant had had an inside track. Another thing that didn't fit was the man in the truck who'd been stalking him. And who was the girl—Karen—who'd asked O'Leary to arrange the meeting? Where did they fit in?

While he was on the subject of why the hell things happened, why the hell had he had sex with Alana Black? Why risk a career he hadn't given up after Kristin Marks, despite his rage and disillusionment, for a few minutes of fucking bliss?

Kyle came back with the food, moving fast, reaching over the seat to set the bags down. He fired up the engine and backed deftly out. The cold car filled with the mingled scents of Chinese food. "Stan's picking up some beer," he said. He rocketed out into the stream of traffic, managing the resulting skid with balletic grace. Only an asshole, and no cop, believed that SUVs didn't slip, slide and skid. Kyle drove with the same intensity he brought to everything. Close to the edge but very competent. People let his taciturnity fool them, thought he was calm and quiet. Burgess knew better. Kyle was as wired and edgy as he was, he just wore it more layers down.

"I can feel your black aura over here," Kyle said. "Keep

it on your side, please. I'm driving."

Burgess growled like a rabid dog. "Aura? Fuckin' new age goo-goo types got auras. Maybe some leftover hippies and crunchy granola types got auras. Cops have tempers. And reasons to lose 'em. Tempers and moods. If I want to get into a bad fuckin' mood, which under the circumstances seems perfectly reasonable, what the hell do you propose to do about it?"

"That's better. Always better to get mad than to get down. That place you go, it's like a tar pit. It'll suck you down 'til me and Stan, together, can't get you out."

"Who made you my keeper?"

"It's a lousy job, but someone's got to do it." A sporty little RAV4 darted out in front of them and began to fishtail. Kyle stomped on the brakes. The Explorer bucked like a bronco but it slowed nicely. Another thing assholes believed—that SUVs could defy the laws of physics. "Jerk doesn't know how to drive, he should stay home!" They went on in silence, 'til Kyle said, "You wanna know who gave me the job? Your mother."

"What the hell?"

"Sorry, pal. It's a sacred trust. One day, I'm visiting and she says to me, 'My Joseph, he gets into these dark places and can't see the way out. Look after him, Terry.' Your mother, even aside from having to put up with you, was a saint. When we were getting divorced, and Wanda was trying to turn the kids against me, I was so mad I wanted to kill her. Your mother kept me straight. She told me to keep it to myself, see the kids as much as possible, and let them know I loved them. That I'd always be there. That I was steady and calm and wouldn't change."

Kyle stomped on the brake, spun around a car that had just popped out of a parking space in front of them, and back into his lane. "She said the kids were getting enough anger and hate at home and if I could keep my bad feelings out of my relationship with them, they'd see the truth, no matter what Wanda did. She was right. I've got a better relationship with them than Wanda does. So I've got no choice. Your mother wanted me to do something, I gotta do it. You don't like it, tough."

It had been Kyle, not the shrink, who'd gotten him through Kristin Marks. Knowing when to show up. When he needed to be alone and when he couldn't be. When his gun was looking tasty. Kyle who had organized his friends to baby-sit. All elaborately casual. All carefully choreographed. All extremely hard and dangerous, since he'd been like a ticking bomb. The rage and despair he'd felt then had been monumental. The reason he had so little furniture. He'd destroyed the rest. But Kyle had never told him this.

"Thank you."

Thank you and I'm sorry. Two phrases a lot of people weren't able to use. He tried to use them both. Another legacy from his mother. From a night he'd found her weeping in the kitchen, back before his father left, holding a dishcloth filled with ice against her bruised cheek. "There's something broken in that man, Joseph," she'd said. "Such a fear of being grateful or beholden. It pains him so much to think he ought to say he's sorry, or to be thankful, he just explodes. You're so like him in some ways. I'm hoping this won't be one of them."

It was, and it wasn't. He'd gotten the explosive temper and he'd learned to control it. He'd learned to say thank you and sorry. But he wasn't sure that there wasn't something broken in him, just like in his father, something that kept him from ever getting close to women. Maybe he was too afraid he'd hurt them. Too painfully aware of the seeds of it in himself, and too aware of the consequences.

Despite Kyle's instructions, he couldn't help his mood tonight. One of the downsides of getting overtired. All day he'd had flashes of Kristin's body lying in that dump. It had happened before. He was supposed to meditate, practice relaxation exercises, take a day off, and if all else failed, get some help. He was in the middle of a fucking murder investigation. He didn't have time. Burgess sighed deeply, feeling his gloom settle in around him like a black velvet shroud.

CHAPTER TWENTY-THREE

They parked and went inside without speaking. Kyle set the food down, opened the cupboard, took out three plates. "Think we'll get through the evening without more hell breaking loose?" Burgess asked, shrugging off his coat.

"I wouldn't mind, but I wouldn't lay odds on it, either."

Burgess removed his shoes by stepping on the backs and wiggling his feet out. They were a loss anyway, ringed with grayish-white salt marks. His wet socks left footprints on the floor. He dumped some ice in a glass and poured the bourbon. An able one-handed drinker. "Want some, Ter?"

"Sure."

Perry carried in two six-packs, set them on the table, popped the top on his first.

"We're predicting the future here," Kyle said. "The immediate future. What comes next, you think?"

Perry buried his fingers in his blond curls and closed his eyes, producing a great imitation of ecstatic wonder. "I see fire. I see gorgeous babes cavorting with men in bandanas while mongrel dogs frisk and whine. I see fat-cat doctors counting their loot and tipsy rich men smirking." He tipped up the can and drank. "Seriously? How about O'Leary dead."

"That's a good guess." Burgess poured a second bourbon and handed it to Kyle. "When and where?"

"What about by whom?" Kyle said. "Let's eat, okay? Cold Chinese sucks."

They carried everything to the living room, filling plates

as Kyle knelt by the VCR, slipped on gloves, and started the first tape.

Burgess ate shrimp fried rice and General Gau's chicken and watched a naked girl cavort athletically atop a fat, red-faced man. Black-haired, fresh-faced. One of O'Leary's girls. Alana had called her Lulu. At first, the man lay like a beached whale, doing little more than puffing and watching the girl's lithe body. Gradually, his hips began to move, then his hands rose and started kneading the pert, bouncing breasts. Finally, braying like a donkey, his wobbling thighs jouncing, he grabbed her waist and climaxed with a series of violent groans, collapsing back against the pillows with closed eyes.

Lulu brushed the man's chest with her nipples, his lips with hers. "Oh, Mr. O'Sullivan, that was good!" The video faded to crackling black and white.

"Oh, Mr. O'Sullivan," Perry mimicked. "It's like screwing your high school principal. That do anything for you, Joe?"

"I'm not sitting here with my hat over my lap. Are there any more spareribs?"

"Looking for something with a little bone in it?"

"Stan, you're sick, you know that?"

"Me? Guy on the screen is the sick fuck. Cheerleader's skirt? Pink cotton panties. An undershirt? She's a C-cup if she's an inch. C-cup girls don't wear undershirts."

"Where've you been, Stan?" Burgess asked. "All that staring and drooling you do and you haven't noticed. These days, D-cup girls wear skinny little tank tops with no bras at all. My fourteen-year-old niece looks more like a hooker than Lulu does. Never mind pink cotton. I think she wears thongs." He shook his head. "I don't get thongs. Seem like a permanent wedgie to me."

"But when you slide your hand over her ass, it's pure ass," Stan Perry said. "That's why the boys wear those baggy pants. To hide their chronic hard-ons." He leaned forward eagerly. "I'm ready for the next one."

"So yours isn't chronic, it's intermittent?" Kyle suggested. "Better call your girlfriend. Maybe she can see you later." Kyle fanned himself with his hand.

"Anybody recognize that guy?" Burgess interrupted.

"Identifying characteristics," Perry said, "two hundred and fifty pounds of pink blubber. Blue eyes. Blue? Yeah. Gray hair. Graying mustache. Prominent yellow teeth. Big nose with broken veins. Fat fingers. Gold signet ring. Prop it upright and dress it in a suit, and what've we got? William O'Sullivan, president of NorEast Bank. Right?"

"Give the boy a stuffed bear," Kyle said. "We've got another winner."

"No shit!" Perry took another beer from the six-pack beside his chair. It was his third. "This would be the moment for someone to chuck a bomb through the window, wouldn't it? Can we see the next one? Please?"

"Nobody wants to critique the cinematography?" Burgess asked.

"No, Joe. Stanley here wants to play 'pecker, pecker, who's got the pecker.' "

"Screw you, Kyle."

"I don't think so."

Burgess got the Jack Daniels. Refilled his glass and Kyle's. Settled into his chair as Kyle carefully removed the first tape and inserted another. The second was much like the first, except the man was older and skinnier and Lulu looked completely bored. No one recognized the man. "Skip the rest," Stan suggested. They went on to number three.

This time, Lulu actually seemed a little interested in the proceedings. Her client was a nicely made man in his mid-thirties with a handsome, familiar-looking face. He was tied to the bedposts with what looked like golden silk ropes. "Curtain ties," Burgess said. "Dr. Lee said that was probably what was used on Pleasant. Too bad we didn't find them."

"Why?" Kyle asked. "You wanted to try them out?"

"Channel 13," Perry said. "Newscaster. Oh, shit!"

"Watch your language, Stan," Kyle said. "You're going to start doing that on the job, and you know how the chief feels."

"Thought I *was* on the job."

At that moment, as he writhed and grunted, the man's toupee popped off and landed on the pillow, looking like some small, furry animal. Lulu screamed and the man tried to grab it, but was restrained by the ropes on his hands. "America's funniest home videos, here we come!" Perry crowed. "Vince would love this. Should we call him?"

"Right now, Vince is reading *The Lion, the Witch and the Wardrobe* to the twins. Little does he know," Burgess said. "Anyway, it's the captain who'd love it."

"Cote would soil his nappy," Perry said. "Let's see number four."

Lulu again. It confirmed his impression from the autopsy that Pleasant had been a well-built man. Well-built, energetic, greedy and demanding. A man who took his sex seriously and meant to get his money's worth. Unlike the other men, who'd been content to be serviced, he directed Lulu's attentions with brief, curt instructions. Despite the sustained and vigorous sex, including a variety of positions challenging the participants' dexterity, Burgess's reaction wasn't vicarious titillation, but distaste. He couldn't help substituting Jen Kelly for Lulu, her small, delicate body being rammed so violently, her sad blue eyes searching that cold face for signs that she was pleasing him, her long blonde hair pooling over his thighs as she performed.

This wasn't the video he'd hoped for. He'd wanted the one made the night Pleasant died, so he could get a look at the mystery girl, Karen. This must be a tape from an earlier time. He'd now seen Lulu from every angle imaginable, felt as depleted as if he'd had her himself. Kyle had become so bored he'd picked up the letters and was reading through them. Only Perry was still watching.

"Let's take a quick look at the other two and call it a night," Burgess suggested.

"Kinda like that giant ice cream sundae they dare you to try and eat, isn't it?" Kyle said. "Halfway through, you've had so much damned sugar and syrup you're sick of it."

"I don't know. I wouldn't mind one of those sundaes. Long as she kept her mouth shut," Perry said.

"She keeps her mouth shut and you miss half the fun," Burgess said.

"Long as she didn't talk," Perry amended.

Kyle set the letters on the floor, crossed the room, and put in another tape. This time he stayed by the machine, assuming, as Burgess did, that they were only going to take a peek at these next two. Once again there was the shabby room, the great big bed with the black satin bedspread, the heap of leopard print pillows. This time the girl was wearing matching leopard print panties and bra, her back to the camera, a man's big hand on her shoulder, slowly pulling down one strap, then the other. But the girl wasn't Lulu and Burgess felt a visceral shock twinge through him as he realized what he was seeing.

"Oh, sweet Jesus," Kyle breathed, settling back on his

heels. "A dirty-minded cop's dreams come true."

The hands undid the bra, dropped it onto the floor, and moved the girl to the bed. The man's head came into view. A big head, graying, distinguished. Dr. Ken Bailey leaned forward and took one of her nipples into his mouth, a gigantic babe being suckled by an earth mother, kneading the other breast with his fingers, his hands an obscene white against the tawny skin. Stan Perry made a low moaning sound, like a warning dog. Burgess looked away.

Kyle took a deep breath and hit the pause button. "Just when you think there are no surprises, along comes a blockbuster." In the dim room, the bluish white light from the screen illuminated the planes of his face, giving him a ghostly look. Dark hair, slumped shoulders in a dark jacket, white skin, white shirt, white walls, a black and white portrait of a weary homicide detective. Above him, Burgess's black and white portraits of empty crime scenes ringed the walls.

"Hold on. I'm out of the loop. Who the hell's that on the tape?" Perry asked. "I recognized Alana Black, America's number one wet dream, but who's the guy?"

"Dr. Kenneth Bailey, senior guy at Pine State Radiology. In the words of Pleasant's wife, 'the closest thing to a boss' her husband had," Burgess explained. He poured himself a third drink, knowing that after a certain point, it was like drinking poison. His father's poison. Held the bottle up. "Terry?"

"Like to, but I'd better not. You think Pleasant set him up?"

"To the extent that you can rape the willing. Let's just say Dr. Bailey was naïve about the level of his partner's deception. It's a common mistake—thinking that a guy who'll cheat on his wife can still be relied on to be your good buddy, because cheating a wife isn't like cheating a friend. No wonder Bailey's angry. He got screwed more ways than one."

"I wonder what kind of car he drives?"

"Shouldn't be hard to find out." Burgess held out his radio. "While you're at it, find out what Ted Shaw drives."

"Shaw?"

"Said he'd bailed his son-in-law out of one financial scrape, cleaned up after some sexual shenanigans. Wanted me to let him know if there was anything else he needed to clean up. Suppose the financial scrape was buying an incriminating videotape?"

Kyle scooped up the radio and moved back into the light, pulling his notebook from his pocket. "Might as well ask about O'Sullivan and the news guy while I'm at it." He hesitated. "Hold on. We might as well look at number six." He put it in. Hit play. Lulu again, with a man none of them recognized. Kyle hit stop and got on the radio.

Burgess took a sip from the glass and leaned back in his chair, letting the hot, sweet liquor roll over his tongue. It would be so easy to lose himself in a bottle. Such a cop cliché. Such a family cliché. If it weren't for the fear of becoming his father, he'd do this more often. Nothing took the edge off better. Nothing was more soothing. Nothing worked better on physical pain, not even Dr. Shorter's pills. And nothing came close, for psychic pain. He loved the feel of Alana Black's hands on his body; perhaps even more, he loved the feel of a thin, slick layer of bourbon between himself and his demons.

Perry had picked up one of the letters and was reading it, tipping it toward the lamp and peering at the words. Beer in one hand, heartbreak in the other. It was the balance they always kept in their lives. Keep your professional distance.

237

Give your all to the job and don't get involved. In a way, they had more in common with Dr. Ken Bailey and the crew over at the Maine Med than those guys gave them credit for. All of them had had to learn professional detachment.

Burgess took another drink and looked at Kyle. "What kind of car?"

"Bailey? Mercedes. 1999. Black. Sedan."

"And Shaw?"

"Lexus. The big one. Dark green."

"The other two?"

Kyle sighed. "Two more Mercedes."

"Joe, did you read any of these?" Perry asked, thrusting a couple at him. "Seriously, we should talk to some of these people."

Burgess picked up the first letter. "That's what Terry said."

"Well, what are we doing tomorrow?"

"You're going to the courthouse, doing financial stuff, and I have a drug angle for you to check out. And there's O'Leary's mother. I'm doing phone records. Maybe Terry can do some."

"Hold on, Joe." Perry shook his head, his natural aggression fueled by beer. "Screw financial records. People don't kill about money when they can recover it other ways. Pleasant had a house, a fancy car, a business. People kill for hate. For revenge."

"I'm with Stan on this one," Kyle said.

Burgess shrugged. Two smart cops with the same gut reaction. Who was he to argue? But he liked to follow things to the end, and right now, they were following sex and hookers, videotapes and big, important men. Drugs and money. Did it really make any difference what order they did things in, when there were no clear winners? He sighed.

"How many letters we got?"

Perry counted. "Fifteen."

"Gimme those." Kyle took them, scanning quickly through them.

"Fifteen?" Burgess said. "Wouldn't you think a warning flag would have gone up? Maybe all doctors get many complaints, but this sounds like a lot to me." He thought about the letter he hadn't written. Was this the tip of the iceberg? Were there dozens of other people out there, nursing grudges, brooding on their secret hate? He tipped his glass up and swallowed it in one fiery gulp. "Unless something changes in the next twelve hours, it's as good a way as any to spend tomorrow, I guess. Give me my five."

Kyle handed him five letters, and started stacking containers and plates. "Bedtime, boys and girls," he said. "We've got a big day tomorrow. Joe, you gonna get a driver? If I drive, we only cover half as much ground."

"I'll call Vince, get him to find me someone. I could do it."

"Don't push it, Joe, when there's no need." He dangled the car keys. "I'll bring these back to you in the morning, along with your car."

Stan picked up the remaining six-pack and his five letters. "Thanks for a lovely evening," he said. "And good hunting."

"Drive carefully," Kyle said. "Real carefully. We need you at work tomorrow."

"Yes, Dad. I know. Otherwise I won't get the car this weekend, right? And I'll have to wash the dog?"

"Otherwise, you might find yourself over at the jailhouse, singing the blues."

"I can't sing."

"Then I hope you can drive."

Kyle watched until Stan's car had pulled out of the driveway and disappeared down the street. "Not too bad," he said. "And he doesn't have far to go."

Burgess was standing by the counter, reading one of his letters. "Jesus, Terry. Talking to these people is going to be like picking scabs off their wounds."

"Like we've never done that before? Picking at scabs is what we do for a living. You going to be okay getting undressed without your nurse?"

"That's not funny, Ter. She doesn't keep her mouth shut, I could lose my job."

Kyle gave him a look. "I'm not sure about leaving you alone, Joe."

"Think I can't handle it?"

"Oh, I think you can get your jammies on and brush your teeth. I'm more worried about what happens when you close your eyes. About that crazy fucker look you've been wearing, the one that just got turned up a couple degrees. Get a grip, Joe. She's a hooker."

He didn't want to get into this. There was enough crap floating around already. "Maybe I just won't close 'em."

"Do me a favor," Kyle said, and held out his hand. Burgess wouldn't have done this for anyone else, but Kyle understood what could happen to a crazy fucker alone in the dark with Kristin Marks. He gave Kyle his gun. "Thanks," Kyle said. "See you in the morning. Oh, one more thing."

Burgess gave him the bourbon, bowing slightly. "Will there be anything else, sir?"

"I sure hope not." Kyle paused, using silence for emphasis. "Call if you need me, okay?"

"Okay." He watched Kyle's stooped shoulders disappear through the door, heard the thump of feet on the stairs. Then the downstairs door opened with a creak and shut with a bang, and he was alone.

He left a message for Melia that he'd need a driver in the morning. Then he considered what to do. There was more bourbon in the cupboard, but he wasn't in the mood to drink it. There was another gun, too. But that was down in the basement, in a locked box, and the key was in the attic. Games detectives play. Especially ones who are prone to depression.

He turned on the bedroom light, opened the closet, and stared at the dozens of pictures of Kristin Marks, dead and alive. In the center was the newspaper photo of her casket being carried out of the church, so small and white, carried by six men bent low by the burden of their grief, her parents coming behind it. The black and white picture didn't show all the vivid ugliness of the day. Kristin's father, Daniel, a huge, gentle man, walking with a Frankenstein stiffness that reflected his stunned state. Beside him, held up by her two sisters, Kristin's mother, Anna, her face swollen with weeping.

Burgess was right behind them, a burly cop in uniform with his head bent. He had to keep his head bent. He couldn't keep his rage off his face. A rarity for him. Cops learn early on how to manage their faces. But this case had been different. In all his years of police work, hers was the only autopsy he ever left to throw up. Not because of the autopsy itself, but because of the information the ME was giving about her violation, and the details his own experience provided about how she'd suffered. One of his nieces had been nine at the time. Every time he looked at her, he felt his stomach roll.

He closed the closet door and looked at the stark black and white picture of the empty landfill at dawn. Maybe he should sleep. He was so tired he felt dizzy, and the alcohol hadn't helped. It had been a long time since his last pill and he hurt, but he didn't feel like medicine. It made the dreams worse and tonight there was already enough stuff stirring. He didn't want to take it with him into sleep. A warm bath might ease the aches without the dullness, and was a good way to lull himself to sleep. He filled the tub and put Emmylou Harris into his portable CD player.

He put the headphones on, and slid into the water, steeping like a human tea bag. He couldn't hear the phone, or someone knocking at the door, or the explosion signaling the end of the world. Gradually, the heat penetrated his muscles, loosening the tension in his back and in his neck. Consciously, he monitored his breathing, practiced relaxing, willing the demons to loosen their little claws, fly away and leave him in peace. Alone with Emmylou. In the end, they did.

Chapter Twenty-four

Morning came too soon, an indeterminate day with a light gray sky promising sun and threatening showers. The radio announcer gave the odds of precipitation at 30 percent, the temperature at 34. Burgess woke without a headache, enough to warrant a mild celebration, though his swollen arm felt worse than ever. Win a few, lose a few. Struggling into his clothes, he could have used the services of his nurse, if not the complications, and he blessed the folks at L.L.Bean who had thoughtfully made boots with zippers.

He fixed a pot of coffee and contemplated the choices: leftover Chinese, leftover pizza, or a bagel and cream cheese. The bagel won. While it was toasting, he picked up the letters. Last night's hasty division had seemed random, but it wasn't. Kyle had given him ones that were geographically coherent. No surprise. Kyle was a fast processor and efficient at allocating resources. Burgess got out his Maine Guide and Atlas, mapped the route, then picked up the phone and called the letter writers. He wasn't traveling to Bath and Boothbay Harbor unless he had someone to see.

Maybe it was his lucky day—he wouldn't know until later—but he found four out of five of the letter writers, and they agreed to see him. He asked for directions, made notes, and snapped his notebook shut. Following protocol, he called the local police departments, telling them who he was going to see and why and that he didn't need to bother them for a local escort.

He felt like a man recovering from the flu, more tired

and lethargic than sick, without much enthusiasm for the day's activities. This would pass. He'd never been able to resist the excitement of the chase. Hour by hour it might wear him down, but he loved the adrenaline and the challenge of pitting himself against the bad guys. And Kyle's certainty that today would bring results was contagious.

He'd barely started his coffee when Kyle pounded on the door, handed over his gun and his bourbon, and assessed him with tired eyes.

"You get some sleep?" Kyle asked.

"A lot. You?" Kyle looked exhausted.

"One of the kids got sick. Wanda gave me a choice— baby-sit the one at home, or take the other to the doctor. I chose baby-sit, figuring I'd get some rest, but she got sick, too. I must have changed her clothes four times and the bed three, and I had to wash all the sheets and blankets and clothes. After about three hours of that, I was dead on my feet. Then Wanda came back with the other kid and she needed a story, too. That took up most of the night. At least she called. Half the time, she deliberately screws things up so I don't get to see them, but God forbid I'm a day late with the support check."

"You want a bagel and coffee? Leftover Chinese?"

"Bagel and coffee sounds good. I didn't have time to eat. Your driver's bringing the car," he said. "You hear the news? Video store got firebombed last night. Total loss."

Burgess put another bagel in the toaster, poured coffee, and pushed it across the table. "Wasn't that one of Stan's psychic predictions? Anybody hurt?"

"It was after midnight."

"Crime lab get their stuff?"

"Yeah. We ever find O'Leary, we've got all we need to put him away. Turns out Mr. Sam Sun had a surveillance camera. Funny how he didn't mention that, isn't it?"

"So how did we know?"

"The divine Andrea learned about it from Mai Phung. Sent someone right over to get the tape. Didn't give Sun a chance to argue."

"She's a good cop."

"She'd be great for Stan. Wonder if he's ever thought of it," Kyle said.

"Can't be many women Stan's missed. Why not for you?"

"Bad luck with women."

"You've got the wrong attitude," Burgess said. "You'll never meet anybody if you put yourself in that box—ugly old guy whose child support keeps him broke."

"You're a fine one to talk. You got a social life?"

He shook his head. "My work is my life." Kyle made a face. "What did you want to be when you grew up?" Burgess asked, opening the refrigerator.

"A keen-eyed, sharp-witted, ruthless detective. You?"

"A priest. It didn't last. I discovered girls. Butter or cream cheese?"

"I like my girls without butter or cream cheese. At least, I think I do. Been a long time since I've had one, with or without. I've got enough trouble with Wanda. Sometimes she's fine, other times she's sharpening her stiletto and trying to decide which ribs to stick it between. Doesn't have anything to do with my behavior."

"Know what you mean. With me, it's my sisters. Where you off to today?"

"The Lewiston/Auburn area. Stan's here in Portland and points south."

"When shall we three meet again?"

"Haven't I heard those words somewhere before?"

"Sister Philomena. The room where the wind always rattled the windows. I could see those witches when she had us reading this stuff."

"Yeah. They looked just like her. So, back at the station, end of the day, unless somebody gets stuck?" Burgess nodded. "You clear this frolic with Vince?"

"He said gut instinct was as good as anything else at this point, only would we please, for God's sake, bring him something. He's got Cote nipping at his heels like a border collie. Add the chief on top of that, and he's feeling like the guy on the bottom of the clown pyramid."

"Clown pyramid. I like that." Kyle rubbed his weary eyes. "Not like we aren't trying." Doorbell rang. "That'll be your driver. Want me to get it?"

"That's okay." Burgess went downstairs, found a nervous-looking Remy Aucoin on the mat, his hand resting on his gun. "Thought you came to drive, not shoot me." The hand lifted and dropped. "Come on in. Want coffee?"

Aucoin looked like it was a hard decision. "If we've got time, sir. Yes. I would."

"Bagel?"

"No. Thank you, sir. I ate."

"Gonna be an awfully long day if you keep calling me 'sir.' Try Joe. I don't bite, you know."

Aucoin looked doubtful. He greeted Kyle with deference, sat at the table, and accepted the coffee, refusing cream and sugar, keeping his eyes on the cup. It looked like, sir or not, it was going to be a long day. Maybe the kid would get over this. And there were virtues to a quiet companion.

Burgess shoved his pills into his coat pocket and pulled it on. Life was damned hard with only one good arm. Not the first time he'd learned that lesson. Once in 'Nam, with some shrapnel. Once in a domestic, getting a knife from a guy determined to kill his wife. He checked his pocket for gloves and gathered up the letters. "Ready?"

They trooped downstairs and out into a mild morning. It felt good after the cold of the last few days, but the streets and sidewalks were turning into mushy soup that backed up storm drains and turned intersections and low spots into vast black lakes the consistency of blender margaritas. Passing cars threw bucketfuls onto each other's windshields. It got better once they were on the highway, and there were great views of mudflats trimmed with patches of snow and heaped-up slabs of blue ice, streams meandering through them like languid brown snakes.

"Brunswick, Bath, Wiscasset and Boothbay Harbor," Burgess said. "And we're in no rush."

It was odd not driving. He'd traveled this route often, usually in a hurry, his mind on other things, where he'd just been, where he was going. Today he could just take in the light glistening on the tide flats, the pale gold of cattails and marsh grass, the idiocy of other drivers. Between Falmouth and Brunswick, he could have written thirty tickets.

"May I ask you something?" Aucoin said.

"Sure."

"Why'd you become a cop?"

So much for the quiet ride. Except for the shrink, and women in bars, no one had asked that in a long time. He'd been a cop longer than Aucoin had been alive. "I was just back from Vietnam. Wasn't ready to go to college. Thought it would be good to do something that made people safe. I was a big, strong guy whose major skills were using a gun and getting along with other guys. Police department's a lot like the military. It felt comfortable."

"You still like it?"

"Most days."

"Does it get boring?"

"Not for me."

"You always want to be a detective?"

"Thought I wanted to be on patrol, early out, forever. Got an adrenaline rush every shift, watching night fall on the city. My city. The crazy Russian roulette of traffic stops. Never knowing what was coming." He considered. "Detective stuff found me. I was good with people. Knew the streets and the players. They kept pressuring me to try it. I did and I got hooked. Why? You want to be a detective?"

"I think so." Aucoin cleared his throat. "No second thoughts?"

Burgess wasn't big on sharing his private thoughts, but the kid was sincere. "Everyone has second thoughts, Remy. We're not machines. You just have to believe in what you do and keep trying to do your best. Try to keep the bad stuff in perspective. Don't kid yourself. There will be bad stuff. Sometimes . . ." But today he wanted to be looking ahead. And the kid would learn this soon enough.

Aucoin had the good sense not to press him. They rode in silence until they got to Brunswick, and Burgess read off his directions. Aucoin stopped in front of a small, well-tended white house with a screened porch and a touch of gingerbread around the eaves. Burgess walked up the neatly shoveled walk, crossed the porch, and rang the bell. A bird-like old man opened the door. He wore corduroy slacks, a dull brown cardigan with leather elbow patches over a blue shirt, and felt slippers. Retired Bowdoin professor, Burgess guessed.

"Detective Burgess? Please come in." Burgess followed him into a hot, airless house that smelled of menthol and frying. There were piles of books and papers everywhere, the books bristling with page markers. "The other officer isn't coming in?" the man said. "I suppose you brought him along in case you had to arrest me." His laugh was mirthless and forced. He had papery white skin and looked tired and cranky. He sat in a sagging chair that was covered by a garish afghan and waved his hand toward the couch. "Please sit down. Careful! Watch the cat."

A black cat curled in a corner of the dark sofa gave a meow of protest as it jumped to the floor and stalked away, head and tail high. Burgess checked for more animals before sitting, then held out the letter. "Did you write this, Mr. Merrifield?"

The hand that took the letter was age-spotted and unsteady. Merrifield pulled glasses from his sweater pocket and read the letter. He sighed, read it again, then handed it back. "Yes. I wrote it. After Aggie . . . my wife, Agatha, died. Why do you ask?"

"You were complaining about the way Dr. Pleasant treated your wife."

"Yes," Merrifield said impatiently. "So?"

"Earlier this week, Dr. Pleasant was killed. We're exploring all the possibilities, including people who didn't like him."

"Well, I'm certainly in that category. My wife, Aggie . . ." He rose, slowly, ungracefully, crossed the room, and picked up a framed picture from the bookcase.

Burgess studied the picture. Agatha Merrifield was holding a baby in her arms. She was smiling. The baby was smiling. They were surrounded by blooming flowers. She was a short, blocky woman with no-nonsense hair, a firm jaw, and a face that had smiled more than it had frowned.

"She was the light of my life," Merrifield said. "That's my granddaughter. Also Aggie. Possibly the only Agatha in her generation." He took the picture and sank down into his chair, the frame in his lap. "All I wanted for her was that the process be conducted with dignity. With respect for who she was. She was a woman who graced life, detective. She was entitled to be granted grace in return."

He turned the picture face down. "It's not whether he could or couldn't save her. That's not why I disliked . . . no, let's not blunt the truth . . . why I hated Dr. Pleasant. It's that he never acknowledged her existence as a human being. It hurt her terribly. Under his care—and I use the word ironically—she wasn't Agatha Merrifield, who had lived and loved and taught for forty years. Who had changed lives and written beautiful poetry. She was the nine-forty. Not a person. A time slot. He rang up patients like the counter girl in a busy diner. Ka-ching. Ka-ching. Next. He didn't see them. Just drew pictures on their bodies, cooked their cells, and took their money, always looking down the line for the next dollar."

He sighed. "I'm an old man. I don't drive at night. I hardly drive at all any more. Without Aggie around to re-mind me of who I am, I'm becoming someone who was. A faded old duffer spinning in a slow circle with my papers and my books. Living alone with a cat. She would have said, 'Remember the time . . .' and the past and present would have connected. Come alive. Without her, I move through these rooms and all I can stir up is the dust." He bent his head.

"I'm sorry to have done this to you, Mr. Merrifield. But I had to ask."

"It's all right. I understand."

"You have a child? Children?" Merrifield nodded. "Are they nearby?"

"Nice try, detective. They didn't kill him either, though they won't be saddened by the news. Leland is in Switzer-land. He's in the foreign service. Mallory's an attorney in

Japan. Neither of them has been back in the States in months. Not since the memorial service. And Aggie is only a baby."

The interview was over. Merrifield followed Burgess to the door. "I appreciate your visit," he said. "Perhaps it's petty and hateful of me, but I take pleasure in knowing that someone had the courage to do what I so badly wanted to do. Aggie wouldn't approve. But I think we men understand more about vengeance."

The door closed behind him, and Burgess, relieved to be out of that bad-smelling, overheated house, sucked in a great lungful of cool air. Yes, he thought, we men understand a lot about vengeance, or at least the desire for it. He tucked the letter away, closed his notebook, and headed toward the car. Then, reconsidering, walked to the garage and looked in the window. Professor Merrifield drove a stodgy white Volvo.

He got in the car and nodded at Aucoin, dozing behind the wheel. "Bath," he said.

The sign hanging from the lamppost read: "Wee Folks Day Care." The driveway, crowded with small, colorful plastic vehicles, looked like a Lilliputian parking lot. One car was half on top of another in a manner suggesting a collision. Aucoin looked sullen in a way that suggested he resented being left behind. Burgess wasn't up to coping with any extraneous emotions—seeing all these sad, bruised people would be enough. If what the kid wanted was to become a better cop, why not let him watch?

"You want to come with me?"

"Sure." Aucoin unfastened his seatbelt eagerly.

Together they went up the walk and Burgess rang the bell. The woman who answered had a baby on her hip, two slightly larger children clinging to her legs. "Sergeant Burgess and Officer Aucoin, Portland police," he said.

"Come on in," she said, stepping back. "And I'm not apologizing for how the place looks. Always looks like this. Probably always will. Kitchen's this way. You want some coffee? I've got coffee cake and it's homemade, too."

They followed her into the kitchen, stepping carefully over scattered toys and books. It was a big room with brownish paneling and yellow Formica countertops. One wall was glass and sliders, opening to a deck. Below, a yard sloped steeply away. There was a round oak table in the center, a row of four high chairs along one wall, one corner given over to a miniature kitchen, with a sink, stove, refrigerator, cupboard and table. Three small girls were busy preparing an imaginary meal.

The woman nodded toward the activity. "Give 'em ten, fifteen years, and see if you can get three women in the same kitchen gettin' along like that."

She was about to set the baby down when Aucoin held out his arms. "May I?"

"Sure." She handed him the baby. "His name's Declan. And one of you is bound to be arresting him before he's fifteen. Looks like a doll-baby, but he's bad to the bone." She said it with satisfaction, as though born to be bad was the best type of boy. Aucoin took the future juvenile delinquent to the window to show him some birds at a feeder.

The woman stared after them with a grin. "Maybe it's some sorta male bonding thing. Declan's father's a cop. Cream and sugar?"

"Declan's yours?"

She nodded. "Thought I was too old but life's a funny thing." She bent down and detached the two clinging children from her legs, dumping one in a high chair and the other into the playpen. The one in the pen howled, and one of the girls came over and started making faces. The howling stopped. She dropped a handful of Cheerios in front of the other, and the child, solemn-faced, began eating them one by one. "Always like a three-ring circus around here. You got kids?"

He shook his head. "Too young until I was too old. I've got nieces and a nephew." He sat at the table and pulled out another letter. "You're Sherri Davis?"

"Since I married Donnie Davis. Used to be Sherri Elwell. But that was a while back. Never married Declan's father. Not yet, anyways. Tired of changing my name. What you got there?" He handed her the letter. She set it on the counter, poured three cups of coffee, got out cream and sugar, and three spoons. "Here's the cake," she said.

Aucoin was rubbing his chin over the baby's downy hair and making silly little noises, the baby giggling with delight. He joined them at the table, scooping up a couple toys on the way, holding the baby on his lap.

"You ever decide to give up being a cop, go into daycare, you call me first," Sherri said. "There aren't near enough men around who are good with kids. Or willing to show it. You want cake?" The toddler in the playpen started to fuss. She picked him up and set him on the changing table. "Phew!" she said. "Luke, you are a little stinker, aren't you? Don't worry, detective. You're next."

"Take your time," he said. "Remy's still bonding." Aucoin gave him a worried look. He'd temporarily forgotten about Bad Joe Burgess, the meanest cop in Portland, who had once been the most popular baby-sitter in his neighborhood. Many a meal had been laid on the table courtesy of his baby-sitting, when his father had drunk up the grocery money. But that was not for publication.

She put the child back in the pen and gave him a bowl

and a wooden spoon. "Future drummer," she said. "You'll see. Now, what did you want to know about this letter?"

"Your late husband was one of Dr. Pleasant's patients?"

"Donnie? Yeah. Guess I shouldn't have written it, huh? My sister says I shoot my mouth off too much. But I believe in speaking my mind. And what I thought's right there. That he didn't do Donnie any favors, and he sure didn't know a hell of a lot about human beings for someone who's a doctor. Am I in some kind of trouble? Is it like, a crime or something to criticize a doctor?"

She looked at the letter again, biting her lip as she reread what she'd written. "So I said I'd like to kick his ass all over Portland." She shrugged. "Donnie was a good man. Didn't deserve that crap. The cancer or that doctor's attitude. I didn't mean that about cutting him up for lobster bait. I'm usually pretty good at keepin' my temper. Have to, around these guys." She picked up her mug. "So why are you here?"

"Dr. Pleasant was killed a few days ago."

The mug paused in midair. "Killed like murdered?" He nodded. "Sorry. I never read newspapers. Just one more thing to pile up. Which you can see I don't need. Don't watch TV, either. By the end of a day, I like some peace and quiet. But you don't think . . ." The mug finished its journey to the table, making a rather rough landing. She stared at him with worried brown eyes. "You don't think that I . . ."

The child in the high chair started pounding on the tray. "Juice, juice, juice, juice."

She grabbed a sippy cup and held it out. "Here, Charlie. Here's your juice."

Declan burped loudly, beginning to fuss as he nuzzled Aucoin's shirt. "Give him here," she said. "This is one case where you haven't got what it takes." She pulled up her sweater and popped the baby underneath. When he was settled, her eyes traveled back to Burgess. "Why me?" she asked. "Why would you think I'd do something like that?"

"We've got a number of these letters. We're checking everybody out. When a person gets killed, we look to see who might have had a grudge."

"Oh, I've got a grudge all right. Person you care about gets treated bad, it sticks with you. I just don't see how more people dyin' is supposed to make things better." Over in the corner, a squabble broke out over a saucepan. "Officer Aucoin, I think we've got us a domestic dispute." She winked at Burgess. "As good a way to train cops as any," she said, handing the letter back. "I wish you luck finding who did it, but it wasn't me. I kept hopin' something would come along, make him see the light. Healin' isn't just about medicine and machines. Guess not, huh?"

"Did your husband have any friends or relatives who might have wanted to get back at Dr. Pleasant?"

"His brother, Lenny, was some pissed, but Lenny's too disorganized to get himself down to Portland to kill someone. By the time he'd got his gun and his dog and couple six-packs, and got on the road, he'd get distracted. Drink the beer. Lose the dog. Shoot out some street lights and come home."

Burgess wrote down an address for the brother. Put his coffee cup in the sink, folded his napkin so the crumbs wouldn't spill, and threw it in the trash. "Thank you for your time." He gave her a card. "If you think of anything." In the corner, three adoring girls were serving Aucoin tea. He looked so young and appealing and optimistic. Burgess wondered if he'd ever been any of those things. "Remy, you got things sorted out over there?"

"At this moment, polygamy looks very appealing."

"Their combined ages aren't old enough for you."

"I'm coming, sir." Aucoin untangled his long legs and bid his harem farewell. "Thanks for the coffee and cake."

"You're welcome. You're both welcome. And good luck," she said. "I think."

One of the little girls toddled up to Burgess and tugged on his pants. "Did you got a boo-boo on your head?" she asked. He nodded. "Does it need a kiss?" In the end, it needed three kisses to avert female rivalry.

"Where next?" Aucoin asked, when they were back in the car.

"Wiscasset."

"That was fun."

"Yes and no. Talking to nice people is fun. She even made good coffee, which is rare. Be better if we didn't have a murder to solve. If they weren't all hurting so much."

"Sorry, sir."

"Goddammit, Aucoin. You say 'sir' once more, I'll push you out and drive myself."

"Sorry, sir."

Burgess had to laugh. "I told you. I don't bite."

"Are you planning to stop for lunch?"

"You hungry?"

"I will be. I'm like my Uncle Guy. Eat all the time, never gain weight."

"You're lucky. I miss about half my meals, and look at me."

The interview in Wiscasset was brutal—the emotional equivalent of rubbing himself and the bereft family with sandpaper. Young mother dead, leaving her own grieving mother. Heartbroken, listless husband. Motherless twins. He left there drained, ready to sit in a dark bar and drink himself into oblivion. But he'd come this far. Might as well finish what he'd started, so he gave Aucoin the nod and they headed for Boothbay Harbor.

CHAPTER TWENTY-FIVE

If this was paint-by-number, the picture of Pleasant was pretty clear. Had the man had any idea how much he was disliked? Had he cared? And was that knowledge bringing them any closer to solving the homicide? The killer remained a blur.

The road was a swooping roller-coaster ride to a nice place way at the end of a peninsula. You could see the water from all over town, and the harbor and the ocean beyond looked exactly like Maine was supposed to look—a sheltered, rocky cove opening to a broad expanse of blue water dotted with little tree-covered islands and boats of all sizes and descriptions. He'd brought his nieces here when they were little—go for a boat ride, buy some souvenirs and fudge. In summer, the town got clogged up with traffic and pedestrians. Now, in February, things were cold and quiet.

He directed Aucoin through town, past the hospital, to a small cottage high on a spruce-clad point. Aucoin pulled out a Tom Clancy paperback. "Picked this up in Wiscasset. I figured you'd get tired, wouldn't want me tagging along."

Burgess nodded. "You figured right. That last one about did me in." He shut the door and walked up the icy stone path to the house. There were cross-country skis in a rack beside the door, a pair of snowshoes on a nail. He knocked. It was so dark inside he could barely see the woman who answered. "Sergeant Burgess, Portland police," he said.

"You're the detective?" she asked. He followed her down a dim flight of stairs and through a door, stopping suddenly, blinded by the brightness. He put his hand up to shield his eyes. The room he was in was two stories high, with glass on three sides. On the fourth side, on the second level, was a balcony. From the balcony hung a series of bright quilts. In the center of the room a quilt was laid out on a huge counter. Nearby, on a smaller table, was a sewing machine.

"Sorry," she said. "It's a mean trick, but I can't help it. People think they're coming to a little shack in the woods and then they find themselves here." She waved a hand around. "This is where I live. Where I work. Come sit down, detective." He followed her to a sitting area in front of the windows. On a small raised hearth, a white enamel stove threw off masses of heat. On top sat a cast-iron pot shaped like a dragon with steam pouring from its mouth. The oversized denim sofas were deep and inviting. The huge coffee table was piled with magazines and books.

"Just shove some of that stuff aside if you want to put your feet up," she said.

"That's okay."

"Can I fix you some tea? Conventional? Gerbil?"

"Gerbil?"

"Sorry. That's what my traditional friends call it. Herbal? I've never entertained a policeman before. Maybe you'd prefer coffee?"

So he was being entertained. "Tea is fine."

"I'll just be a minute. The water's hot." She disappeared through a door in the wall. She was a middle-sized, middle-aged woman with sun-streaked brown hair, probably artificial sun, and a smart, friendly face. Worn blue jeans fit snugly over a nice bottom. She wore a man's flannel shirt over a thermal undershirt. Cozy-looking thick red socks. No wedding ring. Her name was Sarah Merchant.

She was back in minutes with a tray. The teapot was

covered with a tea cozy his mother would have loved, bright colors and a cat. The mugs were a blueberry pattern. A matching plate held an assortment of cookies. "Girl Scouts," she said. "I can't say no, and then I eat the damned things. On a bad night, I can do in a whole box of the mint ones. You want sugar or honey? It's Firelight orange spice. Good with honey." She smiled as she bent to pour. "Sound like a commercial, don't I?" She slid his mug toward him, along with the honey and a spoon. "You were cryptic on the phone this morning. To what do I owe the pleasure of this visit?"

"What do you think?"

"Dr. Stephen Pleasant. May he roast in hell."

"You believe in hell?"

"Hope, maybe? Hell or purgatory. I'd like him to be treated to a few thousand years of his own brand of supercilious indifference. From what I've read, I imagine his death was reasonably quick. In a just world, he would have been incompetently misdiagnosed, more incompetently mistreated, and finally died a horrible and lingering death at the hands of clumsy nurses and exhausted interns and residents. Maybe desperately ringing his call bell and getting no human response."

"Guess you didn't like him, huh?"

She leaned forward, gripping her cup. "About most things, I am very balanced. But not on the subject of Dr. Pleasant."

She'd had a lot of time since his call to brood about this. "Did you kill him?"

"If I had, it would have been slow and horrible, and I haven't got the stomach for that. I'm pretty good at remembering and hating, but I'd be bad at execution. Too much of a coward. I didn't even sue the bastard."

"Why did you hate him so much?"

"Do," she corrected. "It's an ongoing thing. He killed my sister."

"Your sister?"

"Skip the bullshit. You know this or you wouldn't be here. Somehow, you've found my letter. There's no other way you could have known. I don't run ads in the *Press Herald*." She swept her hair back with both hands, held it a moment, then let go with a sigh. "It's been six years since my sister put her life in that jerk's hands. Six years. I hear that normal people get over things. Are sad for a while and then move on. Well, I've been sad for six years. I've moved on, but I'm not over it. I'm not sure I'm ever going to be. You ever do the death by cancer thing?"

He hadn't provoked this, except by coming. This wasn't about him or his questions. He'd started this case thinking his own feelings about Pleasant weren't relevant. Everything that had happened since was proving him wrong. He understood what was going on here better than he understood most of the things he did. For example, he knew little about Sarah Merchant except that they had too much in common. That if he stayed here long, there wouldn't be enough oxygen in the room for both of them.

"Ms. Merchant. What do you do for a living?"

She took a deep breath. Smiled her understanding. "I used to be a banker. Now I make memorial quilts."

"Memorial quilts?"

"I'll have to show you. I made one when my sister died. Showed it to a few people. They told other people, and suddenly, the phone was ringing. It was . . ." She stared out the window. When she spoke again, her voice was strained by that closing of the throat one can't control. "It was such a surprise. I made my first one as therapy for myself because of all the feelings I had no place to put. Then I discovered how many people needed to do some tangible thing."

She pulled out a tissue and wiped her eyes. Gray-green eyes exactly the color of the shirt she wore. Her eyes rose to his face, studied it, fell again. She lifted her mug with both hands and took a sip. "I'm not going to be able to say this well. I think about it. I live it. But I speak about it awkwardly. Too close, detective, even now."

She swallowed. "When someone dies, the people left behind need ways to remember them. People want to perform tangible acts of respect, of memorializing, that don't end with funeral services. That's why people with money donate buildings or scholarships. People with less money give books. So the person's name goes on. But it's more than that. What we really want for people we've loved is for their stories to go on. For the goodness of them, the special things that made them who they were, not to die. We want something we can show to other people, and say, 'This is who my loved one was.' "

She lowered the mug, which she'd been holding before her like a shield. "Do you know what I mean?"

He felt stirred as he rarely did and unsettled by it. His job was to unsettle others. He was the one who pried and probed, stirred up emotions and caused desired responses. He knew exactly what she was talking about. He wanted to stay and share stories. To run from here before she pulled him into her emotional firestorm. He wanted to stop her from saying more. To grab her and wring out a confession.

"Show me your sister's quilt," he said.

She led him back up the stairs, through the dark entry, and into a bedroom. She flipped some switches, illuminating a quilt on one wall. In the center was a big square with a tombstone on it. A large black tombstone with

261

grayish black wings. In the center, embroidered in white, the name, Carman Merchant, and the dates of her birth and death. The other squares varied. Some were color photographs copied onto fabric. Some were fabric pictures, some extremely simple, others elaborate. There were two pink panels, marking the births of baby girls. Four panels together made an elaborate embroidered vegetable garden, surrounded by a white picket fence.

"That stuff where you make the pictures out of cloth. What's it called?"

"Appliqué."

His eyes roved over the pictures—one simply an enormous blueberry, another a potato. There were fish poles and cigarettes and sewing machines. A stack of books. Pies with lattice crusts and loaves of bread. A pizza. A shapely waitress staggering under the weight of a tray. A mother sledding down a hill with two children. A dog. A red heart with an arrow through it and two sets of initials, like kids made in grade school.

"If I say my sister died, she was a very special person, you don't know anything about her. If I show you this quilt, you know things about her life, her children, the fact that she was in love. You know about her cooking. Her green thumb. Carman could hold her hand out over a patch of ground and plants would spring up to touch it."

Burgess stared at the quilt and thought of his mother. She would have loved this. He saw Carman Merchant's story and wanted his mother's life so tenderly sewn and quilted and appliquéd and embroidered. He wanted a wall for his mother. A wall for Kristin Marks. Her life had been brief, yet he could think of a dozen things for her quilt. He thought about Sarah Merchant's wall and his closet door. Their shrines.

He turned away, looking instead at the framed pictures on her dresser. Sarah and her sister and her sister's children. Sarah and a handsome guy posing against a truck with a black dog. Husband? Boyfriend?

He repeated his question. "Did you kill him?"

"Let me show you some others," she said. "Downstairs."

She walked him along the wall, showing him the three quilts hanging from the railing. "These are waiting to be picked up. This first one is . . . well, why don't you tell me?"

But he was here for a purpose. He was tired. And this walk down memory lane was tearing the scabs off his wounds. "The quilts," he said, feeling the constriction in his throat, hearing it in his voice. "How long do they take?"

"Each one is different. A few weeks. A month, perhaps."

"You can't make a living."

"I do make a living. You'd be surprised what people will pay for something like this. For something that matters . . . all that money they spend on fancy caskets and gravestones . . ." She interrupted herself. "I don't need much. I have a little money. I do it to make a connection, because it matters."

She pulled off the heavy flannel shirt and flung it over the back of the sofa. The tight thermal shirt outlined her body. She was smaller than he'd first thought, with a compact female roundness that was very appealing. God, he was like a bear waking up from hibernation. So long not noticing women much, suddenly they were everywhere, filling his wintry landscape with buttocks and breasts. Chris Perlin, yesterday, and now, Sarah Merchant. This case had shaken him, stirred up his own bad memories and violent impulses. Violence and lust, he knew, were close on the emotional spectrum.

She sat across from him, her face sad, her arms wrapped

263

tightly around her body. Six years later, it still hurt. He asked his question again. "Did you kill Dr. Pleasant?"

She shook her head. "I considered it but I'm not brave enough. I've been trying to work out my anger through the quilts. By helping other people with their anger. And sorrow. Sometimes it feels like I have this anger inside . . ." She made a circle with her fingers and rested it on her stomach. "Here. Like a big ball of yarn. I'm drawing it out, bit by bit, unrolling the ball, so that the hurt and anger get smaller. It takes so long."

"Do you know of anyone else who might have wanted to harm Dr. Pleasant?"

She tensed. "Wanted to? Or would?"

"Someone who might have killed him."

It was getting dark. The water was deepening into an angry lead color. It looked cold and unfriendly. Even in the warm room, he felt the chill of it.

"Someone who wanted to? I don't know," she said, finally. And then, as though that gave too much away, "No. No. Of course I don't." Too loudly. He could tell by the stiffening in her body, the way she drew back, that she regretted the words the instant they left her lips.

Aucoin would have to wait. He opened his notebook. "Who is it, Sarah?"

She walked to the window and stared out at the water, her body outlined against the light. "No one. I told you. I have no idea who killed him."

"I think you have a pretty good idea."

Tension had erased all ease from her body. In the silence, the woodstove popped. Waves slapped the rocks. And he could hear her breathing.

At last she said, "I don't know, detective. I need to think about this. I'm not saying I know something, but even if I did, it's a pretty serious business, telling a cop that someone you know might have information about a murder. I mean, it's really up to them to decide whether to talk to you, isn't it?" She kept her back to him. "I think it's time for you to go."

Someone she knew pretty well. Someone who, if it wasn't Sarah herself, shared the same reason for hating Pleasant. "It's not okay to kill people, Sarah," he said, using her name, trying to reach her.

She turned, but now she'd mastered her face and it gave nothing away.

"It wasn't okay for him to make a fatal mistake, if that's what you think he did," Burgess continued. "But even if that happened, it's not remedied by killing him. We have rules about killing, a social compact we have to keep, or everything becomes chaos and safety becomes random."

She listened politely, but he felt his words bouncing off a blank wall. He was being too abstract. "Look what you've been saying. Six years of sorrow and anger. Maybe that can make you, or this person you know, think revenge could be a cure. But it isn't, Sarah. I've seen the corrosive effects of revenge. It's not sweet or satisfying. It doesn't end anything. The one who kills Pleasant is dragged down to his level. If you kill him because he killed your sister, you become like him. You lose your reason for hating him. Your justification."

"So hating's okay, but acting on it isn't? Doesn't hating end up just as corrosive?"

"I'm a cop, Sarah. I've seen people so bad the whole society would be better off if they were dead. I can't let myself start thinking that it's okay to make those judgments and act on them. None of us can. You know that." He watched her face for understanding or agreement. All he saw was sadness.

He searched for another approach. He was supposed to be good at getting people to talk. It was especially frustrating because he liked this woman, felt a kinship with her. But that was personal. He was here because he was a cop on a job, with a cop's distrust and caution, facing another woman who had something he wanted and wouldn't give it to him. He understood divided loyalties, but sometimes he wanted to grab the whole damned world and shake it.

The bright room had grown gloomy. Eventually it would all be dark except the glowing eye of the stove, the eerie white plume of steam from the dragon's mouth. Across from him hung the banners of three lives. They, too, would fade into darkness. This whole place was about memory and loss and sorrow. There was too damned much pain here. He wanted her cooperation. He needed to get out. The gut instincts of three good cops had led him through a painful day to this room. He didn't want to leave without getting what he'd come for.

"Will you tell me?" he asked. She didn't answer. "Will you at least talk to this other person? Ask if they'll talk to me?"

She moved to a lamp and turned it on, bathing their part of the room in warm yellow light, illuminating a long blonde hair on the cushion beside him. Too long to be hers, and too blonde. Casually, he wrapped it around his finger. Slipped the finger into his pocket. Felt the hair unwrap.

"I'll think about it," she said. "But I'm not sure I agree with you. I think sometimes it's okay to take matters into your own hands. As you said, there are people out there who do more harm than good. It's not my decision. We're talking about other people's choices, about an anger that's even stronger than ours. Or maybe a hate." She refused to look at him. "I'll see if there's anything to tell you."

He'd been tantalizingly close. He snapped his notebook shut, shoved it in his pocket, and stood up.

She stood, too. "You're angry," she said.

"I'm frustrated. A man is dead and it's my job to find his killer. I've spent my day showing up on people's doorsteps and reminding them of their sorrow. Sometimes that's what I have to do to find the answers. You're not making it easy."

"But living with hate isn't easy, is it?" She lifted her arms, as though she was going to embrace him, then dropped them again. She wasn't trying to be seductive yet he felt seduced. There was something here that he longed for. Comfort, maybe, or understanding. The neutral expression she'd put on had gone. She looked wounded. It took effort not to put an arm around her. Not to say he understood.

"I wish I *could* make it easier," she said, stepping away. "How do I reach you?"

He gave her a card, writing his home number on the back. Something he never did. "Call me," he said. "Any time."

"I will. God," she said, "it's gloomy in here, isn't it?"

He didn't answer. He followed her up the stairs—this time she put on a light—and across the small hall to the door. "My sister," she said softly. "Carman was so funny sometimes. She had this way of . . . I don't know . . . giving me a look . . . when someone was being pompous. It would just crack me up. And she was such an iconoclast. I'd get all puffed up about being a banker and she'd skewer *me* with one of those looks. God, I miss her."

"I have to go," he said.

"Of course *you* have to go. You can come here, push your way into my life and stir everything up. Then you can walk away, while I'll be up half the night, remembering. I wonder how you can do it?"

He reached out a hand to comfort her, then pulled back, wanting her to stew in this. Wanting her to decide to help him. To do the right thing. "I do it because a man is dead. I wish . . ." But he didn't know what he wished, so he left it there, not looking back as he went down the slippery stone path to the car.

CHAPTER TWENTY-SIX

The motor was running, the radio on, and Aucoin was happily reading his book. He snapped it shut when Burgess got in. "Excuse me, sir," he said, "but you look beat."

Beat? He felt flayed. Utterly drained. In the center of his exhaustion, the questions raised by Sarah Merchant pricked and irritated like a splinter. "Day's not over yet. Remember this when you think about being a detective. Digging up old hurts and tromping through people's private lives, it's not always a hell of a lot of fun. Nor is knowing people are holding out on you and you can't break them down. Anyone looking for me?"

"Stan Perry."

"See if you can find him." He got an evidence envelope, wrote on the outside, pulled the hair from his pocket, and slipped it in. He tilted the seat back and closed his eyes. His arm was a big hot ache going right to the bone. He had to deal with it before he could think. He swallowed a pill with the only liquid available—warm root beer. It was enough to gag a maggot.

"Here's Detective Perry," Aucoin said, handing him the phone and turning off the radio.

"Other than a couple people who wished they could claim credit, my day was a bust," Stan said. "How about yours?"

"Maybe not. I'm still figuring that out. You hear from Terry?"

"Yeah. His was a bust, too. Says he feels like scum, doing that to people."

"Ole Terry's getting soft, I guess."

"I feel like scum, too. Don't you?"

"I'll get over it. You let this get to you, you might as well go back to property crimes. Harder to feel sorry for a guy who's lost a jackhammer or VCR."

"You've got that right. Look, Terry wants to know can we go to the steakhouse? Run down the day and where we go from here over some decent food? I think he's feeling carnivorous."

Sounded like Kyle was feeling explosive, needed calming down. Right now, tearing into something rare and bloody sounded good. "Fine with me. Where are you?"

"Back at the shop."

"Can you go by Salerno's again, flash Pleasant's picture around, see if anyone on the night crew remembers him?"

"No problem. See you in . . . how long? Hour and a half?"

"Closer to an hour. Aucoin drives fast."

"Terry's gone over to that drug store. One the old lady told you about? Following up on prescription records. So he can fill you in on that."

"Back to the station," Burgess told Aucoin. "Feel free to speed."

He hadn't expected to sleep with so much on his mind, but the hum of the tires was like a lullaby. Not even the gaudy magnificence of a winter sunset could keep his eyes open. He dreamed about a quilting bee, sitting around his living room with Kyle and Perry, his cousin Sam, the Cape Elizabeth chief, and a few other cops. All of them in uniform, bristling with brass and badges, the flesh of their necks red against the tight collars. They had his mother's bone china tea cups beside them, his sister's quilting frame set up, big clumsy hands dragging needles in and out of

some soft gray-green fabric the color of Sarah Merchant's
eyes.

He woke because someone was shaking him. They were
back at the station, Aucoin bent stork-like over him, looking
anxious. "What's wrong?"

"I couldn't wake you, sir."

It was hard coming back, leaving the pleasing fantasy of
a group of men with tattered spirits gathering to stitch them
back together and returning to this mire of unanswered
questions. "I'm okay," he said. "Sleep did me good."

Aucoin relaxed then. He gathered up his book and his
trash, smiling shyly as he got out. "Thanks. I enjoyed it,
sir."

"Don't call me 'sir.' "

Aucoin looked around, full of wonder at being part of
the copshop. "Have to, sir."

How did they do it? How did they keep suckering them
into this job, with its bad pay and lousy hours? When he
was a baby cop, he'd just come back from Vietnam, full of
bad memories and bad dreams, coming into a society not
supportive of cops or vets. He'd bounced between wonder
and cynicism like a yo-yo. Couldn't ever remember feeling
the pure pleasure that Aucoin did. But he remembered the
adrenaline rush. He'd been an adrenaline junkie. Still was.

"Right." He held out his hand for the keys.

"I could stick around," Aucoin offered. "Drive you to
the steakhouse? I don't mind."

"You working tonight? Late out?" Aucoin nodded. Even
if the kid got overtime, the schedule was brutal. "Give yourself a break. Go to the gym, work the kinks out before you
have to get back behind the wheel. Or catch a few winks."
Aucoin gave him the keys, then turned and walked away.
Upright and jaunty. He'd just survived a whole day with the

meanest cop in Portland and the old fart wasn't so bad. Burgess put the keys in his pocket and followed Aucoin inside. Not particularly upright—even with the pills, his arm hurt like a bastard—and not jaunty. He had too much on his mind.

Upstairs, he dumped himself into his chair and pulled the evidence envelope out of his pocket. He was thinking about getting up when Stan Perry strolled in. Another upright, jaunty soul. Goddamned kids. Much as he liked this young detective, he hated the way Stan made him feel his age. Wouldn't trade his experience—most of it, anyway—but he'd give anything for a second wind and working knees. He handed Perry the envelope. "Can you take this to the lab? Get someone to compare it to the ones in Dr. Pleasant's hand."

Perry seized it eagerly. "So maybe your day wasn't unproductive. I'll call down. Maybe Wink's still around."

It was too soon to get excited. But just as the day had been set in motion by a gut instinct, this hair represented another. He expected a match. He started through his messages. Couple from his sister. Six from Cote. No information, just to please call. He tried Cote's office, car and home. Didn't find him anywhere. Left messages all three places, genuflecting to authority.

Stan was back before he'd looked through his in-box or finished the messages. "Wink's playing with his Superglue right now. When he's done, he'll take a look. Oh, and something else. I ran down a hunch."

"Hunches. Gut feelings. Man, we are such pros."

"What have we done now?" Kyle asked, coming to join them.

"Stan's got a hunch."

Kyle touched his palms together in silent applause. "Let's hear it."

"To put you in the loop . . ." Perry began, in a perfect imitation of Cote's pompous voice. "What if O'Leary was the one who whacked Pleasant?"

"Why do the video if he's planning to whack the guy?" Kyle asked.

"Maybe our boy O'Leary liked two scoops? Whack Pleasant, then sell the tape to his grieving widow. Maybe he blackmailed the wife and her rich daddy and Pleasant didn't even know. And then I'm thinking, what would incentivize our boy to whack one of his best clients?"

"Money," Kyle said.

"Exactly. So I figure if he's got a bank account, it's probably at a bank near his house, right? I call over to that bank and sure enough, I find a sweet young thing who doesn't know she's not supposed to spill the beans just 'cause I say I'm a cop investigating a murder. I ask her to look at deposits in O'Leary's bank account, which she does, and lo and behold—the day Pleasant gets whacked, O'Leary deposits six thousand dollars."

"Can we trace it?" Burgess asked.

"Cash."

"Could be drug money," Burgess said, "but I'd love to know whether Dr. Ken Bailey or Ted Shaw made a cash withdrawal in that amount around that time."

"It's a thought," Kyle agreed. "But what about the widow or her stepdaddy?"

"Shaw probably keeps that kind of cash around as mad money," Perry said.

"Six thousand's not that much," Burgess said. "Have to be bigger money to kill a cash cow like Pleasant. Three blow jobs a week, plus all that Oxycontin. O'Leary's not that stupid."

"He is stupid. He's a thug, not a businessman," Kyle

said, swaying wearily, but not sitting down. "Probably not thinking ahead. His kind don't."

"Then I wonder why we haven't found him," Burgess said. "Guys like that tend to stay close to home."

"That's what his momma said. I called her. She's worried. So maybe somebody's whacked him," Perry suggested. "But who?"

"Another scumbag for hire, or . . ." Kyle smiled diabolically. "Dr. Bailey kills him with a lethal injection of potassium, cuts him up in tiny pieces and feeds him to the fishes." His sunken eyes glittered wickedly. "Full fathom five O'Leary lies—"

"I think you've been working too hard, Terry," Burgess said. "We need to take you out for a nice dinner and send you to bed."

"All alone?" Kyle said forlornly. He looked pathetic, red eyes, lids at half-mast, clothes rumpled. He needed a shave. Any day after five he needed a shave. All that testosterone going to waste. If this didn't break soon, they'd have to take a day off or they'd be at each other's throats.

"Joe knows some nice hookers," Perry said. "There's bound to be one who'll take on an ugly mutt like you if you pay her enough."

"Who's up for steak?" Burgess said.

"Through Cote's heart? I am," Stan said. "He leaves me all these messages and when I call, all he wants to know is where we are. Like we're his kids or something. Like dispatch didn't know."

"The image is too unpleasant," Kyle said. "I'm not going there."

"It won't be any fun, dining without you."

"Put a sock in it, Stan, will ya?" Burgess said. "Who's driving?"

"If we got Aucoin to drive us, we could all drink ourselves into a stupor," Perry said. "How was it, today, Joe? Did he genuflect and kiss your feet?"

"He's not a bad kid."

"Oho!" Perry slapped Kyle on the shoulder. "Mad dog Burgess likes the kid."

"Put a sock in it, Stan," he repeated. "I'll drive. But one of you has to cut my steak."

The steakhouse was all dim lights, dark wood, and ample, high-backed booths, country-western in the background. The hostess led them to a corner in the back, smiling at Perry as she lifted the amber glass shade and lit their candle. "Been a while, Stan."

He shrugged apologetically. "Got a promotion, Tina. Better title. Longer hours. Same money. Go figure, huh?"

"Yeah?" She let the question hang in the air a minute while she passed out menus. "I just figured you were a play-the-field kinda guy." She swept the table with a look, taking them in, weighing them like they'd weighed her. A woman who liked to know what she was up against. "You all cops?" When no one answered, she gave a lopsided grin. "Oh yeah. Like you'd tell me, right? Michelle will be your waitress tonight. Make Stan keep his hands off her. His hands go anywhere . . ." She gave just the faintest suggestion of a shimmy. "It's right here."

She strode away, leaving Perry staring admiringly after her. She wore a short, tight black dress and high heels. Nice rear view.

"Wipe your mouth, Stan," Kyle said. "You're drooling."

"I love redheads," Perry murmured, shaking his head at his folly. "Why haven't I called her? She never whined."

They were bent over their menus when a voice asked, "Can I get any of you gentlemen a drink?"

Perry and Kyle lit up. If the hostess was the appetizer, Michelle was the main dish. The costume for waitresses was conventional—short black skirt, white shirt, a little black bow tie, but she'd converted it into something distinct and unforgettable. A swishy black skirt with a visible white lace petticoat, and a tucked-front white blouse that gave new meaning to the expression "stuffed shirt." Lovely long legs. When she left to get their wine, a chorus of sighs went around.

"Anyone want to talk about the day?" Burgess asked. When no one answered, he said, "Yeah, like you'd tell me, right?"

"Not now, Joe," Kyle said. "I think I'm in love."

She reminded Burgess of a girl he'd dated in high school. Same innocent face with impossibly sexy lips, same honey-blonde ponytail, even the same touch of blue eye shadow. He looked at Kyle, who was visibly smitten, and remembered getting up the courage to ask for a date. Standing at the mirror, rehearsing his request, trying to imagine that small, delicate body pressed against his own massive one. Back then he'd felt bigger than he did now, and wondered how it all worked? How did big guys like him get together with small girls without hurting them? He'd asked for a date, all tight throat and dry mouth, and she'd said yes. The first time he'd touched her breast he'd gotten dizzy.

When Michelle came back with the wine, Perry flashed his badge at her. "I wonder if you'd mind answering a few questions?"

She stopped struggling to extract the cork. "About what?"

"Are you married?" She shook her head. "Engaged?" Another negative. "Living with someone?"

"That's really none of your business."

"Please?"

"No."

"Well, then," Perry said. "I'd like to introduce you to a really nice guy. You got anything against cops?"

She'd been trying not to smile, now she gave it up. "My uncle's a cop."

"Michelle, I'd like you to meet my friend, Terry Kyle. Detective Kyle. Portland police. Terry, this is Michelle."

"Pleased to meet you, detective," she said, reaching a hand across the table. Kyle had no choice but to reach back. She turned up the wattage on her smile and held on to his hand. "I wondered if you'd ever get up the nerve to introduce yourself. You married?" He shook his head. "Engaged?" Another shake. "Living with someone?"

"Nope."

"I get off at eleven," she said. "Maybe you could give me a ride home." She dropped his hand and finished with the wine, pouring for Kyle first. Watching attentively while he tasted it, then pouring for the others. She pulled out her order pad. "You all know what you want?" They ordered New York sirloins, medium rare, baked potatoes, and salad. "I'll go get you some bread," she said. "Be right back." She winked at Kyle.

"What am I missing here?" Burgess asked.

"You're the detective," Perry said.

"Running on fumes right now. How about Terry's been coming here and mooning over Michelle, but he's too shy to do anything, so Stan decides he's going to help out? This dinner isn't about talking shop or food. We're playing the dating game. What am I, by the way, the chaperone?"

"That's right. When's the last time you picked up a girl in a bar? Jesus, Joe, you live like a fuckin' monk," Perry said. "You're so goddamned smart, tell me this—are we getting anywhere with this fucking case?"

"Think we're getting closer. Want me to run it down for you?"

Perry drained his glass and refilled it, his eyes on the hostess, who'd paused after seating another party to let him admire her. "Maybe later."

"Oh, right," Kyle said. "You're so eager to be the world's best detective you'd eat dog food if it'd help you get ahead, but you don't wanna listen to Joe Burgess, who was solving crimes while you were still peddling your tricycle?"

"Give it a rest," Stan snapped.

"I want to hear it," Kyle said. "This mean you got something today, Joe?"

"A woman who really hated Pleasant. One long blonde hair and a big stonewall. I'm peeking through a crack . . ." They'd come to talk, but he wasn't ready. This was too nebulous. And despite the elevated lust levels, they were still too irritable. "So we got nothing on O'Leary?"

Kyle sighed. "You heard Stan. His mother hasn't seen him. His girlfriend hasn't seen him. His scumbag friends haven't seen him. He's vanished off the face of the earth. O'Leary's like a lot of dumb guys, keeps regular habits, so something's going on."

"Other than that he knows the cops are looking for him?" Perry said.

"Something to check—what size shoes he wears. What kind," Burgess said. "Dani's print is an eleven Reebok."

Kyle was quiet but not morose like he'd been earlier. The slouch was gone and his eyes were open. There was even the touch of a smile on the narrow mouth. He was arranging his forks so the tines lined up. "O'Leary as the killer doesn't make sense," he said suddenly. "If he was pimping for Pleasant and moving the drugs, he was making too much money. Just look at Oscar Libby. Pleasant prescribes a month's supply of eighty-milligram pills just days before he dies. Call it maybe fifty pills, with a street value of eighty bucks per, you've got four thousand dollars. Even if he got only half the money, that's not bad. And that's only one patient. We ask around, I bet we find Pleasant was writing scripts for O'Leary, too, and maybe some of his girls. I've got another idea."

"You said he was stupid," Perry said, reaching for the wine bottle. "Why not go for the quick buck?"

"Wait," Burgess said.

Michelle set a basket of rolls in front of Kyle. "I'll be right back with your salads." She rested her hand lightly on Kyle's shoulder. Burgess hoped the poor guy could hold his thought in the face of the obvious rush he was experiencing. "You need anything else?"

They shook their heads, but as soon as she was out of hearing range, Perry said, "Yeah, honey. He needs a blow job. Quick!"

"Don't," Kyle said.

"Your theory?" Burgess reminded him.

"The mystery girl. She set it up for the guy in the truck. He did Pleasant, then he did O'Leary because O'Leary knew too much about Pleasant's dirty business."

"Then how come we got nothin' on this guy in the truck? You're making this too complicated," Stan said. "Your mystery girl's just a hooker. That's all a wild goose chase."

"She was looking for Pleasant," Burgess said quietly. "Asked to be set up with him. Couple different people saw her and the guy. And nobody we talked to, none of the hookers or pimps, had ever seen her before."

"Too fuckin' weird. Mystery girls. Mystery guys. Maybe the guy was O'Leary?" Perry suggested.

"This guy had dark, curly hair. Hazel eyes. Handsome," Burgess said. "That sound like O'Leary to you? This is a guy who tells Alana Black he's not interested in sex."

279

"Then who the hell is he?" Stan said.

"Hold on," Kyle interrupted. "Getting back to O'Leary for a minute. If he wasn't acting on his own, who hired him, Joe?"

"Couple good possibilities are Shaw or Bailey. Guys with big money looking for the easy solution to a blackmailer? Or what about Jack Kelly? He's not rich, but he loved his daughter. And he was way pissed at Pleasant."

"What about the wife?" Kyle began, but Perry interrupted.

"Salerno's. Guy who owns the place remembered Pleasant coming in there. Came in with a girl. A real babe, the guy said. Stacked. Blonde. It was close to closing time. They ate pizza, mooned about like lovers, then left."

"Doesn't sound like Pleasant. I keep hearing cold and indifferent," Burgess said.

"Me, too," Kyle said.

Perry shrugged. "He ID'd the photo. Maybe this girl was something special. Or it was the transforming power of love. Not that he hadn't already been in every available orifice and paid for the privilege. How the hell should I know?"

"You sound cranky, Stan," Kyle said quietly.

"Why the hell shouldn't I? I spend the whole fuckin' day rubbing people's faces in their own sorrow and here we haven't any of us got the balls to march out to his big house and ask Ted fuckin' big shot Shaw if he offed his son-in-law. If we were to even suggest it, Cote would soil his pants, wouldn't he, Joe?"

"You'd be back in uniform, working traffic. I'd be pushing papers and writing some damned report on the correlation between traffic stops and the age, race and sex of the drivers. And only Terry here would be left to carry the torch of justice."

"How come he gets to stay?"

Kyle was right. Perry did sound cranky. And Kyle, despite the magic of Michelle's presence, wasn't far behind. "Terry's our secret weapon. Cote thinks Terry's a quiet little goody-goody."

"Where the fuck's he been?" Perry muttered.

Kyle snorted and moved his spoon over to join his forks, carefully adding it to the line, then flipped back the napkin and took a roll. "Skipped lunch," he said. "Too depressed to eat. God, what a rotten day!"

"Anybody see the surveillance tape from the video store yet?" Burgess asked. "Or the results of the door-to-door on that street? Any news about the car?"

"We were on the fucking road," Stan complained. "You know that. We were at drug stores and pizza joints. We haven't exactly been sitting on our butts pushing papers. You're beginning to sound like that ass-wipe Cote."

He'd rather die. Burgess held up his hands. "Okay. Okay. I'm sorry," he said. "I know it's been a lousy day. Let's just eat."

Michelle hurried up with their salads, looking flustered. Some of her hair had come out of her ponytail and her tie was askew. "Couple guys being jerks, tried to make me sit with them." She shrugged. "It happens." There was a run in her stocking, like someone had grabbed her leg with rough fingers.

Kyle reached for *her* hand. "Hey," he said, half rising, "want me to talk to them?"

She gave him that smile again, eyelids coming down shyly over her eyes and didn't pull her hand back. "It's under control. I think. But thanks."

"You let me know." Reluctantly, he let go and dropped back into his seat.

They ate their salads in silence. Finished the wine and ordered another bottle, food becoming a substitute for conversation, a space between where they'd been and where they hoped to go. Kyle broke the silence. "We working tonight?"

"We've been working."

"Later?" He was a man with a plan.

Burgess shook his head. "I'm going back. See if the lab has anything for me. You can ride back with me to get your cars, but unless something breaks, you might as well get some rest." He smiled. "Or whatever."

"I'm hoping for whatever," Perry said. "Aren't you, Terry?"

Kyle just smiled.

When the check came, Burgess slapped down his credit card. "This one's on me."

"Thanks, Dad," Perry said. " 'Preciate it."

Burgess thought he had it just right. All evening he'd felt like a father out with his grown sons, putting up with their bad moods and flirtations, alternating between wanting to reel them in, and hoping they were going to get laid. He hoped they'd come back, pick up Tina and Michelle, and have some fun. Hoped nothing would happen so he'd have to call them away, though he had an uneasy feeling it might. He looked at his watch, amazed at the hour. The place was almost empty. Something to that old adage about time flying when you're having fun. "Let's go, kids. It's late."

There was a pause at the door, while Kyle and Perry said goodnight to their respective ladies and firmed up plans for later. The door was just closing behind them when a voice, unmistakably Michelle's, yelled, "Hey! Stop that! Let me go."

The two aggressive young businessmen who were trying

to force Michelle to join them by grabbing her and dragging her into the booth were surprised to find themselves facing three men with guns on their belts. Michelle was liberated, and, in the interest of avoiding further calamity, she was removed from the premises by the police, and placed in the back seat of an official vehicle. She and Kyle billed and cooed all the way back to the station.

By the time he'd parked and thrown the car into gear, Burgess had had his fill of human contact. He left them to sort things out, and went upstairs to check his messages. Hoping Sarah Merchant had decided to do the right thing. Knowing she hadn't.

CHAPTER TWENTY-SEVEN

Some people think there's nothing lonelier than an office in the middle of the night, but Burgess liked the emptiness, the distant building sounds around him. During the day, it was all commotion. At night, walls creaked and the elevator whirred and clocks ticked. Doors shut with metallic thuds, latches clicked, casters on chairs whizzed audibly across plastic rug protectors. You could hear a piece of paper fall into a trash can.

He checked his voice mail. Nothing from Cote, which didn't surprise him, nor from Wink, which did. He called down to the lab. Got Wink's weary, "Devlin, crime lab."

"It's Joe. Got anything for me?"

"I'm not here," Devlin said. "I went home hours ago." He snorted. "Sorry. Haven't gotten to it, Joe. All hell's been breaking loose tonight. I was going to leave it 'til morning, but what the heck. Why don't you come down and we'll have a look."

The hair had been shimmering in the back of his mind all evening. He walked downstairs. Devlin was standing at the counter, adjusting a microscope. "It's all set up," he said. "Take a look. Left one was taken from Pleasant's hand. Right's the one you gave me tonight."

Burgess hesitated. For Devlin it was all in a day's work, but he had such high hopes for these two strands. He needed a match. A solid clue to Pleasant's killer. Ever since he'd leaned into that car, shivering in the wind, intent on rescuing those fragile golden hairs, he'd been working toward this moment. Since he'd seen the awful look on Pleasant's face, the ugly state of degradation the body had been left in, the very literal way he'd been caught with his pants down. Recalled the ultimate irony—that as he'd leaned into the car, the oldies station had been playing "It's My Party." Little Leslie Gore. A delicious piece of sick cop humor.

He walked to the microscope and peered in, the initial distorted, underwater quality resolving into amazing clarity. If Devlin hadn't told him, he never would have known he was looking at hair. "Looks like two feathers to me." He stared until his eyes watered. "Two yellow feathers. You're going to have to tell me. Have we got a match here or not?"

"You're no fun," Devlin said. "Don't you want to guess?"

Burgess sighed. So many days gone, so many people seen, so far from cracking this thing. "I'm too old, too tired and way too deep into this for fun, Wink. I'm just praying for a break before we start tearing each other's throats out. As for guessing, at this point, I'd be grateful for something better than a guess."

"Sorry," Devlin said soberly. "Do enough of this, sometimes I forget this isn't just about what we discover down here." He paused. "Congratulations, detective. Looks like you've got yourself a match."

Burgess patted Devlin on the shoulder. "Good job, Wink. Now if I can just find the person who shed that hair."

Devlin smiled. "Nice to be able to deliver some good news. And by the way, only the one on the right was shed. The one on the left was pulled, which means, with luck, DNA. I'll write it up and then I'm going home. Which is what you should do, too. Tomorrow will be here before you know it."

"I think it already is."

Burgess walked back upstairs, sat down, and reached for the phone. Then he put it down again. It was after midnight. Calling Sarah Merchant could wait until morning. Instead, he called his cousin Sam, the Cape Elizabeth cop. Not troubled about making this call after midnight. His cousin slept as badly, and as rarely, as he did. He smiled, as usual, when the voice that sounded like his own said, "Burgess."

"It's Joe," he said.

"I thought you'd call me sooner."

"Been busy."

"Yeah. Hear you got a nasty one. I know you didn't call to chat. What's up?"

"Ted Shaw."

"You like him for it? He doesn't strike me as the hands-on type."

"I like him in the background, pulling strings."

"Sounds more like it." Burgess heard the rustle of a cigarette being pulled from a package, the click of a lighter. Heard the intake of breath and the long, slow exhale. Sam had never been in a rush to do anything, even as a kid. Smartest person Joe knew who still smoked. "God, I love these things. So, cuz, what do you want from me?"

"I'd like to know if anything unusual happens out there. Any extra cars, visitors, commotion, noise. Digging in the yard."

"Think he's going to bury a body or something?"

"That's exactly what I think, but I've got no leverage to get in the door."

"Man doesn't exactly invite the casual chat, does he? Well, we don't get much excitement out here. Boys'll be happy to have something to do. Discreetly, of course. I'll give 'em the word. See if anything turns up." He coughed again, and spoke to his dog. "I'll do that before I take this damned canine out for her walk. If this is how getting old's gonna be, I think I'd like to be shot. She's got everything failing, has to be taken out every few hours, still thinks she's a beautiful puppy. You see what a nice night it is?"

"Haven't had the pleasure. You come up with anything, call me right away, okay? And tell Miriam I said hello."

He put the phone down, newly energized. This was how he'd expected to feel the past couple days. He couldn't tell whether it was the rejuvenating pleasure of a new lead, or the restorative powers of steak. Either way, he wasn't complaining. It hurt like a bastard but he could use his arm again, could get around without a baby-sitter. When he stood up, his body came with him. He felt lighter and freer, maybe because he was finally alone and it was night. These were a few of his favorite things.

He stared at his in-basket, overflowing with papers, things that needed looking at, stuff to go in the case file. He shuffled through it idly, sorting it into piles, dialing his home machine to check messages. Wedged at the side was a note from Remy Aucoin with a field interview card attached. There were a couple messages from Sandy, asking him to call. His eyes were scanning Aucoin's note when his sister's voice exploded off the tape: "Goddammit, Joe! You can't just drop this girl in my lap and disappear. I've called and called. At home. At work. You're never there, or you won't return my calls. She needs to see you, to talk to you. Don't you understand?"

There was a silence, and then, before it cut off, she was back, still explosive. "You call me, Joe, whenever you get this message. I don't care what time it is. If she takes off just because you won't be responsible, it's your fault!" The message ended abruptly. There was another message, immediately afterward. This time Sandy's voice was more subdued. "Please. She's so nervous and edgy she's making me crazy. If she takes off, and something happens to her, I'll blame you."

He reached for the phone, then decided to finish Aucoin's note first. Anything was better than Sandy's wrath. Her mood would not be improved by the fact that it was nearly one a.m. He picked up the note. "Sgt. Burgess, wondered if I'd missed anything, so I went back through the cards and found this. Maybe it will help. Aucoin."

The card, dated a month before, was not an interview but only a field observation. Suspicious vehicle. Seen in the area before, with a male subject in the driver's seat. Old GMC pickup. White cap on the back. And a license number. Feeling like a hunting dog on a fresh scent, he got the owner's name and address and wrote the information in his notebook. Then he called Sandy.

Her husband Mike answered, a sleepy, anxiety-edged hello. "Sorry, Mike," he said. "It's Joe. I need to talk with Sandy."

Mike didn't say anything, but Burgess could hear soft voices and rustling sounds as Sandy was roused. When she finally did come on the line, his sister began with a sigh, a silence, and then, "It's too late. She's gone."

He couldn't say, "Why didn't you call me," because she'd tried. "When?"

"Couple hours ago."

"Any idea where she went?"

"None. She left you a note, though."

He was heading north anyway. "I'll be right over."

"What's your hurry?" Rustling sheets. "Sorry. I just get tired of all the drama, Joe. Some of us try to live normal lives, you know?"

"My line of work, I don't bump up against much of that."

"Sorry," she murmured. "I'll make some coffee. See you when you get here."

He went through his routine automatically. Checked his gun. His badge. His cuffs. Put his notebook in his pocket. Got a freshly charged radio. Told dispatch where to find him. Then he went downstairs—the stairs, not the elevator—to the garage. Still no chance to see what the night was like, just the gritty cold and damp of concrete. He started the engine and drove out into the black velvet night. Through the quiet streets. Down Franklin and onto 295 north, heading first to his sister's, then north toward Boothbay Harbor and points beyond. It was time for some answers.

When Sandy answered the door, puffy and rumpled from sleep, the hall dim behind her, he was rocked by the sense that he was seeing his mother. He'd never noticed the strong resemblance before. It happened when you were too close to things. They were both tall and dark, broad-shouldered women with ample bodies and fine, long legs. Sandy had their mother's thick, dark hair and sad brown eyes. She even wore the same pale green robe.

"That Mom's robe?" he asked.

"You've got a hell of a memory," she said. "You ought to try living in the present." She slammed two cups down on the counter. "Cream and sugar?"

"You're the one wearing the robe."

Her eyes narrowed. "Cream and sugar?" He nodded. "Hungry? There's pie."

"What kind?"

"This isn't a restaurant."

"Give it a rest, Sandy. I know you're pissed. I'm sorry, okay?"

She jerked her chin toward the table. "Sit." She poured

coffee into his mug, put the half and half and the sugar bowl in front of him, and lifted the foil off the pie plate. She cut a big wedge of apple pie and dumped on a big scoop of ice cream, like his mother had done countless times after their nocturnal perambulations. She put the ice cream away, covered the pie, and brought him his slice, sitting down across from him. "That girl matters to me," she said. "I wish you hadn't gone and messed with her head."

"What about my head?"

"You're the grownup."

"She's a grownup."

"She's a screwed-up kid who wants the world to think she's tough. And she worships the ground you walk on."

"I told you how it happened. I regret it. Deeply. But I was drugged and half-asleep and she got naked and got in my bed. So I'm a flawed human being. We agree on that. The important thing is, it's the middle of the night and she may be at risk. You got the letter?"

"What was she doing there?"

"She and Kyle thought I needed looking after."

His sister sighed. "Terry should have known better. Eat. I'll get the letter." She crossed the room and pulled a plain white envelope from her purse.

"You read it?" he asked.

"Wasn't addressed to me."

He unfolded the pages and read them. Alana had careful girlish penmanship—readable, a little oversized, with circles for dots and long tails on the ends of words. "Dear Copman," it began, "you hurt my feelings bad." He hunched his shoulders, acutely aware of his sister's scrutiny. "But I know you've got a lot on your mind right now. I only wish you'd called me or something so I didn't feel so used. Not like I'm not used to that, huh? Maybe I deserved it, though, because you know what? I lied to you again. Like if lying is not telling the whole thing, I mean."

Girlish language, too. She hadn't been constrained by the formalities of the work world. She just wrote like she thought. "Here's what I didn't tell the truth about. The night Dr. Pleasant got killed, I saw a guy in a truck drop that other girl off at Dunkin' Donuts. I think maybe it was the same guy I told you about. The one who picked me up and asked about the doctor that time? I didn't really see him but the truck looked the same. I know you're getting real mad at me reading this because you're wondering why I didn't tell you this, right?"

Right, Alana, I am pissed at you. "You want to know why I did it?" He read her explanation but he already knew. "I did it because I thought you'd keep coming back and I could give you little bits and it would be fun. Fun for me to see you and fun because you'd be proud of the way I kept remembering things. I was going to help you solve the case. At my place, when I saw how wore out you were, I was going to tell you, but I was mad about that other woman. Then I was going to tell you after we left Dunkin' Donuts but you got beat up. Things happened too fast and then you dumped me here and I never got another chance to talk to you. You didn't call and I was going crazy."

There was a blot where the ink was smeared. He hoped it wasn't a tear, expected it was. "It's not like Sandy isn't nice. I love her and she never makes me feel like I'm bad or anything, and your nieces are the sweetest kids. I wish they were my sisters. Maybe if I'd had a family like that I never would have ended up how I did. But that's the way it is. I love you, Joe. I know you'll never love me back. I mean, like, I know you love me and all that, only not the way I want. I want to make you breakfast and fuck your brains out and give you babies. And you want me to be a nice girl with a nice job and a safe life with someone who is not you. So screw that, okay?"

"You're blushing," his sister said. "I thought she was giving you important information but it looks like she's saying how good you are in bed. Or how bad."

He raised his eyes from the page. "I'm good."

"Nice to think there are some men out there who know what they're doing."

"That's me. BMOC. Hunky football player, started practicing on cheerleaders when you were still humming happily to your Crayolas."

"Guys who use 'on' instead of 'with' generally don't know what they're doing."

"Some of us advance from 'on' to 'with' over time. Any idea where she went?" Sandy shrugged. "You find her a massage program?"

"Nice of you to ask. I busted my butt, called in some favors, spent hours on the phone, and yes, I found a program. Maybe we could even have persuaded her to try it, if you hadn't played the strong silent type. People take work, you know. Sustained work. Human interactions of all sorts, not just sex, go better with continued contact, not just wham, bam, thank you, ma'am. I'm going back to bed. Good luck finding her." She left the room, the scent of her anger lingering in the air like ozone.

He went back to the letter. "That other girl was a babe. Made me feel fat and ugly. But she was no whore. She came there to hook up with Pleasant and she wasn't leaving without him. Don't worry about me. I'm not going home. I'm gonna stay with a friend. See if I can get my head straight. Then I'll call you. Love always. Alana. P.S. I don't know who grabbed me. The guy from the truck or that asshole O'Leary. He was all wrapped up in a coat and hat and everything. Same with the guy who was watching the house. I just said it was the guy from the truck because that made the best story. And he was there at DD dropping the girl off. DD. Ha! Just like me. Tits to die for. Right, copman?"

He caught a glimpse of white on the back stairs. "Hey, pipsqueak," he said. "Get in here and give your old uncle a hug."

His niece came in, totally unself-conscious about the body budding under her red and white Minnie Mouse nightshirt, and gave him a hug. She was going to be drop-dead gorgeous. And he was aware of the irony of his reaction—the same loathsome cop who would sleep with Alana Black would kill any boy who dared to put his hands on this girl. She surveyed the bandage on his head and his unshaven face with disapproval. "You look like hell, Uncle Joe," she said, her voice surprisingly low and husky. She wanted to be a singer.

"You get some pie?" He nodded. "Mom makes good pie." She cut herself a piece and curled up on the chair across from him. Eating like a kid. Crumbs around her mouth, spilling onto her nightshirt. She bounced up, poured herself a glass of milk, and sat back down. "Mom's mad at you again, isn't she?"

"I'm a jerk."

"She says. Mom likes things orderly. Proper. 'Normal' is a word she uses a lot. You aren't orderly and normal. Neither's Alana. Do you want to know where she went?"

She didn't look at him when she said it. She was bent over her plate, her dark hair forming two great wings along her face. All he could see was her forehead and the arches of her brows. Her brows were darker now, but her forehead

293

was as smooth as that first day Sandy had dumped her into his arms, saying, "Here. Take her. This is probably as close as you're ever going to get to kids. Time to learn to change a diaper." He'd been amazed at the perfection of those tiny arched brows in her funny little face.

"Where?"

She looked up, her eyes dancing. "What'll you give me?"

"A night in juvenile detention if you don't spit it out."

She made a face. "Tough guy, aren't you? She's got a friend. Denise something, up in Brunswick. She wrote the number down on a pad of paper. Tore it off, but the number went through. You want it?" She held out a folded sheet of paper, crisscrossed with pale pencil illuminating a scrawled phone number. "She was picked up in a maroon and white Plymouth Duster about nine-thirty. There was a guy driving and a woman in the passenger seat." She gave him the license number.

He reached across the table and shook her hand. "You're a fine detective," he said. "I can't wait until you join the department."

"I'm holding out for the FBI."

"Those stiffs? Give me a break."

"Mom'll have a bird if I don't go to college."

"Most cops go to college these days, kiddo."

"I know. You going to find Alana? Because, like, I really worry about her, you know? Sometimes she's more of a little kid than me."

"Than I," he corrected.

"Yeah," she agreed, cocking her head like a bird. "Even more of a kid than you."

He took the papers she'd given him and Alana's letter, put his dishes in the sink, and let himself out. Walking to his car, a thought hit him like a sudden sharp pain. If Sandy was becoming their mother, was he becoming their father? A blunt, selfish man who rode rough-shod over everyone in his life? With that pleasant thought to ponder, he got back in the car, contacted dispatch, and asked for a name and address on Alana's phone number and the car license. Then he headed back to the highway.

CHAPTER TWENTY-EIGHT

The truck noted on Aucoin's field observation card was registered to a Randall Noyes, with a Warren address. Knowing he was going into unfamiliar territory with a maze of back roads, Burgess called the Knox County Sheriff's Department for directions. The response he got was cooperative, detailed, and remarkably uncurious. He appreciated that. This time of night, he wasn't interested in spending time on the phone.

He took Route 1 north to 90, turned off 90 onto something small and twisty, and from there onto something smaller and twistier, winding its way uphill and down on pavement the texture of crunchy peanut butter. Even with snow on the ground, he could see the crumbling edges drop off abruptly into deep ditches. If he got a wheel over, it would sink through the snow into sand and gravel so soft not even frost could hold it together. Not a road for the faint of heart. He thought of Maude Libby, with her proper hat and the pleasure she took in driving her Oscar's truck.

Eventually he rounded a steep curve and found the mailbox he was looking for. He pulled into the yard, engine running, taking it in. A small bluish-white box of a house with a porch on the end. A snow-covered shape in the yard might have been a bird feeder, another a dog house. Closer to the porch, a tarp-swathed mound was almost certainly a motorcycle. Despite the dog house, there was no dog in evidence. No truck, either. The small outbuilding wasn't big enough for a garage. House and yard were still and dark.

Leaving the car running, he mounted the steps and knocked. After a decent interval, allowing for the hour, he knocked again. No answer. He got his flashlight and circled the house, peering in the windows. There were four rooms, kitchen, living room and two bedrooms. Both beds neatly made and empty.

He went back up the steps and tried the door. Unlocked. Wiping his feet carefully, he walked into the kitchen. It was a spare place, nothing on the counters but a microwave. The floor and counters were clean. No dishes in the sink. A bare table with two chairs. A few papers and bills addressed to Randall Noyes in a kitchen drawer. He opened the refrigerator. A little food, fairly fresh. Three beers. Four jars of Hellman's mayo. No mold, rot, spills or crumbs. So far, this guy was up for the Betty Crocker Homemaker Award.

Living room was the same. Sofa, chair and TV. One lamp. No books or magazines. No pictures. No shoes on the floor, no dirt on the carpet. And he'd thought his place didn't look lived in. He checked the bigger bedroom, hearing the words "monk's cell" in his brain. Clothes on hangers or neatly folded. There was no life in this house other than the bare necessities of food, clothing and shelter. By leaving no stamp of his personality, Randall Noyes had left the indelible stamp of a man withdrawn from life.

Burgess had stopped using the flashlight. There were no neighbors and there was no traffic. He went into the other bedroom, turned on the light and looked around. It had the unused quality of a guest room. Everything was neat and slightly dusty and impersonal. Everything except a large framed picture on the wall and a few more on the small dresser beneath it, the only pictures in the house.

He studied the picture on the wall. The woman he'd seen in photographs at Sarah Merchant's house. Carman

Merchant. She was sitting in a chair in the living room he'd just passed through, backed by soft green curtains, her elbow resting on the arm of a chair. She wasn't beautiful. Not even as pretty as her sister, Sarah. But she had a memorable face. Humor, lurking, impish, mocking, danced in her dark blue eyes and around her mouth. A deep, wry wisdom at people's foolishness. Look at that face and you had to know. Why are you laughing, Carman? What do you see that we don't? She'd probably made a lot of people uncomfortable. But not the man who lived here.

On the dresser top beneath the picture were a few more photos, a folded bit of black lingerie, a small silver earring shaped like a feather. A bowl of smooth rocks, beach glass, fish hooks, and other odd items. A black metal candleholder with a large cut-out of a starfish held the melted remnants of a candle. He looked around the room, at the spare furniture, the enlarged photograph, the small collection of items and he knew. These were her things. This was her bed. Carman Merchant had been dead six years and this was still her room. He was looking at a shrine.

For the second time that night, he felt recognition as a sharp pain. A sharper pain this time. He closed his eyes and turned away. He understood about shrines and honoring your debts to the dead. About life getting stalled and roadblocks in the mind. How a major life event can suck up all your emotions and leave you stuck in an endless loop of what ifs and if onlys, praying for something to change the unchangeable.

He stumbled down the steps and across the icy yard, jumped in the Explorer and backed out of the driveway, skittering noisily over the rutted ground and onto the rough pavement, then slammed it into gear and headed back the way he'd come. Too fast for the road and a man with only one good arm. Trying with foolish, adolescent speed to get away from something inside his own head.

The rest of the drive was a blur. Luckily there were no deer or moose in the road and no wavering drunks. He was alone in the darkness, gripping the wheel with unnecessary intensity as he rushed through the yellow cone of light and the surrounding blackness toward Boothbay Harbor. That long drive down the peninsula was torture, just as the road to Randall Noyes's house had been. Most Maine roads needed at least two hands on the wheel, clear eyes, and a mind on the business at hand. He had none of these.

It was willpower that finally brought him to a stop in Sarah Merchant's driveway, in the chilly stillness of the ending night. He turned off his lights and crept along the last bit of road, switched off the dome light and got out, leaving the door slightly ajar. He let his eyes adjust to the dark and went up the walk, hoping a patch of ice didn't send him ass over teakettle.

The door, when he slowly turned the knob, opened as though he were expected. The dim entry was lit by a candle in a holder with the cut-out of a moose. He went carefully down the stairs, instinctively finding the knob at the bottom, and walked into the big room that had startled him earlier, a time that seemed not hours but eons ago. As he'd imagined, the stove's red eye glowed in the darkness and the dragon's steam rose in an eerie plume.

He stood with his back against the wall, unsure why he'd come down here when his goal was to find Sarah Merchant. Maybe because even when he was breaking rules right and left, marching into a woman's bedroom in the middle of the night went too far? More likely because, even with a tired brain and body, his cop's instinct still worked. He would find her here.

"Come sit down," she said, only a voice in the darkness. "Don't put the light on. It is you, detective, isn't it?" She sounded resigned. He was expected even if unwelcome.

He sat where he had sat earlier, the weight of his body sinking down into the cushions, rested his head against the sofa back and closed his eyes. No longer energized. He felt a million tired years old and saddened by what he was about to do. He took a deep breath, acutely aware of his chest expanding, of the fact that he was still alive, though this night was filled with the dead. His body seemed starved for oxygen. Had he been holding his breath, anticipating this moment?

"Tell me about Randall Noyes."

There was rustling in the darkness. The scratch of a match. She leaned forward and lit a candle. This holder had the silhouette of a loon. "What about him?" she asked. Her shadowed face seemed youthful and mysterious. "Why can't you leave this alone? Leave us alone?"

"You know why," he said.

"There's nothing I can do to help you. I said I'd think about it. I did. I have nothing to tell you."

He wanted to grab her and shake the complacency out of her voice, reacting not to her certainty but to his own. "That's not all there is to it. A man is dead."

"So what? Lots of people are dead." There was a scent rising, from her or from the candle. Something green and soothing.

He didn't want her soothed. "Maybe you think it's all right, what happened to Dr. Pleasant, because of what happened to your sister, but it's not. It's like Romeo and Juliet," he said. "The Hatfields and McCoys. Somebody harms one of yours. You've been wronged, so to get revenge, you harm one of theirs. Now Dr. Pleasant's wife, his children, the innocent victims of your crime, are hurting like you did. Have a reason to want revenge of their own. Where does it stop, Sarah?"

"It wasn't my revenge crime. And anyway, people aren't like that."

This reminded him of nights in Vietnam, the seemingly normal conversation fraught with emotional undercurrents, the overarching sense of danger, the whole situation crazy. "You're like that. Randall Noyes is like that. Patient. Watchful. Calculating."

She shifted angrily. "You don't know Randy. Yes, he's patient. I thought that was supposed to be a virtue." She snapped the wooden matchstick between her fingers with a look that said she wished she could do the same to him.

"The man's a saint," she said. "Best thing that ever happened to Carman. God, she loved that man. Even when she was so sick, she just lit up around him. He was the same with her. Most people forget, let things drift back into memory, but not Randy. I swear he loves her as much today. And I have to think . . ." There was a choke in her voice, a hesitation. "Her spirit's out there somewhere, loving him right back."

"Where can I find him?" Burgess asked.

"Randy's gone."

"Gone where?"

"I don't know. Just gone. I only hope he's gone to a different place, not done something to himself. He's still hurting so much."

"I need to find him."

"Randy didn't do anything, unless watching and hating someone are crimes, which I don't believe they are. The poor man's been through enough."

At the least, the poor man might have helped set up a

murder. He thought she knew and didn't care. The connection he'd felt to Sarah Merchant was gone. Not feeling hopeful, he asked his next question. "Who's the girl? The lovely one with the long blonde hair." Then, suddenly, he knew. "Carman had daughters, didn't she?" She didn't answer. "I'm going to find her, Sarah. Your cooperation could make things easier."

"That's cop bullshit. How is it easier if she's arrested today instead of next week or next month or next year, when she didn't do anything?"

"What do you mean, didn't do anything? They went looking for him, your niece and Randall Noyes, because of how he treated Carman. They stalked him. They set him up. She was there in the car that night. I can prove all that, and Stephen Pleasant is dead."

He waited. Most people would have rushed in with a bunch of excuses and explanations, but she stayed silent. "Look," he said, trying to humor her, "if you know of something to explain her behavior, some reason it wasn't murder, you should tell me."

"Why?"

"Person's in a better position when they're forthcoming, when they voluntarily explain instead of offering their story as an excuse only after they're tracked down and arrested."

"I'm supposed to believe that?"

Her angry defensiveness made him angry in return, something he was trained not to be, not even at four in the morning after a day of dragging people to their sorrow and rubbing their noses in it. Cops, like doctors, sometimes had to cause pain to get a good result. That didn't make it easy. He raised his voice. "I don't care what you believe, Ms. Merchant. I just want to find your niece and get this over with."

"And then what? She goes off to the horrors of some dirty jail and you go home to bed? Maybe your life gets easier, maybe hers is ruined." A log in the stove snapped and she jumped. "You want me to help with that? Maybe I'm dense, but I fail to see the advantage. Right now she's free. Hasn't got the whole state talking about how she dressed up like a hooker and screwed this guy so she could get him alone and jam a poker down his throat. Even if she proves her innocence, which you'll make it damned hard to do, she'll never live that down."

A low moan filled the silence between them as she realized what she'd just said. "Oh, Lord," she breathed. "Lord. I am so damned stupid."

"A fireplace poker," he said. "Thank you. I was thinking curtain rod. Randall Noyes is pretty handy with metal, isn't he? He make these candle-holders?"

"I would like you to leave," she said, trying for firmness. Her voice was shaky.

"I'll just bet you would," he said. "I wish I had some of the crime scene pictures with me. You've probably got some sanitized vision of your sweet and lovely niece performing her quick and efficient kill and marching proudly away. But it wasn't anything like that. Know how he died? He drowned in his own blood. And the lengths she was willing to go to? Oral sex. Anal sex. Lesbian sex. There's a video of the sex party."

She stood up, no longer trying to disguise the tremble in her voice. "I want you to go!" Her voice rising. "Get out of my house! You want to come back, show me a warrant. Otherwise, leave me and what's left of my family alone!"

"You think death only touches you?" Raising his own voice. "Stephen Pleasant had a daughter who loved him. You know something about daughters who love their parents, don't you? A wife who loved him, and a brand-new baby son. Now they're suffering like you and Randall Noyes and your niece are suffering. Is that what you wanted, to make other innocent people suffer? Is it really such a good thing you've accomplished?"

"Get out!" Her voice shatteringly loud in the quiet darkness.

Feet pounded on the stairs. The door burst open, a light came on, and a young woman rushed in. She wore the same nightshirt his niece had worn, but there was nothing budding about this body. This girl had bloomed. Her long blonde hair was tousled with sleep, her blue eyes still heavy-lidded. "Aunt Sarah?" she asked in a puzzled voice. "What's going on?"

He was watching the wrong person. Behind him, he heard the distinctive sound of a gun being readied, turned to find Sarah Merchant pointing a shotgun at his chest. His first regret was not wearing a vest. His second, that he'd only told the dispatcher about Warren and not about coming here. That he hadn't followed protocol. His third, that he hadn't finished writing his reports, and the letter and other information leading here were in his notebook and in the car. He'd been cocky. Careless. Too independent. If someone working for him had been this slipshod, he'd have taken their head off. Maybe that's what was in store for him.

Not the first time he'd been on the receiving end of a loaded gun. He'd been shot at twice. Two misses. That didn't make him feel better now. Staring at the wavering barrel never got any easier, and he didn't believe in third time lucky. He wondered how it felt to be blown apart. He'd seen it enough—bodies torn and shredded. Men he'd loved reduced to dripping hunks of meat. There was a cold sickness in his stomach. He had to remind himself to breathe.

He watched her hands carefully, alert for signs of movement, alarmed by their unsteadiness. She gripped the gun with a familiarity that said she'd handled guns before, but he was sure she'd never pointed one at another human being. Her tense face and white knuckles said she was as likely to shoot him by accident as by deliberation. Had he misjudged her? Were the three of them in this together?

"Throw your gun over here," she said. "And don't try any tricks. The safety's off and I have my hand on the trigger. Even if you shoot me, you're coming along." Her voice spiked with panic. A bad situation behind a trigger. Not a good time to be heroic. He pulled out the gun, bent down slowly, and pushed it toward her. Hating her for it, more so because earlier he'd found her attractive, because she was making him feel like such a fool. A cop never gives up his gun.

"Kara," she said, "this is Detective Burgess from the Portland Police Department. He came to arrest you. Get dressed and get the hell out of here."

The girl started to go and then turned, twisting her body with an agility granted only to the young, giving her aunt a puzzled look. "But Aunt Sarah . . . shouldn't I . . . shouldn't we . . . tell him what happened?"

"He doesn't care what happened, Kara. He won't believe you. He just wants to make an arrest. Now go!"

"Hey!" he said, taking a step toward her. "Wait, Kara, that's not true! She's wrong. I do care what happened."

The girl turned and ran.

"Don't move!" Sarah Merchant stepped forward, tripped on a corner of the rug, and stumbled. The gun exploded as Burgess dove sideways. The window behind him dissolved, showering him with glass. He lay on and among the sharp fragments, stunned by the loudness and proximity of the blast, pain from his bad arm and his new wounds surging through him, feeling the flow of warm blood and the rush of cold night air.

He didn't lie there long. The kickback had knocked Sarah Merchant off her feet. She was sitting on the floor, still holding the shotgun, an astonished expression on her face. He dove for his own gun, which now lay between them, picked it up, and pointed it at her. Holding it steady, he walked slowly forward, grabbed the shotgun, and tossed it through the broken window. Overhead, feet pounded across the floor. The front door slammed, followed by the distant surge of an engine.

She must have used birdshot. Otherwise, at this range, it would have punched right through him. Otherwise, he'd be screaming and writhing on the floor as he bled out and the bad guys would have won. So he didn't think he was going to die, but now that his heartbeat had slowed enough to let him reconnect with his surroundings, he was in a world of hurt. Adrenaline plays strange tricks. It could be worse than it seemed.

He felt cold and dizzy and disoriented, wanting to lie down and rest, but there was too much cop in him. He'd come to get information and he was going to get it. "Look," he said, trying not to sound as pathetic or pissed off as he felt, "she's gone, okay? If I promise not to go rushing after her, will you answer some questions for me? Please? I don't think you meant to shoot me." Get her talking, get what he needed. He could arrest her later.

She stared in amazement. Then, slowly, as if she were as stunned and damaged as he felt, she walked to the couch and sat down. "I've shot you?" she said, disbelieving, looking down at her hands. She unclasped them and flexed her fingers, watching them curiously. "I thought the damned thing wasn't loaded." She rose slowly, came a few steps forward, studying him. "Oh, man," she muttered. "Oh, man. This is unbelievable. I just shot a cop." Then, in the way people said crazy things at times like this, "That was a thousand-dollar window."

Fuck your window, lady. Blood stained the leg of his corduroy pants, darkening the loden green to reddish black. She bent toward it, her face echoing his pain. Then, as though it wasn't a charitable gesture but only curiosity, she rose again and walked unsteadily out of the room, her hand over her mouth. He could hear her somewhere nearby being sick.

He needed to sit, but her couches were so nice. He must be worse off than he thought. The woman shoots him and he worries about her upholstery. Abruptly, he was too exhausted to care. He shuffled across the glass-strewn floor, his blood-soaked pants slapping against his leg, and more fell than sat. An expensive night for Sarah Merchant. She'd blown out her window. He was wrecking her couch.

She came back as far as the doorway, leaning against the doorframe, holding a towel in her hands. "I'm sorry," she said. "Really. Abandoning you like that . . . living alone, I guess, I'm too used to taking care of myself . . . too unused to taking care of others. I . . ." Disjointed, sharing his shock. Her hand fluttered to her head, taking the towel with it, like an exhausted soldier waving the flag of surrender. "I never meant to. I really didn't know it was loaded. There's nothing I can say, is there? One day I'm living a perfectly ordinary life and then, suddenly, everything goes to hell."

The towel fluttered again as she wiped her eyes. "You're bleeding on my couch."

"Should have thought of that before you shot me," he said. "Sit down. We need to talk."

Chapter Twenty-nine

Her gaze darted toward the phone. "You must need an ambulance?"

He waved her off, wincing at the effort. Jesus, God, that hurt! "Let's just get this over with." Her fluttery behavior made him nervous. He liked her better tough.

She hovered there, desperate to do something to make amends. As if she could. "Would you like something warm to drink? Some coffee, tea, aspirin?" She bit her lip at the stupidity of offering aspirin to a gun-shot man.

"A blanket?"

"Right," she said. "Pain. Injury. Shock. I'm being an idiot, aren't I?" She looked at him, thoughtfully. "Do you think you could make it upstairs to my bed if I helped? It's better than down here with all that cold pouring in." She crossed the room and offered her shoulder as a crutch.

He just wanted her story so he could get out of here and go home. Drag his injured body back to his cave and lick his wounds. "Here is fine."

"I'll call the ambulance," she said, scooping up a woolen throw from the arm of the couch and offering it to him.

"Let's get our business done, first."

"But you're hurt."

"I'm pissed as hell, too, and now I've got the gun. So humor me, okay?"

"Okay." She glanced around the room as she tried not to look at the blood. "I honestly didn't know it was loaded."

When people said "honestly," did that mean the rest of

the time they lied? He wanted to get out his notebook, but he had only one good arm. Memory would have to do. "You know stuff about the murder the public doesn't. Were you there?" She shook her head. "Then how do you know?"

"Kara told me what they were planning to do."

"Before or after?" She didn't answer. "Kara told you what happened that night, about murdering Dr. Pleasant?"

"She didn't kill him."

"She told you what happened that night?" Sarah nodded. "Did Randall Noyes kill him?" He'd never interviewed someone while bleeding on to their furniture before. Position and power balances and eye contact were all-important.

"Randy didn't do it, either," she said.

Her goddamned stalling made him jerk with frustration and his body screamed in protest. Adrenaline was mysterious. It could carry you into danger and out again, sustaining you against all reason. Then, like a date who'd had a bad time, it dumped you and took off. He wanted to get through this before he got dumped. "Look," he said, "can you just, for Christ's sake, stop screwing around and tell me what happened."

"I can't stand this," she said.

"*You* can't stand this?" He closed his eyes. It felt like his body had sprung five new leaks. Or one big one. "Lady, what's your problem? You don't point guns at people if you don't want to hurt them. That's how it works."

"Are you trying to make me feel worse?"

"I don't give a rat's ass how you feel. You expected me. You had a gun waiting. What the fuck did you think? Now tell me the story. The sooner you talk, the sooner I go. Then you won't have to watch."

She grabbed for control and missed. "Oh, Jesus," she said, covering her face with her hands. "I didn't mean to—"

"Skip the fuckin' mea culpa. Tell me the truth, and maybe I won't arrest you."

Her hands dropped. She stared at him, horrified. "Arrest me?" Then, "You aren't going to die on me, are you?"

Like it would be even more inconsiderate to saddle her with a body. "In your dreams. Now talk."

She swallowed hard. "I don't know how to tell this without making Kara look worse than she is."

"She went out to kill someone. You can't make that look like a Sunday school picnic."

Sarah bowed her head, then lifted it, looking over at the hanging quilts. "Yes. Okay. Kara and Randall did go looking for Dr. Pleasant. It was Kara's idea. Randy would have gone on forever, spinning in his own small, sad circle. Terrible waste of a good man."

"Goddammit! Will you please—"

"Sorry. When they found him, they decided they were going to . . ." Her voice faltered. "Going to kill him. They figured the way to do it was to entice him into a sexual situation in his car. And that's what they did."

"But you said—"

"I'm not finished." Despite the blanket, he was shivering. "Obviously, you know about the first part of the evening." She sighed. "How that girl could be so stupid, I don't know. She has a three-point-eight average. But she's been brooding for six years. She was there when her mother died. Something like that leaves a mark."

He'd been there. Done that. Knew all about the mark. But he wasn't here to get dragged back down into memories. When his need for self-protection butted up against his cop's instinct for solving a crime, he put the job first. "The story."

"Kara contacted some thug . . . some pimp, I suppose

. . . that Randy'd located. Poor guy. Going down there and picking up hookers . . . the whole thing was so sordid. Kara asked this guy if he could set her up with Dr. Pleasant. I suppose some money changed hands, she didn't tell me. That night, she got the call that this creep had set up a party with Pleasant."

She pushed her hair behind her ears with nervous fingers. "I'm sorry. I know you want this neatly folded and delivered, like laundry, and I'm doing a crappy job. I just want to explain how Kara isn't a bad kid or an evil person and this isn't what you think."

"Why don't you let me be the judge of that?"

It was morning. Outside, in the growing light, twittering birds were coming to the feeder. He felt like shit, furious at himself for letting her shoot him. Some cop he was, couldn't cover his own ass. At least his anger kept him awake, fighting the desire to let go and curl himself around his pain, even if he was too full of wounded rage to let her tell it her way.

Upstairs, a door opened and slammed shut. Quick footsteps came down the stairs. Sarah Merchant's hand went to her mouth, watching the girl come in.

"I couldn't do it," she said, shrugging off her jacket. "I couldn't just run away and leave you to deal with my mess, Aunt Sarah." She wore jeans and a blue sweater the color of her eyes. Even in the dim light and to Burgess's jaundiced eyes, she was beautiful.

She crossed the room and knelt by her aunt's feet, putting her head in Sarah Merchant's lap. Then she rose and turned to look at him. "This is so weird," she said. "A cop all wrapped up like a granny. What'd you do? Shoot him?"

Sarah's "yes" was a low, choked sound.

The girl looked at him again. Then, though she didn't actually roll up her sleeves, he saw a mental transformation from skittish girl to woman in charge. She tied back her hair and pulled away his blanket. "Kara Allison, R.N." A whisper of hesitation. "Almost. Where are you hit?"

"Never mind that. Tell me about the night Pleasant was killed."

"In good time," she said calmly. She opened his jacket, moving him with professional skill, then she started working on his shirt, unbuttoning and untucking so that she was staring at his blood-soaked T-shirt. She rolled it up, looking with dismay at his bloody torso. "Aunt Sarah, have you called an ambulance?"

"He won't let me. Says he came here to ask questions and that's what he's going to do." Her niece's return had restored some of Sarah Merchant's composure.

"Tough guy, huh?" Kara said. "If I tell my story, will you let us get you some help?"

"Just tell the goddamned story," he said.

"This is all my fault," she said. She pulled down his shirt, closed his coat, and stepped back. "Make you a deal," she said. So goddamned cool.

"You're hardly in a position—"

"Neither are you. I'll tell you what happened if you'll let me call a doctor."

"Let's just get the talking over with," he grunted, "before we invite other people to the party. I'm okay."

She studied his face and checked his pulse. He gritted his teeth, not wanting her touching him. No comfort from the enemy. "Aunt Sarah, we need a warmer blanket, some tea and orange juice."

Sarah Merchant was glad to leave the room.

Kara Allison took her place on the couch. "You have a

312

peculiar idea about what constitutes okay." When he didn't respond, she said, "The story, huh? It's pretty sordid." Sitting there, she became a nervous young girl again. These women morphed in a way that seemed unreal, though he knew it was reality. "And I'm supposed to want to help people. Like you. To make things better. But then . . ."

Her pause was long and considered. "That's what Pleasant was supposed to do, too. But he never gave a damn about the people he treated." Her lip was trembling and her eyes swam with tears. She wiped them away with the back of her hand. "I'm not proud of what I did."

"Hold on. Are you about to confess?" He struggled to sit up straighter, to rise to the formality of the occasion.

"Stay still," she ordered. "I really don't know. You'll have to hear it and decide."

"Then I've got to tell you about your rights."

"Miranda?" she said. "Don't bother. I'll waive it."

"I have to—"

"Just let me get this off my chest, okay?"

"I need a formal waiver," he insisted. "You have to sign something."

"You're kidding. I can't just say it?"

"Under the circumstances, I'd like it in writing."

Sarah Merchant came in with a tray, a blanket under her arm. Kara took the blanket and tucked it around him. "Aunt Sarah," she said, "will you be a witness that I understand and am waiving Miranda rights?"

Sarah Merchant gave him a poisonous look. "I don't think you want to do that, Kara."

Screw her and her crazy-ass entitled attitude, Burgess thought. Woman oughta be on her way to jail and she's whining about rights and procedure.

"I'm fine," Kara said.

313

Her aunt turned and left the room.

Awkwardly, he fumbled his notebook out, unfolded a waiver form, and passed it to her. She read it over and signed it. "This really isn't necessary," she said.

"It's procedure," he said wearily, putting it back in his pocket. It wasn't. This situation didn't fit the criteria, but he'd rather be safe than sorry. "Go ahead."

"I started out doing this for Randy, because of how it's ruined his life, and he's such a good guy. Then I was doing it for me. Now I see all I've done is cause trouble to people I love, like Aunt Sarah. That's not what was supposed to happen, you know?" Looking for understanding. He didn't understand. "It was all my idea. Finding him. Setting him up. The weapon. The whole thing. Randy just did what I asked."

"From the beginning," Burgess said.

She looked down at her clenched hands. "My mother died when I was fifteen. She had cervical cancer, but what she died of was complications of Dr. Pleasant." Something hard and raw had come into her voice. "We were very poor and she didn't bother with medical care. She got it for us but not herself. That's how she was. Always giving. She would have given away the shirt on her back if she thought it would help somebody, but she didn't have a clue about how to care for herself."

Like his own mother, he thought.

"She could be wise, and infinitely generous, but life scared her. She couldn't handle stress. I see now that she was probably a little bit crazy, so she self-medicated. She drank." Kara pulled a strand of hair loose and began winding it around her finger. Like Alana. Like a hundred girls he'd interviewed. Something older women didn't do. "She was getting radiation for her cancer. She'd dwindled down to the tiniest little thing. Always in pain and sick. The pain wasn't managed. Her health wasn't managed. Her doctor didn't pay any attention, gave her welfare medicine . . ."

Her hands pressed against her stomach. "I'm sorry," she said. "I still can't . . . give me a minute, okay?" She walked to the window, her arms wrapped tightly around her body. The room was cold. She picked up her coat and put it on. "What I remember of that time is a muddle. I have a confused sense of not understanding what was going on, of being sad and scared and feeling this terrible helplessness, but I have pictures in my mind. How scared she was. Her anger when the doctors treated her like a moron. The nights she cried."

He wanted to tell her to cut to the chase, but if she needed to tell the whole story, he'd listen.

"The last part of her treatment . . ." She swallowed. Started over, her voice softer. "What was supposed to be the last part of her treatment . . . she went into the hospital for a procedure where they isolate the patient and deliver a dose of radiation directly to the spot with this cesium rod. She was supposed to stay very, very still."

She let the tears come. "My mother was an alcoholic. They knew that. They'd sent her away, refused her treatment before because she'd been drinking. But they didn't monitor her. They didn't sedate her. They told her she had to lie there for forty-eight hours, perfectly still, and then they went away and left her." Kara shook her head. "She got restless and delirious. Punctured her uterus with the rod. Collapsed on the floor and bled."

Her voice dropped to a whisper. "It was a long time before they found her and then it was too late. They put her in intensive care to treat her, the DTs, the shock. We sat beside her for three weeks, in that room with all the machines.

315

The nurses braided her hair up with ribbons. She looked so cute, only she wasn't really there." Absently, Kara's fingers gathered clumps of hair and started braiding.

"There were tubes everywhere. Her hands and feet swelled up. Once or twice, it seemed like she responded to Randy's voice, but . . ." The silence of memory lay heavily between them. "All those days and nights. Waiting and hoping. She never woke up. One day, she's trying to get things done around the house before she goes into the hospital, and the next, it's all over. We never got to say good-bye."

Kara shook her head, as if the suddenness and finality of what had happened still shocked her. "It was his carelessness that killed her. What he knew and didn't bother to pay attention to. That's why . . ." The challenging blue eyes met his, fierce and angry. "That's why it had to be a rod, you see. As ye sow, so also shall ye reap."

Had he just heard a confession? Burgess closed his eyes against her pain and his own. Against the memories of intensive care. The hope you clung to when the result seemed inevitable, your own pain so vivid you longed for your own dose of morphine. The way the urge for revenge could grow in the cold confines of that place, fueled by the respirator's *sotto voce* mantra. Hate, hate, hate.

"Tell me about that night."

"We'd been watching Dr. Pleasant. I say we . . . mostly it was Randy. We knew his habits. Picking up girls and having them . . . uh . . . service him in his car. We'd found this creep O'Leary who sometimes fixed him up with girls. I told O'Leary I wanted to party with Dr. Pleasant. He said he'd let me know. I suppose he hoped to recruit me or something. One night he called. Said to meet him at the donut place."

She grabbed a handful of tissues. "It's amazing what you

can bring yourself to do . . ." There was a loud thud. A bird crashed into the glass, fell to the ground, flopped a few times, and lay still. "Oh no!" she said, her hand to her mouth. "I should go see—"

"Finish the story." Pain had settled in at an almost intolerable level. He was somewhere in never-never land, hanging on by his fingernails. He needed to finish this.

She told this part like it was about someone else. "O'Leary picked me up and took me to this grungy apartment. There was another girl there. I didn't get her name. Part black, I think. Pretty in a rather bovine way. We . . . well, you probably know what we did. I'm no prude but I can barely make myself say it, let alone believe I did it, and I made sure I left with Dr. Pleasant. It wasn't hard to do."

"Go on."

"We went out for pizza, and he was flirting like a date. I suggested we go somewhere and park."

"All this time, Randy was following you?" She nodded. "Who had the weapon?"

"I did. Randy made it. He has a little machine shop in his garage."

Evidence. Tool marks. Little shreds of metal.

"We parked where he was found. He gave me another fifty dollars and I started getting him . . . uh . . . excited. I had the rod hidden in the lining of my coat. When I thought it was the right moment, I pulled it out and . . ." She stared out at the fallen bird. "All that trouble and planning. All those years of hating. Then when I was there with a weapon in my hand, I couldn't bring myself to use it."

"Somebody killed him."

"I want to show you something." She showed him the heel of her left hand. It was swollen, with purple and yellow bruises. Then she stood, unzipped her jeans, and pulled

317

them down. "Look at my knees," she said. He did his best to concentrate on the scabbed-over cuts and the big, dark bruises and not on her long, strong thighs.

"So?"

"I'm sitting there wanting to stab this man I've hated so long. I've got the weapon out, ready to kill him, and I'm paralyzed. My brain is saying 'do it, do it, do it,' and my hands won't move. Suddenly, this man jerks the door open, grabs me and drags me out of the car. When I'm out, he pulls the rod out of my hand and flings me away like I was a little bit of fluff. I got these bruises when I landed. He ducked into the car with the rod in his hand, and I got out of there without waiting to see what happened. I found Randy, got in the truck, and we drove away."

She bent down and pulled up her pants. Burgess watched with a twinge of regret as her thighs disappeared. Regret that her wounds had made her so callous. Long-ago wounds, not the ones she'd shown him. "Tell me about the man."

"It was only a couple seconds," she said. "He was big. Strong."

"What'd he look like?"

"I don't know. He was wearing a mask with eyeholes over his face and he had his collar turned up. You know what that night was like."

"Gloves?"

"I think so."

"How big?"

She considered. "Over six feet. An inch or two. Ran maybe two hundred and twenty? But that's a guess. It happened so fast."

"Could it have been O'Leary?"

She shook her head. "I don't know."

"What kind of coat?"

"It was dark. I saw him for a few seconds." Burgess waited. "Dark," she said. "Wool. Short. A jacket, not a coat."

"Anything else?" She shook her head. "He say anything? Anything at all?"

"Not that I heard."

"He grabbed you and threw you out of the car and you ran away?" She nodded. "You went there to kill Dr. Pleasant, but this guy shows up and you run like a scared bunny? After all your planning?" Another nod. "Let's back up. While you were getting out the weapon, what was Dr. Pleasant doing?"

For a second, she seemed at a loss. "What do you mean?"

"You know what I mean."

"Sitting there with his eyes closed, feeling good."

"You had to stop what you were doing, get out the weapon. He didn't ask why?"

"No."

"How did the man who pulled you from the car know you had a weapon?"

"How the hell should I know? I guess he was watching through the window."

"And this whole time, Pleasant just sits there, waiting to be killed?"

"I wasn't taking any chances. I used roofies."

Rohypnol, just as Dani had surmised. "The guy who grabbed you, did you notice his car?" She shook her head. "Notice anything about him?"

She stared at her hands. Brought them up and twisted them thoughtfully. Then, slowly, "He had tattoos on his wrists."

"It's a hell of a story," Burgess said. He sighed, wishing

she were a better storyteller or a better liar. Moved by her story about her mother, a story he knew was heartfelt, unconvinced by the ending. He wanted to tell her to run along and play and not be naughty again. Knew that was what she expected. Knew, regardless of his sympathies, that he couldn't condone homicide.

"It's true," she snapped.

"Then why didn't you come to us and tell it?" he snapped back.

"You know why."

He wasn't sure he did. "Think Randy might have seen anything?"

"I don't even know where Randy is. I'm pretty worried about him. He brought me back here, had some coffee, staring out the window like a man who's already moved on, and then left. I don't think he said more than a few words. I've called him a bunch of times. He's not there."

"I asked if you thought he might have seen anything."

"I don't know. I doubt it."

"Could the man have been Randy?"

"How could he be killing someone in a car when he was waiting for me down the street in his truck?"

"Was he waiting down the street?"

"Yes. Yes, goddammit, he was!"

"Did Randy hate him as much as you did?" She nodded. "But this man who pulled you out of the car was not Randall Noyes? Seeing that you were unable to complete the act, he didn't take over and do it himself?"

"No. I already told you. No. Randy doesn't have tattoos. You're a real pain in the ass, you know that?"

"You tell me how you went out to kill a man. I'm a cop. What do you expect me to do, congratulate you?"

She probably did. Despite the sad story and the "frank"

confession, there was no remorse or regret. No doubt or uncertainty. Everybody lied in threatening situations, lied to cops. The problem was knowing when it mattered. Could she have seen tattoos in a split second on a man wearing a coat and gloves as she was being unexpectedly hauled out of a car? Could a man outside have seen in through iced-up windows? Was it realistic to think the doors had been unlocked and then this phantom killer had locked them? Was she lying for herself? Covering for Noyes?

He felt like he'd run a long race and reached the end only to find someone had stolen the finish line. Now it was his job to find it. That, at least, could wait until later. He closed his eyes, silently cursing the whole damned case.

CHAPTER THIRTY

When he opened his eyes, she was dialing the phone. "What are you doing?"

"Calling the doctor."

"Forget it," he said. "We're going to Portland." His words seemed far away.

She tossed her shining hair, arranging herself to give him the full benefit of her drop-dead figure. "I'm not going to Portland."

It was wasted effort. She could have stripped off all her clothes and not have gotten a rise out of him. He was beyond any synaptic response except finishing the task at hand. "Willingly or unwillingly, you're coming," he said. "The easy way is you get in the car and ride. You talk to us. You go home. The hard way is someone guards you until I get a warrant and you go to Portland in handcuffs. Your choice."

Slowly, she hung up. "God!" she said. "I just poured out my guts to you and you're arresting me?"

Much as he wanted to strong-arm her, he'd have a better shot at cooperation and a useful statement if he could get her to come willingly. "I'd rather you came voluntarily."

Sarah Merchant spoke from the doorway. "You're going to what? Make her go to Portland. Forget it."

"You're the one I ought to arrest," he said.

"I don't believe this."

"Believe it." What planet did they come from? Why would a person who'd admitted plotting a crime, stalking a victim, setting up the victim, manufacturing a weapon, and going to the murder scene with the weapon, find it odd when he didn't believe her *deus ex machina* explanation of the ultimate result? Why would a woman who'd shot a cop assume all would be forgiven because she was nice? "And go get me that picture of you and Randall Noyes."

She turned and stalked out of the room. Banging angrily up the stairs and back down again. Like he gave a damn.

He took the picture from her, shoved it in his pocket, and got cautiously to his feet. Would he make it across the room and up the stairs without falling flat on his face? How do you arrest someone when they can knock you over with a feather? That, he supposed, was why he had a gun. He limped to the phone and called Kyle. Woke him. He could tell by the sleepy tones and the woman's question in the background. "Write this down, okay?"

Bless Kyle, he didn't complain about the hour or what he'd been dragged away from. "Shoot," he said. Unfortunate choice of words.

Burgess gave him an economical shorthand version and said he'd be there in an hour and a half. Told him to wake Stan and send him to Brunswick to get Alana. Somehow this whole damned thing was coming together in the next twenty-four hours, or he was going to die trying. He felt like that might be preferable to his current state.

"You sound like hell, Joe," Kyle said. "Been up all night?"

"Up all night. Got kinda shot up. Tell you when I get there. Get a home address for Dr. Kenneth Bailey. And queue up that video store surveillance tape."

"Will there be anything else, sir?"

"Maybe some Band-Aids. We'll see." He turned to Kara Allison. "Let's go."

Sarah Merchant stepped in front of her niece. Shorter, rounder, and considerably more frightened. When she put a hand on his arm, he smelled that herbal scent again. Wished things had gone differently. A woman looks less attractive after she's shot you. "Look, detective, she's been cooperative. She's done everything you asked. Answered every question. What more do you want?"

"To get it all on the record. A proper interview by a cop who isn't bleeding and hasn't been up all night. A signed, formal statement. So we can eliminate her as a suspect." Didn't add that he wanted fingerprints, a polygraph, hair and saliva samples and information concerning the whereabouts of Randall Noyes, or that he wanted his best interrogation team working on her.

"You don't need handcuffs for that!" she said. "I'll drive her down later."

"Of course I don't need handcuffs. But it took me days of tracking to get here. She's the closest thing I've got to an eyewitness. I'm not letting her out of my sight until I get her statement."

"She's not going." Sarah folded her arms stubbornly.

"What are you going to do? Shoot me again? One more word of argument and I *am* arresting *you*. Assault on a police officer is not a small thing."

Sarah stared in amazement. In her mind, shooting another person should be overlooked if done for a good reason. Yet she'd probably be surprised to learn she was no different from most of the criminals he dealt with. They all had good reasons. Among his favorites, a man who'd shot his brother, explaining, "I hadda shoot him. He wouldn't give me the remote."

"If I collapse at the wheel, it would be good to have a nurse along."

Kara gave him a look. If it was meaningful, the meaning was lost on him. He was beyond subtlety and nuance. "Okay," she said. "I'll come if it'll help straighten things out." She gave her aunt a quick hug. "Don't worry. I'll be fine. I'll be calling you to come get me in no time." Then, with a pointed look at Burgess, she said, "You'd better call me a lawyer. A good one." With a disdainful toss of her head, she started up the stairs.

He followed slowly, bracing himself against the wall, his feet leaden as he climbed the stairs and trudged to the car. He folded himself cautiously in, skipping the seatbelt. He didn't need that rubbing over his punctured skin.

It was still early and the traffic was light. A mercy. He wasn't so much driving as staying upright behind the wheel, keeping the vehicle pointed in the right direction, every bump and pothole a jarring agony. The places where the pellets had bored into him felt red and raw. By the time they pulled into the police garage, he was gritting his teeth so hard his jaw ached. He stopped as close to the door as he could and turned off the engine. Radioed for someone to come get her.

He was no longer a sentient being, inhabiting the sphere of sheer endurance, a static-filled place where the travel time between brain and response was surreally slow. His call brought both Kyle and Perry. Perry took charge of Kara, nodding at his quick summary.

"Get her story on tape," Burgess said. "Right away."

Kyle took one look and dragged him out, propelling him around and into the passenger seat, cutting off his protests with a brusque, "Stan and Vince know what to do."

He closed his eyes and let Kyle take charge. Glad to let someone else be on first for a while. When they got to the hospital, he roused himself long enough to say, "Don't let them admit me." Assisted by Demerol, he dozed through the medical indignities as they pried out the shot.

He would probably have slept the whole day away, despite the gathering of witnesses he'd orchestrated, if he hadn't felt someone's fingers traveling lightly over his face. Even with a cop's instinct for waking quickly, he struggled. He finally opened his eyes to find Chris Perlin wearing a look of sweet concern. She put two warm hands on his bare chest, pressing him gently back against the mattress. "Don't get up," she whispered. "I'm sorry. I didn't mean to wake you."

"Water?"

"I'll get some," she said. Again, he tried to push himself up. She put a restraining hand on his chest. She wore gray sweatpants and a gray sweatshirt with a picture of Tigger on it. Her hair hung loose and shiny down her back. It was Saturday. He'd rousted Kyle and Perry out of their beds shortly after dawn on a Saturday morning, so immersed in the case he'd lost track of time. Her hand stayed on his chest, warm and solid. "Promise you'll stay put?"

She was back in what his mother would have called "two shakes of a lamb's tail," fitting the straw between his lips.

"That's so good," he said. "Where's Terry?"

"Went back to work. They're supposed to call when you're ready to go."

"I'm ready." He hated being away from the action, lying on this table like a slab of meat embellished with large patches of tape. Raw meat. Lotta tape.

"Not quite." There was a hint of teasing in her voice. "You're a bit underdressed for February." She set her hand on his chest and let it travel south, stopping just a tad below his navel. Nothing came between her skin and his. "I think they're bringing you some clothes."

He shivered at her touch, wanting to pull her down next to him and hold her there. Feeling a rare longing, not for sex, but for closeness.

"Why are you here?" he asked. "It's Saturday."

"Fate," she said. "Kid in the apartment downstairs twisted his ankle on the ice. He couldn't drive, so I brought him in. Heard you were here, so I decided to see for myself."

"See all you wanted?"

She laughed, a rich, mellow sound. "Not nearly. I was going to offer my services as a private duty nurse, but knowing the little I do about you, I'm betting the only way I'd get to nurse you would be if I wore running shoes and a bulletproof vest. Even then I'd probably have to hustle to keep up."

"I'm not Superman." He felt like Hamburger Man.

"I'm not usually this forward," she said. "It's just—"

Remy Aucoin opened the door, the lights behind him illuminating his fair hair like a halo. He held out a duffel bag. "Excuse me, ma'am. Sir? I brought some clothes. Detective Kyle thought you might need 'em. He said if you need a ride back to the station, or home, I'm to drive you, sir."

"Officer," Chris said, taking the bag. "Give us a couple minutes, will you? I'll get the detective dressed and he's all yours."

"Yes, ma'am," Aucoin said. "I'll be right outside."

"That's a sweet boy," she said, unzipping the bag and setting it on a chair.

"You were saying something about being forward?" he prompted.

"Right. I'm not. But I went home after our . . . my . . . lunch . . . after we talked, and I thought about you. About how there's more to you than most of the men I meet."

"Yeah," he said. "Thirty or forty extra pounds."

"That's not what I meant. I was thinking about decency. And depth." She touched his bare shoulder. "Let's get you upright and see what happens."

"You get me upright, we both know what happens."

"Later," she said, guiding him slowly to a sitting position and helping him swing his legs off the table. "It comes to that, I don't want anything on your mind but me. Okay. Hold it right there." She got him into underwear and socks, got his shirt on, slipped his pants over his feet. "Time to stand up. And take it easy. I mean it. You might be dizzy."

He slid onto the floor, swaying, slightly exaggerating his need for help. She tucked her shoulder under his and wrapped an arm around his waist. "That's good," she said, taking her time, pressing her body against his before bending to help with his pants. She tucked in his shirt. "There. Now the shoes. Your friend Terry took your gun, I think. All that cop stuff. Except your wallet."

Paper rustled as she slipped a hand into his pocket. "My phone number," she said. "Call me up. I can cook. I can tap dance. I play a mean round of Ping-Pong. I'm into kick boxing. I like to go fishing, listen to women singing the blues and I read Mary Oliver's poetry. A little something . . ." Her voice dropped into a lower, more intimate register. "For everyone." She backed him slowly up against the table, put her arms around his neck, and kissed him. "I think a less forward woman would never get anywhere with you."

He pulled her tighter and kissed her back. The door opened. Aucoin again. "Excuse me, sir. I have your wallet." Burgess went right on kissing Chris Perlin. Didn't even look up. "I'll be outside." The door closed again.

"How am I going to go back to work?" he complained, finally breaking away.

"You ought to be going to bed."

"Don't I know it." He patted his pocket. "I'll call you."

"I hope so," she said. "Do something for me, will you? Stay out of the emergency room. You got away this time without damaging anything vital, but you're pushing your luck. Take it easy for the rest of the day. You got elephants that need stopping, bad guys who need tossing through windows, let someone else do it. There are other cops in town."

"I'll do my best," he said.

"I'm sure you always do." She picked up her purse, hesitated, then pulled out a folded sheet of 8½x11 paper. She unfolded it and showed him a big red heart. "This was on my door this morning. A sign, maybe?" She walked to the door and opened it. "Officer? Your patient is ready." She left without looking back.

Valentine's Day. One of Portland's closely guarded secrets. Every February 14th, Portlanders woke to find the secret Valentine had left these hearts all over town. Burgess had one of his own, at home in a drawer, from 1986. Somewhere in town, a big red heart was hanging. While he was mired in death, life went on.

Aucoin stared after her, grinning. "Man," he said, "that's the kind of nursing care you always dream about."

"Yeah," Burgess agreed. "Almost makes facing a loaded shotgun worthwhile." As they passed the fire station, he saw a big red heart hanging from the flagpole.

Kyle was in an interview room with Kara Allison, Stan Perry watching on the monitor, waiting to take his turn. Melia, who ought to have been home with his kids, hadn't even allowed himself a dress-down Saturday. His suit was immaculate, his tie was straight, his shoes spotless. He and Perry watched as Kyle took Kara Allison through her story.

"It's the third time," Melia said. "He can't shake her.

But it never varies. It's almost word for word. Real people don't work like that. There's something plastic about her, something unreal about the whole thing. I see why you brought her in. Get past that blonde façade, you could be looking at a stone-cold killer. Goes out to screw Pleasant just for the chance to whack him. You like her for it?"

Burgess nodded. Kara Allison seemed remarkably unfazed by the questioning. Most people, even the pros, would be a little frazzled by now. "Told you this one was going to be a bitch. I like her for it—like her a lot—but she could be telling the truth. But is it the truth or the truth up to where the mystery guy jerks open the door? You do a poly?"

"Yeah. Borderline. Inconclusive. She's a cool one, though. I've got a guy working on a warrant for her place. Love to get my hands on what she was wearing that night."

"Probably long gone," Burgess said. "Anyone look at the crime scene photos? See if there's anything to corroborate her story that she was flung down in the snow? Anything that puts a mystery guy in the car?"

Melia shook his head. "They took a hell of a lot of stuff out of that car but they're waiting for something to match it to. You got some prints you want Wink or Dani to run a match on, we can do it Monday. Got no crime lab people to spare. We're already breaking the bank on overtime, and as for the rest of us—been kinda busy around here."

"Alana?"

"Interview three. Cooling her heels. She said we could take our time. She brought a book to read." Melia grinned. "*The Happy Hooker*." He turned to Perry. "Why don't you give Kyle a break?"

Burgess shook his head. "Anyone check that surveillance tape yet?"

"Stan queued it up but no one's had time to look at it yet. It's in the conference room." Melia sat back and studied him. A cop's assessment. He knew Vince was taking in the way he moved, the way he sounded, as well as how he looked and what he said—the speed of his reflexes and the speed of his synapses.

"I pass?" he asked.

"Makes me hurt just looking at you. What are you trying to prove, Joe? You're not a kid anymore. We're neither of us kids anymore. Don't bounce back like we used to." He cleared his throat, looked out the window toward Saturday and the normal life they hadn't chosen. Toward a place where your customers didn't do unspeakable things to each other and you didn't have much risk of finding yourself on the wrong end of a gun. He straightened his tie as though he could impose the same order on the world he imposed on himself.

"I'm wasting my breath but I've gotta say this. You could go home. Get some rest. Sometimes you have to let up. Believe it or not, Stan and Terry are competent detectives."

"I know that. We trained 'em, Vince."

Melia wasn't done. Like Burgess, he took a paternal interest in his people. And though they were colleagues, rank made Burgess one of his people. "When's the last time you ate? I could send out for something."

"Know anyone who delivers chicken soup and weak tea? I'm not up to much else, just want to play this thing out and crash."

"Tea I can do," Melia said. "Wanna see that video?"

"Yeah. I'll just stick my head in, say hello to Alana. Anything on Randall Noyes?"

"Stan talked with the local cops. Guy works for the highway department. Absolutely straight arrow, except for a few brawls right after his fiancée died. He hasn't been at work all week. Taking some vacation time."

"Lawyer show up for Kara Allison?" Melia shook his head. "She tell us where to find Noyes?"

"Says she doesn't know."

Burgess shrugged. "Whole damned world acts like we were born yesterday."

He found Alana engaged in animated conversation with a pair of riveted young cops, one of whom was Remy Aucoin. Aucoin spotted him first and took a step backward, his face flushing red. Alana looked up and grinned. She wore a pair of faded jeans that confirmed his belief that jeans were about the sexiest piece of clothing ever, and a copper-colored thermal top cut low and tight.

" 'Lo, copman. Long time no see." Her visual assessment wasn't much less probing than Melia's; her conclusions, judging from the concern on her face, not much different. "Jesus, Joe. You don't know the meaning of 'take it easy,' do you?"

"Had to go get patched back together," he said. "Think you can wait on me another couple minutes? I've got to take a quick look at some TV."

"Nothing on except cartoons, but you run along. I'm fine."

"I see you are." He couldn't help himself. When he looked at her, he saw her on tape with Ken Bailey, naked with those big hands all over her. Saw Bailey's mouth where his own had been. Proof of the truth of the old saying, a picture is worth a thousand words. A picture could hurt more, too. He knew it was irrational. She'd been a hooker as long as he'd known her. It was just one of those guy things—one thing to know it in the abstract, another to have it brought home in living color. "I won't be long," he said.

"You're mad at me."

He didn't respond. He went into the conference room and turned on the TV. The air was a stomach-turning mix of coffee, pizza, and old sweat. He hit play and waited, Vince beside him. It was ugly and graphic and played out about the way the high school kids had said. It also matched what little bit of statement they'd gotten from Mai Phung. With video like this, they didn't need a statement. They ever caught up with O'Leary, he was going away for a long time. Burgess rewound and watched again, looking for anything that might help identify the car O'Leary had come in or the driver of that car.

Nothing. He backed it up farther and tried again. This time, he got a fairly good picture of a dark car nosing into the curb, stopping, and rolling out of range. A good enough picture to see the hood ornament on the car. A Mercedes. He moved slowly forward and was rewarded again. A glimpse of a man who might have gotten out of the car and was heading toward the convenience store. A man whose tall frame and confident bearing looked familiar.

The convenience store might also have a surveillance camera. He pulled out his notebook, looked up the store, and called. "Burgess, Portland police, following up on the video store assault across the street. Does your store have a surveillance camera?" In response to an affirmative, he asked, "Still have the video from that day?"

She hesitated. "I think my husband saved it, just in case. I'll ask." Just in case what? He knew cops had been in. "Yeah," she said. "He's got it. What do you want us to do?"

"I'll send an officer over," he said. "Thanks."

"Wait," she said, eagerly. "Is there any reward or anything? We were hoping."

"Sorry, ma'am," he said. "But the department appreciates your help."

He got her name and hung up. Looked at Melia. "They were saving it for a reward." Melia rolled his eyes. "Aucoin working today or just here out of the goodness of his heart?"

"Goodness of his heart."

"Mind if I send him on an errand?"

"Hey," Vince said, "he's here for you."

"Right now, I'd say he's here for Alana." With his possessive male caveman reactions ascendant, he couldn't help feeling a little jaded and cynical about Alana. Knew, with time, he'd get over it. Cautiously, he levered his bulk out of the chair and shuffled off to find Aucoin.

CHAPTER THIRTY-ONE

Burgess shambled into Alana's presence, sat down in the chair, pulled out his notebook and turned on the tape, refusing to look at her. "Talk to me about the guy in the truck."

"I told you all I know about him," she said, puzzled, not used to him being so distant. "Which wasn't much. Look, I'm sorry I ran away, but it's like, no big deal. You know me. It's not like there are any secrets."

"That's exactly what it's like, Alana. The games you play. The stuff you don't tell me. Sometimes it matters. When things are real—like people getting dead, people getting hurt, lives getting ruined. Whether you care or not, other people matter."

She folded her arms and stuck out her chin. "I know that."

"Do you? The night Pleasant got killed, you saw a guy drop the second girl off in the parking lot. A guy you thought you'd seen before. A guy who had picked you up once, looking to connect with Dr. Pleasant. Right?" She nodded. He set the picture of Noyes down in front of her. "Is this the guy?"

She picked it up gingerly. "That's him."

"All right. You saw him in the parking lot the night Pleasant was killed. He dropped off the blonde and O'Leary picked her up. See any interaction between them, her and the guy?" Alana shook her head. "Then what?"

"I told you. We went back to O'Leary's and had a

party," she said. "What's with you today, Joe? You're so mean."

The door opened. Kyle came quietly in and sat down without speaking.

"This isn't a game," Burgess said. He wanted to grab her and shake her even though it would hurt him more than it would hurt her. "I'm trying to find a murderer."

"The guy in the truck followed us," she said sullenly. "O'Leary, the dumb shit, didn't even notice. Did you find him yet, Joe? Because I'm not going home until—"

"We're going to catch him and put him away, but we need your help."

"But you *haven't* caught him."

"What was O'Leary driving?"

"Some sport utility. Jeep, maybe? Maroon."

"Have you seen him since that night?" She shook her head. "Any idea where we might find him?"

"Not a clue. Ask Lulu. She might know. She likes the bastard."

"Does O'Leary have tattoos?"

She looked surprised. "Yeah. All over. On his neck and on his arms. He's got snakes around here." She circled her wrist with her hand. "Real fancy snakes."

He tossed another picture down. "Ever seen this man?" She glanced at it indifferently. "No."

"Don't lie to me, Alana. I'm in a bad mood today."

"I've never seen him."

"You've fucked him."

She shrugged, pretty pissed off herself. "I've fucked a lot of guys. Most of 'em not real memorable."

"I've seen it on video," he said. "Thought you didn't go for pimps. So why were you screwing this guy at O'Leary's place? Why let him tape it?"

Alana fidgeted on her chair, studying a room where there was nothing to see. "I already said. To keep O'Leary happy." He waited. There was more. "Money."

"Blackmail?" A shrug. "Why you? Why not Lulu?"

She smiled indulgently, like he was a moron who needed things explained. "He liked big tits and Lulu's well . . . she's okay, but . . . God, that guy liked to fuck. There's nothing like a hungry man, is there, Joe?" She lifted her shoulders and stuck out her chest.

Kyle, who'd been sitting quietly, got up and stepped between them, parking a hip on the edge of the desk, his lank body still and slack except for his angry eyes. "You want us to put you out of business, Alana? Is that it?"

"Oh, fuck you, Terry. I wasn't talking to you."

Kyle grabbed her arm and jerked her up out of her chair, sticking his face in hers. "No more games, you hear, or so help me, I'll see that every time you go out to suck some cock, you end up in jail." He tightened his grip. "We've got no patience with this shit."

He let her go and she dropped breathlessly back into her chair. "What's gotten into you?"

"Guess I've had enough of lying, scheming women," Kyle said. "Enough screwing around. You keep giving Joe this shit and I'll show you what a hard time really is. Joe, you want a Coke?" Burgess nodded and Kyle left.

Alana stared after him forlornly. "Jeez. Even Terry. And he's usually so nice."

"You knew it was being taped?" Burgess asked. A nod. "What did O'Leary do with the tape?"

"He didn't tell me."

"You said you did it for money. If it was just trick money, why make the tape? Were you going to get some money if he sold it?"

"Yeah. He was going to sell it and give me a cut. I guess the guy was some VIP."

"So this was recent?"

She nodded. "Few weeks, a month."

"Did O'Leary often make tapes of you?"

"That was the first time. Pleasant was the second." She flicked her tongue at him. "You saw the tape? Did I look good?" He'd had enough. Better to let Kyle do this. He shoved back his chair and got up. She came after him, grabbed his hand. "Look, Joe. I'm sorry. But it's not like you don't know who I am. What I do."

"What you do is tell so many lies you wouldn't know the truth if it bit you on the ass." He jerked his hand away. "Any idea how the guy found O'Leary?"

"O'Leary said Pleasant set it up. Wanted a special evening for his friend."

Burgess stabbed Bailey's picture. "This guy."

"Yeah. That guy. So I gave him a special evening."

He switched off the tape. "Thank you, Ms. Black."

She stuck out her chin. "Think you could find me a Coke? That guy Remy was getting me one, but he disappeared. And Terry didn't even ask me."

"Terry doesn't like you much today, Alana, and I sent Remy on an errand."

"To get him away from me?"

Like the whole fucking world revolved around her! "Because I was too damned tired to do it myself."

She tried to massage his neck. He moved away. "I don't get it," she said. "You see me on tape fucking some guy and suddenly I can't touch you?"

"Give it a rest."

She flexed her fingers. Wanting to touch him. Believing that's all it would take. That men weren't like women.

Didn't need to be in the mood. He said he'd find someone to drive her home.

Melia was arguing with a guy in the hall. The dull suit, briefcase and belligerence all screamed lawyer. Burgess stopped.

". . . absolutely no right to question my client without me being here," the suit said. "This smacks of police harassment. I demand to see her at once and that all further interrogation cease."

"She's a cooperative witness being *interviewed* in connection with a homicide investigation. She's here of her own free will. *Voluntarily*," Melia said. "What's your problem, Chambers?"

Chambers had a smart face, a receding hairline, and an abundance of attitude. Probably an associate at one of the big firms. It explained his late arrival. Hard to find VIPs on a Saturday, and then the VIPs had had to find Chambers and put him on the case. Burgess did a lot of crime, including white collar, and hadn't seen him around. Sarah Merchant's version of "best" had been "most expensive." Maybe that was how bankers thought. The best criminal defense lawyers usually weren't the big firm types. There was definitely a "lie down with dogs, get up with fleas" quality about criminal defense.

"You guys are my problem," Chambers said. "From what her aunt said, you guys think she's a suspect. She should have been warned."

"She was."

"Kara's just a kid. A few mumbled words from a threatening cop in the middle of the night. That doesn't mean squat and you know it."

Burgess fumbled out his notebook, opened it on the closest desktop, fished out her signed waiver and gave it to

Melia. "Going to see how Stan's doing," he said.

Melia read the paper and nodded. He didn't smile. Cops don't exchange triumphant smiles in front of asshole lawyers, but his eyes were satisfied. "I'll make you a copy of this," he told Chambers.

Chambers snatched at the paper. "Let me see that."

Melia turned, his eyes cold. "I'll make you a copy," he repeated. Chambers got the message.

Kyle was watching Stan and Kara Allison on the monitor. Kyle handed him a Coke. "Sorry about sticking my oar in, but she was being such a bitch. How you doin'?"

"Been better."

"Know what you mean. Hard to leave a warm bed for this." His tired face lit, softened, thinking about Michelle. "She's an angel, Joe."

"Glad to hear something's going right." Burgess shifted his stiff shoulders cautiously. "Vince and I looked at the video store tape. Got the car that delivered O'Leary—Mercedes. Aucoin's getting the surveillance tape from the convenience store across the street. We might get a picture of the driver."

"There's progress."

"We could use some. Alana says that Randall Noyes, the guy in the truck, followed O'Leary when he drove Kara Allison to her rendezvous with Pleasant."

"How could O'Leary not notice?"

"Because he's stupid. I want Noyes," Burgess said. "I want him bad. I want to know what he saw." Remy Aucoin appeared in the doorway and Burgess held out his hand for the convenience store tape. "Thanks, Remy. Let's go watch this sucker. Remy, we're ready to cut Alana Black loose. You want to give her a ride home?"

Aucoin lit up like a child offered ice cream. "Happy to, sir."

"You're bad, Joe," Kyle said. "Mood she's in, she'll eat him alive."

"If he wants to try flying close to the light, try not to get burned, that's a good test for him. Let's leave 'em to it, go to the movies."

The tape had a date and time line, which helped narrow their search. After they watched the clerk snap her gum and pull up her bra straps a dozen times, the door opened and a tall man in a dark overcoat came in and walked past the counter. His face was turned toward the door, his hat hiding his profile. "Come on, baby," Kyle crooned, making a little coaxing motion with his hand. "Let us see your face."

Burgess leaned forward eagerly. The man approached the counter again, dropped his purchases on it, and turned toward the camera as he fished in his pocket for his wallet.

"No way," Kyle burst out. "No fucking way!"

Burgess hit the pause button. They stared at Dr. Kenneth Bailey.

"Go get Vince," Burgess said. "He needs to see this."

CHAPTER THIRTY-TWO

"Only an hour before," Burgess said, "this guy's shoving me around, trying to throw me out of his hospital. *His* hospital. Soon as Terry and I leave, he and O'Leary jump in his car and head for the video store where O'Leary tries to rape that girl."

Melia stared at the screen, fingering his tie and frowning. When they finished, he nodded. "You've got witnesses and video that put him with the suspect at the scene of an assault and attempted rape. You want to talk to Dr. Bailey, I've got no problem."

Burgess saw a problem. "Captain Cote," he said, "wants to be informed when we're thinking about bugging a VIP. Meaning, wants a chance to warn Bailey that we're coming. Wants a chance to screw things up again."

Melia frowned. He knew how Burgess felt, but rank was rank. "You check with him before you went larking off to Boothbay last night to get yourself shot?"

"I tried to return his six messages," Burgess grunted. "He couldn't be found." Something like this, he knew, Cote would expect them to make a greater effort to find him, but Burgess wasn't coming this far and taking this kind of punishment only to have the thing snatched away from him.

"You left messages, right?" Burgess nodded, hoping Melia'd make the right call. "So when you get there, leave a message on his voice mail."

"That going to cover your ass, too?"

Melia gave him a lightweight version of the look he'd given the lawyer. "I'm not worried about my ass," he said. "Why don't you guys get going. Give your cousin a courtesy call, let him know you're coming." Burgess and Kyle stood up. "Anything special you'd like me to do with these women you've dragged in?" Melia said.

"Aucoin's taking Alana home."

Melia rolled his eyes. "And the other one?"

"Kara Allison? Find out what she was wearing and where it is now. Then put it in the affidavit and the warrant to search her place. Do whatever it takes to hold her until we get back. Either she's the doer or a material witness. She walks out that door, she's gone." Cop's instinct again. "Stan's burned out." He shrugged. "You might give it a whirl yourself. Keep asking about Randall Noyes. Maybe she'll get tired, let something slip."

Melia's laugh was short. "Don't hold your breath. She's not a woman, she's a robot." He headed for the door. "You guys be careful. I don't want Burgess any more ventilated than he already is."

"Vince," Kyle said, "we're on our way to see a respected physician. Friend of the governor. There's no danger."

"A respected physician who transported a pimp and blackmailer so he could commit an assault," Burgess said. "Who's the star of an incriminating videotape. Who hates my guts."

"You're wearing vests. My orders," Melia said. "Like Joe should have last night."

"We live and learn," Burgess said. Last night's exploits made him a textbook case of cop carelessness, but every cop made mistakes, the ones that could get you killed. Every cop.

He and Kyle went down to their lockers and got their

vests. Burgess got out his leather jacket. It was stiff and heavy but his other one was dead and he wasn't calling on Bailey in a snowmobile suit. He grabbed the nearest phone, dialed the familiar number. "Sam? It's Joe . . ."

"Been keeping an eye on the place, cuz. Nothing happening."

"This is just a heads up. Couple of us coming out to see one of your citizens. Dr. Kenneth Bailey."

"Great guy, Dr. Bailey," his cousin said. "Saw him at the hardware store a while ago, pickin' up some cement to mend a patio. A big Rubbermaid container to store boating equipment in. Enough duct tape to wrap a mummy. Some folks use duct tape for everything. I told him it was too cold for cement, but he said his wife was after him . . . and didn't I know how that was?"

Burgess nearly dropped the phone. "Sam," he said. "Let me tell you what I got. We're looking for Kevin O'Leary, the pimp who set up the party for Pleasant the night he died. Well, I got Bailey on surveillance video, two days ago, driving O'Leary to a video store. O'Leary tells the clerk he's come for some tapes they're storing for him. She doesn't know about any videos, so O'Leary assaults her, then Bailey drives him away. We respond to the assault, find O'Leary's homemade tape of Dr. Bailey with a prostitute. Later the store gets firebombed and O'Leary, who's a steady source of drugs, hasn't been seen since."

He waited for his cousin to process all that. "Maybe you want to come with us on this. Get someone over there to watch Bailey's house?"

"Sounds like a plan."

He hung up, filled Kyle in. "We'd better tell Vince. This thing's getting crazy. A big plastic container, cement and duct tape. What's that sound like?"

"Like the man's arrogance knows no bounds." Kyle shook his head. "How dumb does he think we are?"

Melia listened without comment, his face grim. "You called your cousin?"

"He told me about the Rubbermaid and the duct tape. He's waiting for us."

"You better get moving. Take Stan." Burgess nodded. "Be careful. Stay in touch." Melia's smile was brief and thin. "And *not* on my voice mail."

"So Stan," he asked, as they drove over the Million Dollar Bridge toward South Portland and Cape Elizabeth, "you get any sleep last night?"

"What you really wanna know is, did I get laid, right? And the answer is a big, fat *yes*. How 'bout you, Terry?"

Kyle just smiled. "Hey," Stan complained from the back seat. "I can't see his face. What's he doin', Joe?"

"Smiling."

"Fuckin' A," Stan said.

Burgess's cousin was waiting in front of the station. He motioned for them to follow and pulled slowly away from the curb. Kyle followed through a maze of twisty roads, past pleasant, well-maintained houses, stopping at the tall white fence sheltering Bailey's house from the street. Burgess got out and followed Sam up the drive. Waited while Sam knocked. A smiling, pear-shaped woman with graying hair, gray slacks and an oversized gray sweater opened it. "Why, Sam Burgess, what brings you out here? Come to arrest me for leaving too many brownies at the station?"

"You can't do too much of that, Madeline," Sam said, patting his girth. "No. The boys appreciate that. They really do. This is Sergeant Joe Burgess, Portland PD, working on the Stephen Pleasant case. Ken around?"

"Oh, Sam, you just missed him. Ted Shaw called. Something about Jen, I suppose, so he's gone over there. Is it anything I can help you with?"

"Just some follow-up questions," Burgess said.

"I could call over there," she offered. "See when he'll be back."

"No." He struggled to keep from shouting. "No. Thank you, ma'am. It wasn't urgent. I just thought I'd stop, since I was visiting Sam. Save myself a trip . . ."

"Ran into Ken at the hardware store this morning," Sam said jovially, moving smoothly into the breach. "Sorry to hear about your patio falling apart, but I told him this is no time to be trying to use cement."

"Cement?" she said. "Patio? There's nothing wrong with my patio. What on earth was that man talking about?" Mrs. Bailey looked from one to the other, scrutinizing them closely. Burgess tensed against some hard question, some articulated suspicion that might send her to the phone. "Are you two related?" she asked. "You look alike."

"Cousins," Sam said. "I'm the handsome one. We'd better be going. Sorry to have bothered you." He gave her a smile. "And keep those brownies coming."

"You can count on it." She closed the door.

"Guess we're off to Shaw's."

"Let me call first. See if Bailey's there." Sam slipped into his car and used the radio. "Got there about half an hour ago. Drove his car right into the garage."

"Delivering the coffin," Burgess said. "Along with cement to weight it down and duct tape to seal it. A burial at sea, perhaps. Or at the bottom of the garden? Maybe wait 'til dark and dump O'Leary off a pier somewhere."

They wound their way to Shaw's. Burgess, who'd only made the trip at night, marveled at how well some people lived. It was more troubled and challenging, but he preferred Portland. He liked it that his Portland landscape was filled with black and yellow and white faces, faces lined with experience, marked by sorrow or glowing with hope. He knew dozens of street people, some vets he looked after. Had been invited to a Cambodian wedding. People bored him when they were all the same brand.

They pulled into the drive and parked behind a Volvo that looked like Jen Kelly's. Kyle made the call to Cote's machine. Shit! If this was nothing more than Mrs. Bailey thought—a consult with Dr. Bailey about Jen's welfare—he needed his gut examined. His cop's gut. But instinct said he was on the right track here. Once again, he climbed the steps behind Sam. God, his cousin's rear end had gotten big. Was his that bad? Did they now resemble not so much aging football players as hippos? Sam was only two years older, but his hair was gray, neck wrinkled, hands spotted. He watched Sam lift one of those hands to the doorbell. Felt an adrenaline surge. Looked back toward Kyle, sitting there watchful.

Ted Shaw gave them a cold, appraising look, like they were tradesmen coming to the wrong door, which, in his social hierarchy, they probably were. "Sam," he said, ignoring Burgess completely. "I'm busy. My daughter and grandson are here. Could we do whatever it is some other time?"

"No problem, Ted," Sam Burgess said. "You go right on visitin' with Jen. No need to disturb you at all. We had some questions for Ken Bailey. Madeline said he was here."

Shaw looked back into the interior of the house, a space they couldn't see because he blocked the opening. "I don't know why she'd say that. Ken's not here." Behind him rose a baby's cry and a woman's soft voice.

Burgess realized that Perry hadn't been in the car. A typical Perry move. Like an impulsive ten-year-old. Tell him to wait in the car and he can't sit still. He has to get out, just for a minute, to look at something.

Shaw looked down at them. "I'm sorry. I'm busy. Come another time." Ready to shut the door in their faces.

Burgess was suddenly rocked by a wave of dizziness. Instead of fighting it, he saw an opportunity. He let himself sway, staggered into Sam, pushing him toward Shaw and stumbling inside as the door yielded to his weight. Sam, quick to see what was happening, got an arm around his shoulders and helped him to the nearest chair. He rested his head on the chair back and closed his eyes. This better bring them something. Sam's rough handling really hurt.

"Sorry, Sam, Mr. Shaw," Burgess said. "I was on the wrong end of a shotgun last night."

"That's no concern of mine," Shaw said. "Sam, now that you know the person you're looking for isn't here, will you please remove this man from my house."

"I'm sorry, sir," Burgess said, deliberately exaggerating his weakness. "I never expected this or I certainly wouldn't have bothered you. I was fine a minute ago."

Sam fussed over him, loosening his tie, unbuttoning the top button on his shirt. "You sure, Joe?" he asked. "Sure? You look awful. Shouldn't I call an ambulance?"

Quick, light footsteps approached and then Jen Kelly's voice from the other room. "Dad? Can you come here a minute? Dr. Bailey says he needs some help . . ." She hurried into the room, stopping with a gasp. Burgess opened his eyes.

"Chief?" she said. "Detective? What are you doing here?" She stared from one to the other, her hand over her mouth like a child caught in a lie. Then, with a cry, she turned and ran from the room.

"Goddammit, detective, I told you not to upset her,

didn't I?" Shaw bellowed. "Isn't that the one thing I asked of your hopelessly incompetent department? To leave the poor child alone and not upset her? Get out before I call your boss and have you fired."

For what, the unpardonable sin of getting dizzy in a rich man's foyer?

Arriving unannounced for tea?

Upsetting people was what cops did. Burgess smiled politely up at Shaw. "Could you tell Dr. Bailey we're here and ask if he would give us a few minutes?"

"I've asked you to leave, which means you no longer have permission to be in my house. Now go."

Under Sam's worried gaze and Shaw's wilting one, Burgess pushed himself to his feet and stood a minute. "Better," he said. He forced a smile, wanting to grab the arrogant prick by his long, skinny neck and shake him until his cold WASP brain rattled in its patrician cage. "Thank you for your hospitality."

Their host barely gave them time to get through the door. They went down the steps and leaned against the car. "Down the road a block or so?" he suggested. Sam walked to his car, and drove away. Burgess got in, glad to see that Perry was back. Kyle cruised smoothly out of the driveway.

Burgess closed his eyes again. He didn't know what he looked like, but he felt gray and clammy. He felt fragile and explosive, like a Fabergé hand-grenade. "Stan," he said, "next time you decide to go larking, ask permission. Shaw wasn't going to let us in the door. I had to fake a fainting spell just to give you time to get back."

"Sorry, Joe. So I guess you don't wanna know what I saw?"

"Of course I want to know what you saw. I deserve some reward for making an ass of myself in front of a guy like that."

349

Kyle fanned himself with his hand. "Oh, Joseph," he said in an affected voice. "We start rewarding you for making an ass of yourself, and who knows where it will end."

"Up yours," he grunted.

Kyle pulled in behind Sam's car. Sam came and climbed into the back seat with Stan. "So?" Sam said. "What do you want to do, bearing in mind that that's my most prominent citizen you just pissed off."

Perry grinned. "In the garage, on the floor under a tarp, is a human body, or at least pieces of a body—a large lump and some visible legs and feet. Naked legs and bare feet. How many people you know lie down naked on a cement garage floor in February? Besides, they weren't a normal color. The toes and front of the legs were a purplish color, the heels and backs of the legs dead white. What our friends in the ME's office call lividity. You've got a plastic storage container and a man I've been told is Dr. Kenneth Bailey stirring up some cement. I wouldn't wait too long to see what happens."

"And how," Sam asked, "did you happen to be in a position to observe all this?"

Perry's grin broadened. "I was leaning against the car, getting some air, waiting for my superior officer to return from the house, when I heard a cry which sounded like someone in distress, coming from the direction of the garage. I immediately proceeded in the direction of the sound. When I looked through the window to determine whether someone was in need of assistance, I observed Dr. Bailey and the body. Not to mention a maroon Jeep the cops have been looking for, possibly the property of one Kevin O'Leary?"

"No shit, Sherlock," Sam said. "Guess we'd better go

type us up a warrant. You gonna be the affiant?"

"Why the hell not?" Perry said.

"Then let's move. We could just burst in, but under the circumstances, I'd prefer to have a warrant. You happen to note the license number?" Perry nodded.

"I'll stay here with Terry. Keep an eye on things," Burgess said.

"He'll be okay. I've got a guy around the corner. You're coming with me."

"I'm fine," Burgess said.

"Have you seen yourself? You're scary."

"I don't scare these guys."

"They know you're a crazy fucker."

"I didn't scare Shaw."

"Don't be so sure. That's why we've got to move. Because they're going to. Stan and I will do the warrant. You're going to eat some nice chicken soup."

"You're so thoughtful, Sam."

"Stow it, asshole. This little escapade's about to screw up my whole day. Gonna have state police all over my ass."

"Just think," Kyle said. "Your first murder."

"You can put a cork in it, too," Sam snapped. "I got no patience with smart-mouth, big-city detectives."

"Aw, shucks," Kyle said. "Portland's just a small town."

"Come on. Let's move," Sam said. Meaning type up an affidavit and a request for a warrant ASAP and find a willing judge on a Saturday afternoon."

So much for the excitement and danger of discovering a body. The thrill of the chase. Burgess shifted the accumulated bundle of misery he called a body into the back seat of his cousin's car and rested his eyes.

CHAPTER THIRTY-THREE

He woke abruptly when both doors popped open, Sam and Stan Perry jumped in, and the car was rolling. "Got a call, Joe," his cousin said. "Kyle's in trouble."

He fumbled for consciousness and his seatbelt, the car already moving fast. Sam hunched over the wheel, cursing steadily under his breath. "Stan, what's going on?"

"Officer watching the place says a big Suburban came barreling out of Shaw's driveway few minutes ago, drove right into Terry and kept on going. There's an ambulance on the way."

"Deliberate?"

"Looks that way."

"What about the warrant?"

"Got an officer picking it up from the judge at this very moment," Sam growled. "Not that it'll do us much good now. Most likely what we're looking for's in that Suburban."

"Not necessarily," Burgess said. "Sometimes the smart guys make the dumbest mistakes. Your guy follow them?"

"Nah. He stayed behind to call it in and look after Kyle . . ." Sam broke off to control a skid. "No way he'd leave an injured officer to go chasing after bad guys. We've got a BOLO out with the plates and description." He fishtailed through a series of curves, then slammed on his brakes and pulled in behind a flashing patrol car.

Burgess was out before the car had stopped rocking. The driver's door of the Explorer was punched in, the rest of the vehicle untouched. A neat, surgical strike. A young cop, looking a little blue in the cold, stood beside the car.

"How is he?" Burgess asked.

"Looks like a concussion and a broken leg, sir."

He went around to the other door and got in. Kyle lay white and silent in his seat, blood from a gaping head wound dripping down his face. The officer had covered him with a blanket. The running engine kept him warm. It looked bad, but head wounds did. Bad color, tight face and the sound of his breathing spoke pain. Burgess pulled out a handkerchief, gently wiped the blood off Kyle's face, then folded it, and pressed it against the wound. "Terry?" he said. "It's Joe. How you doin'?"

"I'm pretty fucked up." Kyle groaned. "Leg hurts like hell. I should have seen it coming."

"No way you could have," Burgess said, wishing he could take the pain on himself and spare Kyle. "Ambulance should be here any minute. You remember what happened?"

"Asshole drove straight at me, backed up, and took off. It was no accident."

"See who was driving?"

"Bailey. Shaw was in the passenger seat."

"We'll get him, Terry."

"I know . . ." Kyle's voice was fading. "Just wish I could be there." The ambulance arrived in a blaze of light and sound. Burgess started backing out to make way for the EMTs. "Wait, Joe," Kyle whispered. "Don't tell Wanda. It'll scare the girls."

Sam came toward him. Not a happy camper. "Just looked through the garage window. I don't see Stan's tarp-covered body anywhere."

Burgess nodded, unsurprised. "There'll be something in

there. They didn't have time to clean up."

He stood shoulder to shoulder with Stan, watching them load Kyle on a stretcher and put him in the ambulance. "I'll ride with Terry, give Vince the word. Stan'll stay here with you. Terry's going to need some TLC, Stan. You might want to call Michelle."

Stan made that call while Burgess got on his phone to Melia. "Vince, it's hit the fan." He explained what had happened, that Kyle was on the way to the hospital. "Cape Elizabeth cops are about to execute the warrant. Stan's gonna stay here with them. Body's probably gone. Tell hospital security to let us know if Bailey shows up." He snapped the words out, impelled by the anger he felt. "He shows up and I want two of the biggest, meanest cops we got taking him out of there in handcuffs. Kyle said Bailey rammed right into him, then drove away."

The whole rocky ride to Portland, he beat himself up for letting this happen. For leaving Kyle alone while he took a nap like some weary goddamned toddler. He should have been more careful. They might be prominent doctors and even more prominent rich guys, but Bailey was also a video porn star and associate of Kevin O'Leary. Known to be both arrogant and hot-tempered. Shaw's eagerness to rush them out the door hadn't been the product of a desire to bond with his grandson. Bailey'd been doing his dirty work at Shaw's house. Had Jen Kelly known what was going on?

In a kindly, if misplaced gesture, the EMT put a hand on his shoulder. "Take it easy, detective. He's going to be okay."

He paced the waiting room, waiting for Kyle to come back from X-ray. Waiting for someone to let him know they'd found something. Surely a big black Suburban couldn't vanish? Sam and Stan Perry must have found something. Wondering what the hell was going on, when Vince came on the radio. "Call me back, Joe."

He carried his phone out to the parking lot. "What?"

"South Portland police stopped Bailey coming over the bridge. He claims Shaw's having a heart attack and he's bringing him to the hospital. We're following them in."

Something in Melia's voice made him ask, "And?"

"Captain Cote's on his way over."

Given the chance, Cote would ensure that Bailey and Shaw weren't arrested, or even questioned, by intrusive cops before they'd had an opportunity to lawyer up. Burgess saw a week of brutal, soul-sucking work slipping away. More victims sacrificed on the altar of power and expedience. Collateral victims like Mackenzie and Stevie Pleasant and Mai Phung.

"No way. No fucking way," he said. "It doesn't take over an hour from there to here. He was driving a car that left the scene of a personal injury accident. Except it was no accident. Bailey was standing next to a body in that garage and now that body's disappeared. I want him in an interview room. Voluntarily or involuntarily. I want his answers to what he was doing at the video store with O'Leary, and in Shaw's garage with the storage container and the cement, and where the hell that container is now. I want to know what O'Leary's car is doing in that garage. I want his version of where O'Leary is."

"Look, Joe—"

Burgess cut him off. "You're the boss. You can call it any way you want, but I've got a man down and that asshole is not walking away from this. Get him now while he's pissed off and agitated and you might get some answers. Wait 'til he lawyers up and you'll get fuck all."

"Sorry, Joe. The command structure is what it is."

Not sorry enough. He'd been here. Done this. Wasn't doing it again. "Fuck the food chain, Vince," he said. "I swear on my mother's grave that that starfucker's not going to help another killer walk just because he's well-connected. Not gonna kiss ass while my guys work themselves to death trying to solve crimes. If Bailey isn't brought in for questioning, with all we know about him, after running down one of our own officers, then I'll shoot Cote myself, so no other cop will ever have to go through this, and consider it a bullet well spent."

"I didn't hear that," Melia barked back, "and you didn't say it. Now get your ass back to my office. Pronto. Or you'll be out of a job so fast it'll make your head spin."

"I don't have a ride," Burgess said. "Bailey smashed it."

Sorry, Vince. Burgess hit end. Put the phone away, watching the big black car with its police escort roll up to the door, looking like the FBI.

Bailey came in with an arm solicitously around Ted Shaw, medical personnel surging to meet them. "Dr. Bailey," Burgess called in a loud voice, waving his badge. "I have some questions."

Talking meant breathing. Meant control. He had, at best, minutes to make this happen before Cote arrived and screwed things up.

"Not now, detective," Bailey snapped. "This is a medical emergency."

"So was the cop you ran into and left broken and bleeding on the roadside, doctor. Did he not count?" Making no move to get closer or lower his voice. "And it looks like Mr. Shaw's in good hands." Still keeping his distance. Drawing a crowd. "I was wondering what you did with O'Leary's body? Kevin O'Leary, the blackmailer? Pimp? Rapist? The body that was in Mr. Shaw's garage.

You dump it somewhere on your way?"

Understanding what was happening, the officers who'd followed Bailey had placed themselves between him and any exit doors. Bailey marched up to the nearest one, barked a loud, "Excuse me," hesitating when the officer didn't jump out of his way. Perhaps remembering Burgess and Kyle with their hands on their guns?

"Don't want to talk about O'Leary's body? Then how about how you got hooked up with O'Leary in the first place, Dr. Bailey. I have two theories about that. How about this?" Reluctantly, but drawn by the words, Bailey turned back toward him. "You had a problem with your partner, Dr. Pleasant, and his unpleasant habit of reclaiming Oxycontin from deceased patients and selling it to drug addicts, didn't you, Dr. Bailey? Pretty damned embarrassing, wasn't it. Was O'Leary your solution?"

Bailey's face was red. He reached out to push the officer aside, thought better of it, backed away from the unmoving police officer, and moved toward a second door. And a second cop. Burgess went on talking, loud enough so the whole room could hear. "Did you pay Kevin O'Leary to kill your partner, Stephen Pleasant? Dr. Pleasant, as you've said yourself, was ambitious and greedy. Did he get too ambitious and too greedy and you decided he had to be stopped?"

"I didn't . . . Goddammit! Are you refusing to let me leave the room? Am I under arrest?"

"Why would you be under arrest? Just because you deliberately drove your car into a police officer, causing serious injury?" As Bailey hesitated, Burgess continued. "But I think, before you rush away, you might want to hear my second theory." Talking faster and louder now, before Cote, who'd just pulled up, could get from his car to the door. "You got hooked up with O'Leary when he tried to blackmail you about a videotape, didn't you? A videotape of you and a black prostitute named Alana Black, filmed during a sexual encounter arranged by your good friend, Dr. Pleasant. Funny how you can know a guy's cheating on his wife and never think he'll screw you, too, isn't it?"

"Shut up," Bailey ordered, turning on him. "You have no right!" He charged across the room, shoving people out of his way.

"I wonder how your sweet wife, Madeline, would react to a full-color video of you sucking the big brown breast of a voluptuous naked whore? Of you jamming yourself down that girl's throat? I've got that tape, Dr. Bailey. I wonder how Madeline—"

"How dare you bring my wife into this!" Bailey yelled. "Stephen Pleasant was a rotten shit, forcing me to deal with extortionist scum like O'Leary."

"You think you're any better? Harboring a man the police are looking for? Driving O'Leary to that video store where he tried to rape a fifteen-year-old? Willing to do anything to get that tape back? You think other people don't matter, doctor, as long as your own precious ass is protected? Because you're some God-like doctor, you can decide who's worthy to live or die?"

Bailey's big head swiveled around at all the staring faces, his face so scarlet with rage it looked like he was the one in danger of a heart attack. "You shut up!" he said, lifting a big clenched fist. "Goddammit, detective. You shut up! O'Leary was a pimping, drug-dealing, blackmailing scum. He deserved to die."

Captain Cote came through the door just in time to catch that statement and see an enraged Bailey shove several people aside and slam a furious fist into one of the few undamaged parts of his ace homicide detective, in full view of at least six cops and a dozen other witnesses. Burgess, knocked back against the wall and sliding slowly to the floor, folded himself around the pain with an inward smile of triumph. Go ahead and let him walk, you oleaginous starfucker. At least this time, you can't sweep it under the rug.

Chapter Thirty-four

He left the mess at Maine Med in Cote's competent hands. Quickly, and without surprise, Burgess ascertained that the Suburban contained neither O'Leary's body nor the Rubbermaid container. But Burgess was on a roll. No time to stop now. In flagrant defiance of Melia's orders, he hitched a ride to the station, got Stan's car, and drove back to Shaw's house, the endorphin high from having outfoxed Bailey, a pretty good offset to the shrieking voices of his aggravated wounds. He found Perry and Sam sitting in Sam's car while a bunch of self-important state police processed the garage.

"No body," Sam reported. "We got an earring like O'Leary wore. We got his car. We got Bailey buying cement and the storage container. Lying about the cement to a cop. And who knows what these crime scene boys will find?"

"Damn," Burgess said. "Nothing in the Suburban, either. I was hoping—"

"Wait." Perry's eyes lit up. "Pleasant's wife. Who knows what she saw, heard, or even carted off in her little Volvo, to go out with her trash."

"Stan, you're a gem. Let's go see her. Wanna come, Sam?"

"Gotta see this thing through. I'll send someone over in a bit."

Burgess felt giddy. Manic. Like the crazy fucker Kyle always accused him of being. This many hours up on this little sleep, beaten down, broken and shot, wasn't he entitled to be insane? But he hadn't laid a finger on Cote.

He filled Stan in as they drove to Jen Kelly's house. Her Volvo was parked at the door. Burgess walked over and looked in. Three big black trash bags that hadn't been there before. He sighed. Now they had to either get her to agree to let them search, or camp on her doorstep until they got a warrant. Wearily, he mounted the steps and rang the doorbell, absently rubbing the spot where Bailey's fist had landed. Old fart still packed quite a punch.

When she recognized them, she turned on her heel, crossed the hall, and picked up the phone. Burgess, feeling uncharitable, followed her and depressed the phone switch. "You can do that later," he said. "We have to talk."

"No. I don't want to talk to you anymore. I want you out of my house. I want to call my lawyer."

"Why? Were you a party to your husband's death?" Burgess said. "To the death of Kevin O'Leary?"

"I don't know what you're talking about." She folded her arms defensively. "I'm just protecting my privacy."

"And to hell with the murder investigation?" Burgess said. "Do you know what was going on at your father's house today?"

Perry came in and closed the door behind him. She looked from one of them to the other nervously. "What do you want? Why are you here?"

"For starters," Burgess said, "I'd like the truth."

"I've always told you the truth."

"Bullshit!"

"I have!" More like an irate child than a mother with a child of her own.

"You said you last saw your husband at breakfast on the day he died. That wasn't true, was it? I have a witness who saw you at the hospital that night, waiting for him. Who saw you talking to him. Saw you run away in tears and drive out in such a hurry you took the security arm right off."

"I wasn't there," she said.

"I can match the paint," he said. "Your car, the security arm. And once I know that's a lie, why should I believe anything else you say?"

"I wasn't there," she repeated, stubbornly, giving him the full eye treatment, a wide, innocent stare with those big baby-blues. Pretty eyes in a sweet, sweet face. It must have worked for her in the past or she wouldn't bother. But it didn't work on the meanest cop in Portland. He was long past feminine wiles. If he hadn't been, this case would have cured him. Good-looking women seduced you, lied to you, shot you.

"Yes. You were." Burgess felt mean. He was sick of these people who lied and thought it didn't matter. Who killed and thought it didn't matter. Who condoned killing because it was easier and thought that didn't matter. He moved closer to her, into her personal space, and raised his voice. "What do you care about, Jen? Do you care about finding your husband's killer? Do you care that your baby will grow up without a father? That Mackenzie will? Does anything matter to you?"

She brought her arms up defensively in front of her. "No!" she said. "No. I didn't care if anything happened to Stephen. I'm not sorry he's dead. He was horrible to me. I thought he loved me, but he was only in love with my money. With Ted Shaw's money. Stephen wanted the money for this lifestyle, but my father ended up using it to pay off Stephen's blackmailers. All that money wasted to keep me from knowing what I already knew . . . and of course to spare us the embarrassment of having it made public."

"Because Jack Kelly told you?"

"He blames himself. Sure. But after Stephen said he'd stop, I knew because I followed him myself. He was so damned arrogant he didn't even notice! I would have given him another chance. If he'd only tried." She raised her eyes to his again, asking him to share her amazement. Then she lowered them. "But I didn't kill him, detective. After my mother's cancer, I got a new respect for life. And then, after Stevie, it was even greater. I don't think I could ever take a life, no matter how much I hated."

"But you were happy to let your father—your biological father—do it for you."

Her gaze stayed fixed on the floor. "No. I'm sure you don't believe me, but I don't think Ted . . . my father . . . killed Stephen."

"But he or they, he and his friend, Doctor Bailey, killed that man whose body was in the garage tonight. The one they were trying to get rid of."

"Body?" she said uncertainly, looking from one of them to the other. "What are you talking about?"

"Kevin O'Leary," Perry said. "Big, ugly bald guy. Tattoos. Ears like cup handles. Used to come to collect the blackmail. Peddle the drugs."

"Drugs?" she said uncertainly. "I don't understand . . . Stephen didn't . . ." She bit her lip, brought her focus back to his question. "No." She shook her head vigorously. "I never saw anyone like that."

"In the back of your car there are three plastic trash bags," Burgess said. "They weren't there when I looked in your car at your father's place. What's in the bags?"

She took an unsteady step backward. Looked at the phone again, maybe wondering if she could get to it before he could stop her. She put a hand on the wall to brace herself. She'd gone deathly pale. "I don't know about any bags."

Maybe she didn't. It was possible, in their hurry, that her father and Dr. Bailey had dumped the bags in her car, expecting she wouldn't notice. "Come outside with me. I'll show you."

"I can't leave the baby."

"It's right outside the door," Burgess said. "Stan will listen for the baby. Come on." He jerked open the closet, pulled out a coat. "Here. Wear this."

Like an obedient child, she took it and put it on. Pulled gloves from the pocket and followed him down the steps. Walked slowly, warily, toward her car. Very slowly, she put out her hand, grasped the latch, and let the tailgate rise. The light came on and she stared in surprise at the bulging black bags. "They're not mine," she said. "I don't know how they got here."

"Mind if I look inside?"

"No. Of course not."

Burgess tugged on gloves and pulled the nearest bag toward him. It was surprisingly heavy. He knew, as soon as he undid the wire and released the smell, what he was going to find. He looked in and turned away, gagging at the horrific sight and smell. Standing in the shadows at the edge of the dim trunk light, he tried with the sluggish responses of an exhausted body to quell his rising sickness.

"What is it?" she demanded, reaching for the bag. "What?"

His stomach twisted and roiled. Tough-as-nails Burgess, who thought he'd seen it all, was going to be sick like some baby cop. Too busy losing his lunch to serve and protect.

She stepped closer, curious. He tried to stop her, reaching out to grab her hands, to pull her away. "Don't look!" he ordered. "Jen, for God's sake, don't look."

Defiantly, she grabbed the bag and pulled it open. She took one long look at Kevin O'Leary's head and crumpled, with a cry, onto the ground.

Burgess hollered for Stan, then staggered away and was sick behind a bush. The spasms ignited all his injuries. He dragged himself back to the car, aware that he'd finally passed his limit. Exhausted his utility here, there and everywhere, until he got some rest.

Stan rushed down the steps, staring in surprise at the girl on the ground and Burgess's face. "What the hell happened, Joe?"

Burgess gestured toward the closest bag. "Grab some gloves and have a look. It's O'Leary."

Perry jerked on a pair of gloves and peered in. "Holy shit!" He looked a little rocky himself. He knelt beside Jen, put the gloves in his pocket, and touched her face. "Out like a light."

"She was so mad she had to look, Stan. I told her not to, so she marched right over and peered in. Mind bringing her inside? We can't leave her here." Stan slid his arms beneath her, lifted her easily, and carried her into the house.

Burgess followed, envying Perry the ease, remembering when he was young and how good it felt to protect someone pretty and vulnerable like Jen Kelly. Not that they'd protected her from much tonight. She'd seen about the ugliest thing a person can see. She'd had a succession of ugly things lately. Depending on how things shook out, it looked like more ugly things to come.

It didn't take many guesses to figure out who'd cut O'Leary up and stuck him in her car. As nasty a bit of criminal hubris as he'd seen in a long time. Were Bailey and Shaw really so dumb they thought the cops wouldn't look in

Jen's car? Had they thought the cops that dumb? And what about Jen? Paying blackmail to protect her and then doing this?

He called his cousin, since this body was on Sam's watch. Then Melia, who took the news with a stoic grunt. His third call was to Jack Kelly, to whom he suggested the possibility of a physician other than Ken Bailey. By that time, she was in the bathroom, being loudly and wretchedly sick; Perry was in the kitchen, making her some tea; and little Stevie Pleasant was yelling his head off, unimpressed by all the commotion.

Following the sound, Burgess went upstairs—an Everest of a climb—and picked the baby up, laying him on a changing table and fumbling with clumsy hands for the snaps on the tiny blue garment. Fists no bigger than quarters punched the air uncertainly. Dark blue eyes stared up at him as he freed the little feet and pulled off the sodden diaper, got a dry one, and taped it on. Feeling like a giant— he'd forgotten babies could be this small—he removed the wet clothes, powdered the soft skin, and dressed the baby in a clean undershirt and sleeper. He finished, poked the little belly with a finger, and said, "Better?" Stevie Pleasant rewarded him with a big, gummy grin.

"You keep surprising me," Jen said from the doorway. Her skin had a grayish pallor and she drooped like an un-watered flower. He thought she might faint again.

"Sit down," he said. "I'll bring him to you."

"You think you look any better?" She walked unsteadily to the rocking chair and lowered herself into it. "Is this when I confess that I've lied to you?"

"I know you were there that night. At the hospital. Was there something else?"

She shook her head. "I should have known better than to

lie to you. I just wanted so badly to protect my privacy."
She bent her head and her hair fell forward, hiding her face.
"From the first, I knew it was a mistake. There's something
unstoppable about you. You'll just keep rolling forward
until you get where you want to go. Stan says you got shot
last night and yet, here you are. Why?"

So it was Stan already. "Just doing my job," he said.

"Why?" she repeated, shaking back her hair.

"I don't believe in murder."

"You have to win, don't you."

"Look who's on my team."

She raised her head and looked at him, puzzled. "Your
team? I don't understand." She looked so young and pitiful
he wanted to get her warm milk and read her a story. A
happy story. She could have used one.

"I play for the dead," he said. "I'm the only one left who
can score."

"You're crazy," she murmured, bowing her head again.

"Maybe," he agreed. "I called your stepfather. He's
coming over." He carried the baby to her. It almost fit in
the palm of his hand—a human life little bigger than a
roasting chicken. He handed it over and looked around for
a place to sit. Settled for a window seat. "The bag in your
car. I'm sorry you had to see that."

She shrugged as she unbuttoned her blouse. "You tried
to stop me." The baby shifted restlessly and made fussing
noises. "I'm sorry, detective," she said. "I can't talk about
this now. My milk won't let down, and he's hungry."

Burgess shoved himself off the soft seat, finding it hard
to get upright again, so exhausted he felt numb. His feet
seemed a long way from his head, uncertain in their journey
across the room. He entertained no visions of sugarplums,
but thoughts of sleep danced in his head. Finding O'Leary

had released him. He was ready to hand this over.

Unanswered questions buzzed like hornets through his weary brain. They could wait. The state cops would have a long, busy night, working Jen Kelly's car and Ted Shaw's house, but those were not his problems. His problem was still Stephen Pleasant. And Kara Allison. What role, if any, O'Leary had played. If he'd been there—as her statement about the tattooed wrist suggested—there would probably be some evidence in the car. Hair, fibers, something. And if she'd been flung out of the car, there should be marks in the snow. But what *had* happened? Now he'd never get to ask. He could march out there and yell his questions at the severed head, but he'd get no satisfaction.

He sat at the kitchen table, staring at the oil patterns in the coffee Stan had fixed, unable to bear putting anything in his stomach. Jack Kelly came and asked questions he answered without knowing what he said, then went upstairs to take care of Jen. Sam came, got filled in, and left. Some state cops came and did the same. He felt like an icon. The kitchen cop, font of wisdom. He wanted to leave, too, but Stan was still working and he was too tired to drive. He listened to the clock tick and thought about calling a cab. It was a long way to the phone. He was about to do that when someone called his name.

Vince Melia, suit rumpled, hair awry, his tie for once slightly loose, said, "Hey, Joe. Ready to go? Stan's gonna stay a while longer, keep an eye on things. I thought you might need a ride." Melia, who'd earlier cursed him for being an ass, looked benign. Maybe Burgess was redeemed. He had found the person everyone was looking for. In pieces, but found. "Thought we'd go by the hospital and see Terry."

"Sure, Vince. Sure." His body unfolded from the chair, a

slow, tired straightening he felt in every muscle and joint, especially his bad knee. He couldn't straighten his shoulders. His head was too heavy. Someone's big, ugly hands— his own?—carried his cup to the sink. Someone's big, plodding feet carried him out of the room, down the steps, past the whole crime scene commotion, and into Vince's car. How could he pass a crime scene and not even pause, not be drawn to the scent of it, the excitement? Where was that piece of him that believed no one else could do it as well? Maybe someone had taken his self away and left him a loaner to use until his own was repaired and ready to use again.

Vince didn't say anything until they were moving. Then he reached down on the floor, grabbed a can of Coke, and held it out. "Thought you might need this."

"I do. Thanks." It was icy cold. Burgess popped the top, tipped his head back and drank.

"Terry's going to be fine," Melia said. "Leg's broken in two places but they're nice clean breaks. He's some pissed he's missing all the excitement."

"What excitement?"

"Another day, you weren't so many hours out, you hadn't gotten shot up, you'd find this exciting." Burgess grunted. "You wanna go to the hospital or straight home?"

"Hospital."

"How the heck I'm supposed to supervise you if you won't follow orders?"

"Cote would have let him walk. By morning, those bags would have been gone."

"That's why I'm not yelling. Can't value a man for his cop's gut and then complain when he uses it. I hear it was a hell of a performance. You think maybe the girl was telling the truth? That O'Leary did it?"

369

"Be handy, wouldn't it? But no. I don't." He changed the subject. "You get her clothes?"

"Claims she burned them. Didn't want them around to remind her of what an ass she'd been."

"No sign of Randall Noyes?"

"We're still looking. Got any ideas?"

Burgess leaned back in his seat and closed his eyes, sleep tantalizingly close. He drifted toward it and hurled himself out into space. Floating among soft black clouds. A thought, like a bungee cord, snapped him back. "Yeah," he said. "I've got an idea."

"You are a phenomenon," Melia said. "Two seconds ago, you were snoring."

"I am amazing, aren't I? Find out where Carman Merchant is buried and watch the cemetery. Guy like that, loving her the way he does, and all stirred up? He'll go there. Now I *am* going to sleep. Wake me when we get there. I'm sorry about the car."

"Screw the car. It's only a door. They'll have it fixed in no time."

"On what planet? It'll take six weeks to get a door here from Detroit and then it'll be the wrong one. Meanwhile, what do I do for a ride?"

"Got a bright blue Blazer we took off a drug dealer. You can borrow that. It'll make you feel young again."

"Lousy car." Burgess fell asleep.

They parked just outside the entrance and went up to Kyle's room. It was jarring, going from the dark, quiet car to the brightness of the hospital corridors. It was good that Melia was with him. Not so long ago he'd been a patient here himself, getting all the birdshot dug out, but that wasn't what came to him now. Walking these corridors alone at night would have pulled him back into memories of his mother's last days. They were always waiting for him. More so at a time like this, when death was in his head.

It was the middle of the night. Things ought to have been dim and quiet, but Kyle's room was busy, visiting hours unenforced. There were other cops there, along with pizza, coffee, and donuts. Centerpiece to it all, Michelle, in tight black jeans and a turtleneck, her blonde hair loose and lovely, sat beside Terry, holding his hand. Weeks of longing, one night together, and she already looked like a fixture.

Kyle gave him a thin smile and held out his other hand. "Hear I missed some fun."

Burgess shook his head. "It was ugly, and it's not ours anyway. Besides, there's plenty of fun ahead. I haven't heard the fat lady sing."

"We workin' tomorrow?"

Michelle frowned. "Terry, you can't possibly—"

"Forget it," Melia said. "Everybody's taking the day off."

"Oh, sure. Only way you get Burgess to take a day off is handcuff him to his bed."

"I'm seriously considering it."

"I'd bet my personal fortune on Burgess working tomorrow," Kyle said, "only I don't have a personal fortune." He looked lousy but content.

"You call your wife?" Burgess asked.

"And tell her what? Her only concern's whether my paycheck keeps coming."

"That you're going to be fine, just in case it gets in the paper. So the girls won't worry," Melia said. "Want me to call her?"

The pain on Kyle's face was psychic, not physical. Thinking about worrying his girls. About an article in the paper and how badly his ex-wife might handle it.

"I'll call her, Terry," Burgess said.

He walked down the silent corridor, the building looming around him, the stark quality of the light, the concealed mechanical hum, feeling the darkness reach out for him. He felt the tentative licks of its raspy tongue, tasting him like a giant, invisible cat considering whether to sink in its teeth. Knowing it could. That in his present state, he couldn't fight back.

He found an empty lounge with a pay phone. Sat in a chair by the phone, his head in his hands, feeling the weight of this case. What he knew and what he thought he knew. About truth. About life and death. Love and hate. About why he did his job and how he did his job. About the nature of justice. It was good Melia was making him take a day off tomorrow. No one believed he'd take it, but he would. He needed a day to think.

He dropped in some coins and called Kyle's ex-wife. Did his best reassuring number. Urged her to bring the girls to visit tomorrow. Kyle needed to see them. They needed to see him. No, his appearance wasn't shocking. A little bandage on his head, a cast on his leg. And yes, the money would keep right on coming. He disconnected and stayed there, receiver in his hand, his head pressed against the wall, so very tired of people and their complications.

Then, though a man tired of people and their complications ought to have wanted to be alone, he pulled out a piece of paper and dialed a number. "It's Joe Burgess," he said.

"I can't believe this," she said. "You're actually calling me. Where are you?"

"At the hospital."

"I thought I said—"

"Just visiting. I'm going home now. Was hoping you might be free."

"It's after eleven on a Saturday night. That probably means I don't have a date. What did you have in mind?"

"Snuggling?"

"Snuggling?" Her voice did that wonderful thing where it dropped a register and, like a conjurer, called up a response from his astonished body. "That's the best line I've heard in years. Your place or mine?"

"Mine?" He needed to shave. To be in a familiar bed. And he'd bled through his clothes. It sure was an appealing package he was offering.

"Good. Then I won't have to dust or pick up. Give me your address."

He gave his address, then hung up the phone and went back down the corridor to Kyle's room. This time, the darkness kept its distance. He reported to Kyle about the phone call and told Melia he was ready to leave. He was silent on the ride home, thinking about Chris Perlin. Numb and exhausted and yet. His mind and body might be borrowed, but the lust he felt was all his own.

CHAPTER THIRTY-FIVE

She arrived shortly after Melia dropped him off, carrying a small duffel bag and a stainless steel saucepan. She dropped the bag on the floor, set the pan on the stove, and wrapped her arms around his neck. Her fingers were warm on his skin as she gave him a long, tender, peppermint kiss. "I've been thinking about that all day," she said. "That, and this." She tapped the pan. "Chicken soup. I knew you'd need it." She adjusted the gas and slipped off her coat. She wore jeans and an oversized blue sweatshirt.

"There's probably no word for how tired you are," she said. "Take your coat off. Sit down. Make yourself at home." She unzipped his jacket and pulled it off, careful of his arm, watching his face closely for signs of pain. "Sit. Man, this thing weighs a ton, doesn't it? I know. I know." She tipped her head as she spoke. "Your other one got shot full of holes. I saw it, remember?" She steered him into a chair. Knelt down and removed his shoes and socks, lingering there, rubbing his feet.

It felt so good. "You think a man could have an orgasm from having his feet rubbed?" he asked.

"Is that about to happen?"

"Maybe." She was making him breathless.

She lowered his foot. "Soup's ready. You want anything with it? Tea? Crackers?"

"You."

She grinned at him, then turned, her hair hiding her face. "That you got."

374

"Why me?" He liked the shining rain of hair down her back, the way it rippled and shifted as she moved.

"You need rescuing. I rescue people."

Something they had in common. "Then what? You tinker with my heart a little and move on to the next hard case?"

"I'm getting tired of moving on." She ladled soup into a bowl and found crackers. "Too soon to tell, but I could see making a long-term investment. You'd have to shower and shave more often, though. I've got sensitive skin. Sensitive nose, too."

"I'm sorry."

"Don't be." Standing beside him, her breasts were level with his head. She pulled it against them. They were soft and pillowing. "Eat your soup."

"Can't, if you keep distracting me like this."

"Eat. Eat. Mind if I check out your place?"

"Be my guest."

She wandered into the living room, then the bedroom. He heard her opening doors, checking things out. She stuck her head around the door. "Got any clean sheets?" He told her where to find them. "It's pretty spare. You smash it all up in a fit of crazy male anger?"

"Yes."

"Thought so. The pictures. Those empty crime scenes. Interesting. Your job is to fill them in?" He nodded. "Mind if I change the bed?" She rustled away in the other room while he ate his soup. Delicious soup. The first thing he'd eaten since last night's steak. His mother had believed in the healing power of soup. Soup for lost games, soup for broken hearts, soup to heal them all after his father's displays of violence. He pushed back his chair, put his dish in the sink. Went into the bedroom.

375

She was lying on top of the covers, still dressed, reading, looking like she belonged there. "That's Kristin Marks on the closet door, isn't it? A shrine?" He nodded. She came around the bed, her bare feet silent on the floor, her toenails electric blue. She ran her hands lightly up his body from his waist to his shoulders and started unbuttoning his shirt. He shivered under her touch. "If you can love half so well as you can hate, Joe Burgess, I'm a lucky woman." She slipped the shirt off his shoulders, eased it gently over his bad arm and reached for his belt. "And I'm not talking about sex."

He slept on his back, the only position that didn't hurt one of his wounds, a pillow she'd insisted on underneath his arm. She slept beside him on her stomach, one leg thrown over him, one arm across his chest, her head resting on his shoulder. Her hair smelled like apples. She wore a plaid flannel nightgown, but where it rode up and her thigh crossed his, her skin was warm and silky. They didn't make love, yet the room, the air, and the bed were full of sex. Rich and voluptuous and tangible, like night air in the tropics. He inhaled deeply, drawing it in as his body rolled toward the edge of sleep and fell over.

He slept fourteen hours, waking alone in the middle of Sunday afternoon. The apartment was quiet. When he turned to look at the clock, he found a glass of water on the nightstand with a note propped against it. It said: "Take your pills. Wait fifteen minutes. Then take a shower." Below, in smaller letters: "Call me when you're ready for that shower." He took his pills. Needed them, moving set the damaged parts of him on fire. He rested fifteen minutes, until he felt the first tendrils of relief, then called her.

Feet thudded across the floor and the bedroom door opened. She leaned in. "Hi, sleepyhead. Ready for a shower and some breakfast, or whatever it's called when you eat it at this time of day?"

"I stink," he said, "and I'm starving."

"How appealing. I'll give you five minutes and then come wash your back. Okay?"

"I'm no fool," he said.

She gave him a goofy smile. "Is that right?" Then, suddenly serious. "Paper says Dr. Bailey was arrested last night. You have anything to do with that?"

He nodded. "It's not my jurisdiction, but I did a little work on it. I found the body."

"Whose body?"

"Kevin O'Leary. The pimp who set up Pleasant's last evening."

"What does that have to do with Dr. Bailey?"

"It's a long story," he said. "Can I tell it over breakfast?"

She pointed toward the bathroom. "Get cleaned up. I've been waiting to eat with you for about six hours. I'm starving."

"You're an angel," he said.

"Don't get mushy on me."

He kept his smartass replies to himself, concentrating on getting out of bed without yelling. When he finally got on his feet, his legs were like rubber. She must have been a mind reader. Before he was halfway across the room, she was tucking her shoulder under his. "I wasn't thinking," she said, matter-of-factly. "Second day is always worse."

She walked him to the bathroom and left so he could attend to "necessities." Then he stripped off his underwear and turned on the shower. He liked his showers hot. Wondered if she did, too, or if she was one of those people who liked things lukewarm. She didn't seem lukewarm. He let heat sluice down over his back, and picked up the soap.

"Hey," she said, stepping in and closing the door. "Did you start without me?"

"At my age, it takes a while."

Her hair was pinned up with a clip the color of her eyes. "Really," she said, eyes skipping down his body with teasing little glances. "I think the evidence is to the contrary."

"That's just how it is when a man wakes up."

"What man? Rip Van Winkle?"

He pulled her against him, rivulets of water running between them, feeling blessed and confused, for once utterly in the moment.

"Want me to wash your back?" she asked.

"I want to wash your front."

She put her hands behind her head and stuck out her chest in a pin-up girl pose. "Go to it," she said.

He went to it. He'd had an idea of taking things slowly, taking her back to bed and making slow and gentle love to her. A proper first time. It didn't work out like that. They slithered and slid around the shower, exploring with mouths and tongues and soapy fingers. He ended up behind her, his hands cupping her heavy breasts, buried deep inside her, as they nearly knocked the wall down in an uninhibited crescendo that must have been audible blocks away. It left him awestruck and dizzy and needing to go back to bed.

Chris, on the other hand, was energized. "And I thought I was hungry before!" she said. "Aren't you starving?"

He couldn't quite stifle his yawn. "Guys," she sighed. "One little orgasm and you fall flat on your ass."

"Give me a minute," he said. But he was embarrassingly tired. All his bandages were wet and soggy and the tape was peeling. He looked like The Mummy after a rainstorm. "You think these things need redoing?"

Suddenly her assessment was clinical. "Oh, yeah. That was dumb. I got so caught up in . . . uh . . . playing in the shower, I forgot I was assaulting the walking wounded. Go lie down on the bed and I'll fix you right up." She caught his look. "I didn't mean that, idiot. Now shoo!" She unclipped her hair and it came tumbling down, falling almost to her waist. "Not quite Lady Godiva yet." She bent and picked up some panties, then a bra. She started to pull her sweatshirt over her head. "Go on. Beat it. If you fall over, I can't pick you up."

He got in bed, pulling the covers modestly over him. A little late for that, but suddenly he felt shy. And it was cold in the room. He closed his eyes and felt the delicious postcoital tug of sleep. It felt so damned good. There was a chill as she pulled the sheet down, then gentle fingers, and a warning, "Watch out! This is going to hurt," as she pulled the bandages off.

"Goddamn!"

"Sorry." Her cool hand touched his face. "You're just so hairy I can't help it." She patched him back together, murmuring to herself about the status of things. The bottom line seemed to be he was unlovely, but he'd live.

She pulled up the covers, then crawled underneath them, fitting her body to his. She cupped him in her hand and, as old Rip Van Winkle struggled to rise for the second time in 200 years, she whispered, "There are so many things I'd like to do to you, but I think you'd better sleep. I'm going to go eat." Her hand relaxed. Moved away. She slid out of bed.

Burgess fell asleep. If he was being graded him on his performance today, he'd probably get an F. On the bright side, maybe that meant he'd have to take the course again.

CHAPTER THIRTY-SIX

She woke him a few hours later by whispering, "I have to leave." First they made love again the way he'd planned it— a slower, more sedate coupling with condoms and kisses and an exquisite, satisfying sweetness in the way she dug her nails into his shoulders, the way her eyes opened wide, the way she whispered, "Oh my God, Joe. Oh, my God!" like he'd done something right in a way no one ever had before. He came as close in that moment as he ever had to being a fool for love. He would have married her then and there.

She didn't leave until she'd marched him to the table and watched him eat, smiling like his voracious appetite was entirely her fault. Only then, her hook set, did she go, leaving him satisfied and longing. Which, she told him, was how she wanted it. She left the chicken soup in a plastic container and took back her pot. "I'm not moving in," she said. "I'm not leaving my stuff here. You're too cranky and set in your ways to be moved in on quickly. And I'm too proud and independent myself."

"What are you doing tomorrow night?"

"Tap dancing. And you can't come. I love it but I'm a total klutz. If you came and watched, I'd fall and break my ankle. You can pick me up after and buy me a milkshake. We could have a real date. Go somewhere besides bed."

"It's not like we spend our whole time in bed."

"Would if we were here."

He reached out and tangled his hand in her hair. She

tipped back her head and he kissed her. "Where's tap dancing? I'll be there." His mind was with the program—say good-bye, get back to work—his body had other ideas.

Against his will, because he had the good Catholic boy's hang-up about whores and virgins and the prohibitions about mixing them up, he heard Alana's voice in his head. If he ever did find a woman, he'd take her to bed and not come out for years. He wanted to take her back to bed and spend the next week fitted into the curves of her body. This was why he never opened the gates. Wherever his passion went—love, hate, rage, sorrow—there was always too much.

She reached out and rubbed his scratchy cheek. "Tomorrow, you'll shave?"

"Tomorrow I'll shave." Goddammit! He even had sex in his voice. Those thickened vocal cords, that raw need. He wanted to hold her there, beg her not to go.

"Don't think I don't feel it, too," she said. "Scares the hell out of me." She picked up her bag, opened the door, and walked out. He went to the window, watched her get in her car and drive away, then stood and watched her tail-lights until the car was out of sight.

He shaved, poured himself a glass of bourbon and put on Emmylou Harris. Then he sat down to think. In the spaces around the edges of all that had been going on, he'd been thinking, assessing, putting the pieces of the puzzle together. What he had to decide now was what to do with what he knew. Where he was going with it, when lives, fates, and futures hung in the balance and he understood so much about the past.

After an hour he walked into the kitchen, deliberately passing the bourbon bottle, and called Kyle. "Terry? Joe. How you doing?"

"I'm pretty bummed. Wanda came with the kids, took a

381

look at me, and started to cry. That got the girls crying and there wasn't a damned thing I could do about it. I can't get out of bed with this leg. Couldn't pick them up. Couldn't make myself heard over the racket she was making. No matter what I said, she wouldn't get a grip. Just kept bawling. I tried to get them to sit on the bed. At least let me hug them, so they could see I was still me, but she was making such a scene they asked her to leave. So I'm in a wicked good mood. You?"

"I need to talk something through. You up for another visitor?"

"Long as you promise not to cry."

"Scout's honor."

"You get some rest?"

"Fourteen hours."

"How you gonna get here? I wrecked your ride."

"You didn't wreck a damned thing. You have any idea what's going on? I haven't even called in, and nobody's called me."

"Vince had to cut Kara Allison loose. Lawyer raised holy hell. You know the drill."

He was disappointed but not surprised. "I'll call a cab. Need anything?"

"Not unless you've got a spare electric razor and a pair of track pants with those tear-away seams. I'm not going out of here tomorrow in a johnny."

"Don't want the world to see your knobby old knees?"

"Don't want the world to see my knobby old ass. See you when you get here."

He called Melia at home. Got Vince's wife, who asked politely about his condition before hollering in her best soccer coach's voice, "Vince, Joe Burgess on the phone." Gina Melia coached boys' soccer, and she'd never had a losing season. There was a silence, then she said, "I think the twins have got him tied up. I'll rescue him and have him call you back. That okay?"

"I wish I could see it."

"Drop by anytime, Joe," she said. "They'll be happy to tie you up, too. They're learning knots for Cub Scouts. With these guys, that's more than a little scary. Oh. Hold on. Here he comes. Torn and bleeding, but ever the cop. When you coming over for dinner? You could bring someone."

Gina'd been fixing him up for years. Never got it right. Never stopped trying. "Thanks, I'd like that," he said. "Got someone I want you to meet."

"Joe?" Vince was breathless. "What's up?"

"I was feeling out of touch. Looking for an update. Wondering about that Blazer."

"It's in the garage. Keys are on my desk in a credit union coffee cup. Help yourself. Both Bailey and Shaw will be charged, soon as they finish sorting things out."

"Like who did what?"

"Yeah. ME says the cuts looks awfully professional."

"How'd he die?"

"Drug overdose."

"Clever."

"Would have been clever," Melia corrected, "if they'd just left him in a dingy motel room somewhere, or in his car. And if they hadn't bruised the heck out of him, holding him down and shooting him up. Sometimes people get too smart for their own good. Not that it looked much like an accident, after they'd panicked and cut him up."

"They find his clothes? I want those shoes."

"Still looking. You get some rest?" Burgess made an affirmative sound. "Good. See you tomorrow. I've got to get tied up again. You don't know what you're missing."

"Guess not." Melia hadn't mentioned the girl. "You warn Kara Allison to keep herself available?"

"Told her. Told her lawyer. Told her aunt."

"But you don't have anybody watching her?"

"Should I?"

"Too late now. You find out where her mother is buried?"

"Shoot. I forgot all about it."

"Bye, Vince," he said. "Gotta go get that car." He called a cab, then took the elevator to Melia's office. Snagged the keys out of the cup. Got the interview report off Stan Perry's desk and copied down Kara Allison's address and phone number. He called there. Got no answer. Called Sarah Merchant. "It's Joe Burgess," he said. "Is Kara there?" Silence. "You know where she is?"

"No."

"What about Randall Noyes?" Silence. He'd had more animated conversations with half-asleep toll takers on the highway. "Where is your sister buried?" Surprised, she told him. "Thanks," he said.

"Wait. Are you all right?"

He didn't dignify the question with an answer. He checked his in-box, just in case someone had dropped off a confession or some vital piece of evidence while he was sleeping. There was no confession, but Dani Letorneau, who wasn't supposed to be working, had left him a stack of photographs with a note that said: "Take a look at these." What she wanted him to take a look at was a series of blurred footprints, made by high-heeled shoes, going away from the car door. He studied them, nodded, then got up, taking the folder with him.

He went downstairs and found the Blazer. Melia hadn't

been kidding. It was an interesting ride. It was a garish bright blue with loose steering and a jarring affinity for potholes, but it was wheels. He detoured to the mall to get the stuff for Kyle. Then to the hospital. Kyle was watching TV, looking mournful. He brightened when he saw Burgess, and lowered the volume.

"Oh goody. Presents."

"Batman p.j.s and everything you need to make fluffernutters." There were lots of cards and flowers in the room, including a big homemade one from Kyle's daughters and a bunch of Valentine balloons.

Kyle smiled wanly. "I must have died and gone to heaven."

"You're too easily pleased." He handed over the electric razor and the Adidas tracksuit with the zippered sweatshirt and the matching tear-away pants. "You are going to be a fashion plate, my man. Who gave you the balloons?"

"Young Stanley and his redhead brought them. Kid's still high as a kite."

"He ought to be. It was his idea to look in Jen Kelly's car."

"Yeah. Boy's coming along." Kyle put his toys away and gave Burgess a searching look. "I know you love me, and I am truly grateful for this stuff, but that's not why you're here. What's up?"

"Truth and consequences."

"Kara Allison. Someone thought she needed protecting badly enough to shoot you over it." Kyle shrugged. "Did she or didn't she?"

Burgess nodded, back for a second in Sarah Merchant's living room, reliving their mutual surprise when she pointed that gun at him, the sudden glaring pain when it went off. The memory sent a trickle of sweat down his spine. "She says no. You know her story? She says she planned it. Stalked Dr. Pleasant. Spent the evening with him. Made sure she left with him. She says she was there in the car, with the weapon, prepared to do it, and at the last minute, she froze and couldn't."

"Who does she say did it?"

"She says a big man with a ski mask over his face opened the car door, dragged her out, seized the weapon, and then flung her away from the car. She showed me the bruises on her knees."

"Have a seat," Kyle said. "This won't be a brief conversation."

Burgess pulled the visitor's chair close to the bed, and his wounds, like a chorus of spring peepers, all began to clamor at once. He let the aches subside, trying not to think about being here in this hospital. Couldn't avoid it, talking about Kara Allison. This was where their stories intersected. Where their mothers had died. "She hated him in a way I understand too well."

"We'll get to that," Kyle said. "Let's get through her story first. Was this man someone she knew and recognized? Someone she didn't know but could describe? Or some generic bad guy, conveniently pulled out of a hat?"

"Pretty generic. It took, at most, a couple seconds. He wore a mask and gloves. He didn't speak. She said he was big and rough and had tattoos on his wrist."

"What about her accomplice? Randall Noyes?"

"The guy who made the weapon? She says no. We can't find Noyes."

"Got anything that puts O'Leary in the car?"

"Dani's footprint puts someone beside the car. And nothing to match it to. O'Leary could have followed Pleasant that night."

"And we've got O'Leary. So we can do hair matches."

"He shaves his head. And we can't do fibers unless we find his clothes. Or match the footprint without his shoes. But O'Leary had tattoos on his wrists."

Kyle shook his head slowly. Slowly was always best with a concussion. "O'Leary must have other shoes in his closet. You ask Dr. Lee whether a woman could've done it?"

"She could have. Not easily, but hate makes people strong."

"No prints on the weapon?"

"No."

"Blood splatter?"

"It wasn't a spurting wound. He drowned in his blood. And her clothes are gone."

"Convenient. You believe her, Joe?" Burgess shook his head. "But you want to believe her. Why?"

"Because I understand why she wanted to do it. And because I want her story to be true. I want her to have come to the moment and been unable to kill."

"Is there such a thing as a romantic homicide detective, do you think?"

"I don't follow you."

Kyle shrugged. "You don't work for Kara Allison," he said. "You work for Stephen Pleasant. And the people of Portland."

"And I hated Stephen Pleasant."

"Then you shouldn't have taken the case."

"I had the case before I knew it was him. I talked it over with Vince. I didn't think it would matter."

"And does it?"

Burgess shrugged. The room was dim, the building around them growing quiet as the bustle of the day gave way to the slow emptiness of night. His time of day. The time when he liked to sit alone and think. Tonight he didn't want to be alone. His mind was at war. Kristin Marks had taught him to put truth and justice first and not back down from it, even when he couldn't always win. She'd taught him that putting up the good fight mattered, even when it left you hurt and impotent and wondering how to pick yourself up to go on. Yeah. She had taught him about hurt, taking him down into the darkness with her. And she had taught him you had to go on, because the next case mattered, too, or else her death didn't.

So Stephen Pleasant's death mattered. Maybe it mattered more because he didn't want it to matter. Maybe this, and not Kristin Marks, was his true test. Because he, too, had wanted the man to die. The harder the death, the better. Sarah Merchant's fantasy about how Pleasant should have died was something they shared. Now Pleasant was dead and Burgess had a choice. Go forward with the case against Kara Allison, who'd been braver than he, and done what he, in his own darkest thoughts, had longed to do, or hang the thing on Kevin O'Leary, already conveniently dead.

"How likely was it that the car would be unlocked or that the killer would lock it when he was done?" he said. "That someone outside could have seen through iced-up windows? That O'Leary wouldn't have brought his own weapon? And crime scene photos show no sign she was thrown from the car as she claims."

He cleared his throat. "The biggie? Cadaveric spasm. Kara Allison's hair, torn out by the roots, clutched in a death grip in Stephen Pleasant's hand. They had to force the hand open to do fingernail scrapings."

Kyle lay back against his pillow, his skin nearly as pale. "You wouldn't be telling me this if you didn't want to hear what I'm about to say, so fold your hands in your lap, listen to Uncle Terry, and don't argue or interrupt until I'm done."

Burgess folded his hands, bowed his head, and waited.

"Something else your mother said to me. Another sacred trust." Kyle sighed deeply. "She said to me, 'Terry, my Joseph, he's so sure he's right. Sometimes he forgets who is he and tries to play God. Remind him that he's not.' "

"That's not fair," Burgess said. "I'm not . . . I don't . . . I've never . . ."

Kyle put a finger to his lips. "Listen. What do you think you're doing right now? Your job, our job, is to get the facts. That's what we've been busting our butts to do for the last week. We just harvest the potatoes, Joe. We don't make the vodka. The French fries. The Tater Tots. Try to get all the potatoes. Do the best job we can. Put 'em in a basket. Bring 'em to the barn."

"I'm nothing but a goddamned manual laborer?"

"No. You're the best goddamned manual laborer. Which is why I follow you around, snapping at your heels. Because I want to be you someday, asshole. But you start playing God and it all goes down the toilet. You've got to call it like you see it. If Kara Allison did it, she did it. You start editing, you start picking and choosing because you don't like what the facts tell you, and you stop being a detective, become something else. If you want to become a private dick, find facts for money, then go there. But resign first. Because that's not what we do. We find, or we try to find, facts for truth. We don't always succeed or like what we find. And we don't always win. But it's an honorable calling. What you're thinking about doing is not."

It was the longest speech he'd ever heard Kyle make. He got up. "Thanks, Terry."

"I hope that helped."

"Actually, it hurt. But it's what my mother would have called 'good pain.' That woman, rest her soul, believed in the value of suffering."

"A trait you inherited." Kyle was tired. His eyes were drooping. He roused himself, though, to say, "Joe, whatever way you go with this, it's your call."

"Thanks, Terry." He rubbed the back of his neck, which was stiff and sore. "I think we both know where I'm going."

"And the truth shall make you free." Kyle closed his eyes. " 'Night, Joe."

Burgess walked down the hall and into the elevator. He watched the doors close and felt himself carried down. They opened again and he walked the familiar corridors, smelled the familiar air, heard the familiar sounds. Passed different, but familiar, sad faces. The faces of worry and grief, tears repressed, fear pressing on the heart and lungs until breath seemed barely possible. He'd probably never come here without feeling it. He walked through the lobby, staring for a moment at the spot where Bailey had cornered him. A piece of work. What came of playing God.

The automatic doors opened, disgorging him into the cold, black night. He stood a moment, inhaling icy air, gathering himself for the tasks ahead. He hoped Kyle was right. He hoped, and felt the first stirrings of belief, that the truth *would* begin to set him free.

EPILOGUE

Their high-priced lawyers—and they had the finest—did a great job for Ted Shaw and Dr. Kenneth Bailey, but Burgess, having learned his lesson from the Marks case, saw that they didn't walk away unscathed. In his book, someone who delivered a known scumbag to the scene of an attempted rape and then helped him escape again was bad news, rich or not. Those who deliberately ran into one of his officers and then left the scene, who mutilated a corpse and attempted to hide the body, never mind having almost certainly killed the person in the first place, were not going to beat all the raps, even if they did claim they were victims of O'Leary's blackmail and the death was an accident.

With Kristin Marks hovering by his shoulder, and Chris Perlin providing private-duty nursing care, including a variety of soups, warm arms, and one unsuccessful tap dancing lesson, he didn't crash and burn this time. He just plodded along, aided by Kyle and Perry, crossing the "t's" and dotting the "i's" himself, bringing in witnesses and evidence and pulling things together, as relentless as a Mountie.

He found the FedEx driver who could put Bailey in the car at the video store. He bothered the arson investigators until the fire at O'Leary's apartment and the video store firebombing were tied to materials in Shaw's garage. He searched whenever he had spare time for the missing Rubbermaid container. It didn't hurt to fuel the legend that Burgess always got his man.

Getting his woman was harder. Kara Allison disappeared as soon as she was released, and no one was able to trace her. The crime scene photographs showed a blurred trail of high-heeled shoes leaving the scene, and no signs of her having been flung down in the snow as she'd claimed. Stan Perry, acting on one of his hunches, reinterviewed the witness who'd seen someone running down the street the night of Pleasant's murder, and gleaned the omitted detail that the runner had fallen and gotten up. The shoes in O'Leary's closet were 12½. No Reeboks.

In the interests of closure and calming the public nerves, Cote tentatively attributed the murder to Kevin O'Leary, a convicted felon with a long record of assaults, unfortunately dead of a drug overdose before he could be brought to trial. They never found any traces of him in the car. Without the missing shoes, there was only an unidentified footprint and Kara Allison's statement that he'd been at the scene, but with him firmly tied to Pleasant by witnesses linking him both with pimping and receiving and distributing drugs, that was deemed enough.

Burgess was sure her aunt knew where she'd gone, but he couldn't get her to admit it. Once burned, or in this case shot, twice shy, he'd sent Perry and made him wear a vest, but not even the threat of arrest moved her. He had better luck finding the missing clothes. Reasoning that a girl who'd spent her formative years in poverty would have a hard time destroying good clothing, he'd gotten cops to search the clothing donation boxes in the area, as well as what had already been collected. Remy Aucoin, who was taking this personally, found the dress, shoes and coat that she'd been wearing. Lab tests found traces of Pleasant's blood on the coat and dress.

He did find Randy Noyes. Eventually, being a practical

and orderly man, Noyes went back to his job, but Burgess had already found him, as he'd predicted, in the cemetery. Carrying a flask of bourbon, he had walked over to where Noyes knelt, laying a fragrant bouquet of fir and red and white carnations by the headstone.

"I hear she was a very special woman," Burgess said. "I admire your devotion."

"It's not much trouble," Noyes said, brushing snow off the letters in the headstone. "I saw this. Thought she'd like it. She was good with plants."

He opened the flask and passed it over. "Joe Burgess, Portland police."

"I figured."

"Wondered if we could talk about Kara Allison."

Noyes shrugged. He had big shoulders. Looked strong. "I guess." He tipped up the flask and drank, then passed it back, wiping his mouth with his hand. "Nice," he said.

"You want to talk here or go someplace?"

"I know a bar."

The bar was smoky and noisy, air thick with grease, the vinyl sticky. They took a booth at the back and ordered beer. Burgess could see why Alana had called him handsome. They were only a few years apart in age, but Noyes's hair and beard were still dark and he had lively hazel eyes. Most people reacted to a cop asking about a murder with some level of nervousness, but Noyes was calm, with an ease that was almost contagious. Burgess heard Sarah Merchant's words—Noyes was the best thing that had ever happened to her sister.

"Any idea where Kara's gone?"

Noyes shook his head. "Nah. She didn't tell me. Didn't trust me, probably. Figured you'd come along and I'd tell you. She figured right. I'm not much good at lying."

"The whole thing was her idea?" Noyes nodded. "Why'd you go along with it?"

"Promised her mom I'd look after her."

"Funny way of looking after someone."

"Helping them do something important to them? Is it?"

"Helping someone kill another person. It doesn't sound like something her mother would have wanted."

Noyes narrowed his eyes, something in his face and his voice unyielding and completely certain. "You got that wrong. Her mother hated that son-of-a-bitch. Hell, I hated him, too. He deserved to be hated."

"So you admit you were helping her kill him?"

"You aren't getting me to say that. Kara said she wanted to scare the hell out of him. Wanted him to know how it felt to come face-to-face with death. A big bad practical joke."

"You believed that?"

"You met her?" Burgess nodded. Noyes laughed. "She can be pretty persuasive. It sounded reasonable to me. Why not scare the crap out of that arrogant little prick? Another thing. When I looked at Kara, I was seeing Carman. I would have done anything for Carman. Still would. Always will."

"You hated him, but you didn't kill him?"

"I thought about it, right after she died. I was so mad, so hurt, I couldn't think straight. I didn't know what to do. Kill him? Kill myself?" Noyes drank some beer and set the glass down with a thump, tears in his eyes. "I don't think it's something you can understand if you haven't been there."

Burgess looked away. "You know she didn't just scare him and run away."

"She said someone came and threw her out of the car. Took the weapon away and threw her out of the car. She said she turned and ran and never looked back."

"You didn't believe that."

"Hard to. I was standing beside the car in case she needed me. Then I got cold, and she seemed fine, so I went back and sat in the truck." He cleared his throat. "It bothered me, what she was doing in there. Even if she was going to scare him in the end, she shouldn't have given him no pleasure. He didn't deserve it."

"And you could see what was happening from the truck?"

"Not the inside of the car. The windows got all iced-up."

"But the outside?"

"Yup. She got out of the car, ran over to the truck, and we drove away. Fell down once in those stupid shoes."

"There was no big man with tattoos?"

Noyes finished his beer and signaled the waitress for another. "Not unless he came after we left."

The waitress brought another round, gave Noyes a smile. "I'm off in an hour," she said. Noyes just shook his head.

"She tell you what happened?"

"Not exactly." Burgess waited. Noyes hoisted his second beer and drank about a third of it, then lowered the glass, centering it carefully on the soggy napkin. "She said, 'Mom would have been proud. I did it, Randy. I did it. I scared that bastard to death.' "

With Sandy's help, he got Alana Black enrolled in a massage program. Things didn't go smoothly, but he and Alana were used to bumpy roads, and she gradually settled down. Stan Perry was still playing the field, but Kyle and Michelle settled into a pretty steady thing, which drove the PMS queen crazy. That was life. You won some, you lost some.

Often simultaneously. And he hadn't shot Captain Cote.

Two months later, on one of his weekend reconnaissance missions, Burgess found the missing Rubbermaid container. Inside were Kevin O'Leary's clothes, including his shoes. They didn't match the footprints beside the car. Burgess wasn't surprised. He'd already matched them to a pair of Randy Noyes's shoes.

Burgess was a patient man. Someday he'd find Kara Allison. She'd slip up. Make a mistake. Get her prints into the system again. Or come home. And when she did, he'd be ready for her. Mrs. Burgess's boy tried not to play God, but when it came to the chess game of life, he was good at watching and waiting.

ABOUT THE AUTHOR

KATE FLORA is the author of six Thea Kozak mysteries and, as Katharine Clark, the suspense novel, *Steal Away*. Flora has taught writing for the Brown Learning Community, the Maine Writers and Publishers Alliance and at the Cape Cod Writer's Conference. Currently, she teaches for Grub Street in Boston. She is a past international president of Sisters in Crime. *Finding Amy*, a true crime story about a murder in Maine, will be published by UPNE in Spring 2006. She is a partner in Level Best Books, which has published anthologies of crime stories by New England writers. Currently, she is pursuing an MFA in creative writing at Vermont College. When Kate isn't writing, teaching or publishing, she is wrestling with her perennials or seeking new ways to cook vegetables so delicious her husband will actually eat them. Her Web site is: www.kateflora.com.